Forces of Evil

Forces of Evil

Trish Kocialski

RENAISSANCE ALLIANCE PUBLISHING, INC.
Austin, Texas

Copyright © 2000 by Trish Kocialski

ISBN 1-930928-07-6

First Printing 2000

9 8 7 6 5 4 3 2 1

Cover design by Mary Draganis

Published by:

Renaissance Alliance Publishing, Inc.
PMB 167, 3421 W. William Cannon Dr. # 131
Austin, Texas 78745

Find us on the World Wide Web at
http://www.rapbooks.com

Printed in the United States of America

Acknowledgements:

I'd like to thank my staff, Linda, Brian, and John, for being willing characters in this book, especially Linda who kept me on task by constantly asking for the next chapter; my cousin, Joyce, for making sure I didn't murder the English language and creative suggestions; my nieces, Sue and Jill for their encouragement and Molly, for her legal advice and assistance; my editor, Daylene Petersen not only for her editing skills, but for her teaching skills; and to the great folks at Renaissance Alliance Publishing for having faith in my first novel. I'd also like to thank the staff at DRC Physical Therapy and Sports Care for their help in understanding the protocols and prognoses for the injuries sustained by our heroines. Last, but not least, I want to thank my better half, Carol, for helping me become computer literate, teaching me to 'surf' the web for research information, and especially for her support through this whole process.

— Trish Kocialski

Dedication:

To my Mom who taught me at a very early age the importance of finishing any project I start no matter how I think it will turn out.

PART
I

Friday, 0530 hours...The Day After Thanksgiving

Morning came quickly for the young woman. Sunlight was barely creeping into the small cramped bedroom, waking the pride of cats sprawled out on the bed covers. Mewing and stretching served as the alarm clock for the other occupant of the bed. "OK, guys, I get the hint," mumbled the strawberry blonde as she started to get out of the bed. With her eyes still shut, she crawled out, quickly grabbing her tattered, but favorite, flannel robe to guard against the chill of the early morning air.

"Guess I forgot to close the windows again last night," she advised the cats, who were now running back and forth in anticipation of their morning meal. "One of these nights, I'll remember to close that darn window *before* I wake up in the morning!" she admonished herself out loud. *I just like leaving it open so the kids can get some fresh air while I'm out,* she thought. The fact that her companions were cooped up for such long periods without any company while she was at work accounted for her open window theory of "cat entertainment."

Katie worked three jobs to keep herself, and her felines, afloat in the current economic condition of the county. Living in a "tourist paradise" was not all fun and games, at least not for the non-tourist. The locals, who had to eke out their livings in a variety of ways, had to pay the same inflated prices for groceries, gas, fast food, pharmacy items, etc. that the tourists did, only they didn't have the bottomless wallets that the tourists seemed to possess. Since most of the area employers would not hire "full time," thus avoiding paying benefits, Katie worked three part-time jobs to make ends meet. Juggling the schedule for three jobs really took some master planning on her part, but she felt it was definitely worth the effort to keep herself employed in the town of her choosing.

"Let's see. Do you guys want *Captain's Choice* or *Gourmet Grub*?" she asked her attentive felines. "Greouw," answered the chubby tortoise shell cat named Butter, followed by two more meows. "Oh, *Grub* eh? Well, that works for me." She reached over to the top of the counter and grabbed the can opener, a spoon, and three saucers so she could divvy up the can's contents. Butter, Sugar, and Spice all chowed down and then finished with their morning ablutions. Katie watched them, still amazed at their precise motions: two licks of the paw, swipe behind the ear, down the side of the face, repeat three times, switch to the other side. Finally, she decided it was time to attend to her own ablutions. Gathering herself up, she went to the bathroom to grab a quick shower before putting on her waitress outfit for the early morning shift at Burp & Freddie's Diner, a local favorite with the tourist crowd. Emerging from the shower, Katie wiped down the mirror and took a good look at herself. *Not bad. Not bad at all, kiddo. Guess my little homemade exercise regimen is doing the trick. After all, I can't be spending time at the gym with my work schedule!* Katie always took pride in the way she looked, but wanted to be extra cautious that her hidden strength remained just that...hidden. It was important that no one suspect this 5'6" blonde was anything but a single, young woman struggling to earn enough to establish her independence.

****

On her way to Burp & Freddie's, Katie reflected on the current influx of tourists. It was the end of November and the height of deer hunting season. The "tourists" at this time of year were not like their summer counterparts, who were a lot more refined and at least knew what proper behavior meant. This lot was cut from different cloth, or perhaps, it was the season that brought out different mannerisms. They were also not necessarily the best tippers, and hunting season was just starting... *It'll get worse!* Sighing, Katie pulled her pristine, turquoise blue, 1957 Chevy into the back of the parking lot that was used by the hired help. "Another day, another dollar," she quipped to herself. "It's almost not worth it."

Katie had been trying various ways of avoiding the verbal assaults that were typical of this year's batch of hunters. She was the most attractive waitress at the diner and had to put up with the brunt of their crude remarks, which made the job harder for her than for most of her fellow workers. She tried her best not to offend the customers, since her tips were greatly affected by her actions. Still, at times, the crudeness just got to her, and she'd have to do what she deemed necessary to maintain her dignity but not lose her job. She could tell from the moment she walked in that today was going to be one of those days that tested her to the limit.

"Hey, blondie!" A crass young man shouted at her from across the diner. "Bring me another cup of Joe, and put your lips to my cup so's I won't have to use any sugar." He leered and winked at her. Katie assessed the group at table six, and by the looks of their rough beards and grubby attire, hunter number one and his tablemates were obviously up for hunting season. However, their lewd remarks and rude behavior suggested that deer, at least the four footed kind, were not their current target. In addition to her observation of their actions, Katie knew that they smelled like they had spent the entire week so far in every bar room from Libertine to Cairo and back.

Katie switched her focus from her assessment back to the man waiting expectantly for her to bring his refill, and thought, *Yeah right, like I haven't heard that line before. Some men can't even come up with an original line*, she mused. It's not that she didn't like men, exactly; she just didn't like rude, dirty, grungy men, who thought they were God's gift to anything in a skirt! *Well,* she thought, *I know a few guys that occasionally like to wear skirts that would just love it if you'd talk dirty to them!* Smiling at this thought, she walked over to the table and began to pour the requested coffee into the cup.

"Hey, sweet thing, now how about putting them pretty lips on my cup?" the man insisted.

Oops, guess I should have wiped that smile off first before grabbing the coffee pot. Despite her inner disdain, she tried to maintain some distance and make light of the obnoxious request. "Now, why would I want to do that?" the green eyed beauty replied evenly. "If I did that for you, then I'd have to do it for every customer. It's just way too busy for that today, so I guess you'll just have to stick to the more conventional sweeteners that are on the table." She kept her tone congenial, trying to avoid a direct confrontation.

"Well, sweet thing, if you want to make some extra cash, I know a few guys that would love to have you serve them some coffee...back at camp." He winked at her while his buddies chuckled in agreement.

Cringing at that thought, Katie answered, "No thanks, I like pouring coffee here, just fine. 'Catering' is not the way I earn my money." She turned to get away from the table, thinking that the guy was starting to get on her nerves and was probably the type to get more aggressive when he was unable to get a response from her. Unfortunately, he didn't fail to live up to her expectations.

Not willing to take "no" for an answer, the overbearing hunter thought he could convince her to change her mind. As she turned to leave, he reached out and grabbed her arm. "Now, I know I can make it worth your while," he drawled. "A pretty thing like you could make some good money working extra for some fine fellas like us." Smug, he searched his buddies' faces for confirmation. "Yeah, Brad. We could use some domestic help back at camp," replied one of his table buddies, while the rest of the group nodded in the affirmative.

Katie was thoroughly incensed. She had put up with his running commentary, but this physical aggression was way beyond tolerable. For just a moment she had an intense desire to show him a thing or two about grabbing someone, but she was able to curb her natural reactions and responded in keeping with her position. "Hey! What do you think you're doing?" she protested. "You can let go of my arm now!" She began to jerk away from the man. In the process, her other hand sloshed hot coffee over the hunting party, with the majority of it landing on hunter number one: Brad. Matters quickly turned ugly as Brad jumped up and yelled at her. "Bitch!" he screamed, as he began wiping at the area where the coffee had made contact. Katie mentally sighed, anticipating his next move and readying herself to fend off the expected retaliation. However, as he reached out to slap Katie, his hand was stopped in its forward motion by another strong hand clasped around his.

"Now, now, that wouldn't be a wise thing to do, would it?" said a low rumbling voice next to his ear. Brad turned to confront the mysterious voice only to stop short and look into the piercing sapphire blue eyes of a six foot plus beauty who just curled her lip, raised an eyebrow in question, and gave him her best feral smile. Recovering a little, Brad stuttered out, "And just who's gonna stop me? You?"

"Yep," came the very confident reply. "With one hand tied behind my back, if you think that'll help." She made a show of moving one hand behind her back while at the same time exerting pressure against the palm of Brad's hand, bending it back towards his wrist. Her action caused him to bend his knees to stave off some of the pain he was beginning to feel, and a little extra push effectively put him back in his seat.

Wanting to save face with his buddies, and noticing that the entire diner was now watching, Brad glared back at the newcomer, and spat out, "Come on, boys, the bitch isn't worth it. Let's get out of here." As his hand was released, he stared at Katie and under his breath threatened, "Until next time, bitch!" Then they all hurriedly left the diner without paying for their breakfast or leaving a tip.

Katie just stood there gazing at the tall, dark, and very beautiful woman who had intercepted her impending encounter with another batch of jerks that deer season in the Catskills seems to produce on a regular basis. She realized that she had been staring for what seemed like an eternity, when the mystery woman stepped up and asked her in a low, gentle voice if she was okay, and broke the spell. Regaining her composure, Katie nodded and said a simple, "Thank you."

As Katie moved to clean up the now-vacant table, her thoughts went to the tall, dark haired woman. *Wow! That was pretty amazing! Here I thought I was gonna have to come out of my shell to fend off that jerk, and I'm saved by a stranger. And what a stranger! I've never seen such gorgeous eyes in my entire life. I probably would have melted myself if her gaze had fallen on me.* Shaking her head, she went back to the task at hand, noticing they hadn't left any money for their bill. "Damn! " Katie mumbled.

"Pardon me?" The tall woman asked.

"Oh, sorry. I wasn't...It's just that those creeps took off without paying their bill...or leaving me a tip for that matter! My boss is going be really mad at that little display, and I'll have to take the money for their bill out of my tips," she explained.

"Yeah, they were creeps alright. But it's not your fault they skipped out on their bill or that they caused a ruckus," the tall beauty offered. "Why would you be held responsible?"

"It's just the rules here. If your table doesn't pay up, you have to cover the bill. It's the waitress' responsibility to make sure the bill is paid. And, Carl is a real stickler about being nice to the tourists so they'll come back often. He wants us to just smile and put up with all their macho crap. Carl says they don't mean anything by it, that they're just here for a good time, so we should 'be good girls and go along.'" The frustration that Katie felt was evident in her voice as she explained to the woman. She looked up into those mesmerizing eyes and took a deep breath, letting it out slowly. "I'm sorry, I shouldn't be going on like this to you; I don't even know you. But I do want to thank you for stepping in. I can usually handle them with words and put up with the pawing, but it's never gotten this close to being threatening before."

"It's okay," the dark haired woman replied. "Name's Deanna. Dean for short. Glad I could help you, Katie."

"How did you...oh, my name badge," she mumbled as she began to turn a very lovely shade of pink. *Come on, kiddo, get your head back into the game. Don't let a pretty face take your mind off of business. Yeah,* she replied to her thoughts, *but what a drop dead gorgeous face!*

Carl chose that moment to come up, interrupting the silence that lingered between the two women and forcing Katie to go back to the table and continue cleaning it up. He looked at her, and the coffee mess, and began a loud tirade directed at his waitress. "Just what were you thinking... spilling coffee all over them like that? You know they could come back here and slap me with a lawsuit over your carelessness!" He was shouting, heedless of who was listening. "Lord knows, there're enough lawyers in this town who would be more than happy to represent them! And I suppose they took off without leaving the money for their bill?" Having reached the real heart of the issue, he looked directly into Katie's eyes with an inquiring look.

Katie turned to avoid his look and was trying to formulate an answer when Dean offered Carl two twenties. "They musta dropped these on their way out the door," she said, smiling at Katie, all the while trying to control her temper long enough to keep from taking care of Carl, too. *Stay cool, Dean,* she counseled herself. *You've called enough attention to yourself for one day. Yeah, but it was worth it for the look you got from the blonde, wasn't it?* she answered herself, chuckling internally.

Katie picked up the bill that was still lying on the table and handed it over to Carl. "Looks like they left enough to cover the bill and my tip."

"Too bad that tip will have to pay for all the coffee you wasted!" Carl said to Katie as he took the money and the bill and walked to the register.

Katie just sighed and looked toward Dean. Sapphires and emeralds met as Carl walked away, and held just a moment longer before Katie broke the spell and asked Dean if she needed a table or wanted to sit at the counter.

"Counter's fine," Dean replied, "just as long as you're the one waiting on me." *Now where in the world did that come from?* thought Dean. *I thought my pick up days were long over!*

Katie smiled and a soft chuckle escaped as she led Dean over to her section of the counter. "Thanks for covering the bill," she said in all sincerity as she handed Dean a menu.

"Who, me?" Dean arched an eyebrow and pointed a finger to her chest.

"Well, who else would have slipped two twenties from her jeans' pocket when she thought I wasn't looking?" Her green eyes twinkled in response.

"Caught me, eh? Must be getting old," the tall beauty said. "Well, I'll start with a cup of tea, herbal if you've got it"

"Coming right up," Katie said as she went to the beverage area to select the box of herbal tea bags, cup, saucer, and hot water. On her return, she swung by the pastry display and grabbed a couple of fresh honey buns. "Here's the tea selection we have; I hope you'll find something in there that you like. And here's a little something to say 'thanks' for what you did." She smiled sweetly at Dean.

Dean took a glance at the honey buns and quickly wondered if there was more to it than just 'thanks.' Raising an eyebrow, she looked at Katie and gave her a nod of appreciation. "You must be more experienced as a waitress than I thought," she drawled. "Either that, or you can read minds." *And if that's the case,* she pondered, *I had better be really careful here.*

"No, on both counts. You just look like the 'honey bun' type," answered Katie, immediately blushing at her choice of words.

Dean frowned, then let a small smile start in the corners of her mouth and said, "I hope you're not saying I look fat?"

Katie gasped and quickly answered, "Oh, no, no, no...you're absolutely gorge...I mean...you look fantas...umm...no, not at all...it's just...unghhh!" Katie threw up her hands and began to blush even more deeply, then gave up trying to explain as Dean broke out into a hearty chuckle.

"So, can I get you anything else?" Katie inquired while looking around the diner and catching Carl's stern eyes watching her.

"No, not right now," Dean replied, "but maybe more hot water in a little bit. Thanks."

Katie left to take care of her other customers, all the while sneaking glances at Dean every chance she could. The mysterious woman was at least six feet tall, dressed in jeans, cowboy boots, and a black and gold Army sweatshirt. *I think this Dean woman is very interesting. I may need to do a little more dig-*

ging to see what I can find out about her, Katie mused to herself. *You just never know what kind of information you can gather from the most unlikely sources.*

Dean settled down to her honey buns and tea while opening the local paper to scan the news and finish with the real estate section. *Not much in this paper,* she thought. *But I guess an area like this can't support a really good daily anyway. Guess I'll have to do my digging the old fashioned way. Maybe I'll start with that cute waitress. She seems to be the talkative type, and you just never know what kind of information you can gather from the most unlikely sources.*

Dean kept a very watchful eye on the diner and its occupants, assessing each as to age, career, local or tourist, socio-economic indicators, etc. She had a very keen mind and was able to categorize each occupant into his own little box for future reference. Some might be possibilities, others definitely not, but she never discarded anyone. She was very thorough. At the same time, she kept an eye on Katie and was very impressed with the young woman's ability to remember orders without writing them down, and her ability to put customers at ease and draw them into conversations. *A very useful talent that! Definitely worth putting some extra time into that one.* She mulled that thought over and decided, with a smile, that it might even turn out to be fun.

On Katie's next pass, she asked if Dean was ready for that hot water. Dean nodded and when Katie returned, they both began to speak at the same time.

"So, how long..." Dean began, overlapping Katie's, "Do you live..." Politeness winning out, they simultaneously offered, "You first..." After the chuckling stopped, Dean waved the waitress on.

"So, do you live around here, or are you a tourist?" Katie asked.

"Just moving up to this area. I've been assigned to the local community college," Dean responded between sips of her second cup of Mint Medley tea.

"Assigned?" Katie looked at her curiously and fixed on the Army sweatshirt.

"Yeah, I'm the new commander for the ROTC unit at the college. I'll be taking over after the winter break," Dean responded.

"So you're in the Army?" Katie asked, pointing to Dean's sweatshirt.

"Yep. Guess I'm being rewarded for doing such a good job on my last assignment," Dean said sarcastically. "My last CO didn't expect me to outshine his good old boys. So I guess this is his way of saving face with them." *Now why on earth am I telling her this?* Dean thought. *You'd think we were long lost buddies or something. Just stick to the program.*

"Wow! I never met a commander before. What are you? A general or something?" Katie asked with wide eyes.

At this, Dean almost choked on her tea, trying to keep it from spraying on the people sitting next to her at the diners' counter. "Not exactly!" Dean coughed out. "I'm just a lowly lieutenant colonel. Just got the promotion, as a matter of fact. Part of the reason I got this cushy posting." Dean sighed, expressing her evident displeasure with her new assignment.

"So, how long have you been in town?" Katie inquired.

Dean looked at her watch and said with a twinkle in her eye. "About forty-five minutes now. The current commander will be finishing out this semester. I came up early to get settled and see what the area is like."

Oh great! Not in town for even an hour, and she finds me—and trouble. Great impression here! Katie thought to herself. "So do you have a place to stay yet?"

"Just the local Days Inn, until I can find something," Dean offered.

Ah, an opportunity to redeem myself. "Well, it just so happens that my next job...after I get off this shift that is...is as a real estate agent for Catskills Properties." Katie bubbled with this information. "And, I happen to know of several very nice apartments and houses for rent. Unless, of course, you're looking to buy?" Bright green eyes questioned the deep blues opposite her.

"Mmmm, 'no' on the buying, but a definite 'yes' on the renting," Dean drawled. "I'm not looking to settle down here, just get this assignment done."

Carl was walking over towards the two women now, clearly upset with the length of time Katie was taking to serve Dean. "Oh, oh. Better get going to my other tables," Katie whispered. "I get off at one from here and will be at the agency by one thirty if you want to meet me there." She quickly pulled out her agency business card and slid it over to Dean as she walked away.

Carl met her halfway down the counter and stopped her. "I thought I told you not to try and do real estate business on my time," he growled out.

"It's bad enough you've been ignoring your customers for the last five minutes. Now either get to work, or get out!" he huffed at her.

Overhearing this, Dean slowly got up and approached Carl who was now standing alone. "Excuse me, but I just wanted to let you know how much I appreciate your employees here." She smiled sweetly at him. "I'm new in town, and it's not often that a new person is greeted with such warmth and friendliness. It's a credit to you as an employer that you encourage this attitude in your staff," she said, batting her blues at him.

Completely taken aback, Carl puffed his chest out a bit then stuttered out a "Why...thank you," as Dean turned and went to the register to pay her bill. *Guess that'll put his knickers in a knot for a while,* she thought, chuckling to herself as she pocketed the business card and smiled, thinking about one thirty and the beautiful blonde.

Same day, 0930 hours

Dean left the diner and got into her brand new black Dodge Durango 4x4 SUV. Just as she was exiting the parking lot, her cell phone chirped. Sliding the phone out of her belt holder, she answered. "Yeah?" The voice at the other end talked on for a few minutes before Dean replied, "Sunday, o-two-thirty, affirmative," and returned the cell to its holder. *Well, let's see how much time a tour of this town will take,* she thought as she pulled up to one of the few traffic signals in town.

Main Street looked like many other main streets across the country. There were lots of empty storefronts, and several people, mostly young men, standing around in the doorways smoking cigarettes. This main street, like many others, was being swallowed whole into the depths of oblivion thanks to the megamall concept sweeping the country. *Makes it tough for little towns like this to survive. With few businesses to tax, it leaves the homeowner carrying the brunt of the load.* Dean just shook her head as she drove through what once would have been a thriving business section. She wondered what these folks did for a living. She remembered Carl's words about an abundant supply of lawyers in town and noticed that he was absolutely correct. Practically every building in town housed a law office. *Hmm, wonder what keeps them all going.* Dean mused, as she continued her drive out into the country.

It was a glorious November day, with crystalline blue skies above. Considering she was in the Catskills, it was a very mild November day with a temperature in the low sixties. All in all, Dean was starting to perk up. The countryside was lifting the subdued mood which had enveloped her during her drive through town. She reached down and turned the radio on looking for something to sing along with. She hit upon an oldies station playing a marathon of Elvis songs that brought a smile to her face. Soon she was cruising through the country singing along to *Hound Dog, Blue Suede Shoes,* and *Love Me Tender.* That last one brought her mind back to the diner and the green-eyed beauty she was going to meet in another couple of hours.

Now, now, Dean. You've got dirty work to do here, and you don't need to get involved with a civilian and have her get caught in the middle, said her conscience. "Yeah, but I need to get some basic info on this town, and a peek into its citizens, too." she argued out loud. "And what better source than a talkative waitress who must know everyone in town—and a real estate agent to boot!" she concluded. *OK, but try to keep to the K.I.S.S. principle. You wouldn't want to see those pretty green eyes in pain, now would you?* her conscience finished. "Oh, yeah! Exactly what I had in mind...the 'KISS' principle!" She chuckled at her own joke as she started to wind her way back to town.

* * * * * * * * * *

Katie worked extra hard the next few hours—concentrating on her customers, and trying to soothe Carl's ruffled feathers too. But her mind kept wandering back to the enigmatic Dean. *I wonder what it would have been like if I had decided to go that route in college instead of the route I chose? Who knows, maybe I could have been a colonel, too?* She chuckled inwardly at that thought. *Who ever heard of a twenty-eight year old colonel?* Still, she had always had a soft spot for a military uniform. *Mmmm...bet she looks great in her dress uniform. OK, Katie, snap out of it! You've chosen your path in life, and it's not been that bad of a road either,* she admonished herself. *If it hadn't been for the last three months of last year, things would be really peachy. Ok, it wasn't my fault, but we lost a lot of groundwork, and now I've got to start all over. I can do this without Gerry,* she thought, as her eyes started to tear. *Don't go there, kiddo. It wasn't your fault. There's nothing you could have done.* Then her thoughts returned to the tall Army colonel. *Hmmm, too bad I don't know Dean better. She could turn out to be an asset if played right.* Katie continued with her inner conversation all the while she was taking orders and cleaning up the tables.

Table number five was just getting up to leave. As she watched them pull out the money for the check, she caught a glimpse of a gun under the leather jacket of one of the Asian men. Intrigued, she nonchalantly moved closer to see if she could catch a piece of their conversation. "...meeting with...two thirty...Hollow Road." Those were all the pieces she could snatch before they stopped their conversation and motioned her over to pay for their lunch.

"Can I get you anything else?" Katie asked with a sweet smile.

"No, thank you," came the answer in a decidedly Oriental accent.

Katie hesitated and said, "I guess you're not from around here. Are you passing through, or need directions anywhere?" she offered.

"No, we know the area quite well. Thank you," the man answered politely.

"OK then. Thanks for coming in, and maybe we'll see you again. I'll be back with your change in just a minute," she offered as she accepted their money and the check.

"Keep the change," the oldest man said as he and his two partners turned to leave the diner.

Katie nodded her thanks and began to clean up their table, all the while committing their looks to memory. Three Asian males, probably Chinese, two approximately 5' 8", 150 pounds, dark brush cut hair, very neatly attired, business suits, late twenties to early thirties. Third male, the one with the gun under his black leather jacket—5' 10', 300 lbs., shaved head, scar over left eye, mid twenties. She looked up to see what kind of car they drove and saw them get into a black, four-door Lexus with a New York plate. She couldn't read the plate number from this distance, but noticed that the Lexus was trimmed in gold rather than silver. *Hhmm. Now that was interesting,* she thought to herself. *Could be some businessmen up from the city. But with a bodyguard? Definitely have to keep my eyes open for these guys.*

Katie finished up table five and went to the back room to clock out since it was now 1:10 PM. *Better get changed, kiddo, so you can meet your mystery woman!* Her thoughts now focused on Dean, and she found herself smiling at the thought of being able to spend some time with her, even if it was for business. *For some reason,* she mused, *I just felt very comfortable and safe around her.* That realization brought her train of thought to an abrupt stop. *No time for fun and games, kiddo, you've got work to do! Must be just that 'stepping in to help' thing she did this morning. You're just not used to that. Yeah, that's it!*

* * * * * * * * * *

It was now noon, and Dean had some time yet to burn. She decided to stop at the local Wendy's for a quick bite of fast food instead of going back to the diner to watch Katie some more. This was her conscience winning out and losing at the same time. *After all,* thought Dean, *my conscience should reward me for being good...so a nice cheeseburger, fries, and a Frosty should be just the thing!* Dean placed her order and was walking over to a table in the corner when she heard a voice holler, "Dean! Is that really you?" She turned to see an old Army friend sitting at a booth in the middle of the room. Smiling, Dean gave a big nod, then headed over to the table to join her. "Well, Tracy! What in the name of Athena are you doing here?" Dean asked.

"I work here," Tracy replied. Noting Dean's questioning eyebrow, she quickly added, "No, not here. I'm the Park & Rec director in this town. Got out of the Army a few years back. Couldn't stomach the hassles anymore. Finished up as a major though, just before I left," Tracy offered. "How about you? What are you doing in this neck of the woods?"

"I've been assigned as the commander of the ROTC program at the college," Dean supplied. "Guess I finally outrank you! I've just made lieutenant colonel." She winked and chuckled.

"Well, I'll be damned. How on earth did you do that? You're awful young to be a lieutenant colonel," Tracy commented. "Counting on my fingers, you should be a captain at most."

"Just in the right place at the right time. Got put on the fast track for promotion. If you remember, I was just a wet-behind-the-ears first lieutenant last I saw you. Been quite a ride since," Dean stated.

"So, you gave up Intelligence to ride roughshod on kids, eh?" Tracy shook her head. "Doesn't sound like you, old friend."

"Well, you know what it's like to follow orders, Major." Dean looked into Tracy's eyes and the knowledge passed unspoken between the two ex-comrades.

"Well, guess I'll have to take you out to my pride and joy sometime," Tracy offered, breaking the short silence that arose. "Got a park on the top of one of the mountains here. You can see forever in all directions. It's really quite something." Dean nodded, storing the unspoken information for later retrieval.

As the two friends finished their meals, they caught up on the lost time as well as reminisced on some of the shared memories of old times. Curious about the large number of lawyers in town, Dean decided to ask Tracy what the scoop was. "Well," Tracy replied, "it seems that our summer visitors don't know how to drive too well, and we have a rash of auto crashes that result in lots of litigation that keep these guys employed," Tracy explained, chuckling. "You really do need to be very observant on the road in the summertime. We get an awful lot of folks up from the city who are used to driving wildly or not driving at all. Add to that all of the immigrants that work the resorts, and you have quite an eclectic society here in our quaint little town. In fact, I was told that there are approximately fifty-seven different dialects spoken in this county."

Too soon, it was time for Dean to leave for her 1:30 appointment. Almost as an afterthought, Dean asked Tracy, "Do you know a waitress by the name of Katie that works at Burp & Freddie's Diner?"

"Sure," Tracy responded, with a little twinkle in her eyes. "Nice gal. Came here just about eight months ago. Lives over in the trailer court off the main highway going east. Has a great work ethic. Think she's working two or three different jobs," Tracy continued. "A really nice looking gal, too. Has eyes that can look right through you...kinda like yours, Dean," Tracy added.

"How'd you get to know so much about her?" The eyes under discussion were reflecting the twinkle in Tracy's.

Tracy smiled back, "She came in looking for a job when she first got to town. Didn't have anything to offer her at the time. She occasionally takes a class from us, or comes to the women's open gym when she's not working. Pretty good athlete, too. Not what you'd expect after seeing her in the waitress get up," Tracy commented. "There's something about her, though, that just doesn't add up. Haven't been able to put my finger on it yet, but I will," she said. "Why the interest?"

"Just curious. I'm going to meet her now. I ran into her at the diner this morning, and she offered to show me some places to rent. I got the same feeling—about things not adding up, but that could just be habit. Well, thanks for the insight, and the reunion. It's good to know there's a friendly face in town," Dean said, giving Tracy a pat on the back. After getting directions to Catskill Properties, Dean and Tracy parted, agreeing to meet again in the near future.

****

An agent named Tim was at the reception desk in the office when Dean came in. "Hi," he said with a brilliant smile. "How may I help you?"

"I'm here to meet one of your agents," Dean said, a serious look on her face.

"Who's the agent?" he inquired.

Dean pulled out Katie's card, realizing that she had never bothered to read it and only knew Katie's first name. "Umm, Katie Miller," Dean answered.

"She's not here right now, but I'd be glad to help you," Tim offered eagerly, just as Katie came rushing in the front door. "Oh, here she is," Tim acknowledged, with obvious disappointment in his voice.

"Hi!" Katie slowed her steps as she approached Dean. "Sorry I'm late."

"No problem," Dean answered. "I just got here myself."

"Come this way over to my desk, and we can get started," the beautiful blonde said, leading the way back to a corner desk. Dean followed, taking in the small cramped quarters loaded with notebooks and bulletin boards filled with a wide range of houses, businesses, and property descriptions and pictures. Maps of various parts of the town and county filled the rest of the walls. Stacks of flyers providing prospective homeowners with all sorts of information on shopping, churches, insurance agencies, and even the local parks and recreation flyer, topped the tables scattered about the room. Katie eyed the tall woman taking in the organized mess that real estate offices tended to be. "Sorry about the clutter," she offered, "but that's the name of the game in this business. Have a seat, and we'll get some basic information before we make a list of possibilities to view. But first, I need you to fill in some personal information on this sheet." Katie's polite request was business, but her interest was hardly strictly professional.

Dean took the sheet and began filling out the necessary information in her neat printing. While she was occupied with this task, Katie pulled out the rental notebook and began familiarizing herself with the current offerings while covertly watching Dean work on the sheet. *Mmm, nice woman,* she thought, mentally inventorying Dean's assets and filing them for later review. *Probably 6'1", about 165 -170 lbs., nice athletic build, no distinguishing marks or tattoos, about 32 to 34 years old, strong hands, expressive eyebrows, long silky black hair, fantastic blue eyes, inviting lips...whoa! Stick to the basics, kiddo!* Feeling a little heat starting to creep up her neck, Katie decided to keep her eyes in the rental book until Dean was finished.

Dean straightened and handed Katie her sheet wondering where the slight blush on Katie's face came from. Putting that thought out of her mind, she asked when they would be able to check out some possibilities.

"Just as soon as I see what you listed for price range and location. Ah, here we go, Miss Peterson, or should I say Lieutenant Colonel Peterson?" Katie asked with a question in her voice.

"Just Dean will do. I prefer to leave the Colonel part for the job."

"Looks like you prefer a house over a condo or apartment and something in the $800 - $1,200 range. Being close to the college is not as important as your privacy, I see. Same goes for me," Katie commented. "I've got a small trailer out on the east side of town. It's in a really nice park, especially this time of year. Not a lot of neighbors since most of them are senior citizens that fly south for the winter. Not a lot of kids either, but that's okay too I guess, though I do miss hearing the pure laughter of children at play," she said cocking her head to one side.

"I think I know just the place for you. It's located on one of the back roads that will take you to the college. There's a nice stream that runs behind it that I'm told has a reputation as a trout fisherman's paradise...if you like to fish, that is," she inquired with a smile on her pretty face.

"Yeah, I do as a matter of fact. I have a rather unorthodox method, but it puts the fish on the table," Dean answered, fondly remembering her last fishing trip with her brother Thad.

"Well, that's not all. It's set on twenty acres of land, has two bedrooms, one bath, a fieldstone fireplace, eat-in kitchen that has recently been remodeled, a small den/living room combination, loft, and a fully screened porch. There are also two outbuildings: a two-car garage that's semi-attached to the house by a covered carport type of set up, and a small workshed. It's all stone exterior, so there's little maintenance." Katie took a breath. "It has a private road that's only a half mile off the main road. If I remember correctly, it shouldn't be a bad road in the winter, either. I can set you up with a plow service that will come in after a snowfall and clean it out for you, if you like. It even has an auxiliary power system in case of ice storms. Best thing is, it's available immediately," Katie finished with a flourish.

"Sounds good," the tall beauty responded. "Can we take a look at it now? I'd like to get out of the Days Inn as soon as possible."

"Sure thing. I'll get the key and be right back." The blonde got up and went into the back room to retrieve a set of keys.

Hmm, sounds perfect, right down to the auxiliary power supply, Dean thought as she watched the green-eyed woman return with keys in hand and a smile on her face. "My car is right out front," Katie supplied as she reached for her backpack. The two women exited the office and walked over to Katie's car.

"Wow!" Dean whistled. "Nice car you've got here, Ms. Miller. Where'd you find a '57 Chevy in such cherry condition? Did you buy it this way?"

"No, actually, I inherited it from my great aunt. I did give it a new paint job almost a year ago, but the inside is as clean as the day it left the showroom. The mileage is accurate too. Only 28,535 miles! Carl keeps trying to get me to sell it to him, but no way. It's my baby!" Katie purred. "With a solid V8, this baby can really haul as...tires," she corrected quickly.

"Ass is more like it," Dean drawled, smiling back at the embarrassed young woman. "It's definitely a beauty. How is it in snow?"

"Haven't really had a chance to check it out that way, yet. We had a fairly mild spring this year, and I just got it right before I moved up from Virginia." Katie said, mentally kicking herself for giving away more information about herself in the last fifteen minutes than anyone else in town knew or had found out in eight months. *How does she do that?* the blonde asked herself. *I'm babbling on like a nervous beau on a first date.*

"So what did you do in Virginia?" Dean nonchalantly posed the question.

"Uuhh, nothing really. I had just been living there with my great aunt before she passed away," Katie said as she unlocked the door and slid into the driver's seat. Dean got in on the passenger side and enjoyed the room she had for her long legs. "Let's go, shall we?" Katie suggested to Dean, and put the car in gear.

The ride out to the house was fairly short since the agency was on the east side of town too. It took only twelve minutes before they were pulling into the covered space between the house and the garage. Katie jumped out of the car and pulled the house keys from her pants pocket. Unlocking the door, she turned on the lights so Dean would have a good view of the inside. The place was really a bargain at $1,150 a month plus utilities. *Sure wish I could live out here,* she thought wistfully. *The cats would love the big windows, and I'm sure there would be plenty of wildlife to entertain them while I'm gone. But, that would raise too many eyebrows and blow a few holes in my story to boot! No way I'm supposed to be able to afford a place like this.* The '57 Chevy wasn't the only thing Katie had inherited from her aunt. She had a sizable savings account back in Arlington, too.

As Dean entered, she looked around, checking the place out fully as she roamed from room to room.

Security on the windows was pretty tight, the entrance and back exits were of solid construction, and views of the approaching road were very good. The place even had a security system and some basic furniture, not that she required much. And the fireplace was awesome. *I'm looking forward to a nice fire already. Not bad,* she thought, *not bad at all.* She went outside and walked the perimeter of the house, approving the inaccessibility to a rear approach due to the sheer cliff that rose up on the other side of the stream. The out-buildings checked out, too. The shed would come in handy for storing some of the stuff that would be coming in next week, and it was as secure as the house and garage. It even had a small wood stove for heat. The sheltered area in which the house was located might wreak havoc with her cell phone, but once she got the satellite dish in place, her communi-cations system would operate fine.

"Well, I don't think we have to look any further. I'll take it." She smiled warmly at Katie. "Does the furniture stay?" Dean asked hopefully.

"Oh, yeah, I forgot about that. Yes, it does, unless you don't need it. Then we would put it in storage for our client. The kitchen is stocked with plates, cooking utensils, and all the necessary gizmos that you need in a kitchen," she elaborated brightly.

"Great, I really don't have much." *Who are you trying to kid? All you've got is what's packed in your SUV,* she chided herself. "Let's go sign the papers, or whatever we need to do. You said it's available immediately. Does that mean today?"

"Yep. All I need is the lease signed, six months at a time, and first and last month's rent. The security deposit is one thousand. Hope that's not too much at once," she probed carefully. "The utilities are all on, and we can change them over to you on Monday."

"Great." Dean said. "Uncle Sam is pretty good about moving us around. I can cover the security deposit and two months' rent without a problem."

They locked up and got into the Chevy to head back to town. Katie was feeling a little disappointed that her time with Dean was coming to an end so quickly. *Damn! I should have hauled her around to a few other places before coming here. Bad Katie!* Her mental conversation was interrupted when Dean asked her rather loudly if she was okay. "Huh? Oh, sorry. Guess I was just getting all the paperwork together in my head before we get to the office," she stammered. "What were you saying?"

"I was asking you if you could recommend a good Chinese take-out," Dean said, trying to interpret the solemn face that had replaced the blonde's seemingly normal happy disposition. For some reason, Dean was very drawn to this young woman and didn't want to see their time together end. This brought on a more somber demeanor within her, and she began to wonder if the young blonde was having the same reaction.

"Well, there are actually quite a few really good ones in town. But my favorite is next to the grocery store across from the office," she stated, and then had a brainstorm. "If you'd like, after we get the paper-work taken care of, you could go back to the Days Inn and check out. Then pick up any odds and ends you might need to stock the fridge, linen closet, etcetera. After I get off work, I'll stop by my place to feed my cats, then bring some Chinese food over to celebrate your new home." *Getting a little forward aren't you, kiddo? Oh, what the heck, all she can do is say 'no'.*

"Umm, sure. That sounds good to me," Dean answered with a bright smile that almost made Katie shiver visibly. "But, on one condition—I buy. It's the least I can do to show my appreciation for you helping me find a place so quickly. I was really dreading house hunting, but you made it quick and painless. Thanks." She smiled again, and they locked eyes for a brief moment that made the world slow down around them. A horn blaring brought them both back to the world and, back to their own side of the road.

"Oops, sorry about that," the blonde said nervously, aware that something had just passed between them and it gave her a feeling of anticipation that all would be right with the world. The rest of the ride, and the subsequent paperwork, took place without further incident. They parted, each to complete her own separate tasks before they would meet again later that night.

Same day, 1930 hours

Katie's concentration was not what it should have been the rest of the afternoon. At five o'clock, she left the real estate office and headed home to change and feed the cats. As she opened the door to her trailer, she was met by three felines that took turns wrapping themselves around her legs. "Okay, gals, this is what's going to happen. I'm going to feed you, change, and then leave again; and I don't want to find any hairballs in my bed as your way of showing your disgust with me. Okay?" Their response came in the guise of three mews of different octaves and qualities. Butter's came as a normal mew, Sugar's was a quiet chirp, but Spices' was a demanding MEOW! "Okay, okay. I get the picture. Feed you first, talk later!" After feeding her crew, Katie went to her bedroom to change into something more comfortable. She was looking for something that would be comfy but also alluring, and fantasized that the evening would become more than just dinner. *Yeah, like that's a possibility! Still, there's something about her. Something about the way we fall into each other's eyes. It's gotta be more than just a passing feeling. It's like we've been there before or something. A connection of some kind. Come on, Katie, snap to!*

Katie settled on her favorite pair of black jeans and added a deep green silk blouse and her favorite loafers. Not one to wear much jewelry, she added a pair of black pearl studs, fluffed her short hair, and added just a touch of Bill Blass. Satisfied with her reflection in the mirror, Katie went out to the kitchen to rummage for the vanilla candle she just bought last week. *Hhmm, I'll just take this along as a housewarming gift. Who knows, it may come in handy during an ice storm or something...hopefully 'or something!' Especially since there's that back-up power supply,* she conceded with a wry grin.

After final instructions to her cats and turning on the living room light, Katie left the trailer to pick up the Chinese dinners, hoping beyond hope that this evening would become a night to remember.

* * * * * * * * * *

Dean managed to get checked out of the Days Inn in record time. Her bags were still packed since she had just checked in that morning. Stopping to pick up some bare essentials—like bed sheets and towels— didn't take long. Going through the grocery store, however, did. She hated grocery shopping. Especially in a new store where she didn't even know the set up of the aisles. It took her several trips around the store before she finally had the items she wanted. On her way out to the SUV, she noticed the liquor store and thought that she'd add a few more things to her larder. Once her purchases had been completed, she headed out to her new place, happy that she would not have to spend the night in a lonely hotel room. Nor would she have to spend the evening alone.

It's been a long time since you entertained any thoughts of companionship, Dean smiled to herself. *Not that you haven't had any offers. Come on, Dean, be honest—there just hasn't been anyone you cared enough about to want their companionship.* She found herself hoping that the young blonde would turn out to be good company and, if truth be told, she hoped for even more. She couldn't understand it, but there was a definite attraction there. *Hmm, never been drawn to someone so quickly before. It almost feels like déjà vu or something.* "She's so young, though. What would she see in an old war horse like me?" Dean asked herself out loud. "Guess we'll find out."

It didn't take long for Dean to get settled in her new place. The few items she had purchased found their way to linen shelves, bath, and kitchen with ease. She had just enough time to take a quick shower, change, and set up her compact Bose stereo before her company was due to arrive. With some vintage Stan Getz playing in the background, Dean assessed her appearance and gave a nod of approval. She had picked out a pair of black chinos, a sapphire blue blouse, black vest, socks and her favorite cowboy boots. The result was stunning. Her long silky black hair and sapphire eyes complemented the outfit.

She left her bedroom to check on the wine she had opened and set aside to 'breathe.' On her way back to the living room, she caught a glimpse of headlights coming down the road. By the time she walked to the entrance door and released the deadbolts, Katie was getting out of her car with a couple of bags. "Need any help?" Dean called.

"No thanks, I think I've got it all." Katie shut her car door and headed up the slate walkway. As she entered and set the bags down, she pulled out the candle she brought for the housewarming. "Here's a small housewarming present for you. I thought it might come in handy sometime. It's nice to be prepared," Katie said as Dean accepted the small gift.

"Thanks for the nice thought," Dean said. "Of course with that back-up power system, I probably won't need it for light. So how about we light it now and add a little ambiance to the dinner table?" the dark beauty offered with a smile. "Mmm, this stuff smells good. Are you as hungry as I am?" Dean asked the young woman, leading her to the kitchen.

"I could eat a horse," Katie replied. "You don't know how much willpower it took for me to keep from ripping into those bags on the way over here."

"Guess we'd better get you fed then," the tall beauty suggested as they opened up the bags and spread out the feast. Dean asked if Katie would like some wine with dinner, to which the green-eyed blonde eagerly agreed.

"I've got merlot, zinfandel, cabernet, and char-donnay," Dean stated. "Name your poison," she invited the blonde.

"Wow! What'd ya do? Buy out the whole liquor store?" Katie asked in awe.

"Not really, I just didn't know what your tastes would be. I also have some beer just in case you didn't want wine, and soda too, in case you preferred something non-alcoholic," Dean said with a twinkle and a smile.

They settled on the cabernet, since it had already been allowed to breathe, and then attacked the food. Dinner passed quietly as they both concentrated on the food as well as sneaking glances at each other in the candlelight. The women furtively appraised each other during the meal and, if they had compared results, they would have found that their attraction to each other was mutual. It didn't take them long to devour everything in sight, while mentally, each con-cluded that she wouldn't mind pursuing this fledgling friendship a bit further.

"Phew!" Dean said as she pushed away from the table. "I didn't realize how hungry I was. That moo shu veggie dish was great, and the kung pao too."

"Yeah, I enjoyed those too, but the hot and sour soup was a real tummy warmer, and this wine is great," Katie commented as she took a sip of her third glass. She started to clean up the empty little cardboard cartons and put them back into the larger bag. "Guess we can have the fortune cookies later, huh?" she suggested as she plucked them out of the paper sack.

"Sounds good to me," Dean agreed. "I don't have a TV, just my compact stereo system and books right now. Would you mind putting in a few more CD's while I take the trash out?" she asked Katie, who nodded in response.

Katie walked into the living room and over to the bookshelf that held the stereo. Looking through the CD's, she saw quite an eclectic selection. Dean seemed to enjoy all sorts of music. She had CD's from artists like Enya and Ronstadt to Natalie Cole and Yanni. There was even some Nana Mouskuri and Stan Getz. Just about every type of music was available, from musicals, to classical, to country and rock & roll. *So, I guess it's up to me to set the mood, eh? Pretty sneaky, Dean*, she thought to herself. As Dean came back inside, Katie remarked on her collection and asked what kind of music she didn't like.

"I'm not real fond of rap and hard rock, but music that touches my soul is what I like best," Dean answered.

Katie thought to herself that her selections of Cole's *Unforgettable* and *Stardust*, and Ronstadts *'round Midnight*, followed by Chip Davis' *Romance* should be met with approval. She knew she was right when she saw Dean smile as "The Very Thought Of You " started to play.

Nice selection, Dean mused, *and very appropriate, too.* "Say, Katie, I brought some maps in with me. Mind helping me get acquainted with the area?" Dean asked innocently as she brought over the maps and refilled glasses of wine.

"Sure," Katie replied. "Let's spread them out on the floor in front of the fireplace," she suggested. She took her wineglass and the maps from Dean and knelt down on the floor spreading them out in front of her. Dean joined her on the floor, and they both began to look them over as Katie pointed out places of interest, historical sites, and the like.

"This area right here is a recreation area on top of this mountain. There's a heck of a view of almost the entire county from here," she said enthusiastically.

"Really?" Dean asked, enjoying the fire, the wine, and the closeness of the attractive blonde next to her. *She really is beautiful*, thought Dean. *The way the firelight reflects off her golden hair and makes her emerald eyes sparkle like jewels in a treasure chest. I think I could get lost in those eyes forever and never want to be found!* "Have you ever been up there?" she asked as she brought herself back to reality.

"Yeah, lots of times. I go hiking up there whenever I can. The park is officially closed now, but you can park outside and hike up. Except at night. They frown on people up there at night, but I hear they do make exceptions...if it's a good reason," she offered.

"Hhmm, I'll have to remember that. It may be a good site for some night maneuvers for the ROTC class," Dean stated matter-of-factly.

"Ooo, that would be cool," the blonde agreed. "This plateau here," she said pointing to a spot on the map, "gives you about a 300 degree view, and if you walk over to here," again pointing to another spot, "you can catch a 180 degree view that includes the part you missed. I was up there a few weekends ago, and the fall colors were awesome," Katie continued with exuberance. "You should check it out sometime."

"So...would you be interested in giving me a guided tour?" Dean asked, raising an eyebrow and curling her mouth into a smile.

"You bet!" The blonde eagerly responded. "I'm off tomorrow. Would that be too soon?"

"Nope, just right," Dean said, while mentally calculating the view from the mountain relative to her objective at 0230 Sunday morning.

Katie went back to the maps and continued her visual tour of the county for Dean, as well as finishing her fourth glass of wine for the evening. "Well, that's about it," Katie finished, wondering why a Lieutenant Colonel in the Army would need anyone to read a map to her. *Not that I'm complaining*, she thought. *In fact, I'm really enjoying this. It's been so long since I've felt this comfortable with anyone... Maybe it's the wine talking. You have had a bit more than you're used to, kiddo.* Katie rolled over on her back and found herself staring into beautiful sapphire blue eyes, finding them much more intoxicating than the wine. Their eyes locked for a very long time. Each lost in the depths of the other, both wanting more, both hesitating.

Trying to pull herself out of the emerald sea, Dean managed to say, "Well, I guess it's time to see what the fortune cookies have in store for us." She stood up to retrieve them, and then offered Katie her pick first. Katie blushed upon reading hers which brought a raised eyebrow and smile to Dean's face. "So...what's it say?" Dean asked with a disarming smile.

"Uhh...nothing...just the usual," responded a very nervous, blushing Katie. "What'd yours say," she asked quickly to divert Dean's attention away from her.

"Not so fast, young lady," Dean countered. "I'll tell you mine after you tell me yours."

Katie blushed again, and then fabricated, "I'm going on a long trip." She attempted to toss the paper into the fire, but didn't count on the quick reflexes of the tall woman.

"Hhmm...let's see," Dean said as she began to unwrap the small fortune, all the while fending off a slightly inebriated blonde. "*You are going to fall in love with a tall dark stranger,*" Dean read, then stopped, realizing the two women were now in a rather intimate position due to the mock fight over the piece of paper. She coughed and then began to flush a bit herself from the implication of the fortune and the intimate position.

In an attempt to recover, Katie protested, "No fair," then reached out to grab Dean's fortune. She opened it up and read: "*You will soon come to a crossroad in life. Take care to follow the right path.* Yikes," the blonde exclaimed, "I think I like mine better!"

"Well," whispered Dean, "I've never had much faith in fortune telling."

"Yeah, me either," said a now quiet Katie. She glanced at her watch and was surprised to see it was already past midnight. "Umm, guess it's time for me to be going home," she said as she attempted to rise, only to quickly return to the floor as a wave of dizziness hit her. "Whew. Guess I had more wine than I'm used to," the young woman admitted, as she put her hand out in an attempt to make the room stop spinning.

"Don't think you'll be driving anywhere," a very concerned Dean said, as she moved over to support the young blonde. "Why don't you just stay in the guest room for tonight?"

"I really can't," protested the blonde as she slowly stood. "Sugar has seizures, and I've gotta give her her medicine."

"Well, you're definitely not driving home. I've only had two glasses tonight, so I'll take you home," Dean said as she continued to steady the young woman.

"No need, Dean, I can drive home. It's only eight minutes down the road, and I'm not that drunk," Katie protested, feeling a bit embarrassed about her lightheadedness.

"You're right," Dean answered. "It is only eight minutes down the road, so it's no problem for me to take you home... And that's an order, young lady."

"Yes, ma'am!" Katie said with a mock salute that would have put her back on the floor, save for Dean's quick reflexes. Dean's arms caught Katie in a quick smooth action that brought them together in a very close embrace. An embrace that found them unwilling to let go of each other, found them both longing to hold on forever, never letting the moment end. Dean wasn't ready for the sensual shock wave that rolled through her as she felt the lithe body beneath the soft silkiness of Katie's blouse. As emeralds and sapphires met this time, Katie gave in to her desire and tilted her head up, softly placing a tender kiss on Dean's lips.

Dean was taken by surprise by this action, even though all night long she had wanted to do just what the blonde had dared. The feeling that went through her body with that simple kiss ignited a fire that she knew would rage out of control if she allowed herself to submit. Softly, gently, Dean released the emerald-eyed blonde and whispered, "As much as I enjoyed that, I don't think it would be a wise choice for us to continue...especially in your current condition. It wouldn't be right for either of us," she stated, gently brushing the blonde's cheek with her thumb. "You understand that, don't you?"

"Yes...no...yes, I suppose," came the confused answer from Katie. "I hope I didn't...I mean...I don't know why I did that." She continued to stammer. "I just couldn't stop myself. I'm sorry," Katie said as tears began to fill her eyes.

"Shhhh," said Dean, still stroking Katie's cheek while pulling her into a tender embrace. "It's okay, really. But I think it's best we get you home for now." *The sooner, the better, or I'm not going to be able to let you go,* she told herself mentally. *Hell, I must be nuts to be sending you home, but there's just something about you, Katie. Something I'm feeling that*

I've never felt before. And I don't want to ruin any chance of keeping your friendship because I took advantage of you. No, no, my beautiful new friend. If we do become lovers, I want it to be on a mutual and sober basis.

"Okay," Katie replied. "You're sure you don't mind taking me home?" *Noooo*, she mentally protested. *I really don't want to go, or leave the comfort of your arms, ever!*

Dean just shook her head and smiled, then led Katie to her car to begin the short trip to her home.

Saturday, 0130 hours

Six minutes later, Dean was pulling up to the last trailer on the cul-de-sac that was Katie's modest residence. When she put the car in park, Katie suddenly reached over and put her hand on Dean's arm.

"What's wrong?" Dean asked quietly.

"I know I left a light on in the living room, and I just saw the curtains close as we came down the road," Katie said in a very low tone. "I think there's someone in my trailer."

"Could it have been one of the cats?" Dean inquired, while carefully looking around the exterior of the unit and peering at the neighbor's trailers. She noted a beat-up pick-up truck at the trailer to the left, but no vehicle at the trailer on the right, and no lights on in either. "Can you go to the neighbor's while I check it out?" she asked the now very alert blonde.

"No, it wasn't the cats, and I'm the only one here this time of year. At least in this part of the park.

Everyone else has already left for Florida," she commented while noting the pick-up next door. "I don't recognize that truck. There shouldn't be a vehicle there at all," she said in a whisper as she pointed it out.

"Okay, give me your keys. You stay here while I check it out," Dean instructed.

"No, way!" Katie protested. "I'm going with you."

"No, stay here!" commanded the tall beauty. "You're in no condition to be of help. Besides, I'm the one with the military training." Dean exited her SUV and stealthily made her way towards the trailer.

All of Dean's instincts and training were now at full alert. She carefully surveyed the trailer, making a quick circuit around it and checking the back door. Then she returned to the front and walked up on the small porch. She placed the key in the door, noticing the scratches on the frame that indicated a very sloppy forced entry. As the door opened, she heard a sound to her right that could not have been made by one of the cats. She quickly slammed the door open into the head of the man behind it, knocking him to the floor. Then she turned to her left to block a blow coming from a second intruder, did a quick turning kick which connected with his head and sent him to the floor to join his buddy. A third man caught her from behind in a chokehold, while a fourth began to land a series of blows to her abdomen. Dean tightened her abdominals to absorb the blows, while she grabbed for the arms holding her from behind. Using this hold as leverage, she lifted her torso and caught the front attacker in a vise grip between her strong legs. A split second later, her rear attacker released his grip, falling to the floor behind her and providing a cushion for Dean as she fell backward, flipping the man in front over her head and onto the floor. She stood quickly, waiting for the next attack. Hearing the sound behind her, she turned to deliver another blow, but pulled it at the last moment when she recognized the blonde standing behind her.

"Whoa, it's me!" called Katie.

"I thought I told you to stay in the SUV!" Dean said, a bit too harshly.

"Yeah, well, when I heard all the crashing, I thought you needed some help," she explained. "I came in and saw that jerk choking you from behind while the other was pummeling you, so I smacked the guy over the head with my frying pan."

"No wonder he released his grip," Dean said as she raised an eyebrow. "But next time, do what I say. I'm trained to do hand-to-hand, and you're not. Besides, I was in total control of the situation." She softened her voice as she took in the mess she had created in the cramped quarters.

"Okay, but you didn't *look* like you were in control, what with the guy in back and the other guy in front." The blonde agreed verbally, but mentally smiled at the thought of Dean finding out she was a black belt in several martial arts and had finished first in her class at Quantico in hand-to-hand combat.

"I just needed two more seconds, and I would have had them right where I wanted them," Dean protested.

Katie reached over to pick up her table lamp and clicked it back on to survey the faces of the downed perps. "Well, what d'ya know," she remarked, pointing to the first fallen victim. "Isn't that the creep you stopped from hitting me at the diner this morning?"

"Yep," Dean replied, making a tsk tsk sound. "These boys need to learn to play nice. Do you want to call the police while I truss them up?" she asked the green-eyed blonde with a smile.

"Uhh, I think I'd rather just dump them into their truck, if it's okay with you. I really don't want to get the police involved," Katie offered tentatively. *That's all I need,* she thought. *The police might ask a few too many questions and find out more than they need to know.*

"It's okay with me, but are you sure?" Dean lifted an eyebrow in question. "They may come back," she cautioned.

"Oh, I don't think they'll come back here after the whupping they just got," the blonde chuckled.

"Yeah, you're probably right," Dean agreed, joining in the laughter.

Together, they physically dragged the men outside and dumped them into the truck bed. It was beginning to rain, and the men started to come to as the last of them was unceremoniously tossed in.

Dean looked at Brad, grabbed his shirt collar, gave him her most feral smile, and spoke in the most menacing voice possible. "I don't want to see your sorry butts around here again. If I do, you'll get twice the beating you took tonight. Ya got that!"

At that, Brad tumbled out of the truck bed and got behind the wheel. He quickly backed out of the driveway, and then burned rubber out of the trailer park. Dean and Katie watched and laughed at the sight of the other three bodies hanging on for their lives, as Brad swerved back and forth up the road.

"Well, let's get inside before we get soaked," Katie said as she reached for the tall woman's hand and tentatively intertwined her fingers with Dean's. *Mmmm, that was quite some show you put on, Colonel,* Katie thought as she noted the smile of sheer pleasure on Dean's face. *And what a lousy way to sober up quickly!* she added.

"Now, that was fun." Dean was still chuckling and enjoying the warmth that was traveling up her arm from Katie's touch. "Guess I haven't lost my edge."

As they entered the trailer, Katie sighed as she looked at what was left of her living room. "Ugh. What a mess!" Katie exclaimed. Then she went in search of her small charges. "Butter...Sugar...Spice," she called. "You can come out now, it's safe." First Butter appeared—mewing softly, then out came Spice—meowing very loudly, and finally Sugar—chiming in with her trademark chirp. "Come here, guys," Katie said, as she sat on the floor and reached out, stroking them gently. They all immediately tried to fit into her petite lap, but were finally satisfied with just being near their owner. "Tough night, huh?" she asked them. "Did those mean old boys try to hurt you?" MEOW! cried Spice, followed by a chirp and a mew. "Well, you all look okay. How about a treat?" No sooner did she finish the word 'treat,' than they all jumped up and ran to the kitchen.

"I'll start putting your place back in order," Dean said as she watched them leave.

"Thanks." The blonde answered over her shoulder.

By the time Katie returned, all of the furniture was back to where Dean thought it was supposed to go. "Sorry about the vase," Dean said. "When I flipped that last guy over my head, I couldn't exactly pick out his landing spot. I hope it wasn't a valuable piece."

"No, just a vase I've had for a while—sentimental value only," she said sadly. "It was one that my great aunt got in Ireland. It was her favorite," Katie said. Tears began to well up in her emerald eyes as she touched the pieces of vase on the coffee table.

"I'm sorry, Katie. I'll try to get it fixed for you." Dean said slowly as she rubbed Katie's shoulders from behind, very aware of the trembling she felt beneath the sheer silk blouse. She turned the young woman around and pulled Katie into a hug and held her, stroking her short blonde hair as the young woman quietly cried. "Shhh," she said for the second time that night. "I've got you."

"I don't have many things from my aunt—just the car, a few knick knacks, and this vase." the blonde said between sobs. "I guess it could have been worse. At least the cats are okay."

"Yeah, and you are too," Dean interjected, still holding the young woman and not wanting to let go. "I'm glad I was with you," she whispered into the blonde's ear. "Do you have any idea how those guys found out where you live?" The tall woman asked, still stroking the young woman's hair.

"I don't know. Maybe Carl told them," she said thoughtfully.

"Well, I can tell you one thing," the dark beauty added, "this trailer is about as secure as a tin can." She gently released the blonde and walked over to the front door inspecting the lock. "Looks like the frame and lock system are sprung for good. The whole door will have to be replaced before you'll be able to lock it again," Dean added as she opened and closed the door.

"Couldn't be because you used a battering ram on it, could it?" the blonde teased with a twinkle and a smirk, as she started to get over her blues.

"Naw," replied Dean. "If anything, the head butting put it back in shape somewhat," she returned with a chuckle. "Actually, it was that way when I put the key in... it just opened right up without any pressure. That's what alerted me to the creep behind the door. I heard him shuffle to get out of the way as it popped open."

"I guess I can put something in front of the door to hold it closed for the night," Katie said as she surveyed the room looking for something appropriate.

"Think again," came the response from Dean. "You'll not be staying here until the door is fixed. You can just pack up some stuff and come back to my place," she insisted.

"But, what about the cats? I can't leave them here." Katie began to protest, but was silenced by two fingers on her lips.

"They can just come too. I really don't mind. I kinda like the little fur balls anyway," Dean said as she looked down at her feet where a very frisky Spice was winding herself between her legs, leaving a streak of cat hair on her black slacks.

"Oh, I'm sure you like cat hair on your ankles," Katie said, as she bent down to pick up Spice. "I've got a lint remover here somewhere," she said as she walked through the living room looking for it. "Ah, here it is," she exclaimed as she handed it over to Dean.

"Guess you'd better pack that too then," Dean commented drolly, as she retrieved it from Katie's hand and began cleaning off her slacks.

It took Katie nearly fifteen minutes to pack up some things for the night and morning as well as some cat food and medicine for Sugar, litter box, and three cats in two carriers. While she was busy with that, Dean worked on trying to semi-secure the front door, at least for appearance's sake. In the process, she noticed a small hidden door in the wall behind the front entrance that must have come ajar during the short fight. As she reached down to inspect it, Katie caught sight of her and quickly ran up and closed the door before Dean could reach it.

"Oh, that's just the service door for the water shut off" she said rather quickly, as Dean looked at her with a raised eyebrow. *Can't have you poking around in there, now can I?* Katie quipped to herself. *I wouldn't want to explain night vision scopes, a 9mm Glock, ammo, and my night camouflage gear.* "I'm all set now. Can you grab the cats for me?" Katie asked with a smile, determinedly trying to change the subject and take Dean's mind off of the curious little door.

Dean did as she was asked, taking the cat carriers out to the SUV with Katie following right behind her, making it the fastest exit she'd ever witnessed. *Hmm,*

I do believe you're right, Tracy. There's definitely more to her than what meets the eye. We'll see... Dean was thinking as she was propelled from the trailer.

"I really do appreciate this," Katie said with a sincere smile. "I wouldn't have gotten much sleep if I had to stand guard at my front door all night."

"Not a problem," Dean responded, considering the strange change in Katie in the last two minutes. "Is there someone in town or at the trailer park that can fix the damaged door?" she asked, attempting to act nonchalant over the quick exit.

"Yeah, I can call Paul, the trailer park manager, in the morning. I'm sure that either he can fix it, or he'll know someone who can," Katie answered as they pulled into the private road that led to Dean's place.

As they unloaded the cats and Katie's things, the rain began to let up. "I hope that's it for the rain. I'd hate to put off the trip to the park tomorrow," Katie said as she waited for Dean to open the door.

"Yeah, me too," Dean answered.

It didn't take long for the cats to prowl their new home and check out the litter box situation. Katie began to yawn in earnest now, so she was glad when Dean suggested they all try to get some rest for the night. She led Katie to the guest bedroom and said good night, then went to her room to plan her reconnaissance mission for the next evening.

Saturday, 0800 hours

Saturday morning was another beautiful fall day. Bright sunshine was burning off the left over fog from the night before and drying out the grass from the brief rainfall. Dean awoke early and went out for her daily run, leaving the blonde to sleep in. By the time she returned, it was nearly eight o'clock, and the blonde was still sound asleep.

Well, Dean thought, *she had a pretty rough day and a traumatic night. She's probably exhausted.* Dean left her to her dreams while she took her shower.

As soon as Katie heard her hostess return, she rolled over away from the door so Dean wouldn't see that she was awake. At the sound of the shower being turned on, Katie got out of bed and went to her duffel bag and pulled out her cell phone. She dialed and waited for a response at the other end. Once contact was made, she related her escapade of the night before and informed her contact where she was and what her plans for the day were. She also fed her contact the bits of conversation she had picked up from the Asians in the diner. After setting a time to call later that evening, she hung up and replaced her cell in the interior zipper compartment of the duffel. Then she went out to the kitchen just as Dean emerged from the bathroom.

"Hi," Katie said, ruffling her hair a bit as she caught sight of Dean coming out of the bathroom dressed in just her short bathrobe. *Mmmm, that sure is a tempting sight, kiddo. Certainly hope you didn't complicate things last night with that kiss,* Katie reflected.

"Hey," Dean replied, then inquired if the young woman had slept well.

"Oh yeah, I was really beat," Katie replied. "Can I put on some water for tea?" she asked politely.

"Mmm, good idea," Dean said, then asked, "Are you hungry? I picked up some cereal yesterday and some muffins. They're in the cupboard to the right of the sink," she instructed as she walked toward her bedroom.

"Great!" the blonde answered. "I'll set the table while you finish getting dressed."

By the time Dean came out, Katie had the table set, hot water boiling, and a fire started in the fireplace to take the chill out of the air. *Nice,* Dean thought admiring the beautiful young woman. She shook off the thought of what it would be like to have the young blonde there every morning for tea and breakfast.

"So, what time would you like to go up to the park?" Dean asked, as she put a little honey on her muffin. She had dressed for the trip already—Black Watch flannel-lined jeans, a cranberry chamois shirt, and hiking boots.

"Looks like you're ready to go right now, but I guess it depends on how the door repair is going. If it looks good, maybe we can go around noon," Katie responded. "I really should try calling Paul now. May I use your phone?" she asked Dean as she finished her cup of tea.

"Sure thing." Dean got up to retrieve the phone from her bedroom and handed it over to Katie.

After the call was made, Katie took a quick shower, gave Sugar her medicine, scooped the litter box, and then joined Dean in the living room.

"Umm, about last night," Katie began. "I...I'm a little embarrassed about the way I acted, or should I say reacted."

"About what?" Dean asked. "You really know how to show a girl a good time," she said with a chuckle. "I haven't had that much fun in a long time. It's nice to know my skills aren't rusty."

"No, not that," Katie stammered. "I...I meant the kiss."

"Oh, so you didn't mean it then?" Dean lifted an eyebrow as she looked at the young woman, a little disappointment showing in her blue eyes.

Katie registered the disappointment in Dean's eyes and decided to come clean. "No," she stated quietly and moved over to the couch by Dean. "I *meant* that kiss. It's just not usually my nature to act on my emotions so quickly. I'm usually arguing with myself so long that any chance of a relationship with someone disappears. Or to put it more accurately, they disappear," Katie finished, and lowered her eyes to her lap. Raising her eyes again to meet Dean's blue ones, Katie sighed and continued. "I just knew I didn't want that to happen with you, so I took the chance. I just...I..." She wrung her hands as she struggled with her words.

Dean shifted closer to Katie, coming so close that they could each almost feel the other's heart beat. Dean brought her hands up to each side of Katie's face and peered intently into the emerald eyes, then softly whispered, "You're much more courageous than I, Katie Miller. You accomplished what I only thought about last night. You followed through on your desire, and I just fantasized about mine. I meant what I said last night. I did enjoy the kiss. Very much so." Dean came forward the last few inches and softly placed her lips on Katie's.

The wave of emotion that washed over her with that simple kiss was enough to nearly drown her. Their lips lingered together softly, then became more passionate as each pair began to explore further, finally parting as tongues continued the exploration deeper. As their kisses intensified, their bodies also succumbed to one another. Hands gently explored backs, arms, and thighs. It was several minutes before the two women parted, each panting from the release of emotions that had been held in check. Placing their foreheads together, they released a sigh in concert.

"Mmmm, definitely better than my fantasy," Dean commented as she lifted her head and looked into Katie's eyes once more.

"Ohh, yesss!" Katie agreed. "I'm glad we've got that 'I'm really attracted to you' conversation out of the way," she added with a chuckle.

"Yeah, that's always the toughest part," Dean agreed, chuckling with Katie in earnest.

The two women looked at each other, totally enjoying the tenderness of the moment. Katie leaned in towards Dean and placed another soft kiss on her lips, relishing the sensation of her smooth lips. Soon that kiss led to another, and Dean gently guided Katie down on the couch allowing them full contact along the length of their bodies. Dean's lips moved to

Katie's neck, stopping to nibble on an earlobe along the way.

"Ungh," Katie moaned as the heat from Dean's lips started to ignite her very soul. Another moan escaped as Dean's right hand brushed her breast as she began a more earnest exploration of the young woman. "Umm," Katie mumbled, "if we keep this up, we're never going to make it to the mountain."

"Well, that sorta wasn't on my mind, but I guess you're right," Dean whispered into Katie's ear, the warm breath once again eliciting a moan of pleasure from the young woman. "Okay, what do you say, we take it slow. I guess we really should get to know each other before we...umm, ah..." She was silenced by Katie's lips on hers one more time.

"Sounds like a good plan to me, Colonel," Katie answered. "I really should check on my trailer first; then we can take that hike I promised you."

They agreed on their course of action for the rest of the morning: stop by the trailer and check on the repair progress, then over to the deli to get sandwiches and water to take on the hike. Dean also packed along a compass, a pair of field glasses to 'bird watch' with, a digital camera to take 'scenic pictures,' and her telescoping hiking poles. She placed all these and an extra sweatshirt into a compact backpack. They took Dean's SUV rather than the classic antique and headed out to complete their errands and then, on to Walnut Mountain Park.

* * * * * * * * *

"Well, here's the gate." Katie indicated the access at the end of the park road. "We can park over there." She pointed to a small parking area next to the walk-through in the fence. "Then we walk up to the face for the 'big view'." They pulled up next to a mini-van that was loading up a bunch of kids and a dog that had obviously been there for a while already. The kids were really dragging, and the dog's tongue was hanging out from the effort of its exercise activities.

"Great day for a hike," commented the man.

"The view from the top is awesome today!" exclaimed a young girl around twelve years old. "You can see forever," she added gleefully.

"Yeah, we're looking forward to it," replied the blonde as the family finished loading up.

"C'mon." Katie called to Dean as she passed through the walk-through gate.

Katie took off towards the hiking trail at a brisk pace while Dean locked the SUV and grabbed the backpack. It didn't take the tall woman long to catch up to the blonde, and then they settled into an easy hiking pace.

They passed the new soccer fields and watched a family of deer grazing on the grass, then continued up the path towards the west meadow. The climb was not difficult at this level, but soon it moved into the woods and became a more upward trek. The fire road had been recently worked on, which made the climb easier than expected. Just before they came out into the meadow, the path steepened then turned to the right, allowing the women a breathtaking view. With just a few more paces, they were fully into the meadow, which afforded them a generous three hundred degree panorama of the surrounding countryside. The clear day made the view all the more spectacular.

"So... what do you think?" Katie eagerly awaited her companion's reaction.

"It's everything Tracy said it was," Dean answered truthfully.

"Tracy?" Katie inquired. "You mean Park and Rec Tracy?"

"One and the same," Dean replied. "We've been friends for a very long time. Served together in the Army. I was surprised to run into her at Wendy's yesterday. She told me about her 'pride and joy' then," Dean said with a smile on her face.

"Well it certainly is beautiful up here," the blonde commented. "Let's go up to the face and the mountain overlook. It's just up this path." Without waiting for a response, Katie led the way up.

They were back in the woods now, following the 'Low Road' to the overlook, and the path became a bit narrower and much steeper. As they emerged from the woods, Katie turned left and hurried over to the edge. "Wow! What a sight!" she exclaimed. "You really can see forever today."

Dean caught up with her, and the two women just stood and gazed out at the view, completely intoxicated by the sight. Dean reached out and clasped the younger woman around her shoulder. Katie responded with her arm around Dean's waist. "It really is nice up here," Dean said. "I'm glad you were able to share this with me." She pulled Katie into a hug and a promising kiss.

"No problem," Katie replied emphatically. "I'll bring you up here every day, if you'll pay me in kisses like that."

"Mmm, like this?" Dean demonstrated, only lingering longer in the contact.

"Umm...'zactly," the blonde mumbled between their lips.

"Mmm, guess we better be heading along the trail now." Dean's suggestion was half-hearted, not really wanting to relinquish her embracing of the younger woman.

Katie nodded, and they turned around and retraced their steps to where the path came to a "Y" intersection. "The way to the left goes around the other side of the mountain, and eventually comes back down through the north meadow—the area the Civil War re-enacters use for the Union camp," Katie explained. "The way we're going takes you past an old foundation of a turn of the century resort and has an exit on the upper meadow above the water tower. That's the other view I told you about." Katie led Dean into the woods on the chosen path.

Just before the path started to incline again, Katie stopped and pointed to a rock formation through the trees. "See that formation? It's called 'witch's rock' because it looks like a witch's profile." Dean's gaze followed in the direction indicated and she smiled as she recognized a crooked nose and pointed chin with a rock slab overhead that made up the hat.

"Pretty neat," Dean commented, "but if you have any American Indian heritage, you could call it 'Indian Rock'." With a little imagination and some descriptive pointers, Dean detailed the 'Indian.'

"Yeah, you're right." Katie considered the profile. "Wonder if anyone calls it that?"

Dean just shrugged, and they continued their hike. It took another twenty minutes of lazy strolling before they came to the exit for the upper meadow. They would have missed it if Katie had not been there before, since it was between two heavily limbed trees. As they passed through and walked out onto the meadow, they were greeted by another awesome picture created from Mother Nature's palette.

Katie pointed out to the distance saying, "That's Double Top Mountain over there. It's over in the next county, about seventy-five miles away."

Dean reached into her backpack and pulled out her binoculars and made quite a show of viewing the scenery before she locked in on her intended target. "Nice," she commented. She charged the coordinates to her memory before handing the binoculars over to Katie. Taking out her digital camera, she went through the same charade before taking several shots of her objective.

"How about lunch?" she inquired of the blonde woman. "I've worked up an appetite with all this walking and this crisp air."

"Great," responded Katie. "There're some rocks over there that we can use to set our stuff on." She led the way over to the natural table, and the two women spent a leisurely lunch enjoying the view, the sandwiches and each other's company. Dean noted the lay of the land, taking in the terrain with a skilled eye, picked out her observation spot and committed it to memory for her trek later in the evening.

"Guess we'd better start down," Dean suggested, as she packed up the few bits of paper and wrappers that were left from their lunch.

"We can take this track down." Katie pointed to a thin trail behind her. "It's a single track bike trail, but it's used for hiking too. It comes out right by the water tower near the entrance."

Dean nodded and they started the hike back. They soon found themselves back at the entrance where they loaded up the SUV and headed out to the main road.

Once they were in the truck, Katie turned to Dean and said, "I have to work tonight." She paused, and then continued, "I help out a caterer friend sometimes when she needs it. Tonight is one of those nights. But I really wanted to thank you again for last night, and for allowing me to show you the mountain."

"Oh," Dean acknowledged, knowing that she had to 'work,' too. "That actually works out well. I need to meet someone tonight anyway regarding work." *Well, technically that's not a lie,* Dean mused, *but it is a good thing Katie's busy tonight. At least now I won't have to come up with an excuse why I can't see her. Although I'd much rather be snuggling with her than that stand of trees up there.* She completed that thought with a smile on her face. "And you're welcome for last night, and thanks for sharing the mountain with me."

The ride back to Dean's was proceeding in silence, with Dean lost in thought and a smile on her face, until the young woman spoke. "Penny for your thoughts."

"Hhmm?" Dean turned to catch the emerald eyes studying her.

"Well, something put that smile on your face." The green eyes twinkled in question.

"I was just recalling how nice today has turned out," Dean covered. "How about some hot chocolate at my place before you head back?"

"You must be reading my mind." The young woman chuckled.

It took them another five minutes before they turned down the private road leading to Dean's. As Dean opened the door, three, very loud, meowing cats greeted them. "Guess I'd better feed them first, or I'll never get them into the carriers," Katie said as she headed toward the kitchen.

Dean took her backpack into the bedroom then went to the kitchen, where she stopped at the doorway and just watched the beautiful young woman with her charges. *You certainly are a beautiful surprise in my life,* she commented to herself as she continued to watch Katie. Then she walked up behind Katie and placed her arms around her, whispering in her ear, "You are really beautiful."

Katie shivered as she felt Dean's breath warm her ear. Turning in Dean's arms she faced the tall woman, locking ice blues and emerald greens in intimate communication. Dean lowered her head and pulled Katie into a long sensual kiss that ignited their souls and fanned the flames of passion once more. As they separated from the kiss, Dean reached for Katie's hand and quietly led her to her bedroom.

Saturday, 2100 hours

Dean and Tracy had just finished cleaning up the dinner dishes when Tracy's partner came back from walking their German shepherd. "Bbrrrr! It's really getting cold out there," Colleen said as she took off her coat and gloves. "The stars are really something tonight. They're so brilliant when there's no moon."

"Guess I better pull out my thermals," Dean commented to Tracy, "or you're gonna find a frozen body up there in the morning."

"Nah," protested Tracy, "I've gotten soft in my old age. I don't go hiking in the cold anymore, so it would be at least a week or two before we found you." She chuckled and gave Dean a smirk. "That is, unless you've changed your mind about needing some back-up," she asked hopefully. "Then I'll make sure we find your body before you freeze."

"Just get that idea out of your head, Tracy," Dean admonished. "This is just an observation tonight, no need for back-up. So you and Col here just stay warm and snuggled in your bed tonight. Ya got me?" she snarled.

"Yeah, yeah...You forget who you're talking to, Dean. I don't get intimidated by you, remember?" Tracy winked at her and chuckled with Colleen as Dean joined in.

"Well, I'd better get going. Gotta get my stuff together and get up there soon." The tall woman gave Tracy and Colleen a hug. "Thanks for dinner. It was super." She grabbed her coat and headed to the door. "You're sure Byron won't mind if I park my SUV in his driveway?" she asked for the third time.

Tracy shook her head and said, "I already called him to let him know you have permission to be there tonight. Told him you're checking it out for ROTC night maneuvers. He's the one who suggested the driveway," came the chiding reminder.

"Okay. Just wanted to make sure. Thanks again," Dean said as she opened the door.

"Hey," Tracy called softly to Dean, "just remember—it's a carry in, carry out park. Don't leave any bodies behind."

Dean nodded her head, then said, "I promise," as she started up the SUV and headed home.

Once there, Dean went to the bedroom and changed into her gear for the task that faced her. She pulled out her thermals and put them on, glad that she had remembered to pack them, then added her black turtleneck sweater, black jeans, and black rough suede boots. *Without the moon, I shouldn't have to worry about reflections off regular issue boots, but why take a chance?* she thought to herself. She added a black field jacket and black gloves. She'd use the black balaclava tonight instead of face camouflage. *No sense scaring anyone at a stoplight,* she mused. She grabbed her backpack that already held the night vision goggles and her 20x80 binoculars that gave her a field of vision of 1,000 yards. From her gun safe, she chose her 9mm Glock, checked the clip, put the safety back on, then returned it to its holster and added it to the pack with two more clips. *Better to be prepared than not,* she thought. *Not that I'm expecting trouble.* She added a flashlight, then checked her Traser Night Diver watch and decided it was time to go.

With the minimal traffic at this time of night, it took her only a few minutes to get to the park. She pulled into the park supervisor's driveway, picked up her backpack and headed up to the observation point she had selected in the afternoon. The total trip from home to observation point took less than thirty minutes. *Now comes the fun part,* she groaned. *Hurry up and wait. God, how I hate surveillance.* It was now only one thirty and, if her information was correct, she had to wait another sixty minutes before she could expect any action. She took her time getting set up. Attaching the mini tripod to the binoculars, she settled in for the wait.

Having been in that position for at least fifteen minutes, she heard a noise coming up the trail. *Could be some deer moving to keep warm,* she thought. Just to be on the safe side, she moved in closer to her tree cover and slipped on her night vision goggles. There was the noise again, so she concentrated on the area it came from, catching the motion of a person slowly moving towards her. The new arrival was decked out similarly to her, and if it hadn't been for her exceptional hearing, she probably never would have heard the approach. She pulled back behind the tree further, took off the goggles, and waited for him to get nearer. Just as the figure was passing her protected area, she reached out and grabbed the guy from behind. No sooner had she engaged the stranger that she found herself on her back with the darkly clad figure straddling her, her arms pinned by knees, and a forearm across her throat. *What the hell!* she thought. *Who the hell is this guy?!* As she began to run through her release options, she met her attacker's eyes and found the most gorgeous and familiar emerald green eyes peering at her.

"You!" They gasped together. Katie released her captive, recognizing the ice blue eyes that met hers. "What are you doing here?" Again, demanded in unison.

"Looks like we both had to work tonight," Katie observed with a twinkle. "So, Colonel, or is it Colonel? What are we watchin' tonight?" she asked, narrowing her eyes in suspicion.

"It is Colonel, but I'll let you go first, Katie. If it is Katie?" Dean returned with a smile and her own version of a suspicious look.

"Allow me to introduce myself—DEA Special Agent Katie O'Malley." Katie answered truthfully, fairly certain that the woman across from her was not part of the evil she was on assignment to watch. "Now you," she countered.

"Lieutenant Colonel Deanna Peterson, U. S. Army Intelligence." Dean also replied truthfully. "What's the DEA doing here?" The tall woman queried.

"Probably the same thing you're here for, but why is the Army involved?" Katie asked inquisitively, and then added, "You wouldn't happen to have any ID on you, would you?"

"Now, if I did, I wouldn't be a very smart agent, would I?" Dean asked with a bit of sarcasm in her voice before she continued. "I'm here on loan to the NSA. They needed my 'special' skills." Dean looked at her watch and noticed it was almost two o'clock. "We can sort this out later, but I suggest we get to work now," she commanded. Agreeing, both women settled in for the wait. The lodge they were observing was a huge old resort that had been very famous in its day. Now, unfortunately, it was often devoid of guests, but was still a beauty of a piece of property on nearly fifty acres of land. The main lodge was situated in a meadow across the valley from their lookout post. It was three stories high, made of local bluestone, and resembled a castle with round turret-like sections at each corner of the building. The entire place was enclosed by an eight-foot stone wall with two gated entrances on Hollow Road that provided a semicircular driveway at the main entrance. Another entrance off Bluestone Road led to the back entrance by the kitchen and to the outbuildings behind the lodge. Their advantage point allowed them to see over the tall walls, as well as both entrances to the estate.

About two fifteen, the first car arrived. It was the black Lexus that Katie had seen at the diner. "I waited on those guys yesterday," she whispered to Dean. "There were three of them. All Asians. One looked a lot like 'Odd Job' from that old James Bond movie." She described the men and related her observation that one of them had a holster under his jacket. "He was the one carrying," she informed Dean.

"Yeah, his name is Chung. Heavy duty body guard and so-so hit man," Dean said waggling her hand. "The other two are brothers: Sammi and Jimmi Lu. They're part of the Chi-Chong gang out of Bangkok."

"Hey, how come you know all this and the DEA doesn't?" Katie asked, a bit miffed.

"'Cause, that's part of my 'special' skills. Remember, I'm Intelligence," Dean said with a crooked smile and a wink.

About ten minutes later, a Lincoln Town Car pulled in and three more men arrived. These appeared to be American, or at least Caucasian. "Those guys are from the city," Katie said. "I recognize the tall one. He's Johnnie Papp, number two man from a New York mob family. Don't know the other two for sure, but they look familiar." She zoomed in her scope for a better view.

"They should. They're from the Vegas and Chicago branches of the mob—Tony Cabini and Gary Stiller," Dean filled in. "Gary is the short bald one. He's from Chicago."

The next car was a Ford Expedition with three more 'guests'. These guys were from the Colombian Cartel. "Carlos Sanchez, Julio Romero, and Tequez Ruiz," said Katie as she identified the three men. "These guys are really nasty fellas," she commented. "I've seen their files, and they're as slippery as eels."

The final car of this trio had three members of the Yakuza from Tokyo: Hiro Kamoto, Ito Sukazi, and Lin Yamakura. "Well, well," commented Dean. "Guess she's moved up and over in the world."

"You must be talking about the female," Katie correctly surmised, since there was only one female in the group. "Who's she?"

"A few years ago, she was one of the best police officers the Japanese had. Then her brother was killed in a drug bust. It really did a number on her reputation. She tried to clear Kao's name, but it didn't work out the way she wanted. Turned out her brother was in up to his eyeballs in the Yakuza. Even though her record was spotless, her fellow officers turned their backs on her. She became very bitter and promised vengeance for the loss of face their rejection brought to her. I heard she received an offer from the Yakuza. Guess she took it."

As they continued to watch, several more cars dropped off groups of three, all from different drug cartels across the world. Most were male, but there were also a few more females that arrived in the later groups. All in all, there were thirty representatives at this meeting, leaving the final complement breakdown at twenty-five males, and five females. They noted that the drivers for each of the groups unloaded luggage and took it in the lodge. They waited for another hour after the last vehicle unloaded just to be sure they didn't miss anyone.

"Looks like that's it. Quite a gathering of evil, wouldn't ya say?" Dean commented as she looked over at Katie. Katie nodded her head in agreement, and then added, "We might as well head down. I've got to call this in."

"Did you get the plate number of the last car?" Katie asked as she pulled out her note pad.

"Yep. The caddy looks like an Avis rental, Vermont plate 235 HHD," Dean answered the young agent. "C'mon. We'll get back to our vehicles and meet back at my place. I think it's a bit more private and secure than yours, what with 'Billy Bob and the Boys' out looking for you and a good time." The tall beauty chuckled, enjoying a laugh at the DEA agent's expense.

Refusing to rise to the bait, Katie laughed along with Dean. She just shrugged and shook her head. "Guess I just attract that kind."

"Are you putting me in the same category as 'Billy Bob?'" Dean asked, feigning hurt.

"Nooo." Katie said quickly, then saw the smirk on Dean's face and gave her a punch on the arm. The two women made the short hike back down to the main entrance in companionable silence.

"Where did you leave your car?" Dean asked when she didn't see it near the entrance.

"I came in from the other entrance." Katie pointed to a service road to the left of the walk-through. "I'll just hike down there and meet you back at your place."

"Nah. Hop in, I'll give you a lift." Dean opened the back of the SUV to put her backpack away in the secret compartment next to the wheel well. By three thirty, the two women were back at Dean's, dressed in sweats and sipping Mint Medley tea.

"Did you know the DEA would be involved in your case?" Katie asked inquisitively.

"Nope. Did you know the NSA would be here?" Dean rejoined.

"Nope," Katie said with a disgusted shake of her head. "Why can't the agencies learn to work together? We could get so much more accomplished instead of duplicating our efforts. And why is the National Security Agency interested in druggies? I didn't know they were considered a national security risk?"

"Turf issues. And it's never simple," was all the answer Dean could provide at the moment. "So, you don't mind if I check you out then?" Dean asked in all sincerity.

Katie was briefly taken aback with that question, but the longer she thought about it, the more sense it made. "Not as long as you don't mind if I check you out," was her honest reply.

With that, both women pulled out their secure communications equipment and did exactly that. In a span of about ten minutes, they were both satisfied that the other one was the real McCoy.

"Now that the 'cat's out of the bag,' so to speak, my agency wants to cooperate fully with yours," Dean announced. "Not that I wouldn't anyway," she added. Katie nodded, indicating that hers did too, but it would take some time to process all the approvals by both agencies. "By the way...just how did you...? I mean...no one has ever been able to get me down that fast before. Where did you learn how to do that?"

Katie smiled and then chuckled a bit. "Well, I guess I have 'special' skills too." She chuckled some more, and emerald eyes twinkled brightly. "Actually, I got my first black belt at the age of eight. I learned several styles of martial arts and mastered them all before I went to college. They just seemed to come easily. So, when I went through my training at Quantico, well, let's just say they were quite surprised. I finished first in hand-to-hand for my class. They even wanted me to stay there and teach, but I couldn't wait to get out in the field," Katie explained as her eyes misted over. "Maybe I should have, who knows..." She shook herself out of her memories and asked, "So, what's your take on tonight?"

Dean noticed the subtle mood shift, but decided not to explore it at this time and shelved the information for later retrieval. Instead she focussed on the problem at hand. "Not sure, yet. We need to get more information, but that won't be easy. That place is a fortress. We were lucky that the meadow in the park offered us such a good view. Got any ideas?" Dean inquired of the blonde.

"Well, I imagine one of us needs to infiltrate somehow. Maybe get hired for the house staff or something, then plant a few bugs," Katie considered thoughtfully

"No bugs. I'm sure they'll sweep the place on a regular basis. I've got some long distance listening equipment coming in tomorrow. That should work better. It wouldn't hurt to get inside though and check out the place and the security arrangements," Dean agreed. "But you'll have to be the one to go in. I'm sure Lin would recognize me."

"How well does she know you?" Katie asked.

"Uh...mmm...too well, I'm afraid," Dean answered with a slight tint of color coming to her cheeks.

"Oh?" said the blonde a bit testily. *Why is the green-eyed monster showing up now?* Katie thought. *You just met Dean two days ago. Surely she's had other lovers before you. Get over it.* "Sorry," she apologized.

"S'okay." Dean locked eyes with the blonde, and then decided to take the plunge and drop her guard a bit. "Believe me, it was over a long time ago." She moved closer to Katie and put her hand on her cheek, gently caressing it with her thumb. "It's been a very long time since I've made love with anyone; but, today...it was very familiar, like we were old lovers and not new ones. I can't explain it. I've never had an experience like this before," Dean said apprehensively, knowing that this was not the way a professional in the field should be acting. Knowing, but not heeding the warning bells going off in her head.

"Yes, I know what you mean. I felt it too," Katie answered honestly. She reached up and held Dean's hand and kissed the palm. *Damn, here I go breaking one of the biggest rules in the agency: Never get personally involved with your partner. But then, she's not really my partner, now is she?* Before she knew it, she heard herself replying to Dean. "I knew I was attracted to you when I first saw you in the diner, and that I wanted to get to know you better." The blonde asked cautiously, "Does that make sense to you?"

"Absolute sense," Dean said with a smile. "I'd had a similar feeling myself." Then she bent forward and kissed Katie longingly, passionately, and very thoroughly. As lips met, lips and tongues dueled, hands explored zippers and buttons, and articles of clothing soon left a trail leading to the bedroom.

PART
II

Wednesday, 2000 hours

It had been three very busy days since the arrival of the drug cartel representatives. Dean's listening equipment arrived on schedule, along with some more advanced surveillance equipment and, with a little help from Tracy, everything was safely and secretly ensconced on the mountain. Dean was thankful for the good fortune of having found Tracy in such a useful position to be of help. She knew that she could trust her completely, and it helped to make her job that much easier. Dean was now officially a volunteer for the park department on 'park patrol,' which presumed to keep unwanted ATV's and hunters off the mountain. One look at the intimidating Amazon, and most would-be trespassers quickly changed their minds. In two days, the word spread; Dean no longer had to watch over her shoulder for unwanted guests. Hikers still came up occasionally, but Dean usually fed them a line about studying the flora and fauna of the mountain and capturing the sounds of nature for an educational video. Soon even the hikers did not want to interrupt a 'work-in-progress.' It also made her comings and goings acceptable to the neighbors, since she wore official park attire.

Coordinating the stake-out with the DEA agent was also working out quite well. She found the young agent extremely capable and very creative at problem solving. The first problem she attacked was the growing lack of natural cover for the surveillance equipment with the trees and shrubs losing their foliage. It was Katie's idea to use the nature study/video idea as a cover, thus allowing a camouflage structure to be established as a 'blind.' She also managed to get herself hired as a part-time maid at the lodge used by the drug cartels. She would be starting that duty tomorrow, so she quit her jobs at Burp & Freddie's and the real estate office. Those covers had outlived their usefulness, since her targets and their location were now identified. She was now free to do more research on the lodge guests as well as relieve Dean at the 'blind' after dark. Actual surveillance work would be moved indoors once the high-tech equipment was installed.

Today, Dean was spending the morning installing the high-tech equipment that would allow them to observe via remote control. Tracy suggested that they use an empty office at the Parks & Recreation building for their control room. Although Dean did not want to get any civilians involved, it seemed the best location since they were 'volunteers' for the department. It legitimized their comings and goings on the mountain even more. Tracy had insisted that it would be best for the operation's cover; at this time of year, things were so slow at the office that no one would know they were there anyway. Now all that remained was to settle in, and hope that they could figure out what the gathering was all about.

"That's the last of it," Dean signaled to Tracy as she put the last box of equipment into the office. "I'll get started on hooking everything up so Katie can come down off the mountain by lunch time."

"You really like the kid, don't you?" Tracy asked with a sly grin on her face.

"Yeah, I do. She's really quite intelligent and has strengths where I have weaknesses. We seem to be making a good team."

"Excuse me. Did I hear you say you have weaknesses?" Tracy asked with wide eyes.

"Oh come on, Tracy, you of all people know I do!" Dean laughed.

"Yeah, like shoot first and ask questions later?" Tracy offered, then immediately regretted using that particular expression.

Dean just nodded her head and flashed back to her last assignment. It was a typical assignment for her and her 'special' skills. It seemed that her superiors never minded her ruthless tactics because she always produced the desired results. She had been sent to Bosnia to rescue the daughter of a NATO official. The young girl had been kidnapped from her home in England and was being held hostage in Bosnia as leverage to keep the troops under her father's command out of certain areas. This endangered the lives of many NATO forces, among them many American troops. Dean accomplished the job quickly, but the body count was staggering. She had to assume that some of the victims were probably innocent bystanders who just happened to be in the wrong place at the wrong time. Their deaths could have been avoided if she had taken a bit more time to ask questions first and shoot later, but it was a war zone, and many lives were at stake. Innocent people often died in a war; it was to be expected. She did her job efficiently and effectively. In and out, mission accomplished. It earned her the promotion to lieutenant colonel. But the ruthlessness was starting to affect her, and the faces of the dead haunted her dreams.

Tracy looked at the sadness on her friend's face, wondering which particular nightmare she was reliving at that moment. "Sorry, Dean, I used a rather poor choice of words." Tracy reached out and touched her friend's shoulder.

Dean just shook her head and shrugged. "It's not your fault Tracy. I'm the one who made the choice to become what I am. And I'm the one who has to live with that choice. It's just getting harder to live with, is all."

"You know Dean, any time you want to talk, I'm here to listen. I'm not in the Army anymore, so my security clearance may be subject to scrutiny; but if you remember, I have very tight lips," Tracy offered softly as she gave her friend a gentle hug. Tracy remembered the first time she had met Dean.

She was Chief of Patient Administration for a five hundred bed Army hospital in the Midwest and was reviewing the medical records of the current influx of new patients. Dean had just successfully completed her second 'special' assignment and was lucky to get out of it alive. She arrived at the medical facility hanging on by a thread and sporting several new openings in her torso that were not supposed to be there. The loss of blood alone would have doomed an ordinary person. Thank the gods she was extraordinary. Tracy had made a point of visiting this patient on a regular basis to track her progress. Tracking soon led to interest, which then developed into friendship. They had been friends ever since, and their military paths often crossed. Tracy reflected that it was great to see her old friend again, and hoped this assignment would not become a repeat of their original meeting.

"Yeah, and I appreciate it. Maybe someday I'll be able to talk about it, but right now I've got work to do." The tall woman smiled at her friend then went into the small office to begin the final installation of her remote surveillance control room and to look back on her life and its secrets. It occurred to Dean that, since meeting the young blonde, she had changed. She now had something in her life that was worth living for. *That is, if Katie wants me in her life.* Dean knew that her willingness to recklessly exploit her 'special' skills was largely due to a lack of fear and a deep burning rage that, at times, was difficult to control. She could accomplish more than her peers because she never feared death. On the contrary, she dealt it out so often that it almost felt like an old friend. She knew that some day, her time would come; but she never worried about when or where. Now, however, she was finding herself falling helplessly in love. And falling in love was something she had never really expected to happen in her life. Sure, she had had many lovers over the years, but the young agent was different. She was finding herself looking forward to the future. Looking forward to seeing those emerald eyes, hearing her laughter, and feeling her touch. And she was beginning to understand fear.

In the past, Dean had lost partners on assignments and could accept the loss as part of the job. Now though, that would be totally unacceptable. This realization was adding another dimension to her job, and another set of priorities. She feared for Katie's safety, and that was becoming her first priority. She knew the assignment always had to come first, but her heart was telling her otherwise. She just hoped that she would never have to choose between the two.

By twelve thirty, the installation was complete, and Katie was signaled to return to the office. Fifteen minutes later, she walked into the control room and surveyed Dean's handiwork. "Not bad, Colonel. You Army folk sure have the toys." She checked out the room with a low whistle. "This stuff will certainly make the surveillance a lot more comfortable. I'm sure glad we ran into each other. I'll certainly be a lot warmer than I had counted on."

"Well, at least you know some of that appropriations money went to good use." Dean chuckled as she began to run the young agent through the various pieces of equipment and how to use them.

"Wow! That's cool!" the blonde exclaimed, as Dean demonstrated the range of the visual scanning camera. It was so powerful that Dean was able to focus on a clock located on the fireplace mantle in the lodge. It read twelve fifty-five.

"Hmm," Dean murmured, "they need to re-set the clock. It's off by two minutes."

"Of course, it's only good for outside views or when the curtains are open," Katie continued.

"Yep, but wait 'til you see this." Dean punched up another set of controls that showed the occupants walking through the lodge as though they were being x-rayed. "This is a TDSC unit, or thermo-dynamic scanning converter," she said proudly. "If it's a warm body, I can find it. It's similar to the satellite version, only on a smaller scale."

"Now that's really cool." The young agent was very impressed. "How about audio? Can you enhance that?"

"Not as much as I would like. Unfortunately enhancing that also enhances all the other sounds between here and there," the tall woman explained. "I can fine tune on one person, two if they're standing close together. It's not too bad. Listen." She gave the blonde a set of headphones and made some adjustments, highlighting the kitchen area and focusing on one of the warm bodies on the screen. The person selected had a small green dot now showing on the viewing screen indicating the fine tuning to that individual's location. As they watched and listened, a very distant elderly female voice could be heard.

"They said they wanted to change the menu to eggplant parm for the guests from Chicago, and the ones from Japan want fresh sushi," the voice said. "You'd think I'm running a damned restaurant here. Why the hell can't they all eat the same thing?"

"Ya, right," said another voice, only it was much fainter. "I sure don't like running back and forth to the grocery store all day. Where the hell am I going to get fresh fish for sushi at this time of day? It's not like I can run down to the Fulton Fish market just like that." The voice ended with a snap of the fingers.

"Mmm, sounds like dissention among the hired help," Dean commented with a smile.

"Yeah," replied the blonde, "but if you ask me, the vocal reception is awesome."

"Ahh, it's okay for fine spectrum, but it can get pretty garbled on broad spectrum. Are you up for some lunch?" A set of blue eyes peered over to where the blonde was sitting.

"Are you kidding? I'm always up for food." With that, the young agent stood, set down her headphones and opened the door to the outer offices. "Anybody out here interested in food?" she called out.

"Yeah!" came the simultaneous answers from Tracy and her secretary, Linna. Dean, in the meantime, set up the second VCR and tape recorder to capture the events at the lodge while they were at lunch. She always had one set taping, but when it was unattended, she'd turn on the second set. The two agents weren't worried about missing anything at this point in the surveillance, so they decided that both could go for lunch.

Linna wasn't exactly sure what the two women were doing in the next office, but she trusted Tracy, even though her instincts told her they didn't look like scientists. Besides, she really enjoyed the enthusiasm of the younger woman. The tall dark haired woman, on the other hand, was more of an enigma to her, but she was beginning to warm up to her, too. "How about Italian?" Linna suggested. "Gino makes the best bruschetta and calzones in town. One thing this town has lots of, besides lawyers, is restaurants," Linna gaily offered, as they took off for the short ride to Gino's. "Guess it's a good thing we get a lot of city folks wanting to either start or end their careers here in the Catskills."

Forty-five minutes later they were back at the office still enjoying the lingering taste of garlic and Italian sauce. Tracy and Linna went into their respective areas, while Dean and Katie went into theirs. "Let's see what went on while we were gone, shall we?" Dean reached over and rewound the tape, and the two women sat down to watch.

"Hey, Johnnie. What time is this new guy coming in?" Voice #1

"Tonight, around midnight is what I was told," replied Johnnie.

"So. Ya figure we'll find out just what this is all about then?" Voice #1

"Yeah, probably. All I know is that I'm getting really creeped out by some of these dudes here. Of, course some of the broads aren't hard on the eyes, if ya know what I mean!" Johnnie said with a lecherous laugh.

"Ya can forget that, Johnnie. Them broads is colder than an iceberg. If I can't get one of 'em to heat up, nobody can!" Voice #3

Laughter filled the room as the men continued to make crude remarks about the five women in attendance.

Voice #3 spoke again. "Man, you see the size of that one guy! He must go 270 or more. I'd hate to have to tangle with him."

"Nah," Voice #2 said. "This little piece here is a great equalizer. Especially with them armor piercing rounds in it." More laughter.

"Hmm," Dean said. "Guess we can forget about wearing any vests for protection. Never liked them anyway. Too bulky."

"They're just not made for the female body," Katie added with a twinkle of her emerald eyes. "I feel like I'm in a vise when I wear mine, and it takes forever for my breasts to get back to normal."

Dean looked at the blonde with a wicked twinkle of her own, and then scanned the mentioned breasts as her mouth curled up in a smile. "We can't be having any of that now, can we?" she said in a low seductive growl.

The rest of the afternoon and evening was uneventful, although they did pick up a few snatches of conversation that could prove to be useful. Katie went home for a quick nap and to feed the cats and medicate Sugar. She returned to the office around nine o'clock. "Dean?" Katie asked softly.

"Hmm?" Dean answered without looking up.

"Don't you want to catch a nap or something? We still have about three hours before that guy is supposed to show up."

"Nah, I'm fine. I don't want to take the time to go back to the cabin right now. But maybe I'll stretch out on Tracy's couch for a bit," she said, getting up and stretching.

"Let me know if anything develops."

Katie nodded as she accepted the headphones from Dean then settled in for her turn at the console. At about eleven thirty, she walked into Tracy's office and nudged Dean awake. "Hey, gorgeous. Time to get up."

Blue eyes slowly opened and focused on Katie. "Mmm, I must have died and gone to heaven. There's this beautiful angel watching over me." Dean favored her with a big dazzling smile that took Katie's breath away.

"Close, but no cigar," the young woman answered, as she gently stroked Dean's hair. "It's almost midnight. We'd better tune in on the new arrival."

"Spoil sport!" Dean joked.

The two women went back to the surveillance room and donned their headphones in anticipation of the new arrival. At precisely midnight, they saw the black limo pull into the lodge compound. Dean decided it wasn't necessary to use the TDSC unit until Katie infiltrated the lodge tomorrow. It was too dark to make out the face of the arrival, but once he was inside, Dean had no problem identifying him by his voice alone. It was General Andre Kasimov, former director of the KGB and now National Security Director for the new Russian regime.

"Good evening, ladies and gentlemen," the Russian began in a heavy accent. "I'm glad you were all able to make it here for this gathering. And, I'm sure you're all wondering why I have called together such a diverse group." He smiled as he waved his arms slowly around the room indicating the people gathered in the living room. "But, I'm afraid, I will have to ask for your patience just a bit longer. Once my aide Dimitri confirms the security of this estate, I will gladly bring you all into my plans at dinner tomorrow. Until then, I suggest you all get a good night's sleep." With that, Andre exited the living room and went directly to his quarters, reserved for him on the first floor, next to the den. There were immediate mumblings from the other participants after the Russian left. They ran the gamut from curiosity to distrust, but all agreed that the Russian's arrogance was unacceptable. Slowly, each of the representatives left for their own rooms. The last to leave were Lin and Ito.

"So Ito, what do you know of this Russian?" Lin asked her companion.

"He once was KGB, now he's with their National Security. I wonder what he wants from us?" Ito said thoughtfully.

"Maybe he wants part of the action? Wants to eliminate the current drug czars and put himself in their place?" she offered.

"No, no." Ito said emphasizing with a shake of his head. "He could do that without our help. In fact, I have sources that say he IS the drug czar for Russia, only he keeps his identity a secret."

"Hmm. I wonder what he's up to then. Guess we'll find out tomorrow." Then they left, arm in arm, for their rooms.

Kasimov! Dean's conscience whispered. *You old devil. So...we finally meet again.*

With a sigh, Dean said. "I was really hoping we'd get what we needed tonight so you wouldn't have to go in undercover tomorrow. I just don't trust that much evil gathered in one place. *Especially with Kasimov in the picture now,* Dean thought to herself. "That's one very evil man who doesn't know how to play nice. This can't be good," Dean said as she shook her head. "Just what's the old General up to?"

"Well, we'll have to wait until tomorrow, like everyone else. And, you'll be here watching over me, so I'll be safe." Katie placed her hand on Dean's shoulder and gave her a gentle squeeze.

"That's true, but I don't have an army of reinforcements sitting outside that gate to bail you out if necessary," Dean said, as she peered intently into the young agent's emerald eyes. "I wish I could go in, not you. But, just in case, I want you to wear this necklace tomorrow." Dean pulled out a beautiful silver chain with an emerald green stone on it. "This won't show up on any security sweeps, but it will allow me to locate you anywhere in the house. It'll show up as a blue dot on the screen. That way I can pick you out from the rest and keep track of your movements," she added with a grin. "If you notice anything that may be a security issue for us, just cough, and I'll mark the location on the layout map."

"Got it, and don't worry," Katie said as she gave Dean a soft kiss on her forehead, "I have no intention of getting caught. Besides, I can handle myself pretty well, remember?"

"You just got lucky that night. Don't forget there's a hell of a lot more of them," the dark woman said, standing and stretching. "When do you have to be there?"

"I report at six thirty in the morning. I'm the downstairs maid." Katie demonstrated a smile and a curtsy.

"Okay. Just BE careful. Do your maid thing, and don't try to do anything that would be suspicious. Get a feel for the layout and keep your eyes peeled for anything that might be useful," Dean instructed. "I don't want anything to happen to you." She pulled the young agent into a hug and a light kiss.

"Mmm, I'll be fine." Katie formed her answer around Dean's lips. "I don't want anything to happen to me either."

"Looks like we can put the taping machines on until morning. I'll be coming in around five thirty. I'll meet you here before you report in. We can calibrate the necklace then." The tall woman released Katie reluctantly, and then they checked the equipment once more before they locked up the office and left for their respective homes. Tomorrow would be a very long day and both needed to get a good night's rest.

Thursday, 0500 hours

Dean had finished her morning run and was coming out of the shower feeling fairly invigorated considering she had had less than four hours of sleep. She was dressed and on her way by five fifteen. By the time she pulled into the parking lot and unlocked the doors, Katie was right behind her.

"Morning," Dean said. "Nice outfit," she added in a mocking tone, noting the very short skirt of the uniform and the lacy apron.

"Hey!" Katie replied, smacking Dean's arm lightly. "I'm not quite awake yet, so I won't take offense at that remark. How're you feeling this morning?"

"Not bad, considering," the tall woman responded. "Too bad Tracy doesn't have a shower in this place, or I'd have stayed here all night."

"Well, hopefully we'll get to the bottom of this soon," Katie offered. "You could have stayed with me last night. My place is closer," she added with a smile and a wink.

"Yeah, then neither one of us would have gotten any sleep," Dean chuckled.

Dean calibrated the necklace while Katie made some coffee for herself and some tea for Dean. They quickly reviewed the tapes from the past four hours noting that no one had stirred during the night, but activity was beginning in the kitchen.

"Probably the cook getting breakfast ready," Dean commented. "Who are you supposed to report to?"

"Actually, the cook is in charge of the hired help. A Mrs. Ellen Schlott," Katie answered. "I checked her out, and she's clean. A local woman. Been in this area all her life. Only thing on her record is a speeding ticket back in '69."

"Good," Dean said, nodding her head. "Try to keep track of the innocent bystanders. We wouldn't want them to get in the way or get hurt." *Getting a conscience now, eh?* her little voice said sarcastically. *Yes!* she retorted. *Guess it's about time I start asking questions first and shooting later. And I certainly don't want Katie to have to live with any regrets.*

"Well, I'd better be off. Don't want to be late on my first day," Katie said, working up more enthusiasm after drinking two cups of very strong coffee.

The young agent slipped the necklace on, and then winked at Dean before she walked out the door. Dean concentrated on the lodge and scanned all of the rooms. The only action, so far, was in the kitchen. *Guess they're sleeping in today.* Dean mused. *Wish I was sleeping in...with my arms wrapped around a beautiful blonde...instead of being here.* "Whoa," Dean said out loud to no one. "Stick to the program, Dean," she admonished herself, and then went back to the task at hand. She watched as Katie reported to the cook in the kitchen area and listened as she got her duties for the morning. Vacuum the living room first, then the rest of the downstairs except for the living quarters by the den. Then dust and straighten up the rooms. At 9:00 she was to return and set the dining room buffet table with the breakfast items. Katie was given a quick tour of the downstairs, then taken to the pantry that held the cleaning tools and shown where the items were located, and left to do her job.

* * * * * * * * * *

Around 0900 hours, there was a knock on the door. "Come in," Dean said as she switched to the camera for the wildlife on the mountain and played the nature sounds tape over the speakers in the room while she continued to listen to conversations at the lodge on her headphones.

"It's just me," came Linna's voice. "Just thought I'd see if you needed anything."

"Yeah, thanks. I could do with a cup of tea," Dean said, displaying a pleasant smile.

"Any particular kind? We've got all sorts."

"Any Mint Medley?" Dean asked hopefully.

"You bet. Be right back." Linna turned and went to the kitchen area for the cup of tea. Within minutes she was back at the door offering Dean the steaming cup.

"Thanks." Dean gratefully accepted the hot, refreshing beverage.

"So...how long have you been studying nature?" Linna asked in an effort to be friendly, as well as try to find out more about the two mysterious 'scientists.'

"Oh, just a few years now," Dean answered, without offering too much else.

"Has Katie been with you for that long?" Linna continued the inquisition.

"Umm, no. She just joined me recently." The tall woman was starting to get a bit uncomfortable.

"Really? You two just seem like you've been working together for a long time," the secretary commented.

"Well, it's just that we have common interests. You know. Shop talk and all." The blue eyes were now flitting back towards the TV screen. "I really need to get back to work," she said to Linna. "Thanks again for the tea."

"Oh. Yeah. Okay. You're welcome," came the volley of answers as Linna moved to leave the office and closed the door behind her. As she walked back to her office, Linna couldn't help but wonder what was really going on with the women. She couldn't imagine that watching and listening to birds chirping and squirrels chattering and deer munching would be so interesting, and yet, the blue eyes definitely wanted to focus on the screen. Two and two just weren't adding up to four in this case. She also knew that Dean was an old Army friend of Tracy's, and she was dead certain that Tracy's military career did not include ornithology. *Well,* she vowed, *I'll get to the bottom of this mystery one way or another.*

Phew! Dean thought as she flicked the screen back on to the lodge view. *I thought she'd never leave. Now, where in the world was Katie when she coughed those two times?* Presently, Dean located Katie back in the kitchen where she was chatting away with the cook.

"So, Mrs. Schlott. How long have you worked here at the lodge?" Katie asked sweetly.

"Just call me El, sweetie," said the seventy-ish cook. "I've been here workin' for Mr. G for almost fifty years," she said with a sigh. "Through the good times and the bad. We thought we were going to have to find new jobs when the lodge closed this season. The economy isn't what it used to be in the resort world around these parts. Don't know what we'd do if the tourist trade went completely down the toilet. Mr. G wanted to sell it, but then this Mr. Smirnoff rented the lodge for the next six months at three times the going rate, with an option to buy! Well, you know Mr. G wasn't going to pass that up!"

"Wow!" Katie said encouragingly. "Why do you suppose he offered three times the money?"

"Who knows? Rich people don't have to have reasons. Maybe he just liked the place. Then he asked Mr. G if he could make special upgrades to the property. Without cost to Mr. G of course," El said approvingly.

"What kind of upgrades?" the young blonde asked.

"Oh, I don't know exactly," the cook admitted. "Something to do with the wiring and security alarms or something. We weren't here when the work was done. Mr. Smirnoff gave us a five week paid vacation during the renovations, plus a $2,000 dollar bonus," she said proudly. "Me and Ezra went to Disneyland with our grandkids." El nodded in obvious delight. "Had a hoot of a time, too."

"Cool." commented the 'maid.' "That was really generous of Mr. Smirnoff. He must be a really nice man."

"I wouldn't know. I've never met the man. Today will be the first time I meet him face to face," El said with a thoughtful expression. "Did all the set up over the phone with Mr. G."

"Well, I'd better get back to work. I want to make a good impression on such a nice man. Thanks for the coffee, El." Katie put her dusting supplies away and started to help Ezra with the breakfast trays for the buffet.

"Sure thing, sweetie, anytime," the cook responded as she went back to the oven to check on the biscuits.

Wiring and security alarms, thought Katie as she busied herself with the breakfast items. *Nothing stands out as obvious. I'll just take another trip around and see if I can detect anything.*

As she finished putting up the buffet, the guests started to come down the stairs. She smiled as she served coffee and tea to the varied group of men and women, noting that they all seemed a bit on edge. She tried to be as pleasant as possible and even tried to start conversations with some of them, but to no avail. They obviously considered themselves above her station in life and ignored her. The only one who spoke back to her was Lin.

At least she wasn't afraid to comment on the service or the fine weather, Katie noted. And she was, indeed, beautiful, and seemed to be just as curious about her colleagues as Katie was. Katie was just about to ask her another question when Ito came up to Lin and led her away to the far side of the room, speaking to her softly in Japanese. Lin listened intently to his comments then spared a quick glance at Katie. She flushed when she saw Katie watching her, before returning her attention to Ito.

Now what was that all about? Katie thought. *Maybe he's hitting on her.* She pursued that line of thought. *Or maybe she's hitting on me? Hmm, inter-esting.* Then she pulled her attention back to her duties as General Kasimov entered the room.

"Good morning, ladies and gentlemen," he bel-lowed like a benevolent patriarch. "I hope you have been finding your stay here satisfactory. My associ-ate, Natasha, and I will be out for most of the day, however we will return in time for our dinner meet-ing. Dimitri will remain here today to conduct the business I informed you about last night. Please extend him every courtesy so that he may complete his duties by this evening. For those of you that may be interested, I have obtained one-day non-resident hunting permits, secured proper equipment, and have scheduled transportation to a hunting camp nearby. See Natasha directly if you are interested." With that, the general proceeded to the buffet for his breakfast as Natasha handled the eager would-be hunters. Most of the men and three of the women signed up for the hunting party. They all quickly vacated the dining area and headed to their rooms to get ready for the transportation pick-up.

Katie took this all in with a blank expression, but was very glad there would be so many less bodies around in case she had the opportunity to explore. She came out of her thoughts just in time to see the general approach her with his laden plate.

"Bring coffee to my table," he said in a command-ing tone.

"Yes, sir," Katie responded quickly.

When she brought the requested coffee over and placed it on his table, she was startled by him suddenly reaching for her hand. "You are the new maid, I'm told," he said as he released her.

"Yes, sir," Katie said quietly, trying not to show revulsion at his uninvited touch.

"How old are you?" he asked curiously.

"Twenty, sir." she said softly, knowing that she could easily pass for that age.

"Why aren't you at university?"

"My parents are out of work and I need to help support them and my sister until they can find work again," Katie said convincingly. It was the story they had concocted for the job interview.

"You are much too beautiful to be waiting tables and cleaning houses," he said smugly, and returned his hand to hers, beginning to stroke it. "You should be at university, learning to be an actress or a model. Perhaps I could help you." He favored her with a lecherous sneer.

"Thank you, sir. That's very kind of you, but I have my family to think about." Her neck started to shade pink. Not in response to the affection, as he assumed, but with controlled anger at his arrogance and touch. He was a very handsome man in his late fifties, but his pompous attitude would have turned anyone off. She slid her hand out from under his and returned to her station. *Bastard*, she said to herself. *He is not a nice man at all. Wonder if El knows about this. Probably not. Just stay cool, kiddo. Don't blow the cover; play nice with the creeps.*

****

Dean listened intently to the conversation between Katie and Kasimov, anger growing with each word issuing out of the general's mouth. *He hasn't changed a bit, the old bastard!* Dean considered, *I should have warned Katie last night. Well, her reaction is more realistic this way. I probably would have punched him out!* This thought amused Dean as she visualized her scenario with the promiscuous general. Her visualization was interrupted, however, by another knock on the door. "Just a minute," she called, as she got up to see who was at the door. This time it was Tracy.

"Hey," she said as she opened the door for Tracy to enter.

"Dean." Tracy closed the door behind her. "I just wanted to apologize about Linna. She can be a tenacious individual when she sets her mind to something. I don't think she's buying the story about the nature video and I'm sure she suspects our 'scientists' of evildoing. She's been pumping me all morning," Tracy said with a smile. "I've tried to throw her off course and spin some yarns about you being in the animal research division, but I don't think she went for it." She sighed. "I just wanted to forewarn you."

"She was already in here this morning." Dean smirked as Tracy's eyes widened in shock. "Don't worry, she didn't see anything. I switched cameras before she came in." Dean motioned Tracy over to a chair by the console as she returned the headphones to her head.

"So, how's it going?" Tracy asked tentatively.

"Not bad, but still no big news. It involves Kasimov though, so it's got to be a real ball buster," Dean
commented.

"Kasimov! No kidding," Tracy said, then added,
"Isn't he the one responsible for all those holes in you
when we first met?"

"One and the same," Dean nodded. "Evil bastard.
I just can't figure what game he's playing this time.
And with the cartel's involvement, I'm really at a
loss. Any ideas?"

"No, but I'll mull it over," Tracy offered. "Anything I can do to help out in the meantime?"

"Yeah, keep a lid on Linna if you can."

"Tough assignment," Tracy muttered. "But I'll
work on her."

"It's bad enough I've gotten you involved. I just
don't want anyone else to get in the way and get hurt.
I don't think I can live with any more ghosts," Dean
said as she leveled a gaze at Tracy.

Tracy nodded her complete understanding of her
friend's comment. "Roger. I'll do my best."

The two women sat in the control room for a
while longer as Dean explained the new technology to
Tracy. She was really impressed with the quality of
the surveillance equipment and asked several questions regarding the range, quality, and penetration
abilities. The TDSC unit was the highlight as they
both tracked the blue dot representing Katie through
the lodge.

****

After cleaning up the dining area from breakfast, Katie was instructed to help the upstairs maid, Darla, clean the sleeping rooms. The handful of guests that remained were in the game room—either reading, watching TV, or playing some billiards. The only ones that remained were Lin and Ito, Tony Cabrini, Julio Romero, Rafael Lonzo and Trina Carbona from the Sicilian group, and of course Dimitri. As she went up the stairs she noticed a small circle just under the first step below the first landing. Katie quickly looked around, and then dropped some of her cleaning supplies on the stairs so she could get a closer look. *Hmm. Definitely a security device of some kind,* she thought. *Probably a laser beam, by the looks of it.* She quickly picked up her things and checked the rest of the steps as she went up. There were eight more of them on the way, all in slightly different locations and at seemingly different angles. She coughed as she stepped on the last stair at the top. She'd have to remember to check the bottom stairs for any she might have missed.

She met Darla in the first room and helped the young girl with that one. Once finished, Katie suggested that they split up so they could get done faster, and Darla eagerly agreed. Katie opted to take the rooms on the left side of the hallway, and Darla took the right side. She figured that tomorrow they could switch sides, and she'd have had access to all the rooms. At each room, she systematically searched as she changed the sheets and cleaned. *Well it looks as though these guys didn't bring a whole lot of anything but clothes,* Katie thought, as she continued her search. *Maybe they were instructed not to bring any-*

*thing, or else they weren't carrying anything impor-
tant with them.* She knew they had weapons because
of the conversation about the armor piercing bullets
the night before. *Maybe each room has a personal
safe?* she conjectured, as she still found no evidence
of anything out of the ordinary, not even any sign of
security devices. She decided to pump El at lunch
and see what she could find out.

Once the rooms were done, the two maids had
only the hall to clean before lunch would be served at
one p.m. Katie was just about done when she noticed
a series of circles similar to the ones on the stairs.
These were cleverly hidden in knotholes in the pine
wainscoting of the hallway. She coughed again. She
also noticed strategically placed pillars with statues
of Greek gods and goddesses in the corners. Taking
her duster, she decided to give them the once over.
Eureka! she shouted in her mind. Each of the statues
had miniscule camera lenses inserted in the hollows
of the eyes. Figuring she might be watched, she continued her cleaning with added vigor and coughed at
the fictitious dust she stirred up. *Maybe the old bastard will give me a raise for the extra effort,* she
thought as she began to whistle softly as she worked.

Lunch was served precisely at one o'clock, and
during that time, Katie tried to strike up a conversation with the remaining guests. She noticed Lin
watching her, so she made an effort to go to her table
to see if anything else was required.

"Can I get you anything else?" she inquired of the
two occupants at the table.

"Yes," replied Lin. "I would like some more tea, please." She focused her gaze directly into the emerald eyes of the young agent and smiled.

It took a second before Katie responded, and as she turned to get the requested tea, she noticed Lin was smiling broadly now. Ito noticed it, too, and shook his head in admiration, then commented to his tablemate in Japanese.

Katie returned with the tea and asked if there would be anything else. Lin said no, but she would be sure to let her know if she needed anything, then smiled a very gracious smile at the young agent. *Phew! That was intense.* Katie thought to herself. *I wonder if she's on to me? Her look felt like she could see clear through me. But then, if she had, I might not be standing here wondering about it. I wonder what she's up to...*

After lunch, Katie and Darla helped clean the dining area and the kitchen with Ezra and El. As she completed her tasks, she tried to pump El for any information that might be useful, noting that some of the women had some very nice looking jewelry on and wondering if the renovations included personal safes or if there was a general safe for that sort of thing.

"Why no, sweetie. That wouldn't be necessary, since they're already in each of the rooms." The cook smiled at the concern the young maid was showing for her guests.

"Really?" Katie said, playing the wide-eyed role. "I sure didn't see any when I was helping Darla."

"Well, Mr. G was a stickler for that kind of thing after a diamond necklace was 'liberated' from one of his guests back in the '50's. Isn't that right Ezra?" She turned to her husband for confirmation.

"Yep. Mr. G had them installed in each bathroom behind the mirrors. I think some of them still work," he added thoughtfully.

"Wow!" Katie said. "I bet this place has lots of little nooks and crannies for hiding things. Just like in the old gangster movie's on TV."

"Oh my, yes." The cook loved to reminisce about the good old days. "Mr. G's father was thought to have been in the Dutch Schultz mob during the '20's, but it was never proved. He did have a speakeasy in the lodge though. All the bigwigs in the county came here. My mother was a cook here then. She used to tell us some pretty wild stories of goings on in that speakeasy. My older sister and I grew up in this lodge in the thirties and forties," El said wistfully, then got up and started to get things ready for dinner. "Well, sweetie, your shift is done for today. I'll see you tomorrow," she added with a smile.

****

It was nearly three o'clock and time for Katie to go off duty. Dean and Tracy made arrangements to grab a quick early dinner with Katie as soon as she came in, then Tracy went back to her office. Katie had changed out of her maid uniform before arriving at the office. She bounced in and waved to Linna and Tracy before entering the office where Dean had been keeping track of her.

"Nice move, interrogating the cook." Dean smiled appreciatively.

"She's a sweet old thing and should be a good source as long as I can keep her from getting suspicious," Katie said, smiling back.

"Yeah, but don't try to ask too many questions. It may look suspicious. Let's grab Tracy and have some dinner before the show starts this evening," Dean suggested.

"Gods, that sounds good. I'm starving." Katie then added, "El may be a good cook, but the hired help doesn't get to taste much of it."

Dean reset the tapes, and then they left the room, locking the office door behind them. In the outer office, they caught up with Tracy and then left for dinner. They selected a lone table in the corner of Mac's Bar, placed their order, and then went over the events of the day. Katie told them about the laser beams and secret cameras, then filled them in on the inhabitants. As she related her meeting with Kasimov, her anger returned and it took some persuasion by both Dean and Tracy to get her to cool down again. Finally, she recounted the incidents with Lin.

"So, what's that all about?" she asked Dean. "Any ideas?"

"Well, we did hear her comment to Ito," Dean said as she eyed Tracy.

"Yeah, but that was in Japanese," Katie said looking at Dean then Tracy, as they both tried to look elsewhere. "Let me guess, you two understand Japanese."

"Uhh, yeah," Tracy muttered as she looked at Dean for help.

"Don't look at me, Tracy. You're the one spilling the beans about understanding Japanese," Dean said with a grin.

"So, spit it out" Katie locked her emerald eyes on Tracy.

"Well...uh...I mean...we didn't get it all. They were talking real quietly," Tracy hedged.

"Seems Lin is attracted to you...and Ito thought it might be fun to have a three way," Dean informed the blonde nonchalantly. "Not that I blame her. You are very attractive."

"Yeah," chimed in Tracy hoping to redeem herself. "You can't blame her for that."

"Oh, great." The blonde was now thoroughly embarrassed. "Now I won't be able to look her in the eye without blushing."

"Well, if it's any consolation, your blush is rather sexy," Dean concluded with a sly grin and a wink at the blonde. This got the intended result as Katie proceeded to blush profusely.

After a round of laughter, Katie turned the conversation back to the security at the lodge. She had not found a security control room, but she hadn't really had much time to look. She would try to explore other areas of the house tomorrow, if at all possible. Finally, the three women discussed possible scenarios if they ever had to enter the lodge in secret.

"I don't know, Dean," Katie interjected. "I sure hope we won't have to go in there. There seems to be an awful lot of laser beam and security cameras around that place. It'd be a tough one to crack if we can't locate the control room."

"I gotta agree with Katie on that one," Tracy added. "I'm sure there's even more stuff that she hasn't seen yet."

"Well, hopefully we'll get what we need tonight and not have to go in there at all," Dean said as their food arrived.

The rest of dinner was spent in pleasant conversation, including an update on Linna by Tracy. "I had a talk with her about your office. I told her that there was a lot of very expensive equipment in there that was very delicate given the difficulty of the subject matter. I suggested that she not bother you two when you're in there because the sound settings were so sensitive, yadda yadda," Tracy said, punctuating her speech with her hands. "She's pretty darn smart, and I'm sure she didn't buy it; but I warned her to not bother you two, and she agreed."

"Good enough for me," Dean said.

"Me too," Katie nodded.

"Well, I'm gonna run by my trailer and feed the cats and get Sugar's medicine down her. Are you going back to the office now?" Katie asked Dean.

"No, I'm going to go by my place first. I need to pick up some things. I'll meet you back there at 1730 okay?" Katie nodded in agreement as Dean paid the bill. The three women left Mac's Bar and walked the three blocks back to the office. When they got there, Tracy asked if they'd mind if she came back in the evening to listen in with them. Both agents agreed, then Tracy went into the office, and the two women left to carry out their errands.

Thursday, 1900 hours

The three women were listening and watching intently as the activity level in the lodge began to increase. They were in TDSC mode since it was too dark for the regular camera, and this made it more difficult to match voices with images. As Dean scanned the house, she noted that an area next to the den showed up black on the screen, indicating that it could not be penetrated by the scan.

"Any idea what's in that space?" Dean inquired of Katie.

"I think that's the area that Kasimov uses for his quarters." The blonde studied the screen. "Why can't we get penetration?"

"There are a few substances that will block the scan. Most are way too expensive, like titanium shielding, but the most likely culprit is concrete. It has to be at least two feet thick, though," Dean elaborated. "Didn't El mention that there used to be a speakeasy in the lodge?" she inquired of the young agent.

"Yeah. She did, but she didn't say where," Katie answered. "You think it's next to the den?"

"Could be, but my guess would be that the room next to the den is empty. See the layout? It doesn't even look big enough to be a bedroom. More like a false front, if you ask me. My instincts say that it leads down to the cellar to the old speakeasy."

"But what about the penetration? Wouldn't it be too expensive to line that room with titanium?" Tracy asked as she reviewed the layout of the lodge.

"That's why my gut tells me the whole cellar is probably thick concrete, but they'd still have to use a thin titanium shield on the staircase and door," Dean said as she continued her scanning. "It would make sense for a speakeasy to be in the cellar. More room for guests, and there's probably a hidden walkout for emergency egress. It probably only took a few more inches of concrete all around the room to make it impenetrable. That's what I would have done," she concluded with a nod.

"Makes sense," Tracy commented. "That way he's sure to have a secure area that would house the control room and whatever else he has up his sleeve." As an afterthought Tracy added, "Did you ever run across Dimitri during the day?"

"As a matter of fact, no," replied the blonde. "I thought that was a bit weird too, since he was supposed to be doing a security check."

"He did it all from the control room. New scanning equipment similar to the TDSC could scan the rooms through the fiber optics in the camera lenses," Dean advised. "Probably has a lens in every room."

"I wonder if he caught me interrogating El and Ezra?" the blonde considered aloud.

"He very well could have." Dean turned, and her eyes gave away the concern she felt. "You'd better stick to just visual examination and not try to pump El and Ezra tomorrow. Just be the hired maid and talk about weather, cleaning, that kind of stuff, nothing more."

About to give Katie a hug, Dean noticed that the voices in the lodge suddenly became quiet as two images spontaneously appeared outside the den. She focused her full attention on the tableau before them. "That about cinches it," she said to her comrades. "Andre and Natasha just 'appeared' on the screen."

The women watched as the two images entered the dining area that was located across from Kasimov's room.

"Good evening, my friends. I hope everyone had a successful day?" Kasimov asked in his heavily accented English.

Murmurs came from the assembled guests on how many deer the hunters had returned with, followed by thanks for planning that event. It had obviously had the intended effect, since most comments about their host that the women could pick up were more gracious than the ones they had heard earlier...

"Yep, he's a smooth one all right," Tracy commented.

"Thank you, my friends!" Kasimov said. "Now let us finish our cocktails, then have a good meal, before we get to the reason why you have been asked here."

The general made his rounds of the group, stopping and chatting with people as he made his way to his table. Sounds of chairs sliding on the floor as guests seated themselves could be heard, followed by those of utensils and plates making contact. The sounds of dinner being served and consumed mingled with laughter and numerous overlapping conversations, making it almost impossible to distinguish any pertinent information. The two agents and park director just sat and waited for dinner to be over.

They were brought out of their temporary day-dreaming by the tinkling of a utensil on a glass. "Okay, here we go." Dean flipped the recorders on.

"Ladies and gentlemen," General Kasimov bellowed over the group, "the time you have been waiting for is now upon us." He smiled broadly. "Tonight I am going to present you with the opportunity of a lifetime. There has been a major push by each of your governments to crack down on drug trafficking. A global 'war on drugs', if you will. Although many of you are still competing successfully, many more of you are not. And soon, all governments will begin to win this war through their cooperative efforts. The tide is turning against you."

"Tonight, I am prepared to offer you a new drug for your arsenal that is so potent, so dependable, and so easy to produce and distribute that you may not believe its potential. Scientists at our National Security Research Division stumbled upon it and discarded it as potentially unstable and highly destructive. I, however, have rescued this substance and, with the help of my dedicated personal staff, have restructured its make-up to make it the most powerful mind control substance this planet will ever see."

"Think of it, my friends. The ability to control anyone's mind, their actions or reactions. The possibilities are limitless. YOU could control your governments! YOU could take over all legitimate or illegitimate businesses in your countries! YOU could become the elite in your country! YOU have the potential to become the wealthiest people on this planet!" Kasimov paused for effect as murmured conversation arose among his guests.

"General!" called out Johnnie Papp, "why are you offering this to us? Why don't you take over the planet yourself?" Numerous voices affirmed the wide-spread interest in the answer to Johnnie's question.

"Because, I do not have an army at my command." The general's answer clearly depicted the declining status of the military in his country. "We are no longer the super power we once were. We have become complacent and soft!" he said with disgust. "Those of you that agree to my terms will become my army. And yes, I intend to 'take over the planet', as you say. But I need your help." With a smile, he widened his arms to gather in his flock.

Julio Romero stood and asked, "What's it gonna cost us, señor?"

"Excellent question, Mr. Romero." The general smiled at the delegate in question, then continued. "My friends, I am not a greedy man. My price to you would be the production costs of the drug and a pitiful twenty-five percent of your profits." He put all of his charm into the offer. "Oh, and I forgot to mention—the cost of production is less than the cost of a pack of American cigarettes, for an amount that would control twenty individuals for one month." The general beamed.

Lin raised her hand and got the general's attention. "General, you say this is a mind control drug. Just how is it administered, and will you be giving a demonstration of its effectiveness?"

"Of course, my beautiful lady. You would not marry a man without trying him out first, now would you?" He smiled lecherously.

"General, I would not 'try out' a man for any reason," came the tart response. "Please answer my question."

A bit taken aback, the general continued. "Administration can be accomplished by almost any means—inhalation, ingestion, injection, or topical application—whatever the situation may require for expediency." He smiled at the Oriental woman before continuing. "And yes, I will be providing a demonstration."

"What are your 'terms', other than payment?" came another question from the back of the room.

"Another excellent question. My conditions are three-fold. Firstly, that I will select your first targets. After that, you are free to select your own. Secondly, your cartel's people will all form an alliance with me and will follow my commands without question, and finally, the matter of pay-ment that we already discussed."

"What's to stop you from using the drug on us?" shouted another cartel member, this one from Canada.

"Nothing, really. I could have used it on all of you already, but I would rather have a voluntary cooperation than a contrived one. It's much cleaner that way, you see." Again, he smiled and poured on the charm. "Any other questions?"

There were a few more questions: concerns about time frames for target selection, delivery of the drug, and—of course—the 'demonstration'.

"Ah yes, the demonstration." The general became seri-ous as he looked through the group. "There was only one expedient way to prove the effects of this drug," he contin-ued, scanning the group intently. "I requested your superi-ors to send three of the most trusted individuals in their organizations. Three people beyond reproach, who could not be swayed by money or power, but were totally dedi-cated to the cartel."

The group all nodded in understanding. The general looked around the room again, and then waved a hand across the group.

"You are each dedicated to your organization. No one in this group would consider doing anything that would jeopardize the lives of anyone in their company. Correct?"

Heads nodded in agreement, then they started to com-prehend what the general was leading up to.

"One person in each of your small groups was given this drug. Please understand this is not hypnosis or sub-liminal transference. I merely need to suggest an action, and these individuals will carry that action out. They respond to my voice because I have arranged it thusly for this demonstration."

The group was becoming a lot more nervous at the general's implications.

"In order to manipulate each of the selected individuals, I personally talked to them after they ingested the drug so they would, in this situation, respond to only my voice." The general paused for effect. "Mr. Cabini and Mr. Sanchez, please come forward."

The two men immediately stood and came to the general's table. "Gentlemen, please remove your revolvers from your holsters and attach your silencers." The two men did so. "Now place the barrel of your revolver to your temple." They complied once more. "Now...pull the trigger." Immediately two muffled 'pffts' were heard, followed by two thuds as the men dropped to the floor, very dead.

Johnnie Papp was the first one to his feet, followed closely by Romero.

"Just what the hell are you doing, General?" shouted Papp.

"Yeah!" Romero echoed. "You just blew away two of our own, you bastard!"

"Your own? I think not," the general said calmly as he held up his hands. "Dimitri discovered that these two members of your group were very well placed agents. What better way to demonstrate the power of this drug than on undercover agents, don't you agree?" The general smiled at the two men.

"You're nuts!" cried out Papp. "I've known Tony for five years. What proof have you got?"

The general pulled out two miniature communication devices and other items that were immediately recognized as standard FBI issue. "I take it you recognize these?" the general asked, referring to the devices. "I had Dimitri trace their last communication to the Bureau headquarters. Luckily, he was able to jam the transmission so it could not be received. I would be happy to share a tape of their foiled communication if you wish."

"Holy shit!" whispered Tracy. "Did you guys know there were FBI agents there?"

The two agents looked at each other shaking their heads.

"We didn't know *we* were on the same case, so it doesn't surprise me that the FBI was there too," Dean commented.

"Here's another reason why the agencies should talk to one another. Maybe we could have done something to protect them," Katie said, obviously affected by the deaths.

"Don't go there, Katie." Dean turned to the young agent and reached out to pull her into a hug. "There's nothing we would have been able to do to stop this. We had no idea what the general was doing with the cartels in the first place."

"I...I know. I just have a difficult time understanding the evil man can do to man. I know it's there, seen it happen, but still..." Katie said with a sigh.

The women returned their attention to the lodge as Kasimov began speaking again.

"Now, my friends, I suggest you go back to your rooms and consider my proposal. Tomorrow, you will contact your superiors with my offer, and tomorrow evening I will expect their responses," Kasimov told his guests. "In the meantime, Dimitri will take care of this unpleasantness." He gestured toward the two bodies on the floor.

The next sounds they heard were the sounds of the assembled guests leaving the dining area and ascending the stairs. This was followed by Kasimov's instructions to dump the bodies in the woods at the hunting camp. Then silence.

"Do you suppose we could find their bodies?" Katie asked hopefully. "If they have families, I'd like them to be able to have their loved ones back and not have them wondering what went wrong, or where they are."

"I suppose we can try to follow Dimitri. I just don't want to jeopardize our assignment," Dean said hesitantly. "We'll give it a try, but I won't take a chance on being recognized."

"Fair enough, and thank you." The blonde gave Dean an appreciative hug.

"Take the park truck," Tracy offered. "I've been known to wander around the countryside in it checking the parks and such, so if the vehicle is spotted, it won't arouse suspicion."

"Are you sure?" Blue eyes settled on Tracy.

"Yeah, no problem. I'll lock up. You two get going so you don't miss him," Tracy answered as she handed Dean the keys.

"Okay, thanks." Dean quickly put new tapes into the machines, and then the two agents left to follow Dimitri. Tracy stayed at the office long enough to make sure the building was secure and locked, then headed home herself.

****

Dean and Katie got into the truck and quickly reached the intersection where they hoped to pick up Dimitri's van. They only had to wait a couple of minutes before they spotted the van turning onto Route 17 going east. They followed him discreetly as he exited on Route 55, heading towards the reservoirs. He kept going past the Neversink Reservoir then turned off on a county road leading up towards Slide Mountain. There wasn't a lot of traffic they could hide in, so the agents were forced to hang back quite a distance. They almost missed the dirt road that Dimitri had taken. Luckily it hadn't rained since Saturday, so they saw the dust cloud raised by the vehicle and then could pick out the taillights in the distance. They immediately turned off their headlights and were about to turn in, when they saw the brake lights go on; then the lights went out. Dean drove past the dirt road a short ways before she pulled into a turn off. They extinguished their lights, quickly exited the truck, and covered the distance back to the dirt road in seconds.

"We'd better stay close to the woods for cover," Dean whispered as she led the way.

Soon they were opposite the van, and Dimitri was just returning from the path that led off to the right. He reached back into the van and hoisted the other body over his shoulder, then headed down the path again.

"He couldn't have gone too far down that path, so let's just wait here until he leaves, and then we'll go retrieve the bodies," the tall woman whispered.

In a few minutes, Dimitri returned, entered the van, turned it around and headed back down the dirt road. Reaching the main highway, he quickly turned left to return to the lodge.

"Our truck is far enough out of sight, isn't it?" The blonde was still whispering.

"Yeah, and it was pulled over far enough around the curve that there's no way he would have seen it," Dean responded. "I'll go get the truck; you wait here."

****

It wasn't long before Dean was back with the truck, backing it up the dirt road to where Katie was waiting. She grabbed a flashlight from the glove box, and then joined Katie to look for the bodies. It took them nearly twenty minutes to find them. Dimitri had done a good job of hiding them beneath several boughs of evergreens. It took them another twenty minutes to pack them back to the truck. They wrapped the bodies in a tarp they found behind the seat.

"What now?" Katie asked.

"We'll take them to my place. I'll put them in the shed, and then call it in. I'm sure they'll have some-one out here before daybreak. Once I get the call in, we'll go back to the office and run through the record-ings, just in case. Then we'll go back to my place and wait for the feds." Dean looked at the young blonde, and then added, "If you'd rather go back to your trailer, I'd understand."

"No, I'd rather be with you. After all, retrieving their bodies was my idea," the blonde said sadly. "I wonder if they had families...lovers..." Her voice

trailed off as the tragedy took its toll on her composure. "Oh, Dean," she said between heaves, "I'll
never get used to needless, violent death. Maybe I
should have stayed at Quantico as an instructor and
not have to face these tragedies."

"Mmm," the dark-haired woman said as she gathered the blonde into her arms. "I've got you, and I'll
do my best to protect you. Nothing like this will ever
happen to you, I promise." Dean knew with every
fiber of her being, that she would do her utmost to
keep that promise or die trying. Trying for a lighter
note, she added, "Besides, if you had stayed at Quantico, I never would have met you." That simple
reminder brought a smile to the young woman's face
as she looked up and gently placed a kiss on Dean's
lips, lingering there to enjoy the sense of well-being
she felt while in her lover's arms.

They got back in the truck and headed to Dean's.
It didn't take long to unload the bodies and lock them
in the shed. They completed the rest of their tasks
and were back in Dean's cabin before midnight.

"I don't think you should be going back to the
lodge in the morning." The blue eyes pierced the
blonde's emerald ones with determination. "We have
what we need. There's no need for you to risk main-
taining your presence there."

"I don't agree, Dean. We still don't know where
he keeps the drug, and it would be very helpful if we
could get our hands on a sample so we could try to
come up with something to counteract it," the blonde
persisted. "Besides, won't it look suspicious if, all of
a sudden, I quit? It might make him bolt if he thought

there were more agents around that Dimitri hadn't
discovered."

"Well, they may be able to get some information
about the drug from the autopsies," the tall woman
offered. "Besides, I think it's too dangerous now."

"No Dean, it's more dangerous if I *don't* show up.
You said he's a sly bastard. He'll figure it out; you
know it!" Katie said, feeling a bit agitated that the
colonel did not think she could handle it. "I can do
this! I'm a highly trained professional. Just because
I get upset at needless death doesn't mean I can't do
my job!"

"Hold on," Dean said quickly. "I never said I
didn't think you could do your job. I...I just don't
want to see anything happen to you." The blue eyes
closed, and Dean took a deep breath before she continued. "I've seen more than my share of death,
Katie. I was the cause of much of it. I have demons
of my own to deal with, and I don't know what I
would do if it were your body that I had to drag out of
that ravine." She sighed heavily and moved closer to
the young woman. "I just can't lose you, not now, not
ever."

"Oh, Dean," Katie said softly, placing her hands
on Dean's cheeks. "I can't lose you either. I'll be
careful, and you'll be watching over me the whole
time. I promise I'll hightail it right out of there if I
get any inkling that they may be suspicious." The
emerald eyes fell into the pools of blue as both
women leaned into each other.

They stood that way for several minutes, just
holding each other and enjoying each other's warmth.
Finally Dean led the young woman over to the sofa in

front of the fireplace. She lit the kindling under the logs for the fire that had been laid earlier and watched as it spread. She stood and walked over to the sofa, then quietly sat down next to Katie to wait for the FBI to come and claim their own. Katie turned and softly kissed Dean, then stretched out on the sofa putting her head in Dean's lap. The older agent softly stroked the blonde hair until Katie gave in and finally fell asleep.

They were both awakened by a knock on the door at two-thirty. A black van sat in the driveway, and the three men at the door were each holding out their FBI badges. Dean recognized the oldest one. "Hey, Sid," she said with a sad smile. "Sorry to have to run into you like this." She held the door open to allow them in. Sid introduced the other two men, and then asked where the bodies were. Dean gave them the key to the shed, and the two men left to take care of the bodies.

"We really appreciate you recovering them for us." Sid looked at her with sad brown eyes.

"Yeah, well, I wish we could have gotten them out of there alive," Dean said. "But there was no way to tell what was coming down until it was too late."

Dean introduced the sleepy DEA agent, and the two women filled in the lead FBI agent. It took about an hour to update him. "Here, my boss said to give these to you. They'll give you the blow by blow of what the bastard is doing. At least up 'til tonight," she qualified, as she gave him a copy of the audio and visual recordings of the events of the night. "I don't know exactly what he's planning to do, yet. We'll keep you informed."

"Thanks." Sid shook her hand, then Katie's. "Their families will appreciate what you did for them." The two women nodded, then Sid went to the van, and it disappeared into the dark.

"It's too late to go back to the trailer," Katie said as she was led back into the house. "Mind if I stay the night?"

"No, I was just going to suggest that," Dean answered, leading the blonde to her room.

Friday, 1100 hours

The morning had been fairly uneventful. At the lodge, Katie had been assigned to similar duties as the day before. Today, she was even more discreet in her visual inspection of the premises. She had not seen Kasimov at all since her arrival. Heeding Dean and Tracy's suggestions from the night before, she refrained from pumping El or Ezra. The only communication she had with them was what they initiated. Her lack of communication went unnoticed since she was kept busy the entire morning.

Attendance at breakfast was minus a few guests, besides the two agents disposed of the night before. Katie assumed that they were all still contacting their superiors about Kasimov's offer. With fewer people at breakfast, she was already on her cleaning rounds with Darla upstairs. As per her plan from the previous day, today she took the other side of the hall. Things were going quite well until she got to the last room. It was Lin's room, and she was still in it.

Katie knocked on the door and heard Lin say, "Come." As soon as she heard Lin's voice, she knew she was in trouble. *I should have taken this side yes-*

terday, she thought to herself. *Now I've got to face this woman! Well, better get this over with.*

"Hi," Katie said as she entered. "I didn't know anyone was here. I'll come back later." She quickly turned to leave.

"No. Please, I won't be in your way. I'm just finishing up some Haiku. Just pretend I'm not here and go about your business," Lin said with a sweet smile.

"Oh...okay, if you don't mind." Katie answered a bit hesitantly at first, then immediately started cleaning the room.

"Would you mind starting with the bath? Then when you're done in there, I can go in and shower and leave you to finish your work."

"Uhh, no problem." Going into the bathroom, Katie started cleaning quickly and vigorously. It took her half the time she normally would have taken. As she exited the bath, she was stopped cold in her tracks as she came face to face with a very beautiful, and very naked, Lin.

"Oops, sorry," Katie said quickly, as she blushed in embarrassment. *Shit!* Her mind screamed. *What the hell is this all about!* "I'll just...umm...excuse me," Katie stammered as she tried to get past the ex-cop and pull her eyes off of the woman's breasts.

"Oh, no need to rush off on my account," Lin said seductively. "Haven't you ever seen a naked woman before?"

Back at the office, Dean nearly started an electrical fire as the tea she had just taken a very large sip of came exploding out of her mouth and all over the console. *What the hell? What on earth is she up to this time?*

****

"Well...yeah...it's just that you're a guest, and, I...uh...I need to get back to work," Katie said, once more trying to get around the woman.

Lin continued to block her way. "What's a beautiful young woman like you doing here working for minimum wage? You should be doing something exotic, something adventurous, like being a spy," Lin said as she began to laugh.

Katie didn't know what to say, but she was suddenly glad that she was still blushing to cover her astonishment at the suggestion of her being a spy.

"No, ma'am," Katie said quickly. "I just can't wait to marry Billy and have lots of babies. That'll be plenty of excitement for me." *Where the hell did that come from? I sound like some backwoods boob from the Ozarks for God's sake!* She quickly took advantage of Lin's laughing state and brushed past her. "I'll be back later to clean your room," she said, as she picked up her things and left. *Shit, shit, shit!* Katie said to herself as she contemplated what had just transpired. *Oh Dean! I bet you got an earful on that one. Too bad you couldn't see the view!* she mused. As she started to polish the tables and dust the statues in the hall, Katie stuck her hand in her apron pocket to get out a tissue, but came out with a folded piece of paper instead. *That wasn't there before I went in Lin's room,* she thought, then quickly put it back in her pocket and pulled out the tissue, aware that she might be watched. *I'll read it later, much later.*

The rest of the afternoon went by without any more incidents. She was able to go back to finish cleaning Lin's room after the young Oriental came out, pausing to wink at Katie before heading down the stairs. At three o'clock, she left the lodge with little more information to add to what she had already gathered the day before. By the time she reached the Parks and Recreation office, it was nearly three thirty. As she opened the office door, Dean turned around and gave her one of those raised eyebrow, 'what in the hell was that all about' looks.

"Sooo..." Dean said, trying desperately to keep a blank expression on her face.

"Well," Katie shut the door and took the seat next to Dean, "I had a very uneventful day." Despite her words, she was smiling her own version of the 'cat that ate the canary' smile back at Dean. She also noticed the wet spots on the carpet and wondered what had happened.

"Uneventful, eh?" Dean inquired. "So, you run into naked women—excuse me—gorgeous, naked women every day, huh?" She lifted her eyebrow even higher.

"Oh, it's a regular happening for me." Her emerald eyes twinkled mischievously. "Guess I just attract that type."

"Yeah, that type and the Billy Bob type." Dean chuckled. "...marry Billy and have lots of babies," Dean said, mimicking a Katie-ish voice.

"Stop that!" Katie said as she slapped Dean's arm. "It was all I could come up with at the time." Almost as an afterthought, she added, "She is really beautiful, you know."

"Oh, I know all right. That's why I lost my tea all over the console!" Dean confessed.

"So...that's why the carpet is wet." It was Katie's turn to chuckle. "Anyway, it just took me by surprise. I have no clue as to what's in that woman's mind." Then Katie related finding the note in her apron pocket.

"So, what's it say?"

"I haven't read it yet. I was afraid I would be caught on camera," Katie explained.

She pulled out the note and began to read it.

> *I don't know who you are or whom you're working for, but I recognized your necklace at breakfast yesterday. I'm hoping you're working with Major Peterson, and you will be able to get this message to her.*

"Damn!" Dean smacked her head. "I completely forgot that we used the same necklace on a case in the Philippines. Oh, Katie, I'm sorry. I really put you in jeopardy here."

"Don't be; obviously I'm still alive," Katie said, reaching out to touch Dean's arm in reassurance, then continuing to read the note.

> *Kasimov is planning on taking over the world with a new mind control drug he has developed. Drug cartels are to become his private army. I'm acting as a representative for the Yakusa...*

Katie finished reading the note that told pretty much the same story they already knew except for the additional information that Lin was working as an independent, trying to reclaim her family honor by destroying the Yakusa. It ended with Lin asking Katie to contact Major Peterson and meet her in her room again tomorrow.

"Well, well." Dean reflected on this new development. "I'm glad she didn't turn. I always felt she was good to the core. I just hope they don't catch on to her and dispose of her the same way as the two FBI agents. Guess you'll have to meet her again tomorrow."

"Well, I hope it won't be under the same circumstances," Katie said, starting to blush again.

"Guess you'll just have to take your chances," Dean said with a broad smile. "Don't worry, she's a pro. Just go with whatever she presents you, okay?"

"Yeah, easy for you to say," Katie retorted as she stuck her tongue out.

The two women reviewed the new information on camera locations that Katie had found that day. After that, they reset the tape machines and locked up the office. It was almost four thirty, so they decided to get some dinner before they came back for the evening's report to Kasimov from the cartels' upper echelon.

At 1900 hours, they were back in the office waiting for the action to begin. Kasimov appeared at seven thirty, and dinner progressed without any announcements. After dinner, drinks were served in the den. That was where he made an initial announcement that he would be taking the group to his quarters to discuss the vote of the cartels, assign initial targets, and discuss the distribution of the drug.

"General," came Lin's voice over the headphones, "Don't you think it will be a bit crowded in your quarters? Why not discuss it out here?"

"My dear woman, things are not always what they appear," the general said cryptically. "There will be more than enough room for all of us, and in light of last night's departure of two of our guests, I believe it is the most secure place in this lodge," he concluded as he led the way to his quarters.

"Shit!" The two women said in unison as they watched the ethereal bodies on the screen disappear into the blackness that was Kasimov's quarters.

"Now what?" Katie asked in desperation. "We can't penetrate that area!"

"Good thing Lin made contact. We'll have to rely on your meeting with her tomorrow to fill us in," the tall agent replied. "We may as well call it a night. I'm sure he'll impose a code of silence on them once they exit his quarters."

"Looks like we have the night off, Colonel." Katie smiled affectionately at the tall woman.

"Your place, or mine?" Dean asked with a smile.

"Yours," Katie determined. "But, after I stop at the trailer to take care of the brood and pick up some of my things."

****

The evening found the two women curled up on the sofa together in front of a cozy fire. Soft music played in the background, a bottle of cabernet, opened and half-consumed, sat on the side table. Dean was lightly stroking and playing with Katie's hair, humming along to the tune.

"You really have a great voice," Katie said, looking up into Dean's blue eyes. "I couldn't carry a tune if it was in a bucket," she chuckled.

"Well, I did say I have 'special' skills, didn't I?" The ice blues twinkled back at the emeralds.

"Why do you suppose Lin wanted me to contact you specifically?" The question came out before Katie could call it back. *Don't go there, Katie. Let the green-eyed monster just crawl back into his cave!* the young blonde thought to herself. *I'm sure it's just for professional reasons...I hope!*

"Don't know, love. Probably because she trusts me." The tall woman was seemingly unaware of Katie's concern. "We got into a very tight situation in the Philippine's, and we came to trust each other implicitly."

"How long were you and she..." Katie let the word trail off.

"Lovers?" Dean finished for her. "I was assigned out there for about eighteen months. We were lovers for six of them."

"Why did it end?" Katie asked again, and then added, "If you want to talk about it, that is."

"It's okay, I don't mind," Dean admitted. "Actually, I thought about that a lot when I got back to the States. It was her decision, not mine," she continued. "I tried to get her to come back to the States with me, but she refused, citing her family as her reason. Her family was very traditional. She broke that tradition by joining the police force and felt that she owed it to them to remain there. That was just before all hell broke loose with her brother." The blue eyes became distant as she began again. "Lin really loved her brother. It broke her heart to uncover the truth. Her father was so dishonored that he took his own life. Her mother followed shortly after that, more from a broken heart than anything else. Lin's the last of her line, and I can understand her drive to redeem her family honor."

"Wow," Katie said softly. "That's a really tragic story." She paused a long time before she asked the next question. "Are you still in love with her?" Green eyes focused intently on the blues above her.

"No," came the quiet response. "I was younger then, and Lin was very young too. We were both new to the world of women loving women, and we rode the waves of passion as though there were no tomorrow." She sighed heavily. "I realize now that it was lust, not love, driving our desires for each other; so no, I'm not in love with her, never was."

A wave of relief swamped over Katie's heart at that moment. She had been wondering about Lin since Dean had first mentioned her. Now she decided to proceed with her next question.

"Do you think you might be in falling in love with me?" the blonde asked timidly, as she searched the blue eyes for affirmation.

It was almost an eternity before Dean answered. Then she slowly spoke. "I've been asking myself that same question since I met you." She paused. "I don't know if I have been truly in love with anyone at any time in my life." Again, another pause. "All I know is that when I look at you, my heart smiles. When I touch you, my body sings. And when I make love with you, my spirit soars." Dean's smile broadened as Katie found her confirmation in the blue eyes.

"That's the most beautiful thing I've ever heard," Katie whispered as tears welled up in her eyes. "And I love you, too," she concluded, emphasizing each word as she pulled Dean down into a kiss that lingered softly as the young woman surrendered herself to her lover and allowed both of their spirits to soar.

Saturday, 0600 hours

This was Katie's third day of work at the lodge. She and Dean rose early so that they could get in a morning run before she had to report to work. Dean had just gotten out of the shower and was drying her long black hair, as Katie fixed a quick breakfast of toasted bagels with cream cheese and hot tea.

"Now remember," Dean called from the bathroom. "Let Lin make the contact. Don't try to force the meeting. Let it come naturally."

"Got it!" the young agent called back. "Are you almost ready? I'd like to get there..."

Her words were lost as she was held from behind in a loving embrace. She turned and placed a kiss on the waiting lips. "You can move as quietly as a cat, you know that?" the young woman observed.

"Yep. It's another of my 'special' skills," the tall agent responded as she snatched a bagel and travel mug of tea. "What are you waiting for? You're gonna be late." She pretended to scold the blonde.

Katie just smiled, grabbing her bagel and mug of tea as the two women left the house and got into their separate cars. By the time Katie arrived at the lodge, Dean was already sitting at the console reviewing the tapes from the night before. "Just as I thought," she spoke to herself. "Nothing here of importance. It was a good night to take off." She focused her attention on the sounds from the lodge. It was a foggy morning, so she was using the TDSC unit for video input. Katie's blue dot appeared to be in the kitchen. This was verified by the voice of El welcoming her.

"Good morning El, Ezra," Katie said as she announced herself.

"Good morning, sweetie," said El, returning the salutation. "Coffee's ready. Would you like some? And I've got some raisin bran muffins coming out of the oven in about two minutes."

"Boy! That sounds good to me," Katie answered, as she put her coat up in the mudroom. "I think the weather's changing. It's pretty foggy out today."

"Supposed to turn cold and maybe even get snow in the higher elevations tonight," came the contribution from Ezra. "Winter'll be here soon." He stood to leave. "Better get more firewood chopped and stacked."

"What's on my duty list today?" Katie asked El as she poured herself some coffee, then helped her put the muffins on the cooling racks.

"Same as usual, sweetie. That Oriental lady asked to have some ginger tea brought to her room. She's not feeling too well today," El commented, then asked, "Would you mind taking it up to her? Darla's not here yet."

"No problem," Katie replied. She walked over to the counter where El had set out the tray and a small teapot

that smelled of ginger tea. She added a teacup and saucer. "Do you use sugar with ginger tea?" she asked El.
    "Some do, some don't. Better take it with you," El
answered. "Here, put this nice hot muffin on a plate for her.
Maybe the aroma will entice her into having a bite to eat."

    Katie finished fixing the tray, then went up the
back stairs to the second floor and Lin's room. *Well,*
that was pretty quick, Katie thought to herself as she
ascended the stairs. *Okay, just go with the flow. Let*
her make the first move, like Dean said. She got to
Lin's room and knocked twice.
    "Maid," she said softly, so as not to wake any of
the other guests in rooms near Lin's.
    "Come," came the muffled voice from inside the
room.
    Katie entered and found Lin still in bed. When
Lin saw her, she motioned for Katie to put the tray on
the table by the bed. As Katie did what was
requested, she noticed that Lin was watching her
intently. *She's probably wondering if I got and read*
the note. Katie considered how to let her know, and
then she hit upon an idea.
    "Ma'am, are you feeling any better?" she inquired
of the Oriental woman, then sat on the bed next to her
and gave her a smile and a wink. "I don't have a ther-
mometer, but my Mom would put her cheek on mine
to tell if I had a temperature or not. She said using
your hands to feel for a temperature didn't work since
some people always have hot hands, and others
always have cold. May I check?" Katie asked quietly.
    "Why not, it can't hurt. The ginger tea usually
helps though," replied the ex-cop.

Katie leaned over and placed her cheek on Lin's, then whispered ever so softly in her ear. "I got your message and talked with Colonel Peterson. What do you want me to do?" Then added, "Are you really ill?"

Lin whispered back, "Good, come back later with soup or something. I'm fine."

"Well it doesn't feel like you have a temperature," Katie said aloud. "Is there anything else I can get for you?"

"Not right now, thank you. Perhaps a bit later I could have some broth or soup?" Lin also answered in a normal volume. "I'm glad to see I didn't scare you off yesterday," Lin continued with a bit more verve to her voice.

"No, ma'am," Katie replied. "Just took me by surprise is all. I'll be back at lunchtime with some soup."

The rest of the morning followed the same schedule as the previous two days. Katie helped serve breakfast and clean up the dining area, and then helped Darla with the room cleaning before lunch. In the kitchen, El prepared the soup and had a tray ready for Katie to take up to the Oriental woman at lunchtime.

****

Dean spent her morning monitoring the blue dot on the screen and the conversations over the headphones. Whatever had happened last night in Kasimov's quarters was not discussed at all. He had undoubtedly issued a gag order due to the discovery

of the two FBI agents. Around 1000 hours there was
a soft knock on the door.

"Yes?" Dean queried as she switched the camera
view to the park. *Now who would be here on a Saturday?*

"It's just me, Dean," replied Linna. "I just
thought you might like some tea or coffee or something?"

"Come on in," Dean called to the secretary.

"Thanks," Linna said on entering. "Tracy told me
not to disturb you, but I just wanted to say I was sorry
for the interruption the other day."

"No problem, Linna," the agent responded. "It's
just that sometimes, I need to really focus on the
screen so I can re-direct the camera angle. Don't
want to miss any opportunities to capture my prey on
film," the tall woman concluded in a chuckle.

"Yeah, that's what Tracy said. So, you need anything?" Linna asked hopefully.

"Actually, I need to get up and stretch. Sitting
here all day gets really boring." Dean smiled. "How
about I come out there for some tea?" After a pause
she added, "So, what brings you into the office on a
Saturday?"

Um...well...I wanted to apologize, but I didn't
want Tracy to know I bothered you again," the secretary said, smiling. "I brought in some great goodies
from the bakery this morning, kind of a peace offering
I guess. And thanks for not being upset with me."

The two women left the office and went into the
small kitchen area for their morning snack. Linna, all
the while, was sizing up the tall agent in her mind and
kept coming up with the same conclusion—this

woman was more than she appeared to be, and she *was* going to get to the truth one way or another. She'd just have to use a different tack to find out.

By one o'clock, Dean was focusing again on the upcoming meeting between Katie and Lin. *Just what is she going to do to pass on the information?* Dean kept thinking. *What would I do?* She continued that thought until she came up with a plausible scenario. *Well, let's see if I'm right.*

****

Katie walked into the kitchen and asked El if the tray was ready for the Oriental guest. El had just finished pouring the soup in the bowl and nodded to Katie, indicating the tray.

"Now, if she's feeling better, I can make up a sandwich or something real easily," El offered. "That one is too small to miss too many meals. She'll just fade away to nothing in no time."

"I'll ask her when I drop this off," Katie said. "I'm going to tidy up her room while I'm there, so, I may be a while," she cautioned the elderly cook.

"That'll be fine, sweetie. Just take your time. That poor thing probably would like some company after being shut in all morning," the cook offered with a compassionate smile.

"Will do." Katie spoke over her shoulder as she headed up the back stairs. *Yeah, company coming!* the young agent thought to herself. *Now how are we going to communicate with cameras and listening devices in each room?* She arrived at the door and knocked twice.

"It's me, Miss. I've brought your soup." Katie directed her comment to the door, and then waited for a response. Not hearing one, she knocked again and repeated the salutation. Again, there was no response. She then tried the door handle and it was unlocked, so she went in. She could hear the radio playing in the bath, and the shower running. She went to the bathroom door and knocked loudly.

"It's me...Katie. I've brought your soup. Would you like me to put it on the table or by the bed side?" Over the sounds of the shower and the radio, Lin asked Katie to come into the bathroom. Katie put the tray down on the dresser then went in.

"Yes, ma'am," Katie responded. "Do you need a bath towel?" she asked as she entered the bathroom.

It was beginning to get very steamy from the shower, and the radio was even much louder in here. *Hmm,* Katie thought, *good idea, steam up the camera lens and cover our voices with the music! I like it.* As she entered, she found Lin wrapped in a towel.

Lin grabbed another towel from the towel bar and tossed it over her shoulder. Then she approached Katie quickly as the steam continued to build. She leaned in close and whispered to Katie, "Just follow my lead," the Oriental whispered, "We don't have much time." With that, she started to unbutton Katie's blouse and unzip her skirt. This action caused Katie to back up until Lin cautioned her again about the camera lens clouding. "Just trust me," the ex-cop whispered.

"Okay," came the soft response from the young agent. By the time the steam started to reach the camera lens, both women were naked and wrapped in each other's arms.

"Sorry for this approach," whispered Lin "but it's the only way I can get close enough to talk to you without being overheard or arousing suspicion. These jerks are well aware of my supposed 'attraction' to you," she continued. "I've made specific remarks and bets regarding you, and what I wanted to do with you, *after* I saw that necklace. I didn't want to take a chance on another note in case they got suspicious and stopped you before you left. Believe me, this way they won't think anything other than that a little tryst is going on."

Bets? Great, they're taking bets on bedding me? "Okay, now what?" Katie whispered, very aware of the naked body next to hers and the lips pressing against her neck.

"We're going to go into the shower," she instructed the young agent. "Then we will appear to be 'making love' as I fill you in on last night. You okay with this?" she asked, concerned about the stiffness of the body next to her.

"Yeah, I'll survive." She smiled at Lin.

After a brief interlude of 'mild intimacy' in the bathroom, Lin led Katie into the shower. "The steam will keep the lens fogged, and the music and shower noise will help cover our conversation, but they will be able to pick up some visual, albeit foggy, so we may have to appear to be a bit more intimate," Lin said in Katie's ear as she pressed Katie against the glass shower door for effect. "Just try to imagine me as your lover, and he's the one doing this. Okay?"

Hmm, Katie mused, *wait till she finds out he's a she, and her ex-lover to boot! Okay, Dean, you're the one who said to go with what she presents me!* To Lin, she nodded her head and said, "Yeah, got it."

All the while they appeared to be exploring each other, Lin filled Katie in on the revelations in Kasimov's quarters. When the exchange of information was complete, Lin and Katie exited the shower and toweled each other off, as new lovers would do. During that time, they worked through a prearranged script—in deliberately audible voices—regarding their 'attraction' to each other and making promises to meet again. Katie dressed, and then exited the bathroom. Lin, still wrapped in a towel, led Katie to the door and gave her a very convincingly seductive kiss before she left the room. All in all, it was quite an afternoon for the young agent. This bizarre way of passing information was nothing compared to the information she had acquired. Her eagerness to get back to Dean made it difficult for her to finish her shift. This, of course, made the encounter seem even more realistic for the watchers as Katie's nervousness was interpreted as excitement related to Lin's advances.

****

Dean recognized Katie's ethereal body from the blue dot. She watched it merge off and on with another ethereal body as the scenario played for real in her mind. "Bingo!" Dean exclaimed out loud as she finally was able to decipher the verbal repartee that Katie and Lin scripted for the watchers. "Exactly

the tack I would have used! Bravo, my old friend."
She found herself wondering, in more ways than one,
how her partner was reacting to the ruse. In her
career, she had often had to use her body as a means
to an end, and she hoped that the young woman would
be okay with what had just happened. *No time to
worry about that,* she chided herself. *You've got to
learn to trust. Katie will be fine. Right? Right!*

Saturday, 1630 hours

Once Katie arrived at the office, the two agents
decided to put the surveillance cameras into tape
mode and return to Dean's to discuss the information
in more privacy. As they arrived at the cabin, Katie
noticed that Dean had company. Inside the cabin
stood Sugar, Spice, and Butter. All were meowing
vigorously. She tilted her head towards Dean for an
explanation.

"Well," the tall agent started, "it just makes sense
for you to stay here during the rest of this assignment." She began to blush slightly. "It saves time,
and we won't have to worry about Sugar getting her
medicine, and..."

Two fingers gently placed on her lips stopped her
words. "It's fine, really. It just surprised me." Katie
removed the fingers and replaced them with her lips.
"Just how did you get them here today?"

"I had Tracy and Colleen move them over while I
was at the office watching you... and Lin," Dean said
as she raised an eyebrow. "They like cats too, and
would know better what had to come with them. I

asked them to make sure they brought over Sugar's medicine," Dean finished with a slight blush.

"Thank you for thinking of them. They really mean a lot to me. And you're right, things are going to start getting pretty hectic around here." The young blonde bent over to stroke the meowing cats that were now winding in and out of two sets of legs.

"So, what's the story?" Dean pulled the blonde into the living room and onto the sofa.

"You are not going to believe the evil plan this bastard has come up with." Katie took a deep breath and began to reiterate the information Lin had passed on. "The General is going to target some group right after the holidays. He didn't disclose who his targets were, but promised that it would be a 'grand beginning to level the playing field.' Whatever that's supposed to mean! Then he went on to inform them that the drugs are already in place and ready for dispersal at the appointed times. He showed the group the canisters that would be used to deploy the drugs." Katie reached over to the coffee table and picked up a pad and pencil, then began to sketch. "From what Lin told me, they probably look something like this." She showed Dean the pad.

As Dean looked at the pad, her eyebrows furrowed. "Are you certain?" she inquired of Katie. "They look like air tanks of some sort, with slots in the canister."

"Yeah," Katie said, "that's exactly how she described them. She even drew one on the wall of the shower. Stumped her too."

"The shower wall, huh?" Dean asked as she lifted an eyebrow. "Are you okay with what happened?"

"Umm, it was okay. I was a bit nervous at first, but when she started telling me about the meeting, I completely forgot about where we were." The young agent began to blush a bit.

"Umhm?" came the question from Dean.

"Well, it was a bit embarrassing. I'm not exactly used to strange hands roaming over my body, no matter what the reason." The blonde looked up into affectionate blue eyes.

"I'm sorry you had to go through that." The dark-haired-agent reached for the young woman. "If I could have..."

"No, you couldn't have, and it's really okay. Just another part of the job." *Guess it's just one more thing I'll have to get used to if I want to be really successful at this business,* the blonde thought silently.

"So, go on...what else happened?" the blue eyes encouraged. "Where were the drugs manufactured? Did he say? What did he want from the cartels?" The questions started coming fast and furiously.

"Whoa! One question at a time!" the blonde said holding up her hands. "First, the drugs were manufactured right at the lodge. He showed them the lab where they were made. She said there's a veritable maze of rooms down there, kitchens, sleeping rooms, etc. He must have done some heavy duty renovations in those five weeks. She didn't see any scientists around. When she asked, he just smiled and said their work was done for now. Kasimov said the drugs are in a highly concentrated liquid form. One drop could affect hundreds." She shook her head in anger. "Lin said that he claims to have hundreds of those canisters already in place. She figures that each canister holds at least four or five gallons of liquid. That means he plans on drugging millions of people!" Emerald eyes closed as the young body shook in anger. "I don't understand, Dean! How could someone be so evil that he would drug millions of people...and why? Who? Where?"

"Now it's you're turn to slow down." The blue eyes gentled. "Did he say what he wanted from the cartels?"

"Yes, in a way," the young agent proceeded. "After he found out who was in. And incidentally, they were all in. He asked them to have each cartel send at least twenty of their best men to arrive here between Thanksgiving and Christmas. He cautioned them to make sure they were men that were not known to the authorities. He gave each cartel representative a set of instructions. The one he gave to Ito said to have their men filter through Canada—Vancouver, Toronto, Quebec, Montreal, etc.—then cross over the border into the U.S. at various ports of entry to avoid suspicion. His people are to stay in various hotels in the Catskills until it's time to meet for final instructions. The selection of port of entry and hotels is totally up to the cartel."

"Great, that doesn't help us one bit. Did the instructions say where or when to meet?" Dean asked hopefully.

"No, just to have everyone in place by December twenty fourth, and they would be contacted through their cartel representative here."

"There's so much travel during the holidays...customs will be swamped. Chances are it will be impossible to try to identify them all. We're going to need help." Dean mentally ran through a list of her contacts. "Was there anything else?"

"Not really. Lin said some of the men in the group were tired of being cooped up at the lodge and asked if they could leave for some 'entertainment,' or another hunting trip. She said the general was going to have Natasha make arrangements for another hunting trip in a couple of days, but as far as other 'entertainment'—they would be left to their own devices. It would be too risky for them to leave, and even worse to bring anyone in. He also said he would open the indoor shooting range, gym and pool, if they were interested." Katie added with a sly grin, "Guess it's a good thing I'm already spoken for. I just hope they leave Darla alone. She's very young and very naïve."

"Guess so." Dean smiled as she ruffled Katie's blonde hair. "But you and Lin just be careful. Someone else may want to get a piece of your action."

"Like maybe a tall, dark-haired, blue eyed, gorgeous, sexy, lieutenant colonel?" Katie asked suggestively, as she slid closer to Dean and placed a tender kiss on the aforementioned colonel's neck, ears, and lips with each descriptive word she spoke.

"Mmm, maybe." That was about all Dean got out before she took the blonde in her arms and repositioned her on the couch. She held herself over the beautiful blonde, smiling wickedly.

"Why, Colonel. If Ah didn't know better, Ah would think you're trying to take advantage of poor little old me," Katie said in a syrupy Southern accent. Then she reached up and took advantage of her position by pulling the tall agent forcefully down on top of her. Lips met lips, and soon the only conversation heard was the voice of ecstasy that ended in gasps of pleasure.

* * * * * * * * *

At seven p.m., Tracy and Colleen arrived at Dean's bearing dinner—two large supreme pizzas and two six packs of ice cold Molsen's.

"Brrr," exclaimed Tracy as she and Colleen entered the cabin. "I think it's going to snow tonight. Hope you've got plenty of firewood for the fireplace."

"Yep." Dean took their jackets. "Thanks for coming over and bringing dinner."

"Well, we just thought it would be a good thing to do, knowing your cooking skills," Tracy quipped back as she and Col chuckled.

"Hey! I've gotten better, really! Just ask Katie." Dean laughed as she pointed at Katie who was trying to look like she didn't hear a word of the conversation even though she was standing right behind Dean.

They all laughed and went into the kitchen to attack the pizza. Katie had made a spectacular salad to go along with it, and by the time they were finished, not a speck of food remained.

"Wow!" Katie said as she held her stomach. "I didn't realize I was that hungry."

"Geez," added Col, "just what have you two been doing that you haven't had time to eat?"

The two agents, looked at each other then quickly looked away, inspecting various parts of the ceiling as they both began to blush.

"Never mind. Guess you don't need to answer that question," Colleen said, as Tracy joined her in hearty laughter.

Colleen and Katie stayed behind in the kitchen to clean up as Tracy and Dean went into the living room. Dean started a fire before moving to the love seat next to where Tracy was sitting on the sofa. They both sat there for a bit, neither speaking, just staring into the fireplace as small flames from the kindling licked the larger logs. Soon the fire was progressing nicely, and Tracy turned to Dean to ask how the surveillance was going.

"Well, we're at the point now where we're going to have to call in the troops. We're going to need some extra help here to figure out just what that bastard has in mind," Dean informed her old friend. "At least we have a bit of time to work on it. Looks like the timeline is set for Christmas day or later." Dean thoroughly recounted the events of the last twenty-four hours, filling Tracy in on Katie's experience with Lin and the status thus far.

"Are you sure you can trust that woman?" Tracy asked in all sincerity. "After all, she's been with the cartel for how long now?"

"About six years, if I figured it right," Dean stated quietly.

"I don't know, Dean. That's a long time to be exposed to the temptations of a life of crime. Lots of money and unlimited power can sure change people." Her old friend was cautious. "I don't know if I would be able to put Colleen in that kind of a dangerous situation, if you know what I mean."

"Yeah, I've thought of that, too. But I've got to let her. It's important to her to be recognized as a capable professional. And you know something, deep down in my heart, I know she's better than I am," Dean confided.

"No way, Dean!" Tracy protested. "I've seen you do things that I never thought could be done by anyone, and you'd pull them off without even breathing hard!"

"Well, that was then, and this is now. And I'm telling you, Trace, she's damn good. Anyway, back to the problems at hand." The dark-haired agent sighed. "We're going to need someplace to convene, and the office isn't big enough, or, with Linna skulking around, secure enough. Got any ideas?"

Tracy thought quietly for a while as Katie and Colleen came into the room. Colleen sat down next to Tracy then asked if there was anything she could help with.

"We're trying to come up with a good place for Dean and Katie to assemble the troops," Tracy said as Colleen put her arm around her. "Got any ideas?"

Colleen mulled it over for a while then said, "How about the tennis courts up at Hollinger's? It would be perfect. They could come in dressed as contractors. You know—painters, electricians, etc. Everyone knows the department has been given exclusive rights to the old indoor courts...and, since the resort is closed down, there's no one up there anyway."

Tracy looked at Colleen, and then gave her a big hug and a kiss. "Perfect," she agreed, and kissed Col one more time for good measure. "Colleen's right, that place would be perfect. It's up in the old Hollinger's Resort. It's been closed down since before I came here. The department just negotiated the rights to use the indoor tennis courts, but we need to do some renovations to the place before we can use them. I'll take you up there tomorrow, and you can check it out. I'm sure you'll like it." Then she paused and added. "We may have to do something about the heat, though. I'm not sure if the old ceiling heaters still work. I understand they were fairly new just before the closure, but who knows now."

"Great!" Dean and Katie said simultaneously. "Katie's off tomorrow, so we can both go. What time do you want us to meet you?"

"How about 10:00 a.m.? That way most folks will be at church services so we'll be less likely to be seen by commission members or anyone from the town board."

"Sounds good, Tracy. I don't know what we would have done without you. It was pure luck running into you here, but definitely good luck." Dean aimed a smile at her old friend.

****

By the time Tracy and Colleen left, it was nearly midnight. The two women were so exhausted from the stress of the week, that when they laid back in bed they found themselves too tired to do anything but talk.

"Dean?" Katie whispered softly.

"Hmm?" came the soft reply.

"Have you and Tracy ever..."

"No, we haven't. We're really just great friends."

"Oh. She just seems to think you walk on water or something," came the unexpected remark.

"Mmmm, that's because I can!" came the quick retort. "Ufff! What was that for?" Dean complained, as she rubbed her rib cage.

"Being a smart-ass," Katie said as she broke into a chuckle. "Seriously, she does think a lot of you."

"And I think the same of her." Dean rolled over onto her side and rested her head on her propped up hand. "She's seen me overcome odds that even I didn't think I could beat. She's seen me so full of holes that I looked like a sieve. And she's helped me cope with the death and destruction that I have had to face in my job."

"Just what exactly is your job?" Katie asked tentatively. "I know you said you're in Army Intelligence, but most intelligence officers of your rank aren't in the field, they're back where it's safe and warm, and out of harm's way at Operations. What's your story?"

Dean closed her eyes and rolled over onto her back, while her conscience spoke to her. *Well, it's now or never...and she has a right to know the truth about you.* Katie just about gave up on Dean answering her question and was about to speak, when Dean began her story.

"I grew up in the Midwest as the daughter of a Baptist minister. My dad," she began with a disgusted tone, "was a very devout man, at least in front of the congregation. They loved him. He'd give them all the fire and brimstone from the pulpit that they craved. Had the congregation just falling all over themselves to repent of their sins. He really had them eating out of the palm of his hand. He was so kind and caring. So willing to help them and willing to forgive them. I thought he was the best...but I was wrong," Dean said with a bitter smile.

"Why? What happened?" Katie probed softly.

"One night he found my brother in the backseat of our Chrysler...with the deacon's daughter. They were just teenagers...you know, hormones raging and all." Tears began to well up in her eyes. "I really loved my brother Thad. He was seventeen, and I was eighteen. Thought Dad loved us, too." She paused before she went on. "I thought he would start doing the scripture thing, you know...the fire and brimstone...then the 'save the sinner' routine...then the forgiveness. But it didn't turn out that way." Dean sniffed then continued. "He told the young girl to go home and confess her sin and weakness to her father...so she did. After she left, he told Thad to get out of the car and go into the barn. Dad was screaming and hitting him over and over. Thad was crying something terrible. He didn't see me at first, not until Mom came out to see what the commotion was. As soon as he saw us, he yelled at us to go back in the house. Mom immediately turned and went back, but I stayed outside the barn and listened. Dad was furious. I'd never heard him so angry. By the time it was over and Dad went into the house, I crept into the barn to see if I could comfort Thad." As Dean continued, tears flowed from her eyes. "When I saw him lying in the hay...all bloody...I lost it! I did what I could for him, but it was too late. Thad died in my arms."

"Oh, my God, Dean. What happened next? What did you do?" Katie reached out and pulled the tall woman into her arms. Dean gratefully slid into Katie's embrace, glad for the comfort she felt in the young woman's arms.

"I went into the house, full of rage and covered in Thad's blood, and confronted him. I told him that Thad was dead, and it was all his fault. Mom screamed when I went to hit him and that stopped me. I went over to Mom and told her to call the police. She refused, so I went to the phone myself. Before I got the number dialed, he came up behind me and hit me over the head with something. Next thing I knew, I was tied to my bed. I could see the red flashing lights of the police cars outside and could hear muffled voices. After they left, Mom came up and untied me, but asked me not to talk to Dad. The next day I tried to explain to the sheriff what really happened, but Dad had spun a yarn about my walking in on the guys that beat Thad, and how I hadn't been 'right' since. Of course, they believed him, him being the upstanding minister and all."

"Where are your mom and dad now?" The green eyes somehow softened the hurt Dean felt inside.

"Mom's dead. She passed away while I was on one of my missions. Dad, well, he's still out there somewhere, for all I know. He left the ministry a few years after Thad's death. Turned to drink and became one of the souls he used to save. Mom stayed with him 'til she died." Another tear slowly carved a path down Dean's cheek.

"What did you do after Thad's death?" Katie asked catching the tear with her thumb and wiping it away.

"I left. The same day I talked to the sheriff. I couldn't stay there and listen to his sanctimonious crap, so I joined the Army, and found a release for my rage. I was so good that they put me in a special program, put me through college and officer's training. I became a 'problem solver' for Uncle Sam...and boy, am I good at it!" There was irony and self-loathing in her tone.

Dean stopped and turned her head up to face the young agent, hesitating before she continued. The tension coursing through her would not allow her to remain in a static position. She carefully eased out of Katie's embrace and slid from the bed. Her pacing kept a staccato time with the rhythm of her revelations. "I go in and solve problems that normal political and military channels can't. I'm their 'special' weapon. They wind me up and point me towards the problem, and I make it go away. I do whatever is necessary, take out whoever stands in my way; the blood of the innocent as well as the guilty is on my hands. I'm a very efficient machine," she snarled sarcastically.

Unable to risk even a glance at Katie, now that she had begun, Dean needed to purge her conscience. Her voice was filled with tension, but softer, more controlled, as she finished her confession. "My rage at my father started me on this road. I am the fire and brimstone he preached about. I have been judgment day for many souls, evil and innocent. I don't grieve for the evil...but for the innocents that were felled by my hands. I'll never know how many there were; so now, I live with their ghosts."

Dean knelt by the side of the bed next to Katie, her eyes pleading for understanding, and for forgiveness, before they dropped to look at the floor. Sighing heavily, Dean turned away and sat on the floor facing the wall, placing her head in her hands, elbows propped on her knees. Tears began to form in earnest now and slowly cascaded down her cheeks before she continued in a raspy voice. "Lately, I've felt them pulling at me, begging me to stop, but I don't know if I can. I'm not strong enough to stop, to change my life." She turned back, rising to her knees, forcing herself to face Katie, submitting to her judgment. Intense blue eyes searched the emerald green ones above her, then she added, "Katie, you deserved to know what I am, and what I've done, and I won't blame you if you decide to get up and leave. I owed you the truth. I'm ruthless and..."

Katie looked down into Dean's sad blue eyes and gently wiped the tears from her cheeks. "Shhh...you don't owe me anything, Dean. And I seriously doubt if anything you say would cause me to leave you." She tugged Dean up to sit beside her on the bed. "I don't care what you've done in the past—it's over and can't be changed. You had no way of identifying innocent victim from evildoer; you just did your job the best you could. Millions of people, myself included, are depending on you to keep them safe, keep them from the evil living in the likes of people like Kasimov."

"But, I have my own demons to deal with, I've killed innocent people," Dean interrupted.

"Did you know they were innocent at the time?" Katie asked her tortured friend. "And we all have our personal demons to live with."

"No... but they couldn't have all been bad. I'd just go in, guns blazing..." She shut her eyes. "...and see my father's face...see Thad's bloody body." She began to cry in earnest this time.

Katie slid over a bit and pulled Dean down to lie in her embrace. "It's okay love, I've got you. Go ahead, get it out of your system. It's time you grieved for Thad, and...forgave your father," Katie finished with a whisper. Then she held her friend through her tears and sobs, until they both finally fell asleep; a sleep that, for the first time in a very long time, held no ghosts for Dean.

PART
III

Sunday, 0800 hours

Dean slowly opened first one blue eye, then the other. She was amazed to see the sun streaming in the window of her bedroom, realizing that it must be fairly late already. She was more amazed to recognize that she had slept nearly seven hours. Seven hours of solid, blissful sleep...a sleep without any nightmares. Dean surveyed the room without moving as she contemplated the second set of heartbeats and breathing that belonged to the beautiful young agent sharing her bed. *Well, they say that confession is good for the soul...*Dean thought to herself, *and Katie...you are definitely the best thing that's happened to me in a long time. I hope last night didn't change how you feel about me.* Concluding that thought, she looked over at the sleeping woman on whom her head was nestled. She extended her senses to memorize the young woman's scent, the sounds of her breathing, and the rhythm of her heart. She found the last two totally in sync with her own breaths and pulse. *If only we could stay like this forever.* That thought was discarded as Katie opened her eyes and turned her head to look into the most awesome blue eyes she had ever seen.

"Hi." Katie lifted her free arm to brush away an errant lock of Dean's hair.

"Hi," came the response from the dark-haired woman.

"Have you been awake long?" Katie inquired.

"Nope. Just been enjoying the sights and sounds." The reply was followed by a dazzling smile.

"Mmm, sights and sounds huh? Must be that flora and fauna watching is rubbing off on you." The blonde answered with her own version of a dazzling smile.

Dean spoke softly. "Thank you."

"For what?" The green eyes widened in wonder.

"For last night," Dean admitted. "For listening, understanding, and especially for being here with me this morning." She shuddered slightly before she continued. "I was afraid that I was going to wake up alone after sharing my life story last night. I've never before told anyone about what happened with my brother, or about all the horrible things I've done in my life. Not even Tracy knows the full truth, although I think she may have her suspicions."

"Oh Dean, I love you. There's nothing you could say or do that would keep me from loving you. Your past is your past. It's over. I'm not one to judge you or anyone." The blonde pulled Dean into a gentle hug. "In my heart I know that you're a good person. That the things you have done have been for the good of our country and our allies." She smiled down at her blue-eyed lover, and then continued. "And as far as your hatred for your father...it's time you let that go...time to forgive him."

"As I drifted off last night, I think I did forgive him. I remember hearing a soft whisper telling me it was time to forgive him...and I did." She closed her eyes then looked back up into the emerald green ones. "I had my first night of solid sleep in a long time. I met no ghosts from my past, relived no horrors, and experienced no nightmares. Just blessed peaceful sleep."

Katie just smiled at her lover, realizing that it was her whisper that sent the message of forgiveness to Dean. The two women remained in bed in that same position for what seemed like a long time, but was actually only a scant five minutes. It was a five-minute break in their hectic week that they both needed to take advantage of.

Dean was the first to stir. "C'mon, love, let's get our run in and shower before we have breakfast. Then we'll meet Tracy at her place at 1000 hours."

"Yeah, yeah, yeah," came the response from Katie. "Gotta run...gotta eat...gotta go. I'll be glad when this is all over, so I can sleep in for a change!"

"Sleep in," Dean sighed. "What do you call this morning? It's already 0830!" she finished with a chuckle, as she pulled the blonde up and into her arms. "Tell ya what, if you beat me back to the cabin...we'll take a long shower...together." Dean finished the comment with a wink, a smile, and kiss.

Katie jumped out of bed, calling over her shoulder, "You're on," as she very quickly slipped on her sweats, socks and shoes and beat the tall woman out of the house.

Well, we know what gets you up and going, don't we? Dean said to herself as she got herself out of bed and hurried to dress and catch up.

****

Dean was the first one back to the cabin, the blonde just seconds behind her.

"No fair!" called Katie as she entered the cabin on Dean's heels. "You've got longer legs than I have."

"And the three minute head start was...what?" Dean answered with a snicker. "Ok, I'll give in...see ya in the shower." She headed toward the bathroom, slipping off her sweats as she went, shadowed by a smiling young blonde who was also stripping as she followed.

The shower took a good bit of time, and they would probably have still been in it when they were supposed to be at their meeting, except for the fact that the hot water heater was only a forty-gallon model. As it was, they had to skip breakfast in order to be at Tracy's on time. As they pulled into her drive, Tracy and Colleen came out and jumped into the SUV.

"Morning!" Tracy and Col said at the same time, and were answered with a like response from Dean and Katie.

"Just go back out this street and onto the main drag." Tracy pointed as Dean pulled out of the driveway. "Turn right at the stop sign and go out towards Burp & Freddie's."

Dean did as she was instructed, and when they arrived at the intersection where the diner was, Tracy told Dean to turn left and go up the hill. As they reached the top of the hill, the road curved to the right and wound around the hill to the back side. A quarter of a mile from the entrance, Tracy indicated the tennis court building and its adjacent parking lot.

"That's it," she said as they pulled in to park. "I'll unlock the main entrance. It's on this side of the building." Tracy indicated the left side as she stepped out.

The rest of the passengers exited the SUV and followed Tracy into the building. The power was on, so Tracy flipped the switches to illuminate the interior. Then she flipped the master switch for the electric heaters and, to her amazement, they began to click. "Guess we'll see if they produce any heat or not." She crossed her fingers.

The four women walked through the building noting that there were no windows in the court area, but the small office and locker rooms did have glass block windows around the top section of the walls. Inserted at intervals in the glass blocks were narrow ventilation ports. There was no way anyone would be able to enter through the windows. That left the double fire door at the center of the main court building, the fire door in each locker room, the main entrance at the side of the building and an outside door in the office as the only security points.

Dean stood in the middle of the tennis courts and surveyed the building one more time. There were additional ventilation panels in the ceiling, but they would normally only be open in fair weather. They would be easy enough to lock down for their purposes.

"Looks great, Tracy," Dean commented as she turned around one more time, mentally ticking off the five doors and the ceiling vents. "This will work well. That double fire door will allow us to pull in some vehicles too. Keep them out of sight until needed."

Tracy sniffed the air and noted that the smell of long unused heaters was in the air. A definite aroma of hot dust could be detected. "Looks like the heaters are working," she commented with a smile. "Of course, if Uncle Sam wants to contribute towards the cost of heating and the like while you guys are in here, I certainly wouldn't object." She winked at Dean.

"Yeah, we'll get the Enigma Foundation check processed ASAP. In fact, I think I'll requisition some improvements for you, too. Just make a list of what needs to be done, and I'll take care of it." Dean winked back at Tracy.

"Cool!" Tracy commented. "That'll make my day."

Dean and Katie made one final tour through the building, noting where things could be set up, where electrical outlets were, and what other supplies they would need—such as tables and chairs. When they were done the electricity was turned off—including the heaters—and the building was locked.

"Thanks for coming up with this idea, Col," Katie said as she entered the SUV. "It's going to work out great."

"No problem," she answered, then said, "Anybody hungry?" Which led to three raised hands. "Great, me too. We didn't have time to eat breakfast today." Two sets of eyes, one emerald, the other sapphire, looked quizzically at Colleen. "And why were you so busy this morning?" Katie asked with a mischievous tone.

"Uhhh...well...umm...how about the diner up by the reservoir?" Tracy stammered as she and Col started to blush. There was a round of laughter as the SUV wound its way back down to the main highway and turned left for the ride out to the Overview Diner.

****

"This is Agent Shelton." The voice at the other end of the line was familiar.

"Hey Sid," Dean said into the secure phone hook-up. "This is Colonel Peterson."

"Hello, Dean. What can I do for you?" he asked with a slight hesitation in his voice.

"Don't worry, Sid, no more bodies, at least not yet," the colonel replied, hearing the apprehension in Sid's voice. "I just called to update you on the latest information and to see if we can get an interagency task force up here to work on this case. I also need to know the status of the autopsies, and if the drug has been isolated."

"Sure," he replied with obvious relief in his voice. "What do you have?"

Dean proceeded to update him on the information Katie was able to get regarding the logistics of the canisters and the potential targeting of millions of people. She also informed him about the men the cartels would be sending between the holidays and the possibility of a deployment date after the holidays.

Then she asked him if he could put together an interagency task force of agents, scientists, and chem-
ists—anyone the agencies could spare that could help
decipher the clues they had so far.

"I'll put in a call to the director right after we
hang up. I'm sure he'll be willing to put together a
team and contact the other agencies as well. This is
one nasty situation, isn't it?" he inquired of the colonel.

"Yeah, it is," Dean concurred. "I'll contact the
Pentagon and NSA myself, so don't bother with those.
Now what do you have on isolating the drug?"

"Well, it took a bit of sleuthing, but they finally
found it. It never would have shown up on normal
scans, but since you clued us in to its presence they
persisted until they found it," the FBI agent informed
her. "The docs say it's a simple compound but a very
tricky one. So far, they've been able to determine
that its lifecycle *after* ingestion is only 96 hours.
After that, it dissipates. They don't have an antidote
for it yet."

"Well, if it dissipates in 96 hours, that shouldn't
be a major problem. We really need to know what
sets it off, the changes that occur in the mind to allow
such control, and how to stop the reaction," Dean
added. "How are they doing in those areas?"

"Zippo," Sid replied unhappily. "They just found
it last night, so they haven't had much time to analyze
it. They were lucky to find it at all. It was nearly the
96 hour limit when they did. It's a damn good thing
you went after the bodies and got them to us so
quickly, or we'd be batting zero."

"Well, you can thank Katie for that one," Dean told the agent.

"Yeah, do that for me." She could feel his smile through the phone line.

They finished their conversation and set a time to return calls for an okay on the task force. She told him about the building she had arranged for the troops and left him her secure phone number. She hung up and then called her superior, General John James. After updating him, she proceeded with her task force request.

"What do you mean a task force!" the general rumbled. "There's no need to involve the other agencies. The Army and NSA can handle this."

"General, the other agencies are already involved, and they have two dead bodies to prove it." She was holding her temper, then she softened her tone and added, "Besides, Jack, when have you ever doubted my judgement?"

"Well, I haven't yet, but there's always a first time." Nevertheless, he calmed down some. "Oh...all right," he agreed grudgingly. "What do you need from us?"

Dean gave him a list of items, then broached the subject of the 'to do' list for the tennis building. At that, the general really started to balk. "C'mon, Jack. It's not gonna cost that much, and it's the least we can do for Tracy helping out like she has," Dean urged the general sweetly.

"Damn, this has been a very one sided phone call, ya know!" He feigned anger.

"Yeah, but it's for Tracy," the colonel persisted. "Remember when she pulled your butt out of the can at Leonard Wood? If your wife had seen you with that nurse, you'd still be picking buckshot out of your rump!"

"Okay, okay," the general said resignedly, then added, "Just get me my results!"

"I always do," Dean said solemnly, then hung up.

Dean put her phone down and went into the second bedroom where Katie was making her phone calls. She stepped in the room as Katie concluded and flopped back on the bed.

"Phew!" the young agent spat out. "You'd think interagency cooperation was the damn plague the way they hem and haw."

"Oh?" Dean teased raising an eyebrow and smiling brightly. "Why I had no problem at all."

"Yeah, right!" the blonde said, as she threw a pillow at the tall woman. She suddenly realized that this was probably not the wisest move on her part as it was immediately returned, followed by a tall body landing on top of her. The next thing she knew, she was being tickled ferociously.

"Eeiiiieee! Uncle! Uncle!" the blonde cried out. Dean stopped and rolled off her partner as Katie brought her breathing back to normal. "You are really quick," she commented after she regained control.

Dean just smiled and nodded. "Yeah, but you still got the best of me up on the mountain. That was really quite a surprise." She shook her head. "No one, and I mean *no one*, has ever done that to me before. I must be getting old." She chuckled.

"Oh, sure. Blame it on getting old and not my skills." The blonde pouted and then relented. "You really mean that? About no one?"

Dean rolled over onto her right side facing the blonde and pegged her with her steel blue eyes. "Yes, I do. You're *very* good. In fact, you're better than me." She reached out and stroked the blonde's cheek. "And I promise never to sneak up on you like that again," she added with a brilliant smile.

****

By 1700, all the confirmations were made, and the task force members were scheduled to arrive before five in the morning. The requested equipment would all be in place by noon, and operations would be fully active by that time, as well. Dean and Katie were named the lead agents on the case, and all operations would be run through them.

"I'm glad Tracey and Colleen offered to take care of the cats for the duration. I hope Brutus gets along with them. Spice can be a real pistol when she wants to." Katie paused before asking the next question. "Are you going to shut down the surveillance from the P&R office?"

"No, I think I'll leave it up as a back-up," Dean answered as she watched Katie sort the task sheets. "I know Tracy isn't active military anymore, but I value her input. If I take down that console, I'll be cutting her out of the project, and I don't want to do that, at least not yet. If it gets too hot, I may have to reconsider."

"I thought you didn't want to involve civilians," the young agent reminded her.

"I don't, but Tracy is different. She's been such a help so far...and she is ex-military and all." Dean was beginning to wonder why Katie was asking this. "Why?"

"Don't get me wrong, Dean. I like Tracy and value her input, too. In fact, I want her help. I just don't want anything to blow up in her face, so to speak, that she'd lose her job over." Katie smiled at Dean. "You know?"

"Yeah, I thought of that, too. I know she'd understand if we had to shut her out, but it would be such a slap in the face to do it now. I'd like to keep this between you and me, though. The rest of the team doesn't need to know." Both women nodded their heads in affirmation.

"Well, I guess we'll just have to make sure nothing blows up then," Katie resolved as she turned and gave Dean a hug. "Okay, what's next on the list?"

"Now," Dean returned the hug, "we get some rest because from here on out we'll be running on adrenaline. It's a good thing you have Monday off, too. It's going to be a busy day. We'll need to meet the team at the courts by 0500 so that means we have a little less than twelve hours to ourselves."

"Mmm, and I know just how I'd like to fill some of that time." The blonde tugged on the older agent's hand and led her to the bedroom. Three sets of eyes watched the scene intently, then squeezed their eyes shut and began to purr softly.

* * * * * * * * *

Katie was snuggled into the crook of Dean's shoulder, resting her head on the older woman's chest. They were enjoying the quiet and solitude that they knew would be broken in just a few short hours. Dean was gently stroking Katie's hair and admiring the shimmer of each strand as it reflected the light of the moon coming through the bedroom window. "You really are beautiful," Dean whispered into Katie's hair, as she pressed her lips to the blonde's forehead.

"Uh huh, and I bet you say that to all the women in your life," came the adroit response from the beautiful blonde.

"Nah, only the woman I happen to be holding at the time." The older woman chuckled before she got serious. "Katie, please be careful the next few days. Kasimov will be on super alert with the holidays only a few days off. He'll be looking for anything out of the ordinary."

"I will, Dean. I promise." Katie lifted her head to look into Dean's blue eyes. "We've got to find out what's going down though, before it's too late. I don't ever want to be too late again."

"Why do you say that?" Dean caught the intensity of the emerald eyes peering into hers.

Katie shut her eyes and took a long deep breath, exhaling before she began to talk again. "Remember last night when I said we all have our own demons to deal with?"

"Mmmhmm," Dean replied softly.

"Well, about twelve months ago, I was working on this case from another angle." She paused before continuing. "Jerry and I. He was my partner at the time, and I was the senior member. We were working the drug group out of the Chicago area during an undercover op. Jerry was under, and I was his contact. He had been under for several months, and things were looking pretty good." She shook her head as she began to relive the anguish of a job gone sour. "I kept warning him to be careful, to watch which informants he dealt with, but he was adamant that he knew what he was doing. He did have a great record of busts, but that probably led to his downfall in the end." Katie sighed. "Anyway, I was working as a waitress in a coffee shop on the eastside that was used exclusively by the drug ring. He'd come in and put the moves on me to pass on information. Everyone thought I was his 'girl', so they pretty much ignored me. During the last three months, we were so close to getting in. We knew there was going to be a huge meeting of all the drug cartels, and that each one was sending their three best people. He really thought he'd be one of the ones chosen to come to this meeting. Everything was pointing in that direction... until he talked to the wrong snitch." She shivered thinking about the last night. "I never liked Emilio. He was a real creep, if you know what I mean. I told Jerry not to trust him, but I had no reason, no proof. Turned out I was right. The creep was a worm for the cartel working in the land of snitches. His job was to look for troublemakers and people asking too many questions. By the time I got enough proof, I was too late. I found Jerry in his apartment with a knife in his chest, and his mouth full of earthworms. He had a note pinned to his chest addressed to the DEA. It said for them to find a better 'worm' next time." Katie was near tears by the time she finished her story. "I was his superior. I was supposed to keep him safe... and I didn't! I was too late. I should have done something sooner." The young agent was very upset now, and Dean held her tightly. "I should have stopped him...I..."

"Katie, it's not your fault. You told him not to talk to Emilio, and since you were his superior, he should have followed your orders." Dean tried to comfort the young woman. "You can't blame yourself for his blunder. It's over. You just have to live with it and learn from it." Dean cupped Katie's chin and turned her face towards her. "It's like the whisper you sent to me last night—it's time to let go, time to stop beating yourself up over it."

"I know that now. I found out later that he wouldn't have listened to me anyway. He was trying to prove that women didn't belong in the agency, especially not as lead agent on a case. That's why I vowed I'd never be late with proof again." Katie held onto Dean as though her life depended on it. "I won't let you down, Dean. I promise I won't be late!" she said softly as she captured Dean's face with her hands staring purposely into Dean's eyes. Then slowly, gently, she let them slide away from Dean's face.

"I know, love," Dean answered her quietly, "I promise I won't be late either."

Monday, 0430 hours

By four-thirty the two women were up, showered and on their way to the courts. They dressed in their park uniforms just in case anyone saw them enter or leave the courts building. As they pulled up and parked, Katie asked, "So how are these guys going to show up?"

"They're going to come in a variety of construction and maintenance vehicles. I faxed a list that Tracy gave me of local contractors so they could duplicate their truck styles. To the casual observer, they'll look legitimate enough." The tall agent smiled. "But of course, if those particular contractors were to see them, they might be doing double takes. There is just a slight chance that would happen at that hour of the morning, and you saw how far the courts building is from the main road. No one will see the trucks once they're parked by the building."

"Why not use fictitious company names?" the blonde queried.

"The whole town knows that Tracy uses local contractors whenever possible. It's good for the contractors, and good for the department. Stimulates excellent cooperation when she needs it most," Dean answered.

"Pretty smart on Tracy's part. Got to hand it to her, Dean, she's a keeper."

"Yeah, and that's just why I want to keep her on board for as long as possible. You never know when one of her connections will turn out to be valuable. In fact, as much as I'd hate to do it, her secretary may prove to be even more valuable." Dean sighed.

"How's that?" Inquisitive emerald eyes captured ice blue ones in a questioning attitude.

"Well...her husband is the mayor of this little burg and also the police commish! Two people—or in this case, one—you definitely need on your side when push comes to shove," Dean finished.

Katie let out a low whistle. "Well, hopefully we won't get to pushing and shoving!"

They went into the building and turned on the lights and the heaters, then sat back in the small office waiting for the troops to arrive. They didn't have to wait long. At precisely five a.m., the first trucks rolled in. Katie pulled open the double fire door at the back of the building and directed the trucks inside. A few were left outside to provide an impression of work in progress on the old building.

On the inside, work was progressing steadily. A console similar to the one at the P & R office, only bigger, was set up next to the court office windows that looked out on the courts. Within an hour, it was installed and operational. The viewing screens were 36 inches instead of the 19 inch ones back at the P & R building. That really made a big difference in viewing ease. Several long tables were set up, and maps of the entire East Coast were taped up on the walls around the large room. In addition, there were detailed maps of every large city within a two hundred mile radius. Every kind of machine to enhance audio or visual input was there, along with quite an impressive display of ordnance.

Katie had just finished instructing the staff on where the final truck's contents should be set up when she tapped Dean on the shoulder and asked her where she wanted the kitchen sink.

"Very funny," replied Dean. "Hey, ya never know what you might need. Weren't you ever a Girl Scout?" she asked, as she surveyed the room.

"Umm, claymores?" Katie said, raising her arms then shrugging. "I thought those went bye-bye a long time ago."

"Surplus...Jack's just trying to be funny." Dean shook her head and smiled at the young blonde. "But you will like these little beauties." She directed Katie over to a table by the office and lifted the lid on a fairly small container the size of a shoe box. "Take a look at this." Dean handed the item over to Katie.

"A pen?" Katie said in disbelief. "You want me to write a letter or something?"

"No, no. Not just a pen," Dean retrieved it from Katie's hand, "although it does write quite well. Sits in your hand real nice, has a nice smooth writing ba...Ouch! What was that for?" Dean looked at Katie as she rubbed her shoulder.

"Okay, 'Q'. Just what else does it do?" Katie asked as she put her hands on her hips.

Dean just looked at her in puzzlement for a nano second before she got the reference. "Q...yeah, I like that." Then she proceeded. "Well, this black one works like this—if you press the clip down here" Dean demonstrated the correct placement of her fingers. "it becomes a high tech stun gun with enough voltage to put your attacker down for at least five minutes before they get any feeling back, especially in the muscles you hit. It has a range of eight feet, too!" Dean was really getting into this now. "And, it can be used up to five times before it has to be recharged. Cool, huh?" Katie just shook her head in amazement as Dean picked up the red pen. "Now this one works the same way, but it contains one dose of knock out gas. Anyone breathing this stuff in will be in la la land for at least an hour. It has a spread three feet wide and a range six feet forward, so make sure your target is within those parameters. At arm's length, it shouldn't affect you, but hold your breath anyway, just to be sure."

"Geez, Dean, if I was an undercover nerd I could have a whole pocket protector full of these, and no one would be the wiser." Katie chuckled as Dean just shook her head and started to laugh too. "Guess I'll just have to settle for two clipped to my uniform, huh?"

"Yeah, guess so." Dean replaced the pens and pulled the young blonde over to the next box. She pulled out a small jewelry box and opened it to show Katie. "Now these look like a normal pair of black pearl earrings, but if you crush the ball between your fingers like so, and put the crushed material, say…in this lock here, add some moisture, like spit for example…" She did so then moved Katie back from the demonstration. "In about two more seconds…" There was a quiet 'pffft' sound, and the lock fell apart and landed smoldering on the floor. Katie reached down to pick up the broken lock, but was stopped by Dean's hand. "No, don't touch it. It gets really hot, and the residue is very acidic and can cause some nasty burns." She went on to caution Katie not to try crushing the earrings with wet hands.

"Duh!" Katie said, smacking her forehead with the palm of her hand after Dean finished the cautionary remark, earning her a finger wagging by the older woman. "What happens if you're wearing them in the rain…or shower?" Katie asked with raised eyebrows.

"Nothing. They have a coating that protects them until they're crushed," the older agent said with a smile. "Intelligent question, though. You've got exemplary insight into potential problems." Dean was obviously proud of her partner's grasp of the possibilities.

"Okay, so what's next?" Katie prompted, beaming at the compliment.

"Next, is the best friend a maid can have." Dean opened the next box and pulled out a can of furniture polish. It looked just like the cans of lemon furniture polish that Katie had been using at the lodge.

"I get to clean the place up, eh?" Katie said with a twisted smile on her face.

"Sorta, only don't use this can by accident. See how the top swivels, and there's a red dot here and a blue dot on the other side of the neck?" Dean pointed these out to Katie.

"Yeah, the regular cans only have the red dot. You're supposed to make sure the nozzle is pointed in that direction when you use it. Right?"

"Right, only this red dot indicates a knock out gas, so make sure you're holding your breath for at least twenty seconds after you stop pressing the nozzle, if you need to use it. Anyone breathing the gas will be sleeping for an hour, just like the pen gas, so be careful if you use this. Turned toward the blue dot, the nozzle emits a fine powder spray so you can see laser beams in the dark."

"Not bad," Katie said admiring the little 'toys' in Dean's play box. "Got anything else for me?"

"Yeah, but they haven't arrived yet. Should be here by tonight. Let's go see what's up on the screens. They should be just about ready for breakfast by now." The two women went over to the console, slipped on headphones, and toggled them on.

The only action so far was in the kitchen between El and Ezra.

"So Ezra, what do you think of all these guests?" came the cook's voice.

"Kinda strange to me, El, but I really don't care as long as Mr. G gets to keep the place, and we get to keep our jobs," replied her husband.

"Yeah, hon, I know what you mean. It'd be tough for us to start over again someplace else, and we surely can't afford to retire. I just hope nothing goes wrong for Mr. G, and we wind up losing our jobs," El said with a heavy voice before she continued. "Not only that, dear, but what about them two kids we got working here? They need the money, too. Darla is expecting a baby in June, and that Katie is supporting her family and all."

"Yep, would be tough on all of us. But I'll tell ya somethin'...I just don't like the looks of that Smirnoff fella. And those assistants of his are spooky! That one guy never comes out of the cellar. Why, when that water pipe broke week 'fore last, I thought he was gonna have my hide for goin' down there. I'd tried to go down the main stairs but they was locked, so I'd used that old back way from when the cellar was reinforced for a bomb shelter back in the '50s. Didn't mean ta scare him or nothin'. He was just watchin' TV and listenin' ta headphones. Damn good thing that woman showed up and was able to talk to him in his language. She calmed him down long enough for me to fix the pipe. Don't know why the hell anyone would want to live in the cellar when there's all these nice rooms up here!" Ezra finished his tirade with a final "spooky sons a guns, if ya ask me."

"Well, let's get this breakfast out there, they'll be comin' down soon," came El's soft reply.

Sapphire and emerald eyes locked, then Dean spoke. "Well, well, well. We may have a way in after all. And the mystery of penetration is cleared up. Mr. G must be the one responsible for the extra layer of concrete when he reinforced it for a bomb shelter." A wicked gleam came to her eyes as she smiled at Katie. "Wonder if they did anything to block the 'back way', or if Dimitri even knew he came down a back way."

"Hmmm, I'll see if I can find out somehow, if the opportunity ever presents itself," Katie said as she mulled over a few ideas. "Good to know there is one, though. May be useful some day."

The two agents went back to their surveillance for a bit longer, while the rest of the troops finished putting the equipment and gear together. Dean had called for a staff meeting at one o'clock so they would have some time to review the previous night's tapes that they had picked up from the P & R office before they got to the courts this morning. Breakfast was going per normal, so they set the recorders going and decided to review the tapes from last night. It didn't take them long, since the occupants were all asleep. They did note two ethereal bodies moving through the lodge at regular intervals. Perhaps Kasimov brought in some extra help to patrol the lodge. A review of the outside tapes also showed two bodies covering the grounds of the lodge.

"Well, that's a new twist," commented Katie. "We've never picked up human guards before, have we?"

"Nope, first time for everything," Dean replied as she rewound the tapes. "Bet the old general doesn't feel as secure as he'd like, so he brought in the extra help."

"Wonder where they're staying, and just how many of them there are. Didn't pick up any comments about them from El or Ezra." The young blonde tapped the table top with her fingers.

"Probably in the cellar with Dimitri so they don't arouse any suspicion. That's what I'd have done in his place. And there's probably only the four. Any more than that would be hard to keep secret," guessed Dean as she labeled the tapes. "Well, at least we're forewarned about the additional security."

"Might put a crimp in our style though," mused Katie out loud. "In case we have to go in."

"We'll cross that bridge when we get to it. Right now let's go over the agenda for the staff meeting." The two women went into the small office to get ready for the first full meeting of the interagency task force.

****

Linna had just finished doing the deposit of registration fees for the department when Tracy came into her office. "Is the deposit ready?" Tracy sat down in the chair next to Linna's desk.

"All ready for ya, boss." She looked up at Tracy then added nonchalantly, "So, where are our scientists today? Taking the day off?"

"Oh, they're probably up on the mountain getting a closer look. They'll likely be here sometime today," the director said as she took the deposit envelope from her secretary. "Don't forget that I've got that lunch meeting over at the college today. I'll probably just go straight over there from the bank. Do you want me to stop and bring you back some lunch?"

"Nah, I'm going to run out for lunch myself. Got a few errands to run," Linna said, setting up her ploy. "Mind if I take a few extra minutes? I've got a lot of running to do."

"Nope, just make sure you lock up and set the alarm. And don't forget to lock the door to the senior center. Can't have them wandering down here when there's no one around," Tracy instructed as she got up to leave.

"Okay, boss. Have a fun meeting."

"Yeah, right. I love listening to politicians blow their horns," Tracy said as she left the office.

Linna waited a good fifteen minutes just to be sure Tracy didn't come back unexpectedly. Then she went outside and moved her car around back and out of sight. When she came back in, she put the 'out to lunch' sign up, indicating the time of return as one hour from then. She then set the alarm, locked the doors, and turned the lights off. The last thing she did was to unlock the small office that the two women were using as an observation post. Linna took a final look around, and then entered the small office, turning on only the lamp on the desk.

"Okay, now what?" she said out loud. "Now try not to disturb anything," she reminded herself. She went over to the console and sat down, scanning all of the equipment and dials. She noted that the tape machines were running and the sound indicator was making jumping movements as it recorded. "Okay, everything is recording, so don't screw anything up," she told herself. She reached up and turned on the TV screen and put the headphones on her head. *What the hell is this? It certainly isn't a view of the birds and bees!* Linna immediately recognized the view on the first TV screen as the exterior of the Gersch Lodge. *Hmmm, I wonder why it's focused there? Maybe the wind storm last night knocked it off target, and they went up to fix it.* She began to pay attention to the sound coming from the headphones. *Hey, that's El and Ezra's voices. Just what the hell's going on here?* As Linna continued to listen, she found that she could change the direction of the sound device easily, so she began searching out other conversations. The last one she picked up really set her mind whirling.

"Geez, Johnnie, I still can't believe Tony was FBI!"

"Believe it, man! That freaken' general knows his stuff, Gary, so just drop it, will ya?"

"Ya think anyone will find the bodies?"

"Nah, no way. That spook of his was sure to put them somewhere where they won't turn up until they gotta put the bones in a sack to haul them out. Bears or somethin' will get to 'em first."

"No way...bears around here are herbivores not carnivores," Gary corrected. "I learned that on the Discovery Channel," he said proudly.

"Who the fuck cares, Gary. Point is, there won't be much left of them by the time someone finds them."

Man, that was really somethin' the way they blew themselves away! Freakin' crazy if ya ask me."

"Well, I'm tellin' ya, Gary, ya better stop flappin' about it, or they're liable to make you blow yourself away, too. I wouldn't be surprised if this whole place was bugged!"

"OH...MY...GOD...!" Linna exclaimed loudy. *Just what on earth are those two women and Tracy into? Scientists? Horse pucky! Man oh man. Now what do I do?* Linna's mind was racing now as she realized the implications of what she had just over-heard. *Just stay cool, Linna. You know that Tracy wouldn't be involved in anything illegal. These women must be undercover agents of some sort. OH... MY...GOD...! This is so bizarre. Wait 'til I tell Kelly, he'll freak that this stuff is happening in his quiet lit-tle town. No, no...on second thought, I can't tell him. Can't let him know that I know if he knows...huh? Oh Linna, you just had to know, didn't you! Shit, shit, shit!* Linna looked down at her watch and realized that she had been in the room for nearly fifty minutes. *Okay, put everything back to the way it was...huh? Now how was it? Okay, turn off the TV, reset the dial...to where? OH...MY...GOD...! Now what?*

She did the best she could to put things back, then turned off the light and left the room, locking it as she closed the door. She had just disarmed the alarm, turned the lights back on and taken down the 'out to lunch' sign when Tracy opened the outer door and came whistling down the hall to the main office. *Oooo, that was too close!* Linna said to herself as she greeted Tracy at the door.

"You're back early," Linna said with a big ner-vous smile.

"Yeah, well, I showed up and let everyone see my face, then I slipped out the back door. I hate listening to politicians." She shook her head and walked off to her office. "I didn't even want to stay for the free food after, that's how badly I wanted to leave."

"Umm, if you're hungry, we still have some burri-tos in the freezer," Linna offered, while silently trying to calm her rapidly beating heart. "I didn't get a chance to eat, either."

"Sure, sounds good to me." Tracy came back out of her office and joined Linna in the small kitchen area.

Monday, 0130 hours

"Okay, listen up!" Dean called the group together around the tables. She turned on the slide projector, put up the first slide of a local map, and began with the location of the lodge. "We know that the lodge is brimming with audio and visual surveillance throughout. General Kasimov has also recently added four armed guards to supplement his laser beam security. He is using an old 'speakeasy/bomb shelter' in the basement of the lodge for his control center. It can't be penetrated by any of our technology." She produced slides of the lodge layout indicating where this area was located.

"We also know that there are at least twenty eight cartel representatives from across the globe currently residing at the lodge." Dean flashed pictures of each and gave their name and cartel affiliation. She went on to give an overview of General Kasimov's, Natasha's, and Dimitri's roles, displaying their pictures too.

"I'm now going to play the audio tape from the night that agents Cabini and Sanchez were murdered. Please pay close attention and see if you note anything unusual in the tape." She played the tape then asked for comments. No one noticed anything out of the ordinary.

"This is Gus Silver. He's heading up the technology end for us. He's from NSA, but he'll be working with a team comprised from each of the agencies. Okay, Gus, it's up to you and your boys to tear this tape apart for any abnormalities." She nodded at Gus as she handed him a copy of the tape from the night of the incident. Then Dean discussed the subsequent recovery of the agent's bodies and the initial autopsy results. After that, she introduced Dr. Beth Berg, from the DEA, who took over the discussion on their current findings regarding the mind control substance.

"What we have to date is very little," Dr. Berg informed the group as she pulled out a drawing of the chemical makeup of the substance. "We know from what General Kasimov inferred that this substance can be ingested, inhaled, injected, or absorbed through the skin. We also know that once it is in the system, it has a life span of 96 hours. After that, it dissipates and becomes inert." She went over to the blackboard and wrote "four methods of administration" and, below that "96 hours". "We also know that the substance alone will not cause a person to do anything different from their ordinary routine. There has to be a verbal command." She added "verbal command" under the "96 hours" on the blackboard. "Finally, we know that there is something in addition to the verbal command that triggers the drug's effects." She placed a question mark on the blackboard under the other items. "We need to find out what that question mark represents." She emphasized this statement by circling the question mark. "Perhaps if we can find out what this is," she tapped the chalk on the question mark, "we can break the chain of action." She looked over at Dean and then returned to her seat.

"Thanks, Beth," Katie said, as she stood to address the group. "According to our information, this drug of General Kasimov's has already been placed. We estimate that there is enough of this drug out there, ready to be released, with the potential to affect millions of people." Katie paused for effect then continued. "We just don't know where it is or the mode of transmission that will be used, although it is in liquid form rather than gas." Katie went over to a flip chart and produced a drawing of what the canisters supposedly looked like. "This is an approximate drawing of what the canisters that contain the drug look like."

"Looks like an air tank to me," commented a middle-aged agent named Bruce. "But what are those slots for?"

"The nearest we can figure is that the drug will somehow be released through those slots," Katie explained. "Our informant mentioned that there is some sort of device attached to the top of each tank. It's not certain if that device is necessary for the release of the drug, for filling the canisters, or both."

"It may be for both, but my guess is it's gotta be for the release," Bruce observed. "I was a Navy SEAL before I joined the FBI, and have used a lot of air tanks for diving and have seen a lot of chemical warfare canisters. I can't imagine the general sending out his troops to turn on hundreds of tanks to disperse the drug. My bet would be it's either a remote controlled device or a timed device," he stated. "If it's a remote, we might have a chance at stopping the relay before it releases the drug. If it's a timed device, we may be in real trouble trying to find all the canisters to deactivate or remove the timers before they open up."

"Thanks, Bruce." Katie smiled at him. "I'm sure you're right, and my gut tells me that they're probably timers. I can't imagine the general taking a chance of a remote control signal getting disrupted." The group nodded in agreement. "Now we need to find out where he put these canisters, as well as who his targets are. If anyone has any theories on this, I'm all ears." She looked around the group. Not getting any response, Katie added, "Well, keep this information in mind as you work. Any ideas will be greatly appreciated."

"Okay, folks. Time to get to work," Dean said in dismissal, as she stood again. "Dr. Berg, your group will be set up near the locker rooms. The sooner we find out what that question mark represents, the better." Dr. Berg nodded. "Bruce, you and your team will work on the maps and possible targets. Also, work on possible locations for all those canisters of drugs." Bruce also nodded in affirmation. "Gus, you and your boys will be set up here by the consoles. Get me what you can from those tapes, okay?"

"You bet, Colonel." Gus replied.

"All right then...we've got less than a month to crack this before we have a massive event that we won't be able to control. Let's get to work." With that, the task force broke up into their smaller groups and went to work on their respective puzzles.

"Well, that went fairly well," Katie said as she walked over to Dean. "Lets just hope we can get to the bottom of this soon." She looked up into the intense blue eyes of her partner and then said, "I don't want to be late!"

"Me either," came the soft, far off response from Dean. "Me either."

****

At three p.m., the two women left the court building and headed down to the P & R office to fill Tracy in. They decided that it would be better for them to go there than to have Tracy show up at the courts. As they walked into the office, Linna greeted them with a big, though somewhat nervous, smile. "So how's the mountain?" Linna asked as the two agents entered.

"The mountain?" they responded in unison.

"Yeah, Tracy said you were probably up there today, since you didn't come in to the office."

"Oh...that mountain," Katie answered as she recovered from the momentary confusion. "It's fine, just fine. Did a little fine tuning of our equipment, then took a nice walk around."

"Um...yeah," offered Dean. "Just wanted to make sure that wind storm last night didn't knock anything out of whack."

"Is Tracy in?" the young blonde interjected quickly before Linna could quiz them any further.

"Yep, but she has the Commission chairperson in with her right now. She'll only be a bit." Linna got ready to ask another question, but was stopped by a ringing telephone.

The two agents took the opportunity to go into their small office to avoid any further conversation. "Did she seem nervous to you?" Katie asked as they sat down in front of the console.

"Nah, I think I just intimidate her," Dean said with a chuckle.

"You have a tendency to do that to a lot of people." Katie gave her a teasing smile and then put her set of headphones on. She sat there for a while then looked over at Dean. "Did you reset the voice direction on these this morning? I could have sworn we left it on the kitchen area, and it's set for the dining room."

Dean gave her a quizzical look then donned her headphones and listened for a bit. "Nope, I don't think so, but maybe we're just confused with the two set ups now. We were listening to El and Ezra this morning at the courts."

"Yeah, you're probably right," the young agent acknowledged, then refocused her attention on the audio device and scanned the lodge for conversations. Most of them were just normal banter, then her head exploded with the sound of gunfire. "Shit!" she called out as she ripped off the headphones. "That really hurt!"

"What happened?" Dean asked, her blue eyes showing intense concern.

"I think I just found the shooting range. Either that or the place is under siege by automatic weapons fire." Katie held her head and tried to shake out the remaining echoes.

Dean unconsciously looked up at the TV monitor, then back at Katie. "Guess we need to mark that on the layout map so we don't stumble on it again without turning the volume down."

"Good idea," Katie remarked as she lowered the volume, put the headphones back on, and returned to her scanning.

Dean had just started to review the tapes from earlier that day when there was a knock on the door. She got up and opened the door to find Tracy grinning back at her. "Hey." Dean opened the door fully to allow the director in.

Tracy stepped in, closing the door before she spoke. "How's it going at the courts?"

"Not bad. We're all set up, and the task force is working on their specific angles." She paused then shook her head and added. "I just hope we have enough time to crack this one."

"So, aren't you going to ask me why I'm grinning?" Tracy looked at the two women with the biggest Cheshire cat grin she could muster.

"Okay...we bite...why are you grinning?" Katie asked as she took her headphones off.

"I just got a special delivery letter." The director waved it in front their faces. "Want to know what's in it?" The two women just nodded, grinning back at her. "It's a check for $50,000.00 from the Enigma Foundation!"

"Wow," Dean said with wide eyes. "I didn't expect Jack to act that fast. Is that why the commissioner was here?"

"Yep. It came addressed to him, with a nice little letter informing him that an anonymous donor was impressed with my work here and wanted to help us reach some of our improvement goals, so he sent this 'little' donation our way. Cool, huh?"

"Definitely cool," Katie chimed in. "Good cover letter, too."

"Yeah, I thought so too. So what's new?"

They proceeded to update Tracy on the staff briefing including the latest on the autopsy and the canisters. "I hear that Dr. Berg is one of the best in her field. You're lucky they sent her down," Tracy commented when Dean finished her update.

"I asked for her, specifically," Katie offered. "We went through training together at Quantico and have been friends ever since. And you're right, she is the best!"

"That so?" Blue eyes shifted to peer into the emeralds across from her. "Friends, huh?"

The emeralds across from her twinkled as Katie replied, "Yes... *just* friends."

"So..." Tracy decided to interrupt the staring match, "do you really think the canisters are on a timer? 'Cause if they are, you'd better concentrate on counter-acting the drug. I can't imagine having any success in locating and disengaging a timer on 500 canisters!"

"That's what we thought, too," Dean agreed as she broke off her eye contact with Katie, winking as she did so. "Katie thinks that Kasimov wouldn't leave the release of the drug susceptible to any chance of a signal disruption, and I believe she's right."

"So what are the chances of stopping or counter-acting the drug?" Tracy was mentally considering the proverbial needle in the haystack they were going to have to find.

"Well, I just hope Beth can come up with some-thing...and in time. Then we've got to figure out who and where his intended drug victims are, and what they'll be told to do." Katie got up and walked over to Dean and put her hand on Dean's shoulder. "Then *we* have to figure out how to stop it all," she said, giv-ing a squeeze to Dean's shoulder.

"Piece of cake," Dean replied, as she reached up and placed her hand over Katie's.

"Well, ya know if there's anything I can do, just whistle." Tracy stood to leave.

"You've already done more than you should have, but we'll definitely keep you in mind." Dean sighed and added. "If you can put up with it, I'd like to keep this surveillance console active as a back up."

"No problemo." Tracy smiled. "I was hoping you would. I know it's kinda selfish of me, but I'd like to stay in the loop." The two agents smiled and nodded their affirmation as Tracy left the office.

"What say we pack up today's tapes and take them to Gus's boys to review?" Dean suggested as she took the tapes out of the machines and replaced them with fresh ones. "Then we can go grab a bite to eat before we check in for the evening briefing?"

"Sounds like a plan," the young blonde replied as she gave Dean a big hug, then added, "You're not really upset about Beth, are you?"

"Naw...just pulling your leg." Dean bent down to give Katie a very sensual kiss as a simple, but effec-tive, declaration of her affection.

By 1600, they had locked and left the office, thankful that Linna was in Tracy's office and out of ear shot, thus safe from having to make up any more lies to appease the secretary's inquisitive nature. Both women really liked Linna, but both agreed that it was best to keep her in the dark. Little did they know that Linna was just as actively trying to avoid the two agents for fear of having been found out.

* * * * * * * * * *

After a quick trip home, a hastily prepared pasta dinner, and a long, relaxing and highly sensual sojourn in the two person Jacuzzi, the two agents were on their way back to the tennis court building for the evening briefing. There were light flurries in the air, and the flakes were starting to stick to the ground. The weather forecast was predicting a light 'dusting' of snow by morning.

"Let's hope they've got this solved, and it'll be over by the time we get there." Katie expressed this fervent hope in her most positive voice.

"You are a dreamer, aren't you?" Dean casually held her partner's hand then lifted it to her mouth and caressed each of the knuckles with her soft lips.

"Mmmm. Just thinking of better things to be doing right now than meeting with a bunch of stodgy old scientists and super techno twits."

"Techno twits? I don't think they would appreciate you labeling them techno twits," Dean mumbled around the knuckles that were still being caressed. "But, I have to agree with you about thinking of better things we could be doing!"

"Well, hopefully they will have gotten a bit closer to solving this mystery." Katie sighed as Dean released her hand to make the turn onto the road leading into the old resort. By the time the SUV had warmed up, it was time for them to get out and brave the cold again.

An anxiously pacing Gus met them at the door. "I've got some good news, and I've got some bad news," he reported as the two women entered the building.

"Okay," Dean said as she shut the door. "Give me the bad news first."

"The wiring in this place isn't meant for the juice we're drawing. We're gonna to have to shut down the surveillance equipment until we can add more circuits."

Dean shrugged, knowing that the back up system was still on, and then asked for the good news.

"Well, just before we lost power to the surveillance unit, your man Kasimov made an announcement, and..." Green and blue eyes pinned the techno wizard and held their breath. "Seems he's leaving in the morning for the Russian Embassy in Washington until the middle of December."

The two women released their held breaths at the same time and looked at each other. "And that's good news because...?" Katie questioned.

"Well, Bruce was talking it over with his team, and they think they will be able to do a night insertion and examine the control room while Kasimov's gone." He didn't understand the cool reception he was getting to that idea.

"He'll do no such thing," came the quick response from Dean. "Kasimov may be leaving, but I'm sure he won't be taking Dimitri with him." She looked over at Katie and the young agent could see a definite change in the coloration of the blue eyes looking back at her. It was as though Dean's eyes had turned to steel blue, and her neck and face began getting flushed; the anger rising in her partner was almost palpable.

"Well, it makes sense that he's heading for D.C.," the blonde murmured. "Especially if he already has the drug canisters in place. And after all, he is the Russian's Security Director, so why not go to the Embassy? Probably has to put in an appearance so the Russians don't get suspicious."

"Yeah, but don't believe for a minute that I'll give a damn about diplomatic immunity if I can catch his sorry butt in the middle of this. We'll just have to make sure he's in the thick of it and not hiding at the Embassy. I don't want to lose him again." Dean's voice had turned to a very low menacing tone when she spoke, and it alarmed Katie somewhat to see the absolute hatred and anger that surfaced whenever Dean discussed the general. She made a mental note to find out why Kasimov pushed Dean's buttons so easily.

About this time, Bruce came over to the trio. He soon found himself the target of Dean's growing anger as she swiveled her attention towards him. "What makes you think you can decide to do a night insertion?" She challenged him as she pulled herself up to her full 6'1' height and bore down on him with her steely blue stare.

"Uh...I thought..." He started to stammer while backing up a bit, unsure as to the cause of this reaction from his superior.

"I'm the one who does the thinking around here!" the dark-haired woman growled. "Nobody does anything without my permission, ya got that?"

Bruce looked back and forth between Katie and Gus, then back to Dean, not knowing what had brought this mood change about. He was trying desperately to figure out how to get out of this situation with all of his parts in working order when Katie stepped up, obviously trying to defuse the situation before Dean and Bruce came to blows.

"Umm...Dean?" she said softly as she gently placed her hand on a very tense Dean. "I'm sure Bruce wouldn't have done anything without your permission..." she began, as Bruce emphatically nodded his head in agreement.

"No, Colonel, of course not." Bruce held up his hands, partly in self-defense and partly in a bid for time to explain. "My team and I were just talking about the possibility...not planning anything...really..."

Steely blue eyes shifted from Bruce to Katie's entreating emerald eyes, back to Bruce. "Yeah...well, just make sure you pass things through me before you do anything," came the somewhat less hostile response from Dean before she turned and strode off towards the small office that was her private domain. Katie stayed a moment with Bruce and Gus ensuring them that everything would be all right, before she followed Dean to the office.

Katie entered and closed the door quietly behind her. Dean was sitting at her desk with her feet propped up, her back to the door, and her arms crossed in front of her chest. As she came around the desk, she saw that Dean's eyes were closed, and she silently monitored the contractions of the jaw muscles as they clenched and released, then tightened again. She approached carefully, gently placing her hand on the right shoulder, feeling the tension release slightly at her touch.

"Dean...are you alright?" Katie spoke softly as she began to gently massage the older agent's shoulders.

Dean didn't answer at first, only inhaling and exhaling deeply a few times before she spoke. "I'm sorry...I just..."

"It's okay." Katie continued the gentle massage noting the relaxation of Dean's muscles as she did so. "I'm sure you have your reasons."

"No. It's not 'okay'. I shouldn't lose control like that." Dean swiveled around to face the young woman.

"Then, what happened? What set you off?"

"Kasimov sets me off!" Looking at Katie, her steely eyes softened and returned to a warmer blue. "I should have taken him out the first time I saw him...the bastard!"

Katie just waited and let Dean settle down. She wanted to know the story behind the anger, but also wanted to give Dean the space and time to tell her story. She only had to wait a few minutes before Dean was composed enough to begin.

"It was just after I made first lieutenant, about ten years ago. I had an assignment that took me under-cover into Russia. I was to meet my Russian contact and swap some stolen U. S. military computer chips for similar, but altered, computer chips. The chips that were stolen would compromise our missile guidance capabilities severely. The ones I was to replace them with were identical except for one small thing—a virus was implanted in the chip to destroy their computer guidance systems once they installed and activated it. And it worked. They're still trying to recover from that damage. I got in, made the switch, and was home free, except for one thing—Kasimov." Dean sighed and closed her eyes once more as a tear escaped and rolled down her cheek.

"What happened?" the young blonde asked as she gently stroked Dean's cheek and wiped the tear away.

"Somehow, my contact was compromised. I had only met with her twice on the operation, but she was a very likable person. She was full of life, energy and had a terrific sense of humor. And she was very brave. I did my best to try to save her, but it wasn't enough." Another tear fell. "She led them to believe that the op hadn't even begun...that it was scheduled for the following week. Kasimov ordered the chips to be moved and installed in their computer systems immediately. As soon as I found out, I went back and tried to get her out. I found her in the interrogation room." Dean's voice had become raw with emotion as she continued the story. "She was still alive when I found her. Her face was battered almost beyond recognition. She had been tortured, repeatedly raped by the general himself, and left on the floor to die. I held her in my arms as she told me what the general had done and that the op was safe. She begged me to leave her there, but I couldn't. I picked her up and was almost in the clear when Kasimov and his men spotted us and opened fire." Katie sucked in a breath as she saw the pain in Dean's eyes. "I don't know how I managed to make it to the pick up vehicle. I had been hit seventeen times and passed out as the door to the van closed. Next thing I knew, I woke up at General Leonard Wood Army Hospital. That's where I first met Tracy." Dean blinked away the tears, then looked at Katie. "So you see, I too know what it's like to be too late. Through all the beatings, the torture and the rapes, she didn't crack, and that saved the operation. I swore if I ever crossed paths with Kasimov again, I'd even the score for Katarina"

"I understand now why he sets you off so easily," Katie said quietly. "We'll get him this time."

"Yes, we will,if it's the last thing I do." Dean got up and walked to the door.

"Where are you going?" the young agent asked.

"To apologize to Bruce," came the quiet reply as she left the office to find Bruce and mend some fences.

Thursday, 0900 hours

Dean was back at the Parks & Recreation office doing the audio and visual surveillance until the new circuits were installed in the court building. *Oh yeah, Tracy was getting a top notch wiring job on the old building. She'll have more juice than she'll ever know what to do with,* Dean mused as she idly scanned the rooms for pertinent conversation. They also decided to upgrade the heating system and put in a small kitchen while they were at it. *She's going to be preening her feathers for quite a while after this job is over. Couldn't have happened to a better person,* the tall agent thought to herself. *Now all we have to do is get this job over without anyone getting hurt in the process.* Dean mentally reviewed the progress of the past two days.

The teams working at the court building weren't getting very far yet. Dr. Berg had managed to reproduce the drug successfully, but had not been able to isolate the one factor that made it actuate. Several of the staff acted as guinea pigs for the process, but so far no one jumped when commanded. She went over and over the tape from the night the two agents were killed and tried to consider every possible scenario— the kind of food served, the drinks the two men had before dinner, whether or not they smoked, even down to the after dinner mints on the tables. Still there was no progress in finding the elusive trigger.

Gus, on the other hand, was tied up with the electrical installation, so his task was temporarily on hold. The ETA for completion of the new circuitry was Thursday night at best, so he gave the tape back to Dean for review at the P & R office.

Bruce and his team were actively working on their project. They were coming up with lists and lists of possible targets and drug deployment tactics, but the sheer volume of the numbers was starting to stack up against them. The "could be's" were too numerous for the team to check out and eliminate before another stack of possibilities turned up.

What they all needed was a break. Just a little clue. Anything to guide them to the right path. Dean and Katie were trying their best to find that clue. So far, they were batting zero. Katie had been back to the lodge now since Tuesday morning. She managed to have a quick rendezvous with Lin, but even Lin was unable to shed any light. The cartel members were occupying their time with the various diversions provided by the general. The indoor shooting range was constantly in use, as were the game room, gym, sauna, TV lounge, and the pool. Several of the guests took advantage of the acreage surrounding the lodge and spent time outdoors as well. All in all, the general attitude of the cartel was that they were on 'vacation' until further orders came in, so they might as well enjoy themselves—even though many of them were getting a bit antsy from all of the sitting around. Natasha had scheduled several more hunting trips that would carry them through deer season. After the time they had spent in the indoor range, the deer would be well-advised to head for the hills.

At eleven, Tracy knocked on the door to the surveillance office and stepped in when Dean opened the door. "Hey...how's it going?" The director walked over to take a seat at the console.

"All's quiet on the lodge front." Dean handed a set of headphones over to Tracy. "They're still working on the wiring at the courts, Dr. Berg's still at ground zero, and Bruce is seeing possible scenarios everywhere."

"Sounds like a plan coming together," Tracy said with a chuckle. "So how's Katie doing at the lodge?"

"'Bout as well as the rest of us. Still nothing concrete." Dean located the room Katie was in and set the audio to match.

"...you and your sister had fun growing up in this lodge." Katie's voice came over the headphones.

"Yep. Me and Lilly had a lot of fun in this place," El's voice replied.

"What kinds of games did you have to play as kids? Our family plays a lot of board games now, and even when we were kids. Monopoly, Clue, Chinese checkers, that sort of thing. How about you?"

"Oh, we didn't have a lot of money for store bought games. We just played a lot with our imaginations making up games. We did play card games a lot though...and oh my...we'd have lots of fun playing hide and seek in the lodge and out on the grounds."

"Really? You mean the grown ups didn't mind you playing in the lodge?"

"Oh no. Mr. G's parents didn't mind at all. See, we were almost the same age as their kids, so we played a lot with them. As long as we didn't get underfoot or disturb the guests, we pretty much had free reign of the lodge," El said, then added, "This was quite the family place to vacation back then."

"Hide and seek huh? Bet that was fun in a big place like this."

That's my woman, Dean thought to herself, *see what you can find out about this lodge...see if there are any secrets still to be had in the old place.* Dean was mentally urging Katie on with this round of conversation. She looked over at Tracy who was smiling back and giving her a thumbs up signal.

"Oh, it certainly was. Why there were so many places to hide in from the attic to the cellar that we could play all day and not get bored." El was chuckling at the memories of good times past. "Why...my favorite trick was to use the dumbwaiter to get past my sister and the boys." She snickered some more. "They never could figure out how I could get from the attic to the cellar without being seen on the stairs."

"What fun!" Katie said trying to keep the mood going, all the while wondering if the dumbwaiter was still operational. "Sometimes I wish I could use a dumbwaiter to sneak away from some of these guests. Especially some of the men...if you know what I mean," Katie said in a low conspiratorial voice. "It's a good thing Darla is pregnant, or they'd be after her, too."

"Oh, sweetie, I know just what you mean. I'm glad I'm an old hag, or I'd be puttin' a few of them in their place mighty fast," she confided in a whisper.

"Well, I would too, except I really need this job and can't afford to offend anyone. But a few tricks might come in handy."

Dean could almost see the emerald eyes doing their poor puppy dog routine on El, and she chuckled inwardly. *Atta way, Katie. Go for it!*

"Well, I really shouldn't be tellin' ya this, but that old dumbwaiter is still intact and operational. In fact, when no one's here I often use it to cart stuff up and down these floors so's I don't have to carry 'em." El chuckled lightly. "Of course, I'm too old and too big now to fit in it like I used to, but you could fit."

"Wow! That would be really cool, El. Can you tell me where it is?"

Dean could hear the hopefulness in Katie's voice as she and Tracy listened in and watched Katie's blue dot on the screen.

"Sure thing, sweetie. But it's got to be our little secret.
Come with me."

The ethereal body with the blue dot and another
reddish orange body, signifying El, started to move.
The two bodies went into the pantry area where they
stopped.

"It's right here behind this door. Mr. G's dad didn't
want to get rid of it 'cause it was a nice old-fashioned fea-
ture of the lodge, but he didn't want to use it either, so he
built this broom closet in front of it. If I hadn't grown up in
this place, I never woulda' known it was there. See, this
panel just slides over like this..." The women listening in
could hear a creaking, sliding noise. "And there it is," El
finished with a flourish. The space was about five feet
square and five feet high. "You'd hafta scrunch down, but
it's sturdy enough to carry over three hundred pounds.
Built with steel cables and not ropes. They used it to carry
fireplace wood, small pieces of furniture, and the like. And
of course, the bootleg booze!"

"Whoa! That's so cool! So where does it let out?"
Katie's voice could hardly contain her excitement. She
could tell that it was electric by the red and green buttons
and the up and down indicators. She also noted a hand
crank that was probably used prior to it being motorized.

"Well," El began, "it goes clear up to the attic following
the length of the chimney that's here to the right. In the
attic it lets out behind the chimney. Then on the third floor,
which we haven't used for years, it lets out in the bathroom
on this end of the lodge behind the towel rack. You just pull
on the rack, and the door pops open. It's set up pretty cleverly. You'd never know there was a door behind the towel
rack." El paused for a breath before continuing. "Let's see

now...on the second floor, it lets out in the back of the hall linen closet next to that Oriental lady's room, then here on the main floor...then behind the chimney again in the basement. You just push the button for up or down, green for go and red for stop. Each entrance has a call button to bring the dumbwaiter up or down when it's needed."

Bingo! Thought all three women. "I wonder if Kasimov knows about this?" Tracy asked as she looked over at Dean.

"Probably not, from the sounds of the conversation with El," Dean answered back. It almost seemed as though Katie was tuned in to the conversation the two women just had, because in her next sentence she asked if Ezra knew about the dumbwaiter.

"Nope," El said with a proud voice. "I never told Ezra about it. Had to make him wonder how I'd get my linens and things moved up and down so quickly, but it was always my little secret. I'll even bet a week's wages that old Mr. G has forgotten all about it too. Now...it's our little secret!" You could hear the giggles of both women as the creaking and sliding noise indicated the closure of the dumbwaiter.

"Gee, thanks El." Katie's voice came across the headphones. "I promise never to tell anyone." *Except maybe my partner and the task force...And maybe I should tell Lin too, just in case,* Katie mused, as she and El stepped out of the pantry.

"Well, it looks like there's another way into that cellar that no one knows about except El, and now Katie," Dean said as she slipped off her headphones.

"Yeah, that sure is good to know," Tracy said as she removed her headphones too. "Now all you need is an opportunity to get in and out without anyone being the wiser."

"It sure would help if we could find something...anything...that would clue us in on the targets and the location of the drug canisters. I'm not holding my breath though, what with the four added guards and Dimitri." Dean studied the lodge layout and located the approximate position of the dumb-waiter. "Wish we knew more about the layout of the cellar."

"Hmm, that would be helpful. Maybe Katie can get that info from Lin at their next get-together?"

Dean nodded her head and then sighed. "I wish there was a better way for those two to pass information. I know it makes Katie uncomfortable, but at least no one's tumbled to them yet."

"How about you?" Tracy asked with a serious look at her friend. "Does it make you uncomfortable, too?"

Dean thought a minute before she answered her friend. "Yeah...I guess it does. I know it's just a means of passing information, but I can't help feeling a bit..."

"Jealous?" came the suggestion from Tracy. Dean just lowered her head and nodded. "Well, if it's any consolation, I would be jealous too, if it was my Col in that situation."

"Speaking of Colleen," Dean raised her head and lifted an eyebrow. "She's really into technology—computers and audio/visual stuff, right?"

"Right. So?"

"Do you think she'd mind going over the tapes from the night the two FBI agents were killed? I know it's a lot to ask. It is pretty gruesome." Dean shook her head then added, "I guess I'm grabbing at straws for answers. And I'll try to get them any way I can."

"It's okay, Dean. I'm sure she won't mind. What are you looking for?"

"That mind control drug needs some kind of an external stimulus to activate it. We just can't put our finger on it yet. Maybe a fresh point of view will help." Dean shrugged and went to the tape storage area to pull the audio and videotapes from that night. "Here are the originals. We've got plenty of copies out at the courts. And tell Col thanks."

"Sure thing, Dean. I'll give them to her this afternoon. I've got to run by her office anyway, so I'll drop them off after lunch. And speaking of lunch...you interested?"

The two friends left the surveillance room after putting new tapes in the machine. On their way out, Linna asked Tracy if she'd mind stopping at Gino's to pick up an order for her. Linna said she'd call it in so it would be ready for them on the way back to the office. Then she went back to her typing until she was sure they were gone.

Okay, I've got maybe forty-five minutes to do some snooping, Linna thought to herself as she locked the door to the office, put the 'will return' sign on the door, and unlocked the surveillance room. She slipped on the headphones and began to listen.

"Hey El, do you need help putting this grocery order away?"

Linna recognized the voice as Katie's, but wasn't surprised at all. Not after her last peek into this room when she'd figured out that the two women must be undercover cops.

"Sure would appreciate the help. Most of the canned goods go into the cupboards in the pantry. I'll get the rest of these groceries put into the refrigerator."

The secretary recognized that voice as belonging to El Schlott, housekeeper and long time employee at "The Lodge". *I certainly hope that El and Ezra aren't involved in anything illegal. Naahh!* Linna thought as she continued to listen.

"Boy, this sure has been a weird winter so far."

Hmmm, Katie's making with the small talk. Wonder how long she's been working there?

"That's just fine by me," came El's response. "I certainly have learned to appreciate warmer weather, and I'm in no hurry to have winter return."
"I like warmer weather too, but I guess winter will arrive one of these days."
"Ezra says we're gonna have some bad weather soon."
"Oh? What makes him say that?"
"His knees. They always act up when the weather gets bad. He says we're liable to have a nasty storm in the next week or so."
"Well, if he's right, he's a better forecaster than the weather channel!"

Linna could hear both women giggling. *Well, it doesn't sound like much is going on right now. I really don't want to change any of these dials. I almost got caught the last time. Guess I'll just have to try again another time.* Linna took the headphones off and was careful to replace them exactly where she had found them, then left the room locking it behind her.

Thursday, 2000 hours

Dean and Katie were at the court building going through a briefing from the task force on the day's work. So far, no good news had been reported.

"That special breaker box won't be in until morning," Gus commented, as it was his turn to report. "I'm glad you had the console at your other location still operating. We should be back on line by noon tomorrow, then we can take down that other console."

"No need. I'll take care of it myself," Dean cut in.

"Okay, sure. Whatever you think is best."

"I just want you to focus your full attention on solving the mystery on those tapes. The other console is of no significance now," Dean explained as she smiled at Gus. "Now for a little good news." She turned to Katie for her turn to report.

"Today I was having a conversation with El, the housekeeper, and found out about a hidden dumb-waiter." She went on to inform the group about its location, size, and operation before she completed her report.

"That may come in handy if we ever have the opportunity to get in." This came from Bruce as he looked up at Dean for confirmation.

"Yeah, but only *if* we have the opportunity. I don't want to scare Kasimov off before we know more." Dean returned Bruce's look, and he nodded in agreement. "Until then, we won't be using it. Anybody have anything else they want to say?"

No one ventured to add anything else, so Dean called the briefing to a close then she and Katie went into the small office.

"Something's gotta give soon. We don't have much time left," Dean said with a sigh as she sat in her chair. "Did you get anything from Lin today?"

"No, we just kept up our daily contact for the sake of appearances, but she hasn't heard anything, either. She did think that Natasha would be going to join Kasimov for the weekend. That would leave Dimitri and the four guards behind to keep an eye on things."

"She's not thinking of doing anything rash, is she?" Dean lifted an eyebrow as she looked over at Katie.

"I don't think so, but I'll warn her off, if you want me to."

"Just tell her to wait a bit. We don't want to do anything prematurely and scare Kasimov off," Dean said as she stood. "Let's go home and get some rest. We can't do any more here."

Part
IV

Sunday, 1200 hours...Six Days Before Christmas

The physical complex at the court building was actually looking a bit better since the new circuits, heaters, and kitchen were installed. At least everyone seemed to be in a better mood now that they didn't have to put up with the intermittent lack of heat and power, but the pressures of the case were taking their toll. Especially since they had not been able to make much progress in their respective investigations. Bruce and his team were still whittling away at the myriad of possible scenarios, and they were actually making progress. Gus, unfortunately, was still coming up empty on locating any possible catalyst from the tapes, but his team had been preoccupied with the circuitry installation that had taken longer than expected. Now that it was complete, they could focus on their task without interruption. It had been a long week, and the teams were starting to get on each other's nerves.

The tension was so thick that Dean had opted to meet Tracy at the office rather than do her surveillance at the court building. She figured this would give the teams time to work together without having to feel stressed by her presence. Together she and the park director kept an eye on the young agent as she performed her routine at the lodge. As they watched Katie, Dean filled Tracy in on other developments.

Dr. Berg and her team had relocated to the local hospital where they could avail themselves of the necessary medical equipment in the hospital laboratory and pathology departments. General James had pulled some strings with the hospital CEO, who just happened to be an old West Point colleague, and got them in without questions being asked. Dr. Berg was eliminating as many false leads as she could in her quest to find the stimulus for the mind control drug. The team did find that the drug could remain dormant in the body for an undetermined length of time, perhaps even weeks, until it was activated. She assumed that once the stimulus activated it, the ninety-six hour life span would then start ticking away. Unfortunately, they still had not discovered the enigmatic stimulus to test this assumption.

This new information came through a new team member that had been flown in from California. A forensic pathologist whose specialty was on the cellular level, Dr. Leigh Randall discovered that the drug had an affinity for brain tissue. She explained that it was an action similar to that of oxygen attaching itself to the red blood cells until it was needed, when it would be released to the cells requiring it. Only in this case, the elusive stimulus was the cause for detachment of the drug, which would then enable the nervous system to provide the actions indicated by the verbal cues given. Dr. Randall also found that the drug would pool mostly in central nervous system tissue, specifically the gray matter, although it was found in miniscule amounts in other tissues of the body. The ability of the drug to lay dormant in the body for two weeks was not good news. If Kasimov's plan was going to take place sometime between Christmas and New Year's, that meant they had to find out where the drugs had been cached this week. That prospect was looking pretty dim right now.

"How's Col doing with the tape project?" Dean asked during a lull in the surveillance conversations.

"She's really been trying to get you something concrete, but so far—no go. She's not about to give up, though," Tracy added hastily. "She knows how much this assignment means to you."

"Yeah, I'd like to really nail that bastard," Dean said with a feral smile.

Following a pause, Tracy decided to while away the time with mundane conversation. "We're really enjoying Katie's cats. Brutus loves playing with them. How did you adjust to them when they were at your place?"

"Actually, I was becoming pretty fond of them. They all have pretty distinct personalities. We'll both be glad to get them back," Dean said with a smile. "When I was a kid, we always had animals around. We had cats, dogs, cows, horses, and even an old goat." This brought out one of those dazzling smiles that could just take your breath away. "I used to hate going out into the pasture when the goat was around. It used to sneak up on me when I would feed the cows or brush the horses. Wham! She'd butt you right in the old derriere every time." She shook her head chuckling at the memory. "I finally learned to recognize when she was coming. I guess that goat had a lot to do with my ability to perceive would-be attacks from the rear!"

"Col and I really love Brutus. He's a great German Shepherd—really loyal and smart as a whip, too. The other day I taught him how to open the back door using his mouth!" Tracy said with excitement. "He's been bugging me a lot lately to let him out in the backyard, and I just got tired of getting up to let him out."

"What? No doggie door?" Dean said a little sarcastically. "I'll bet it was hard for you to get your mouth open wide enough to grab the handle," she finished, with a soft pat on Tracy's shoulder.

"Verrry funny, Dean and no, no doggie door...too drafty in the winter." Tracy's eyes just twinkled mischievously back at Dean. "Actually, I just sat in my chair and instructed him what to do. Next thing I knew, he walked over to the door, opened it, and let himself out! Cool, eh?"

"Not bad, Tracy. Any chance I can get him on my team?"

"I bet he'd love that! Though he has been acting a bit weird lately. In fact, the cats have been a little on edge in the evenings, too. Must be a change in the weather is coming."

"Hmmm, could be. We've gotten away with really mild weather so far. Can you believe it was almost sixty the other day? I thought the Catskills would be buried in snow by now," Dean said as she switched tacks on the audio surveillance.

"Been that way for two, no, three winters now. Haven't been able to get my cross-country skiing programs going at all. Well, maybe after Christmas."

The two women stopped their conversation to listen in on an interesting one at the lodge.

They didn't recognize the voices as any of the guests or the staff, especially since they were speaking with a very heavy Russian accent.

"Hey, Mika, I hear the General is coming back tonight with that bitch, Natasha."

"That's what I heard too. Maybe we'll get to go home soon. This place gives me the creeps."

"Me too. I hate being in the dungeon all the time. Do you suppose Dimitri will find out we came outside in the daylight?

"I hope not. He would probably kill us on the spot! We'd better get back in."

"Hmmm, interesting. Must have been two of the guards. At least we know that Kasimov is coming back. Maybe we'll get some new information," Dean was saying as she continued to rotate the scanning dial. "I wish there was some way we could alert Lin that he's coming back. Guess we'll have to play it by ear."

Tracy nodded and then the two women continued their surveillance in relative quiet. At three o'clock Tracy left the office to return home, and Dean continued her watch as she waited for Katie to arrive after her shift at the lodge was over. Katie pulled into the parking lot at three-thirty and entered the office. She passed Linna pulling out of the drive just as she turned the corner to pull in.

"Hey, love, how's it going here?" Katie said in a chipper voice as she entered the surveillance office and walked over to give Dean a big hug.

"Same old, same old. But it looks like the lodge is getting company tonight," Dean replied as she stood and took the young woman in her arms. "Tracy and I overheard two of the guards talking. Kasimov and Natasha are coming back tonight." The tall agent leaned her head down and placed a very long, very tender, and very loving kiss on the smaller woman's lips. They lingered that way for a while enjoying the comfort of each other's touch, totally caught up in each other's eyes, before Katie was finally able to speak.

"Mmm, now that's the way I like coming home from work!" She looked up into the gorgeous blue eyes across from her and winked, before she got serious again. "Yeah, Lin already knew about Kasimov and Natasha. Dimitri told them all that there would be a meeting tomorrow after lunch." She paused then asked as an after thought, "Was Linna here earlier?"

"Linna? No, just Tracy. Why?" The blues looked back into the emeralds questioningly.

"Hmm, she was pulling out of the parking lot driveway as I came around the corner. I tried to wave, but she didn't see me."

"Well, maybe she was just cutting through from the back lot," Dean conjectured as the two women sat down to discuss the day.

* * * * * * * * *

Darn! thought Linna as she pulled out of the driveway from the parking lot. *I thought for sure I was going to be able to sneak in for another listen. Sure wish I knew what kind of a schedule they're following. It would definitely make my snooping easier. Guess I'll just have to come back another time.* Linna turned out of the drive and headed home, not seeing the young agent turn the corner and wave.

* * * * * * * * * *

"So...there's going to be another meeting of the reps, eh? Hope he lets a little more out of the bag. We're not doing too well on our end, so anything he can throw us will be a bonus."

"Lin said it's got something to do with their assignments," Katie said as she pulled her chair closer to Dean's.

"Assignments...good. Maybe that'll be the break we need," Dean considered as she pulled Katie out of her chair and into her lap.

"It's a good thing Dimitri told them. Lin was ready to do some serious snooping tonight. She'd figured she could run the shower with the bath door open, fogging both surveillance lenses and then put a fake body in the bed using extra blankets I'd been dropping off. That way, if Dimitri looked in on her room, she'd appear to be sleeping." The blonde made a face at Dean. "I was not looking forward to trying to talk her out of that. She's a very determined woman, ya know."

A shake of the long black tresses accompanied Dean's reply. "All this sitting around and waiting has got to be tough on her. Believe me, if I were in her place, I would have been snooping a long time ago."

"We must be getting close to Kasimov's target date. Does Bruce have any solid scenarios, yet?" Katie asked. She rested her head on Dean's shoulder, enjoying the scent of *White Diamonds* on her lover while she began nibbling on her ear lobe.

"Mmmmm...what?" came the husky reply.

"I said...has Bruce...come up...with any...scenarios?" the blonde repeated, pausing between words to lick, then kiss, and finally, gently, exhale each word into her lover's ear.

The gentle teasing became too much for the older agent to ignore, so she slowly got up carrying the younger—who, incidentally, did not protest the move—in her arms, and walked over to the lone couch. As she sat down on the couch, still holding Katie in her arms, she replied, "I guess we'll just have to wait until later to find out." Then she reached over and pulled the young woman into a kiss that drove all thought of anything other than each other totally and completely out of their minds.

* * * * * * * * *

By 2000 hours, after a quick trip home to eat, shower, and change clothes, the two agents made their way back to the court building at the old resort complex. They informed the teams of the impending return of Kasimov and Natasha and the meeting scheduled for the next day after breakfast. Then each team leader went through a summary of their day's accomplishments. This didn't take long. Bruce was the only one with a fairly lengthy report in which he reviewed the latest scenarios and explained why some had been eliminated.

"In conclusion, I'd have to take an educated guess that whatever's coming down will be in either Albany, Boston, New York City, or Washington, D.C. Otherwise Kasimov would not be based here in the Catskills," Bruce concluded. " By car, Albany and New York City are just an hour and a half away. Boston and D.C. are more like five to six hours out, but still not a bad hike from here. All are a stone's throw, if they use air transportation."

"I doubt that," Dean interjected. "Too many bodies to move to use air. They'll probably move them by car, van or truck."

"Or possibly the train. There are several Metro stations throughout the area," suggested Gus. They all nodded in agreement at Gus's comment.

"Well, at least we've got it narrowed down to four probable target areas. Good work Bruce, but keep on it; we're running out of time," Katie said. "If the good doctors over here are on track with their drug dormancy theory, our possible victims may already be ingesting, inhaling, or absorbing it."

"Yeah," the ex-SEAL replied. "That's just what we were thinking, too."

"Okay then. It should be a quiet evening at the lodge tonight, so you might want to let your teams get some needed rest. Maybe tomorrow we'll get lucky," Dean suggested at the conclusion of the briefing.

Monday, 0530 hours

Dean rolled over and turned off the alarm as Katie turned over and stared at the ceiling. The two women had spent most of the evening going over all of the facts of the case and had come to the same conclusion: they needed a break and they needed it soon. They both agreed that the most logical target areas were Albany or New York City—and the latter was the most probable—only they couldn't rule out D.C. entirely. They also had to assume that the target population had already been exposed to the drug, but "how" was another question. And "who" and "why" were even bigger ones. If the drug had already been disseminated to the target population, then they had to concentrate on finding the elusive stimulus that would make it work.

"Gods, Dean, I hope we can get to the bottom of this soon." Katie sighed as she turned her gaze toward her partner. "There's enough of that drug out there to affect millions of people."

Dean rolled to face her lover and reached over to gently caress Katie's cheek with her strong hand. "I hope so too, love." Then she swallowed hard before she began to speak again. "I want you to be extra cautious from here on out. Don't take any chances, and make sure your 'toys' are on you at all times." She peered intently into the emerald eyes across from her. "We'll be watching every move at the lodge, so if you need help, all you have to do is ask for it."

"I know," came the soft reply as she reached up and held the hand to her cheek. "But we can't be storming the place until we find out what's going down. Otherwise, we've wasted all this time, and Kasimov wins again."

"No way, love, Kasimov will not win this time... I guarantee it!" Dean said with such conviction that Katie truly believed her partner's words.

"All right, Dean." Katie spoke quietly. "Let's get him, together!"

Monday, 1400 hours

Dean and Gus were listening intently to the voices coming from the dining room at the lodge as the meal concluded and Kasimov began to speak.

"Ladies... and gentlemen. Thank you for humoring me and abiding by my request that you not leave the premises. I know that this may have been a very difficult task. Some of you, I'm sure, have enjoyed the time to relax...."

C'mon, c'mon, get to the point, thought a very inwardly anxious, but outwardly cool, Lin as she sat in silence with Ito and Hiro. *Let's get to this new information. I want to end this now!*
The house staff was ordered to remain in the kitchen while Kasimov talked to his guests, and they were all availing themselves of a needed rest and a wonderful lunch. All except for Katie, who appeared to be enjoying the break along with the rest of the staff, while in actuality she wanted to be a fly on the wall. *Guess I'll have to wait to get the scoop from Lin, or the team, later. I just hope this will be the proverbial straw that we've been clutching for.*

"...while others of you are eager to know more about the plans I have in mind." Kasimov paused for effect, knowing that the tension in the room was thick and enjoying every minute of it. "Natasha, please pass out the information to our esteemed partners."

"Damn it!" Dean and Gus's curses exploded along with a silent one from Lin at the lodge. "Now we'll only get a piece of the picture. I hope Katie has an opportunity to meet with Lin this afternoon," the tall agent commented, as Gus nodded in agreement. "Their meetings have not been as frequent as I had hoped, thanks to a meddling Ito. According to Katie, he wants in on their 'action'. They've been putting him off by not meeting as often," Dean elaborated as they both continued to listen.

"Once you have had time to read over your instructions, you will be needing to make arrangements to meet with your people at the prescribed locations. Natasha and I will be leaving in the morning, so if you have any questions I suggest you contact me before we leave. Dimitri will remain here until you have all left per your instructions. If anyone needs to reach me, please contact Dimitri."

The general finished his short speech, and Dean and Gus watched Kasimov's and Natasha's ghostly signatures disappear into the impenetrable labyrinth of the cellar.

"Well, I guess I could try to contact Katie at the lodge," Dean ventured.

Gus thought about that for a moment. "Are you sure that's wise, Colonel?"

Dean just shrugged in response. "It's either that, or wait until tomorrow to find out what the Japanese group's instructions are." She picked up the phone and dialed the number for the lodge.

"The line is probably not secure," Gus reminded the tall agent, who nodded in comprehension as the phone was answered at the other end.

"Gersch Lodge. How can I help you?" came El's very familiar voice.

"Hi. This is Mrs. Miller. Mah daughter Katie is working thar today. May Ah please speak with her?" Dean did a fairly good impression of a woman in her fifties from the South.

"Sure thing, Mrs. Miller." El put her hand over the receiver and called to Katie. "Katie, it's your Mom." She extended the phone to a somewhat startled Katie.

"Um, thanks," Katie managed to get out as she placed the receiver to her ear. "Mom?"

"Hi, sweet pea. I'm sorry ta hafta bother ya'll at work, but Ah need ya ta stop and pick up some of that ol' Japanese shark oil from the health food store on your way home. Your little sister didn't get the message at school today, and your papa really needs that oil."

"Oh, um, sure, Mom. I'll do my best to remember," Katie answered still somewhat off balance.

"Thank ya, sweet pea...love ya!" Dean put the receiver down, smiling to herself.

"Love you too, Mom." Katie replied into the receiver as she handed it back to the waiting El.

"Everything okay at home, sweetie?" El asked, concerned at the confusion on Katie's face.

"Um...ah...actually, yeah," the blonde said, snapping out of her thoughts. "Mom just needs me to bring something home from the store tonight. I was just surprised to hear from her." Katie returned to the table to gather her composure. *Guess that means they didn't get enough information on their end, and they want me to meet with Lin. Okay, I can do that. I just hope that Ito doesn't get in the way today.*

The staff was just finishing up their lunch when Natasha came into the kitchen and gave orders to clear the dining room. When she left, El and Ezra just looked at each other, biting their lips to keep from making any comments. *Hmm, guess they don't like her either,* Katie considered as she picked up her dishes and rinsed them before putting them in the large commercial dishwasher.

"I'll go start clearing the tables," Katie offered.

"Thank you, sweetie." El slowly got up. "Darla will give you a hand just as soon as we finish up in here."

Katie nodded and took a large serving tray with her into the dining room. When she walked in, she saw Lin, Ito and Hiro putting papers back in a manila envelope, then they rose to leave the table. Their table was fairly close to Katie, so she picked the one next to it to start cleaning. Lin watched Katie out of the corner of her eye. When she saw Katie look over, she motioned towards the upstairs. Ito, too, noticed the motion, but did not say anything to his beautiful partner. Instead, he decided that maybe today would be his lucky day, and he walked out of the dining room smiling.

Katie glanced at her watch as she and Darla brought in the last of the lunch dishes from the dining room. It was two-thirty, and she had only a half hour left on her shift. She needed to get upstairs and meet with Lin quickly. She grabbed her cleaning supplies and headed up the back stairs.

"I'm going to finish my rooms now," she called over her shoulder to El. "I've just got a couple left to do, and I promised Ms. Yamakura I would do her room before I left."

"Ok, sweetie, but we can't pay overtime, you know." El watched Katie run up the back stairs. *That gal sure takes her job seriously. And she's been especially attentive to that nice Japanese woman ever since she was sick. Maybe I can talk Mr. G into keeping her on when Ezra and I retire. She'd sure make a good replacement.* El pondered as she busied herself with putting the dishes in the washer. *I might just have to mention that to Mr. G, next time he stops in.*

Katie did a cursory cleaning of Trina Carbon's room, then went over to Lin's room and knocked. "Maid," she called in her usual tone and then she waited for Lin to respond.

"Come." Lin quickly opened the door for Katie. The two women went into the bathroom where Lin already had the shower going. It was effectively fogging the spy lens, and they were able to cover their conversation with just the sound of the running water by keeping close contact and whispering their words.

"I got a message to try to meet you today and bring back the information." Katie whispered in Lin's ear as they embraced.

"Kasimov threw us a curve by giving each group their assignments in separate folders. I can only give you our assignment," Lin informed Katie. "Our group is to meet at a vacant warehouse at 121 Lamont Road outside of Newark, NJ on December 27th. Our job is to familiarize ourselves with the equipment we will need for our part of the project."

"Do you know what the target is yet?"

"No, just that we will be handling the broadcasting part of the project." Lin put her fingers to her lips as a sign of silence. She no sooner gave the signal than the bathroom door opened and Ito came in, grinning at finally catching the two women in an embrace. He was dressed only in his robe and was disappointed to see the two women still fully clothed.

"Ito!" Lin exclaimed. "It is not proper for you to enter my room without my invitation."

"I have been waiting for an invitation to join the two of you for two weeks now, and all I get from you is 'later.' I decided that today would be my lucky day," Ito said with a sneer as he closed the bathroom door behind him and boldly walked over to the two women and began groping at their clothing.

Katie looked at Lin and searched her eyes for a sign of what to do. Not seeing an answer, she decided to take matters in her own hands and reached into her pocket for the red pen. She motioned for Lin to hold her breath then held the pen in front of Ito and released a short burst of the knock out gas. Ito immediately fell to the floor, embarking on a long nap.

The women waited a safe period before they chanced taking a breath. "Wow, that stuff works fast!" Katie whispered, as they checked Ito for any injuries. "He's got a bit of a bump on the back of his head. We'll have to get him into your bed while he sleeps it off. Hopefully, when he wakes, you'll be able to convince him that he slipped on the wet tiles and knocked himself out. That would explain the bump." She smiled up at Lin. "The hard part will be getting him into bed with those surveillance cameras watching. But first, what else was in the assignment papers?"

"That's pretty much it. We're supposed to be in place by the 27th, familiarize ourselves with the equipment we find, then we'll be contacted later with our broadcast materials and time schedule."

"Okay, we can work it out as it unfolds," the young agent whispered. "Now, let's make a good show of getting him into your bed."

* * * * * * * * * *

"So the three of you..." Dean's sentence was cut off quickly by Katie's reply.

"Yeah, the three of us, in Lin's bed, naked as jaybirds, and Lin and I trying to act like he's making love to us! I hope Dimitri enjoyed the show. Do you suppose the DEA would give me hazardous duty pay?" Katie asked with a snicker that was soon joined by hearty laughs from the team leaders.

"Well, at least we know the pen works! Now let's get down to business," Dean said as she wiped the tears of laughter from her eyes. "Gus, get that warehouse pinpointed and see what we can do to get it wired or something. But be careful, Kasimov may have it under surveillance." Gus nodded in understanding. "Bruce, what's the latest on finding those drug cylinders?"

Bruce pulled out a huge map of the tri-state region and spread it out on the table. "Well, it looks like the target area is going to be somewhere around New York City. That's a lot of area and a lot of people to consider."

"It certainly is in sync with the hundreds of canisters that are out there somewhere. Kasimov is *really* targeting millions of people, if the location is right," Katie cut in. "It sure does make things more difficult though. There must be hundreds of targets in that area alone."

"Ya got that right! We're gonna need more information to narrow this down a bit," Bruce concluded.

"Do you suppose he's going to do something involving Newark Airport?" the young blonde asked in amazement. "If he wanted to milk our government for some kind of ransom money, that would be one hell of a hostage situation with all of the holiday travelers and all."

"Could be, but I kinda doubt that. It'd be too easy to reroute traffic around it," the ex-SEAL commented. "But who knows, with a tricky bastard like Kasimov. We'll explore all of the possibilities, but it's gonna take time."

"We haven't got that luxury, Bruce. Do the best you can, as quickly as you can," Dean instructed.

"You've got it, Colonel. We'll get right on it." Bruce rolled up his map and headed over to his team.

Dean looked over at Katie and asked her if she was really okay with the events of the afternoon. "Yeah, I just kept hoping that 'toy' of yours would work like it was supposed to, or I would have been doing some really fast talking about whipping out a pen at him! And I'm really glad you guys couldn't get that on film." Dean put an arm around her partner's shoulder and led her over to the office. "I'm glad, too." Dean gave Katie a gentle pat on the back. "Do you think Lin will be able to get any information from the other guests?"

"I don't know, but I'll see what she can do," Katie offered. "My God, Dean... New York City! How? Exactly where? And why?" She shook her head in disbelief. "Too many possibilities and not enough time."

"I know what you mean. I hope Lin will be able to shed more light on this, or we'll be in deep trouble here," the tall agent acknowledged.

The two agents retreated into their office and spent the rest of the evening poring over the facts,

maps, and team reports. They needed more information to put the pieces together, and time was not on
their side. Nothing seemed to fit right. By 2300
hours, they called it quits for the night and headed
back to Dean's cabin.

Wednesday, 1800 hours

"That's all the information she was able to get out
of the other cartel members. She was just lucky that
Trina Carbon was a bit inebriated last night, or she
might not have gotten that much." Katie finished her
report to the task force members.

"Transformers! Are you sure she said transformers?" Katie nodded. "What on earth is he going to
use those for?" Dean thought out loud. "Anyone
have any ideas?"

No one volunteered any ideas, so Dean added
them to the blackboard along with the original information Dr. Berg had put up. Then she directed her
attention to Bruce and the warehouse recon.

Bruce informed the team leaders that the warehouse was located in a corporate park that had a
pretty tight security set-up. He didn't anticipate any
difficulty in obtaining access, but was concerned that
it might be difficult to wire the place for sound before
the weekend. He was hoping that the number of security guards would be reduced, since it was the Christmas weekend and corporate offices would not be
conducting much business. Unfortunately, having
fewer people around the premises would also make it
more difficult for his men to blend in. Dean warned
him to be extremely cautious so as not to tip their
hand.

Doctors Berg and Randall confirmed that the drug had a longer life expectancy than they originally thought. Their tests indicated that it would remain in the tissues for several weeks before losing its hold on the gray matter of the nervous system, whereupon it would get flushed from the body. They also found that the initial samples recreated by Dr. Berg were still highly potent. Since they would not be able to rely on the drug losing its strength before it was activated, their main focus had to be to stop the flow of the drug to its intended targets before the canisters released it, if they still had time. Work on the antidote was not looking very promising either, but they continued to pursue that avenue, as well.

Gus and his team were still monitoring the lodge and its occupants. He informed the group that he was not able to glean much from the conversations recorded thus far. They provided absolutely no clue to the elusive stimulus that set the drug in motion, so it remained... elusive. He had even contacted his colleagues in Washington to see if they could tap into the Russian Embassy to track Kasimov's moves there, but they weren't successful.

Katie suggested that with Kasimov and Natasha out of town, she and Lin could do a little recon at the lodge utilizing the dumbwaiter entrance into the cellar. They figured that the best time to do it would be at night when the extra guards would be patrolling the grounds, leaving only Dimitri in the cellar. The group discussed the pros and cons of such a move and decided that it should only be used as a last ditch effort prior to the projected weekend departure of the cartel representatives.

Dean concluded the briefing with a reminder that once the representatives left, they'd have to divide their efforts by sending surveillance teams to follow

each group. Any information that they might be able
to come up with before then could mean the difference between success and failure. They all agreed to
redouble their efforts.

In their private office, Dean looked at Katie with
intense blue eyes. "I'm not sure I like the idea of you
and Lin doing any recon while Dimitri and the guards
are still around."

"Well, I'm sure that when they leave, all information regarding Kasimov's plans will depart with
them." Emerald eyes returned the intensity. "Desperate times call for desperate measures." Katie softened
her tone and her look. "I'll be fine. You've given me
just about every 'toy' imaginable to keep me safe.
And that last one is definitely a good insurance policy
against discovery."

"Yeah, but will you be able to use it?" Glacial
blues peered back at the emeralds across from her.

"If I have to, I will," Katie said with certainty.
With that, she crossed the short distance to her partner
and put her arms around Dean's neck. Looking up
into the blues once more, she pulled her down into a
passionate kiss. "We'll be careful, love. I promise."

Dean held the young woman tightly for what
seemed like hours, then slowly released her grasp and
put her forehead against Katie's, noses touching gently. She closed her eyes and inhaled deeply before
opening them and replying. "You'd better be careful,
or so help me...the rivers from here to New York City
will run red with my vengeance!"

In an effort to lighten the mood a bit, Katie
looked up at Dean and winked, then said, "Well,
you're lucky that it's been a mild winter, or the rivers
around here wouldn't be running anywhere." She
paused then pulled away, abruptly smacking herself in

the forehead as she did so. "I can't believe I didn't think of this before!" she said excitedly.

Dean, in the meantime, was totally confused by the unexpected change in her lover. "C'mon!" Katie grabbed Dean's hand and dragged her out of the office and over to where Bruce was working with his team.

"Bruce!" she hollered over as they approached. "Pull out your maps again!"

Bruce looked up when his name was called and saw the two women rushing over to his area. "Yeah, sure." He reached up for the maps and spread them out on the table. Dean and Bruce stood by as Katie reviewed the maps.

"Oh, yeah...yeah," Katie muttered as she pored over the maps. "I think I know how Kasimov is distributing his drug."

Dean, Bruce, and now Gus were watching the young agent as she finally turned to face them. "Look at this map and tell me what you see," Katie said as she moved over to give them all adequate space to view the map she had selected. They looked down at the map, then up at her, then back down at the map. Dean was the first one to get it.

"I think you've got it," Dean said to Katie "It makes perfect sense now."

Bruce and Gus were still looking at the map and then they finally said in unison, "Got what?"

"Look." Katie pointed to the map. "Here, here, here, and finally, here. They're all part of the Catskills Watershed. The watershed is owned by New York City. It's their water supply!" Heads started nodding in understanding. "These three reservoirs," she pointed them out on the map, "the Cannonsville, Pepacton and Neversink send their water into the Roundout. From there, it travels 85 miles through the Delaware Aqueduct to New York City!" The four of them studied the map a bit longer as Katie continued, "What if Kasimov placed those canisters in these reservoirs with a timer to release the drug on a prescribed date? This water is used daily by millions of people in the city. We already know that the drugs in the canisters were highly concentrated; we just didn't factor in the possibility of diluting them before they reached their intended targets." Katie finished speaking, then searched their eyes for comprehension, smiling when she found it.

Dean was the first to comment. "Good work, Katie. This may be the break we've been waiting for." She reached over and gave the blonde a hug.

Bruce spoke up. "But why wouldn't he have just contaminated the water supply with his drugs closer to the city instead of all the way up here?"

"My guess is that it would be easier to do here since there is less security around these reservoirs," the tall agent commented. "Just look at the size of them. There's no way they could be patrolled. It would have been a piece of cake for Kasimov."

"Yeah, and people are still allowed to use them for fishing. Rowboats are on them all the time," Katie supplied. "No one would have taken any notice of him. He could have gained access just about anywhere. He probably placed them right after the scientists filled them in the lab. That way, he didn't have to store them or chance having them discovered before they could be placed."

"Well," said Bruce, "there's only one way to find out if you're right. I'll take a dive team down to the Neversink Reservoir in the morning and check it out. Maybe we'll get lucky and find them still full."

"Better wear full dry suits, Bruce. We don't want any of your team absorbing any of that stuff if it's already in the water," Dean added. "And start closest to the intakes."

"Right you are, Colonel." Bruce departed to prepare his team and get on the phone to have the needed diving equipment sent up from Quantico immediately.

"Chances are, they've already released their loads," Gus said as he looked down at the map again. "But at least we know who will be affected." The enormity of the situation finally hit them. "Millions of people! How on earth are we going to stop millions of people? And when?" Gus asked in a muted whisper, as he raised his head from the map and looked into intense blue eyes.

"We'll just have to figure that out too, my friend." Dean reached out and patted his shoulder. "And, before it's too late."

Thursday, 0700 hours

The dive equipment arrived at 0500 hours, and Bruce and his team checked it all out to insure that it was working properly. By 0700 hours, the team—along with Dean and Gus—were on their way to the Neversink Reservoir in two vans. One held the team and their gear while the other had the communications set-up.

"You know, Bruce," Dean said as the men unloaded their tanks. "We should be thankful that you don't have to chop through a few feet of ice to get in. I guess the mild weather does have its benefits."

"It's still gonna be damn cold, but these suits will help. They're a closed system suit—no water can get in." He smiled as he donned his gear. "Alright, guys, let's do it!" The five-man team entered the water and began their search. The team could communicate with each other using some special gear he had selected. That made the search a bit easier since they could spread out and cover more area, and still stay in contact.

Dean and Gus entered the communications van and waited for the team to report in. While waiting, they discussed the perplexity of the problem they were facing. Kasimov was subjecting millions of people to his mind control drug. Once the drug was stimulated to act on the nervous system, he would literally have an army of people at his command. The sheer thought of the havoc he could wreak was frightening; perhaps that had been his intention all along: to show the world his power by bringing one of the mega centers of the world to its knees. They were running out of time. They had only four days before the cartels would be in place, ready for their instructions. Whatever Kasimov was planning would be happening shortly thereafter. At least Lin was on the inside. That should give them a tiny window of opportunity, provided they knew what to do with it. They had to find out what caused the drug to activate, and they needed a way to neutralize it. Without those two pieces of information, they would be hard pressed to come up with a happy ending.

"Colonel." It was Bruce's voice over the speaker.

"I'm here, Bruce. What have you found?"

"Your partner is right on the money. So far I've found at least a hundred of the canisters." Dean could hear the rest of the team reporting in on the numbers of canisters in their quadrants. "My bet is there must be thousands, not hundreds, of these things."

"Have they released the drug yet?" Gus asked quickly.

"Looks like mine are all empty," came Bruce's reply. The same response was coming in from the rest of his team.

"Okay, Bruce, bring your team in. At least we know the answer to the 'who' part of the question now." Then she added as an afterthought, "And bring one of those canisters up with you."

"Yes, Ma'am," Bruce responded and then gave the order for his team to surface and return to the vehicles.

"Well, Gus, that cinches it!" Dean said as she shook her head in dismay.

****

"We'll do the best we can, Colonel, but you'd better start praying for a miracle," was Dr. Randall's reply to Dean's request to find a means to neutralize the drug. "It certainly would be a lot easier if we knew what activated it."

"Then call in reinforcements!" Dean shouted. "Just get me something I can work with!"

"Colonel...Dean..." came the soft voice of Dr. Berg. "We'll do the best we can. You can count on that. Now that we have an actual specimen of the drug, maybe that will help. Maybe the one we replicated isn't exactly the same. We'll get the answers you need."

"I know...I'm sorry. It's just..." Dean stopped and just shook her head.

"It's okay, Colonel. We're all feeling that way right now." Dr. Berg gave Dean's arm a gentle squeeze, then turned to leave the court building with Dr. Randall.

Dean inhaled slowly to calm her nerves. This was probably the most complex case she had ever worked

in her life. She had had nothing but a string of suc-
cesses her entire military career, and now she was facing failure. She couldn't fail now. Too much was
riding on her ability to know what to do. But what if
she failed? How could she ever face her superiors?
How could she ever face Katie? *Well, damn it all to
hell! I just won't fail. Not now... not ever! I can't let
Kasimov win. Not this time.* Her mind made up, Dean
turned and went over to the surveillance section
where Gus and his crew were working feverishly to
find the drug's stimulus.

"Anything happening at the lodge?" She inquired
as she approached.

"Same old, same old," Gus replied. "Doesn't
seem to be much interaction between the participants.
They must all be getting ready to head out on Saturday morning to meet up with their counterparts."

"Knowing Kasimov, he probably slapped on a gag
order to keep the flow of information between groups
at a minimum," Dean told the technology leader. "As
much as I hate to, I'm going to give Katie permission
to do some sleuthing with Lin tomorrow night.
Maybe then we'll get some answers."

"It's the only thing you can do at this point, Colonel," Gus answered. "That's one sharp young
agent...and with the insider, well...all we can do is
hope."

****

"Their granddaughter had the emergency surgery
this afternoon. She came through with flying colors,
but they want to go to Rochester and see her." Katie
was filling Dean in on the chain of events concerning
the lodge caretakers. "I offered to stay at the lodge

until they come back from Rochester on Monday morning, and Mr. G approved."

Dean just looked at her skeptically. This was too much of a coincidence in her book. "Okay. So you get to stay for a couple of nights. That's good cover for a little snooping, but it just seems too convenient, if you ask me."

"Oh, come on, Dean...how could Kasimov possibly set up an emergency appendectomy?" Katie's emerald eyes pinned Dean's ice blues with a very valid argument.

"You're right, you're right. But I've asked Beth to contact the hospital in Rochester to check it out...just in case." Dean gave in, raising her arms and shaking her long dark hair, but added, "Just, the two of you be careful. Don't take any chances, okay?"

"Yes, Ma'am!" came the retort from Katie as she whipped out a salute causing Dean to grimace a bit, but then smile at her young partner. "I've pretty much got the laser security beams all located, and that can of stuff you gave me will help us out in case I missed some. The dumbwaiter will be our main means of getting up and down between the lodge floors. There are definitely no surveillance cameras or bugs of any kind in it."

"If at all possible, stay away from Dimitri. Don't let him even catch a whiff of you down there. And pay attention to the breaks the guards take. They've been pretty regular so far, but be ready for any change in their routine." The tall agent was all business now as she and Katie went over the plans for the sleuthing, deciding on protocols in case they got into trouble. "We'll keep watching from here, but remember, we can't penetrate the cellar. If you get into trouble, one of you will have to somehow get topside to warn us."

"Is there any kind of a wire I can wear that won't be detected by Dimitri?"

"Can't chance it." The tall agent shook her head. "I don't know how sophisticated his equipment is, but I'd bet it's the best," Dean replied. "At least there won't be too many of the cartel groups left at the lodge tomorrow or Saturday. That's in our favor. Less folks to trip over."

"Well, they'll all be gone by Sunday, so it's now or never," Katie supplied. "I'm sure Dimitri will be closing up shop to meet up with Kasimov and Natasha as soon as the last one is gone."

"Okay. Let's go over this all one more time, but with the rest of the task force." Dean rose and called the teams over to the briefing area. They went over the plan several times before they were all satisfied, and the two Doctor's reviewed the latest weapon in Katie's arsenal with her until she fully understood the ramifications of using it.

"The results are very realistic, and the pain accompanied by its use is too," Beth told her old friend. "Believe me, a bullet is much kinder but, unfortunately, too obvious."

"Last resort only," Katie murmured as she placed the lethal weapon in her backpack. "Too bad I won't have my trusty old Glock with me. I hate using these other things. Just not as comfortable with them, I guess." She raised her head and looked into her old friend's eyes.

"The best thing for you to remember, Katie, is to keep a healthy respect for all weapons." Beth took Katie's hands in hers and gently squeezed them. "Good luck and be safe!" Then the doctor rose and exited the area as Dean approached, returning from a phone call with General James.

"Well," Dean said as she sat down in a chair next to Katie, "that was General James. He's not too happy with our progress."

"Neither am I," commented the blonde, "but it's all we've got for now."

"Oh, he's dealing," Dean informed her. "He just hates it when things go down to the wire."

The two women sat there a bit longer going over the past few weeks in their minds and trying to find that one piece of information that would give them an edge. By 2230 hours, they gave up and decided to head for home and for what might be their last bit of peace and quiet for a while.

Friday, 1000 hours...Christmas Eve Day

"Okay, sweetie, I think Ezra has everything in the car and is ready to go." El looked out the back door window to see Ezra motioning for her to come out. "The caterer will be bringing in all the meals about thirty minutes before they're supposed to be served. Just throw them in the ovens and keep them warm until serving time."

"I really can cook," Katie said for the fifth time.

"I know, sweetie. This will just make things a little easier on you and Darla, that's all." El gave Katie a hug. "Now if you need anything else, just call Mr. G., okay?"

Katie nodded and walked El out to the car. The weather was fairly mild so far, but they were predicting rain, possibly sleet by early evening. Katie opened the door for El and handed her the thermos of coffee she had put together for them. "Just a little something to keep you warm," she said, as El took the offering and smiled. "Now you drive carefully, Ezra.

The weather is supposed to be turning nasty here, but from the looks of it, you should be ahead of it most of the way."

"Yup, it's coming up the coast line... just like a 'Nor'easter. You better hope it stays as rain. It doesn't take much to shut this town down." Ezra started up the old Buick. His parting words were, "Remember where the emergency back-up switch is!" Then he put the car in gear, and they drove off towards the Quickway. Katie waved and watched them go before she headed back indoors. *Just our luck—the weather is deciding to turn now,* she muttered to herself as she walked back into the kitchen. *Well, at least I won't have to drive home in it.*

The caterer arrived precisely thirty minutes before lunch was to be served. It turned out that it was the same caterer that she had worked for in her spare time, so the exchange went pleasantly. Darla and Katie served the lunch and then Darla cleaned up the lunch dishes while Katie went upstairs to tackle the rooms that had been vacated that morning. *Well, instead of the whole group for dinner, we'll be down to only twelve. By tomorrow, we'll be down to only six—Ito's group and the Chi Chong group from China. I think I can handle this.* She was in the middle of finishing Trina's room when she felt a presence behind her. She picked up her clipboard and selected the red pen and nonchalantly started checking off items on her task sheet before she turned around.

"Oh...hi!" She feigned surprise as she bumped into Ito. "Is there anything I can do for you, Mr. Sukazi?"

"Oh no. Not now. But later perhaps we could...?" He let the sentence trail off leaving the innuendo hanging for Katie to pick up.

Inwardly Katie cringed as she picked up his intention, while outwardly she was all charm. "Gee, Mr.
Sukazi...I'd love to, but El and Ezra had a family
emergency to attend to, and they left me in charge. I
couldn't disappoint them by ignoring my duties. It
wouldn't be the honorable thing to do."

It seemed that appealing to 'honor' was the right
tack to use. He said he understood, bowed, and
turned to leave. As he left, he turned over his shoulder and said smiling, "I guess that means that Lin will
be alone tonight."

Damn! thought Katie, *now we've got to deal with
Ito all over again! Maybe Lin can slip him a mickey
or something. Well, her room is next, so maybe we
can come up with a solution.*

****

Back at the courts, Dean and Gus were keeping a
close eye on the lodge and Katie. They were
impressed that Katie had things going so smoothly.
She certainly is a jack of all trades, thought the tall
agent, *definitely good talents for an undercover
agent.* Bruce and the two docs were computing the
odds that the drugs released in the water system
would be too diluted to be effective, while Bruce had
his team checking out the Roundout reservoir for canisters too. They were expected back shortly. Knowing Kasimov, they realized that the odds were in his
favor and not theirs, but they kept hoping anyway.
They all looked up as Bruce's team leader came in.
The dive leader spotted Dean and immediately headed
over to her.

"Colonel." Dave saluted. "I'm afraid the news
isn't good." By this time Bruce, Gus, and the docs
were there to hear Dave's report. "There must be at

least another five to six hundred of those things in the Roundout, too. And if I were a betting man, I'd say they're in all of the reservoirs up here. That bastard wasn't taking any chances."

Dean just nodded at the report. She looked at the docs, but before she had a chance to say anything, Beth said that they'd redouble their efforts to find the stimulus...and Leigh said she'd work on a way to block the drugs reaction on the nervous system.

Dave spoke up again, "There's something else, Colonel. The weather's going to be a factor real soon. Forget the rain and possible sleet that was predicted. We've got a humdinger of a blizzard developing out there."

This piece of information took them all by surprise. Since there were no windows in the building to speak of, they didn't even think of the weather. All eyes immediately turned to the entrance door as the last of the dive team came in. When the door swung open, all they could see was a wall of white behind an ambulatory snowman. Four voices, all on cue, proclaimed a resounding, "Oh Shit!"

* * * * * * * * * *

"Tracy, it's Dell on line one."
"Thanks, Linna, we've been expecting this one." Tracy picked up the phone and began talking with her boss. The weather was not a big surprise for Tracy and her staff. They had been getting ready since seven-thirty in the morning. Linna had an uncanny ability to predict weather—better than the weather-men—so they had already began converting the senior center into an emergency shelter. Byron was busy getting the big park truck loaded with sand, and had already attached the plow. His last job for now was to

bring in the frozen food supply from the park concessions building. By the time Tracy finished her conversation with the Town Supervisor, Linna finished bringing in the last of the blankets.

"Bet he was surprised that we're already ready," Linna said, as she piled the blankets she was carrying on the first available cot.

"Yep! Very impressed to say the least." Tracy gave Linna a big smile. "I don't know how you do it, but you sure make me look good."

"You just be glad I like you, or you wouldn't be looking so good." The two women chuckled as they finished making up the last batch of cots.

"Well, if the power stays up, we won't have too many guests; but if it goes out, we're one of the few buildings in town with a back-up power supply. Speaking of supply, how's the food supply?"

"Byron should be back any minute with the stuff from the concession stand, and with what we have from the nutrition site, we should be okay," Linna replied as they went down the back stairs to the office. "In fact, I think that's him pulling in now."

Just then, Byron came into the hallway carrying several containers of burritos. "We'll get our coats on and give you a hand," Tracy shouted, as she and Linna went to get their gear.

"Man, it's coming down like crazy! It's a good thing I put the chains on," Byron said as the three of them made a short assembly line, passing the boxes of food through the recreation room door. "This one's going to be a real bear! I brought over the ATV, too."

"Good thinking, Byron. Hope you weren't planning on going home tonight," Tracy said over her shoulder. "I'm afraid we're all going to be here for the duration."

"Nah. You've got all my favorite foods here; why should I go home?"

They all laughed and then transferred the boxes once more into the storage room that was, thankfully, unheated and would keep everything good and cold.

****

Having finished Trina's room, Katie went next to Lin's room. Knocking and entering, she found Lin working at her desk. She exchanged pleasantries as she cleaned the room and then went into the bath to clean there. Lin followed her in and asked if she could have some new towels, handing her the dirty ones. As Katie took them, she felt a paper thrust into her hand under the towels. She closed her fist on it and took the dirty towels out to her cart in the hall, managing to transfer the note to her pocket in the process. When she went back in with the clean towels, Lin was back at her desk working on her daily haiku. Katie watched the graceful penmanship as Lin wrote in traditional Japanese style.

"The Japanese symbols are very artistic." Katie stepped closer behind Lin.

"Yes, they are. Each stroke, if not done correctly, can completely change the meaning. I find it very relaxing to work on them," Lin answered as she looked up at Katie.

"I would find that very stressful," Katie commented. "Speaking of stress, I will be staying here tonight for the Schlotts while they are away." Katie leaned down to hide her head from the camera angle and whispered to Lin as she made it appear she was examining the symbols more closely. "Ito has plans for you tonight. Got anything to get rid of him?" Then out loud she said, "I think your haiku are beauti-

ful!" As she raised her head she got a barely percep-
tible nod from Lin who responded with a simple
"Thank you."

"Well, I guess I'd better get back to work. If you
need anything, just let me know." Katie gathered her
cleaning supplies and turned to leave. Lin just continued her graceful strokes on the parchment as the
door closed behind her.

As Katie put her cart back in the linen room, she
transferred the note under the pages on her clipboard,
and began sending the dirty laundry down the chute to
the laundry room next to the pantry in the kitchen.
On her way down the back stairs, she lifted the sheets
of her clipboard and studied the note as though she
was reviewing her checklist of duties. The note said
simply, "must go tonight." Katie was hoping they
could put it off until Saturday, but Lin must have a
good reason for going tonight. *Well, let's hope she
can take care of Ito before midnight when we agreed
to meet.*

The rest of the afternoon went smoothly, especially since there were only the twelve guests left.
Unfortunately, the weather was not going as smoothly
as everything else. Instead of the expected rain and
possible sleet, the precipitation came down in the
form of snow—heavy, wet snow. And it was quickly
piling up. The caterer showed up early with the dinner meal. It was a good thing she had a four wheel
drive vehicle, since there were at least six inches of
the stuff on the ground, and not a let up in sight. Carrie, the caterer, agreed to contact a friend who did
plowing on the side to come and plow the circular
drive by morning so that the guests that were leaving
would be able to do so. Having taken care of that situation, Katie sent Darla home with Carrie so she
wouldn't get stuck at the lodge for the night. *No*

sense having any innocent bystanders around, Katie thought to herself...*just in case.* She took her time cleaning up after dinner so she wouldn't have to wait long before her meeting with Lin. After that, she served espresso and after dinner drinks to the few guests that were still in the lounge. She was about to return to the kitchen when Ito came up to her.

"Excuse me." Ito said with a frown, as he was obviously plagued with an abdominal spasm. "Would you have anything that I might take for an upset stomach?"

"Oh, Mr. Sukazi," Katie answered in a concerned voice. "Are you coming down with something?"

"No, no. I'm sure it's just indigestion. Perhaps the meal was a little too rich for me," he explained, as another spasm took him.

"I'll go see what I can find right away." The young woman headed for the kitchen. "Why don't you go up to your room. I'll bring it to you."

Just then, Lin came up behind Ito. "Ito, are you not well? Perhaps we should postpone our plans for tonight." Concern and caring just oozed from her voice as she looked up at Katie and winked.

"Yes, yes!" he said quickly. "Lin, please go with her and bring the medicine to me."

"Yes, Ito," Lin said as she gently pushed Katie towards the kitchen.

"Will he be okay?" Katie whispered as they entered the kitchen.

Lin just smiled and shrugged, whispering back, "I'm sure it will pass by morning."

Katie went through the cupboards and found some Pepto Bismol and asked Lin if that would do. She merely smiled, then said it probably wouldn't help. Nothing would until it ran its course. Lin took the Pepto and a large spoon, then left to deliver it to Ito.

Guess we won't have to worry about Ito tonight! Katie thought, as she went back into the lounge to see if anyone needed anything else before she called it a night. Most of the guests were concerned about the accumulating snow, but she assured them that the plow would be there at daybreak or sooner, and they would all make their travel connections. *This may just work in our favor*, she thought. *If they can't get out of here, then Kasimov may have to cancel his plans. Well, it's a nice thought, anyway.*

****

Katie spent the rest of the evening in her room, actually the Schlott's apartment, going over her "toys" and making sure the guards did indeed go out on their nocturnal patrol. She picked up the latest addition to her arsenal, cradling it respectfully as she recalled Beth's instructions on how to use it in a close quarters confrontation. Its construction was similar to a field medic's drug administration syringe in its simplicity. Just jab at your opponent and it's in, but the results—an immediate heart attack—were not to be taken lightly. It was as deadly as a well-aimed bullet. Hoping that she wouldn't have to use it, she returned the dose pack to her pocket along with her two pens.

At precisely five minutes before midnight, Katie left the Schlott's modest apartment, passed through the kitchen, and entered the pantry. She stopped to pick up a small flashlight to add to her equipment for the night's sleuthing. Previous surveillance on the lodge showed the guards patrolling from eleven p.m. to five a.m. Of course, they didn't have to put up with a blizzard before. Katie hoped that they would be holed up in the shed outside rather than trying to brave the elements on their normal patrol route. As she slid back the secret panel, she fervently hoped that the dumbwaiter was also a mute. It wouldn't do to make a noisy entrance at the second floor linen closet. Katie switched the flashlight on to look for a light in the small space. There was none, so she kept the flashlight on. She entered the dumbwaiter, slid the hidden panel closed, crossed her fingers, turned the directional lever to up, and hit the green "start" button. To her relief, there was only a soft hum and a slight jerk before the apparatus started its slow climb to the next floor.

Great! How do I know when I'm there? Wonder if it will stop automatically or just keep going? "Now's a fine time to be thinking of that," she muttered to herself. "Guess I'll just find out when it stops." A few seconds passed, and then it finally stopped. Slowly Katie looked at the wall in front of her for any sign of where she was. On the wall, about eye level, she could barely see the number "2". *Aha! Must be on the second floor. Now, how do I get out?*

She gently felt the wall in front for some kind of a latch or locking system and then remembered that the pantry entrance was a sliding panel. She pushed to her left first, without any success and then tried again to her right. This time the panel slid open, and she found herself at the back of the linen closet. The tricky part coming up would be to exit the closet and hug the wall until she reached the statue with the surveillance lens. Once there, she had something that would circumvent the camera.

Gus had designed a holder for a picture she had taken of the hall from that angle. The miracle of digital cameras and computers turned that daytime shot into a nighttime one. She could only hope that Dimitri wasn't looking at that particular camera view when

she made the switch. It took her about five more minutes to complete the set-up and wait long enough to
see if she had aroused a response before she decided it
was safe to go to Lin's room. She had already given
Lin holders and pictures for the two lenses in her
room that were fabricated at the temporary headquarters by Gus and his technology wizards. They were
very believable; Katie only hoped they were in place
before she entered the room.

Lin was waiting by the door when Katie slowly
entered. She almost made a sound when she felt Lin's
hand on her shoulder as she stepped in, but managed
to swallow it. Using hand signals, Katie led Lin to
the linen closet and into the dumbwaiter, before she
spoke.

Katie was finally able to ask Lin why there had
been a change of plans. After Lin explained, Katie
asked her how long ago she made the switch on the
lens.

"About forty-five minutes ago. If Dimitri saw it,
he didn't react to it," Lin replied in a soft voice.

"Good. This thing doesn't make too much noise,
but in the dead of night, he may hear something.
We'd better be prepared for a confrontation when we
get to the cellar." With that, Katie handed Lin an
extra set of pens, one black and one red, and went
through their operation. When they were comfortable
with the set-up, she moved the lever to "down," and
hit the green button. Again there was a slight hum, a
subtle jerk, and the descent. The dumbwaiter stopped
at the first floor; then Katie hit the button once more
to descend into the cellar.

"El said this will let out behind the chimney. Do
you remember where that is in respect to the control
room?"

Lin nodded. "The chimney is in the room they used for a lab. The control room is on the other side of the building. We should be in the clear...at least for a little while."

****

The senior center-turned-relief shelter had only three customers by early evening. A young couple and their child had come in for shelter when they ran out of fuel oil in their small trailer. Linna got them settled down in the back, and she and Tracy were about ready to crash for the night when Tracy's cell phone chirped. She looked at her watch and noted that it was only 9:00 PM. *Maybe it's Col,* Tracy thought, as she flipped open the phone.

"Yeah?" Tracy said into the phone.

"It's Dean. Can you have Byron come up and plow us out first thing in the morning?"

"Sure thing. When do you want it done?" Tracy asked.

"As soon as possible, but at least by daybreak."

"Are you expecting any trouble tonight? I can have Byron run up now and do a quick plow."

"No, nothing on the agenda till tomorrow night, but I'll feel better if we can mobilize if necessary." Dean thanked Tracy then hung up.

"Problems?" Linna inquired.

"Nope." *At least not yet,* Tracy thought. "Time to hit the sack...better get some rest while we can." Then she got up and headed to an empty cot. Byron was already snoozing away and it didn't take long for Tracy to follow. Linna on the other hand, was not tired yet so she decided to watch some TV downstairs.

As she entered the office, she had a second thought and decided to watch a different kind of TV...it was now just after midnight.

****

The task force was pretty much snowed in at the court building. They didn't have the equipment for snow removal, so they were waiting it out until morning when Tracy would send Byron over with the plow truck. After calling Tracy earlier to make the arrangements, Dean had watched the monitor most of the evening. When it appeared that Katie was going to call it a night, she headed to the office. The venture into the cellar was slated for the following night, so she decided to catch a few minutes of shuteye while things were calm. The calm, however, didn't last. She had been asleep for about forty-five minutes when Sarah, one of Gus's team members, came knocking on the office door.

Sarah's voice was subdued so as not to disturb the other agents that were trying to get some sleep. "Colonel. You'd better get out here. There're people on the move in the lodge, and one of them is Katie."

Dean thought she was dreaming at first and then became fully alert when the knock turned into a loud bang. She flew off the cot and ran to the door just about pulling the young female agent off of her feet, as Sarah had decided to open the door at the same time Dean had.

"What did you say?" Dean looked at the startled agent through bloodshot eyes. Sarah caught her breath and repeated her message. "Go get Gus and Bruce," the colonel ordered as she ran to the surveillance sets. A few minutes later, Dean, Bruce, and Gus were glued to the monitor watching the blue dot move from the Schlott's apartment to various stops, until there were now two ethereal bodies moving on the screen.

"What the hell is going on? I thought the recon was set for tomorrow night?" muttered a sleepy Gus.

"Yeah, well, things have a way of changing. Something must have come up, or they would be waiting until tomorrow."

They were glad to hear the whispered comments coming from Lin and Katie. They overheard Lin telling Katie that the change was necessary because Ito had decided to leave for Newark in the morning. Seems he was anxious to get moving, and doing something productive for a change.

"Guess that explains it," Bruce commented. "Now let's hope they can get us some good information and get out without Dimitri or the guards walking in on them."

* * * * * * * * *

The dumbwaiter stopped descending after another few seconds. Lin and Katie waited for an additional thirty seconds before she slid the partition open as quietly as possible. The lab was dark, so Katie hooded the flashlight with her hands to narrow the beam of light. "Are there any windows in this room that could be seen by Dimitri in the control room?"

Lin stopped to think, then shook her head in the negative. She whispered back to Katie that the room was solid concrete, had a row of tables along the back wall and another in the center of the room, then a third row against the next wall. The area to the right was where Kasimov had set up desks and filing cabinets.

The two women cautiously entered the lab, spilling only what light was necessary for them to keep from bumping into things. They silently made their way over to the desks and began going through them one at a time, searching for any information that could possibly be useful. When they got to the third desk, they hit a minor vein of information. Most of it was already known by the doctors working on the drug, but the amount of the drug produced in this lab was enormous.

"My God!" Katie whispered. "He made enough of this stuff to drug half the people on the East Coast!" They waded through some more papers, and Lin found the maps Kasimov had used for the deployment of the canisters. They showed the location of each one of the reservoirs, and the sites where the canisters were dumped. They also listed the release times for each reservoir. "Too bad the guys already went diving this morning," Katie told Lin. "We could have saved them the trouble. Looks like Kasimov wants to get the entire city on this stuff."

Lin nodded as they moved over to the filing cabinets. The first one was unlocked and had a lot of miscellaneous stuff in it, like receipts for chemical deliveries, the canisters and timers, etc. It also had a file on each of the guests at the lodge. Katie was amused to see a file on the staff too. She opened hers and found only the information that she and Dean had planted for her cover story. *Guess he didn't have time to do an in-depth study on me. Too bad, he might have found me interesting reading.*

The second file cabinet was locked. Katie was not expecting to pick any locks, so she hadn't brought her picks with her. Lin, on the other hand, came prepared for any eventuality. She pulled out her set of picks and, in fifteen seconds, had the cabinet unlocked and started going through the top drawer.

"This looks like it might be the mother lode," Katie whispered over her shoulder noting that the files were records of experiments on the mind control drug, most stamped with the word "FAILURE" in red ink. Now all they had to do was find the one that was the winner. It took them less than five minutes to find it.

It was in the third drawer of the four-drawer stack. They took the file over to the closest desk and flipped through it quickly. Katie broke into their perusal of the documents and suggested that they take it up to the kitchen and away from Dimitri, just in case he decided to check the rooms. They moved quickly back to the dumbwaiter, slid the door shut and started to ascend. Once they got back to the kitchen, they sat at the table and started reading. They did not notice the door open, or Dimitri and one of the guards walk in.

"So that's how it's activated!" Katie whispered. "We may have never figured it out in time."

"Yes," Lin said turning the pages to read on.

"Yes...it is rather unique isn't it?" said Dimitri in what seemed like a thunderous voice.

The two women immediately jumped up. Assessing the situation, Lin and Katie stepped away from the table and each other, making their opponents split their efforts too.

****

Dean looked up at Gus when she heard Katie's voice mention the activation of the mind control drug. "Thank God!" Dean said, but before they could turn back to the conversation, the entire building went black. A few red emergency lights went on, throwing an eerie glow over the large room.

"What..." Bruce stammered.

"Oh, shit! Not now!" Dean shouted. "Somebody hit the back-up switch!"

"Damn it!" was the exclamation from Gus, followed by, "There is no back-up switch!"

"What the fuck do you mean?" Dean looked incredulously at him. "You didn't put in an emergency back-up system?"

"Uh...no. Actually, they didn't have one to send up...uumm...it was supposed to come in today," Gus stuttered and started backing up as Dean approached him. "Colonel, it was out of my control...the storm..."

Dean stopped in front of him and pinned him with her ice blue eyes before speaking. "You should have told me. I could have found temporary generators for the essential equipment. Now it's too late."

"Maybe the power will be back up shortly," Bruce offered.

"We'd better hope it is," Dean said as she stalked off to her office to check if the land phones were still working.

****

Linna was in the surveillance room thoroughly engrossed in watching the two ghostly bodies move on the screen. She had realized that the second voice was not Dean's, but assumed that it was another undercover agent. When the agents went into the cellar, she lost them and started to panic, adjusting the dials every which way she could think of. After about ten minutes, she reset the dials to where they had been when she lost them, and found them again. The two women were talking about activating something when she heard another voice over the headphones. The power went off at that instant and then the back-up generator kicked on. She continued to listen to the stranger's voice. He had a very distinguished accent—foreign, but not one that could be easily placed...and he didn't sound friendly. This point was made perfectly clear when she heard him order the women to go with him. She now saw four of the wraithlike bodies on the screen, one with a blue dot on it. Two of them made some quick moves, and she could hear scraping and sounds like blows being struck along with several grunts. One of the larger bodies suddenly became motionless, and the smaller one, with the blue dot, went towards the other two. Then she heard voices again.

"Stop right there, or I'll put a bullet in her!" came the unknown man's voice. The blue dot stopped. "You have some nice moves for a maid!" he said.

"I take karate lessons," Katie shot back and then started to slowly walk forward.

"Don't, Katie. This isn't your fight. I shouldn't have talked you into this," Lin cried out, then turned to address

Dimitri. "Leave her out of this, she's just a little diversion of mine!"

"Really?   Now why should I believe that?" the man's voice interrupted.

Linna could hear the other woman's voice scream and then heard Katie shout for him to stop. As Linna watched the screen, she noticed another body image appear behind the body marked by the blue dot. A voice started to shout and then got muffled. The next thing she heard was a "thunk" and the blue dot was motionless with the new image next to it.

"I'm sure glad to see you, Natasha. How did you get back here?" Dimitri asked as he lifted Lin to carry her to the cellar.

"Andre was getting worried about the snow...wanted to make sure the rest of his cartel people got out in time to meet his deadlines. As soon as the snow stopped, he sent me in his private helicopter to check things out," Natasha told Dimitri as she dragged Katie to the cellar stairs.

"Well, it's a good thing you showed up when you did. Now let's get them back to the cellar."

Linna watched in horror as the bodies all disappeared from the screen along with their voices.

Oh shit! Now what? Do I go get Tracy and tell her? Damn! I can't let this go. Gotta get Tracy. Linna jumped up and ran upstairs to wake Tracy. When she got Tracy awake, she whispered for her to follow her. After she got her downstairs, she quickly told her boss what she had done and the gist of the situation she overheard.

"Damn!" Tracy reached for her phone and dialed Dean's cell phone. It was answered almost immediately.

"Dean, it's Tracy. Have you been watching?"

"Until we lost power. We don't have a back-up in place yet. It was supposed to get here today. What's happening?" Dean asked with a noticeable edge to her voice.

"You need to get here, fast. They've been compromised. I'll get Byron over to pick you up ASAP"

"Right. I'll be ready." Dean hung up and ran out to the court. "Bruce! Over here on the double."

Bruce was there in a heartbeat, and Dean filled him in. They both decided to go to the Parks & Rec office when Byron got there. Bruce went to his second-in-command and filled him in. He gave him instructions for the team to assemble as soon as Byron could get back to plow them out. He grabbed his weapons duffel and went to Dean's office.

"They'll be ready when Byron gets them plowed out, Colonel. We shouldn't need reinforcements. There are only a few of the cartel people left, and five of Kasimov's. We can handle it."

"Okay. But tell them to make it quick." Bruce left to give additional information to his second and then returned to the office. Dean got out her Glock, checked the clip and took extra shells, clips, and her silencer. They were already waiting outside when Byron arrived. The snowfall had stopped, but the wind was beginning to pick up, blowing waist high drifts in the open areas. The trip back only took ten minutes, but to Dean it seemed like an eternity. The roads were thick with snow, and drifts were develop-

ing rapidly. This doubled the normal five-minute
ride, but the big 4X4 truck made it without too much
trouble. As soon as Dean and Bruce got out, Byron
turned the truck around and went back to plow out the
others.

Dean led Bruce to the surveillance room and
found Tracy and Linna waiting there. Quick intros,
then Dean went straight to the tape and rewound the
last hour of tape. They all sat there in silence, listening and watching. When it finished, Dean turned to
Linna.

"I'm sorry," Linna started. "I just couldn't control my curiosity. I knew things weren't right, so I
started poking around in here."

"How long have you been 'poking around'?" Dean
asked, staring at Linna.

"About two weeks, maybe a bit more," she
answered honestly.

Tracy asked the next question. "Who else
knows?"

"No one, honest, just me," Linna went on. "I
didn't even tell Kelly...or Byron."

"Good," Dean cut in. "Linna, I can't approve of
what you've been doing. If you had suspicions, you
should have just come out with it and trusted Tracy.
Your 'poking' could have cost lives." She paused and
then added. "But it looks like this time...you may
have saved some...if we can get there in time. Thank
you." Then she smiled at Linna. "You've got great
instincts. Too bad you're stuck here with Tracy."

Linna breathed a sigh of relief and then asked if
she could be filled in on what the hell was going on.
Tracy and Bruce looked at Dean, who shrugged and

said she might as well know the full story. Tracy filled her in while Dean and Bruce, waiting for the rest of the team to get there, continued the surveillance.

****

When Katie came to, she found herself lying on a cot with her head in Lin's lap. They were locked up in one of the old storage rooms that Kasimov must have converted to very Spartan sleeping quarters, probably for the scientists first, and then for the guards.

"Ooww. That hurts," the young blonde said softly. "How long have I been out?"

"About five minutes," Lin informed her.

"Who hit me? And where did he come from?"

"*She* hit you...Natasha. And she came down the back staircase."

"What? How did she get here? It's been snowing like a banshee in heat all day!" Katie tried to sit up, but the pain sent her back into Lin's lap.

"Sorry, I tried to warn you, but he stopped me," Lin informed Katie. "Looks like you'll just be suffering from a rather nasty bump on your head. You really shouldn't move around too much, just in case you have a concussion, but you do need to stay awake."

"Umm, thanks." Katie stretched and found everything else working okay. "What did she hit me with...a lead pipe?"

"Close...looked like an old-fashioned meat tenderizer mallet, if you ask me. I wonder what she's doing back here?" The Oriental woman shifted on the cot. "I overheard her talking to Dimitri about destroying the files.

"Yeah, well, at least we got a look at one of the ones that counts first," Katie said with a pained chuckle. "Of course, we have to get out of here in order to make any use of it. Too bad Dean can't penetrate the cellar with all that technology. I could just tell her what we found."

"Better yet, Katie, I would rather tell her face to face," Lin said with an amused smile.

"Hey," Katie said smiling back at Lin. "Careful there. That's *my* face you're drooling over!"

"Really? You and Dean?" Lin shook her head in surprise. "So...how is the old war horse?"

"Well, the 'old war horse' is terrific! In fact, she's better than terrific...she's..."

"Okay, I get the picture." Lin stopped abruptly putting her fingers to her lips. "Shhh, someone's coming."

Katie became very still as she heard the door unlock and watched Natasha and one guard, pistol at the ready, come into the room.

Natasha strolled in and walked around the room, eyeing the two women with contempt. "Well, well. Isn't this a cozy picture?" She stopped in front of Lin and then bent low, locking her with eye contact. Lin returned the stare with a raised eyebrow and smiled. This defiant gesture enraged Natasha to the point that she lashed out at Lin with the back of her right hand, sending a violent blow to the ex-cop's cheek, causing her head to snap back and contact the concrete wall. The action caused Katie to try to sit up and charge at

Natasha, only to be stopped by the butt of the guard's
pistol as it made contact with her head. The blow
wasn't enough to cause unconsciousness, but left her
dazed and unable to respond further.

"Dimitri tells me you got the maid to help you.
My, my, you must have hidden talents I'm not aware
of." Natasha looked at Lin with a seductive smile.
"You must tell me your secrets to wooing young
blondes," the Russian said with a venomous hiss.
"Too bad she's going to have to die for you, but, Dimitri might make her last few moments fun!"

"Why don't you just leave her alone? She's just a
kid," the ex-cop said, trying to sound convincing.
"She just offered to help me get in the cellar. She
doesn't deserve to die for that."

"Oh, how touching. You should have thought of
that before you got her to help you!" Natasha spat
out. "Now it's too late for your little tart. We're
leaving now so don't try anything stupid. I have
talked to Andre, and he wants me to bring you back
with me. Seems he has something in mind for you.
Of course, he would prefer it if you arrive in one
piece, however he has left me much latitude in this
regard, should you resist." Natasha turned to the
guard and instructed him to cuff Lin and escort her to
the waiting helicopter. A second guard entered the
room and helped him, roughly dragging her up the
stairs to the main entrance.

Natasha stopped and looked at Katie, then said.
"Your mother should have taught you to beware of
strangers." She laughed and exited the room. She
stopped to give final instructions to Dimitri regarding
the destruction of all of the files and for insuring that

the rest of the cartel member's packed and left for their destinations now, rather than in the morning. She also told him to dispose of the blonde before he left. Then she grabbed her parka and headed to the main entrance. As she opened the door on frigid air, she turned and smiled at Lin. "Sorry, no time to get your coat." Then she and the guards took Lin through the blowing snow towards the helicopter. When the two women were on board, Natasha added another set of cuffs to Lin, locking her to her seat. When the guards were clear, the helicopter rose and headed into the night.

* * * * * * * * *

"Damn it! Where the hell are they!" Dean exclaimed as she paced the office.

"Easy, Colonel...it's only been twenty minutes. It takes ten to get there, and ten to get back. Plus, he's gotta plow them out," Bruce said as he continued the surveillance, switching to the outside camera since it had stopped snowing. "Hey, Colonel, look at this." They looked at the outdoor surveillance camera and watched as he spotted a helicopter in the front of the lodge. As they watched, a figure exited the lodge, followed by two guards dragging another woman.

"That looks like Natasha. What's she doing there?" Tracy asked as they continued to watch. "And who's that they're dragging?"

Dean intensified the camera power and could barely make out long dark hair through the blowing snow caused by the helicopter's props. "It's Lin," she said in a whisper so low she could barely be heard. "But where's Katie?"

Dean backed away from the TV, pain and anger showing in the lines of her face. Tracy looked up and carefully approached her friend. "Dean, she's probably all right." Her words faded as Dean focused her energy again.

"I've got to get over there now!" she said, pacing the room. "Tracy, have you got another plow truck I can use?"

"Only have the one, Dean. Byron will be here soon."

"I can't wait for Byron. I need to get there now!" The volume of Dean's voice was increasing with the level of her anxiety.

"Okay," Tracy said, trying to come up with an alternative. "Wait! Byron brought over the ATV. That'll get you there, but try to stay out of the really deep drifts or you'll get stuck," Tracy offered. "Linna, get the keys for the ATV!"

Linna ran to Tracy's office to get the keys, and Dean grabbed her parka. Bruce wanted to go with her, but Dean refused. She wasn't sure that the ATV would be able to get them both there without getting stuck. She told Bruce to follow her over as soon as Byron got back with the rest of the team. In the meantime, he was to call General James with the information about the helicopter so it could be tracked. Byron and Tracy were to lead the team to the lodge, with the plow truck going first to break through any drifts along the way. When Linna came back with the keys, Dean and Tracy went to the storage room to get the ATV out the side doors. It took three tries to get the cold machine running; then Dean roared off toward the lodge.

* * * * * * * * * *

As soon as Natasha and the guards left with Lin, Katie slowly got up and surveyed her surroundings. The rap to her head was making her very nauseous, and her balance wasn't the best, but her mental capabilities weren't affected. She admired the quick thinking on Lin's part to throw suspicion off of her. Now maybe she'd have a chance to finish the job and, hopefully, still have time to save Lin, too. She checked her pockets and found that she still had both pens and the dose pack. Katie walked over to the door and studied the lock. It was an old-fashioned skeleton key type lock. If she had her picks, she would have been out in no time flat.

Okay, time to try out one of Dean's toys, she thought, then reached up and took off one of the black earrings. She looked around the room and found a piece of paper on the small dresser. Katie carefully crushed the earring over the paper then carried the corrosive over to the door. She carefully poured some of the powder into the keyhole and then put some on the bolt by folding the paper and sliding it into the crack between the door and the frame. She turned around and spotted a half-full water bottle on the dresser. Grabbing the bottle, she folded the paper into a funnel shape and carefully poured a few drops on the two spots where the powder had been placed. In a few seconds, she heard a 'pfft' and slowly pulled on the door handle.

The door opened easily, but she was cautious and only opened it an inch or two until she could see if there was a guard outside the door. There was, but he was sitting in a chair at the end of the hall. She could hear Dimitri talking to someone in the distance, but couldn't see anyone else. She pulled out her red pen and crept quietly out of the room, hugging the wall to stay out of the guard's peripheral vision. When she was close enough, she reached out, held her breath and tapped him on the shoulder. When he turned, he received a face full of knock-out gas and immediately hit the floor.

Cool! Wish I had some of these in high school for all those back seat gropers! She propped the guard back up in the chair and leaned his head on the wall so he appeared to be sleeping at his post. She also relieved him of his pistol and a couple of extra clips of ammo, before she headed down the hall toward the sound of Dimitri's voice.

As Katie crept toward the voices, she began picking up more of the conversation. It appeared that Dimitri had assembled the rest of the cartel members in the cellar to inform them of Lin's betrayal and the need to pack and evacuate the lodge immediately. The only questions seemed to be coming from Ito regarding the disposition of Lin. He was insisting on questioning Katie about her involvement, but Dimitri emphasized the need for him to be leaving with the rest of the guests.

"You will not have to worry about the maid. Her body will eventually be found in the ashes of the lodge." He ordered them to their rooms to pack only their necessities and leave the rest. They were to assemble in the lounge and be ready to leave in five minutes. They could use the two SUV's owned by the lodge to get out of town.

Sorry, Dimitri, I'm afraid there's going to be a slight change of plans. Hmmm. One down, sixteen to go. Guess I'd better wait for the odds to be in my favor. Let's see, after the rest of the cartel leaves, I'll have one guard asleep and three left with Dimitri. Okay, four to one... sounds better! Katie slowly back-tracked down the hall to where the guard was still propped up. She scanned the hall and began checking out the rooms on both sides, finding more of the spartan living quarters. Her head was still pounding and her balance was way off, so she had to rely on the walls for support as she did her search.

When she came to the lab, she noticed a room directly across the hall. Katie cautiously crossed, turned the handle and then entered, closing the door behind her. She leaned back against the door as a wave of nausea almost put her on her knees. When she recovered, she explored the wall by the door, located the light switch and turned it on. To her surprise, this room was anything but spartan. Carpeted in a thick plush, it was easily the size of the lab and contained a couch, king-sized bed, dresser, a workstation complete with a computer, printer, and scanner, phone/fax, TV/VCR and...a safe! It even had its own bathroom. *Okay, let's see if you've left anything on your computer.*

Katie sat down at the workstation, located the power switch and turned it on. It would take a while to completely boot up, so she decided to look through the room in the meantime. The dresser contained a few pieces of clothing; she found nothing taped to the backs or bottoms of the drawers. The workstation was very organized with a place for everything— pens, CD's, paper for the printer, even a few odd books, all in Russian. There was nothing in the trash can by the workstation and nothing left in the bathroom. *Looks like you aren't planning on coming back here, General, so there's probably nothing in the safe either. Well, we'll let Bruce and his boys take a look in there later.* Katie walked over to the TV and started to check out the videos that were left behind. *Figures...nothing but x-rated flicks. Oooo, and what do we have here? A documentary on the United Nations. Interesting.*

The young agent returned to the computer and sat down staring at the screen. *Well, I should have figured. It's in Russian. Okay, looks like Gus will have to tackle this one.* She shut down the computer and checked her watch. It had been seven minutes since she left Dimitri. If he was on schedule, he should have been chasing his charges off into the night by now. *Guess it's time for me to check out the control room.* When she reached the door, she shut the light off, allowed her eyes to adjust to the dark, pulled out the retrieved pistol and switched off the safety. As she slowly opened the door and peeked out, she was surprised to see two guards coming down the hall, checking all the rooms as they went. *Oh, oh. Guess they found sleeping beauty.* Katie silently closed the door and headed towards the bathroom.

****

The distance to the lodge from the Park and Rec office was only seven miles, but on an ATV, going as fast as Dean dared on roads filled with snowdrifts, it was beginning to seem like seventy miles. Being fully exposed to the bitterly cold elements was not a wise choice either, but Dean put her discomfort out of her mind as she plowed through another drift. At least it hadn't started snowing again, and the wind seemed to be dying down. That surely was a good sign. It didn't look as though a plow had been through the roads at all, but Tracy had told her that they had been out since the snow first started to fall. As she turned the last corner toward the lodge, she almost ran head-on into an SUV coming down the road. It didn't have its lights on, and she barely had time to swerve out of the way. When she regained control of the ATV, she noticed a second SUV leaving the lodge driveway. *Abandoning ship, are you? Well, we'll see about that.* Dean had noticed that the second SUV had the lodge logo on the door. She pulled into the first driveway and pulled out her cell phone and called Tracy's number. Linna picked up on the first ring.

"Linna, it's Dean. Call the police and have them stop the two SUV's owned by the lodge. They're just pulling onto Hollow Road now. Warn them that they may be armed and dangerous. Get the State Police called for back-up."

"What do I tell them the reason is for the stop?" Linna asked. "They may not do it on my say-so."

"Okay...your husband is the mayor and the police commissioner. Call him and have him call the police," Dean suggested. "Only do it fast! Tell your husband whatever you have to for now...but get them stopped before they leave town!"

"You've got it!" Linna answered as she hung up.

Dean pulled back out onto the road and headed toward the lodge. About fifty yards from the drive-way, she pulled over and turned off the engine. Going as quickly as she could wading through waist high drifts, Dean noticed that the lodge was completely dark, and that she could not see any of the guards patrolling outside. She assumed that they had either all left, or were inside getting ready to leave. Considering her options, Dean decided to use the kitchen entrance to get in. It was further from the door to the cellar than the front entrance, so if she had to break a little glass to get in, the chances were better that she wouldn't be heard. Also it was closer to the dumb-waiter, which she hoped to use to get into the cellar. When she got to the kitchen door, she was surprised to find it unlocked. *So much for security!* the tall woman thought as she carefully entered, silenced gun drawn.

****

The quick motion to turn towards the bathroom had made Katie's head spin and brought on another wave of nausea. *Not, now, kiddo, gotta get to cover first,* she muttered to herself as she slowed her pace. Losing her balance, she crashed into the chair at the computer station on her way and hit the floor face first, causing her to lose her grasp on the pistol. The guards, hearing the noise, ran to the room, kicked open the door and opened fire into the darkened room, sending shards of wood, plastic and glass flying everywhere. Katie rolled to her left and found herself next to the king-sized bed, then slid under it for protection, not paying attention to the stinging pain in her back. In the light of the gun flashes, she could see her pistol lying just out of reach on the floor at the foot of the bed.

After the deafening barrage stopped, the guards cautiously turned on the light. Their automatic weapon fire had demolished the plush room, and as they entered, Katie could hear their steps as they crunched on the debris. She carefully reached into her pocket for one of her pens, but found none. As she was reaching into the other pocket, a pair of hands appeared under the bed and pulled her out, feet first. Roughly grabbing her right arm and a handful of her hair a guard pulled her to her feet, causing her to scream with pain. He then shifted his hand from her hair to her left arm and held both her arms behind her back. Katie struggled to get free, but the previous two blows to her head had left her too nauseous and weak to effectively defend herself.

The guard holding her spoke to his partner in Russian. They both laughed, and the one in front came up to Katie and smiled, then said in broken English, "Maybe you like Russian man more than Japanese woman? Eh?"

As he reached up to try to kiss her, Katie raised her knee into his crotch with such an explosive force that he reeled backward in pain. Anger showing on

his face, he came at her again, but this time he
punched her in the abdomen, forcing her to bend forward with the pain. His partner, holding her from
behind, laughed and pulled her up again, allowing the
man in front to raise her head and beat her face with
several punches before he quit. Blood was trickling
from cuts to her lips and cheek, and she groaned in
agony, but Katie's spirit was not daunted. As he drew
near for the third time, Katie raised her head and spat
in his face.

****

Dean was in the kitchen, making her way to the
pantry, when she heard the burst of automatic weapons fire. Throwing stealth to the wind, she ran into
the pantry and searched for the dumbwaiter. Finding
it still on the cellar level, she pressed the call button.
"C'mon, c'mon," Dean shouted at the slow moving
elevator. When it stopped, she quickly entered,
changed the direction to "down" and hit the "start"
button. As it arrived in the basement, she found herself in the lab. The lights were on, and she could see
the door was left ajar. She ran to the door and took a
quick look up and down the hall. Seeing no one, she
stepped out.

She was about to move off to the right when she
heard muffled groans coming from the room across
the hall. As Dean peeked around the open door, she
saw Katie spit on a guard in front of her. Dean threw
herself into the room and rolled as she hit the floor,
now aiming at the chest of the guard standing in front
of Katie. He was bringing the butt of his rifle forward

and had just made contact with Katie's left temple when the bullets ripped through him, sending him backwards toward the door. The second guard released Katie, who fell limply to the floor from the third crushing blow she had incurred to her head. Before he could reach for his weapon, Dean had placed five bullets neatly in his chest and directly into his heart.

Dropping her pistol, Dean reached over and pulled Katie into her lap, wiping the blood from her lips and cheek and checking her breathing and pulse. "Katie...Katie...love, I'm here. I'm so sorry I'm late..." Her words fell on unhearing ears as she began to sob, clutching the unconscious blonde to her chest.

Part
V

Bruce and his team arrived at the lodge shortly after Dean and captured Dimitri and the last two guards quickly. The two SUV's were also stopped and all of the passengers were safely locked behind bars at the State Trooper barracks. A news release was planted, describing a terrible traffic accident involving several foreigners who lost control of their SUV's and plunged off the bridge at Bridgeville on the Quickway. A second press release described a fire that had leveled an old resort, killing five men, thought to be guests, and one female staff member. Footage of an old resort fire was shown, and Mr. G, after sufficient encouragement from Gus, Linna, and her husband Kelly, was interviewed lamenting the loss of his family's resort. The resort was located at the end of a private road, and the police cordoned off the area so that no one would be able to tell that the story was a hoax.

When the ambulance arrived, Katie still had not regained consciousness. The paramedics checked her vitals, started an IV drip of 5% saline, and prepared her for the ambulance. Dean asked Tracy to go to the hospital with Katie. She, herself, would catch up once she had secured the lodge. After the ambulance left, Dean and Bruce's team completed a top to bottom search of the lodge. Dimitri had done a very thorough job of destroying the records, and there was little left to give any solid clues as to the event Kasimov had planned. The few items that survived were some samples of the drug, a documentary tape on the United Nations, a calendar with December 27th and 30th highlighted, a safe, and a bullet riddled CPU. Gus was currently trying to get anything he could off of the CPU, but he didn't have high hopes. Bruce had cracked open the safe earlier and found it empty, except for the calendar. The documentary was a complete mystery.

* * * * * * * * * *

It was now 1200 hours. Dean was pacing the floor in the surgery waiting room at Catskill General Hospital. Tracy and Colleen were also there, waiting. When Dean arrived at the hospital, she found that Katie had been taken to surgery to repair a severely dislocated left shoulder and to remove several shards of glass that were deeply embedded in her back. One large piece was dangerously close to her spinal cord.

"Dean," Tracy spoke to her friend, "why don't you come and sit down? You've got to be exhausted." Dean looked over at her, then finally shrugged and sat down heavily next to Tracy, resting her elbows on her knees and her head in her hands. Tracy reached over and started giving her a back rub to try and relax her a bit. "You know, Col and I can stay here, and you could go back and get some rest."

"No. Not until I know what's happening," came the curt reply. They sat there a while longer, just staring out the window at the white landscape...waiting.

Dr. Berg, dressed in scrubs, was the first one through the door, followed by the orthopedic surgeon that was flown up from Walter Reed. Beth introduced Dr. Jack Stein to the three waiting women.

"The surgery went well. All of the shards were removed successfully, including the one close to her spine. The shoulder will take some time to heal completely, but with diligent therapy, it should heal better than new," Dr. Stein finished.

"Had she regained consciousness?" Dean asked hopefully.

"She did, just before surgery. Right now, she's still under from the anesthesia," Dr Stein responded.

"When can I see her?" Dean asked again.

This time, Dr. Berg answered. "She's in the recovery room right now and will be there for at least another couple of hours. Then we'll transfer her up to a private room. You'll be able to see her then. But, Dean, she'll be in and out of it for a while, and she was very disoriented when she regained consciousness." Beth took Dean's hand and led her over to the couch before she continued. "She doesn't remember anything. There's evidence that she took three severe blows to the head. It's a miracle that she woke up at all."

Dean paled at Dr. Berg's words. "She'll...she'll be all right...won't she?" The blue eyes began to tear as a cloak of guilt settled itself around her.

"Only time will tell, Dean." Beth sighed and continued. "Physically, she'll be able to recover fully, but psychologically...well, we'll have to wait and see. Head injuries are extremely difficult to predict. But Katie is young and strong. If anyone can overcome the damage she received, Katie can." Beth hugged Dean, then stood to leave. "Why don't you go get some rest? You can lie down in her room until she comes up from the recovery room. C'mon, I'll take you all up."

Dr. Stein shook their hands, then left to check on Katie in the recovery room. Beth led the three women up to the surgical wing on the third floor. She had secured a private room for Katie that had a sleeper couch and a recliner. The room was a corner unit with two large windows meeting in the corner. It was big, bright and cheery. Before she left, Dr. Berg asked the nurse in charge to have some lunch brought up to the three women. Dean took the recliner, and Tracy and Col settled on the couch.

They sat there in silence for nearly an hour and three-quarters, when the chirp of Dean's cell phone finally interrupted the quiet. "Yeah?" Dean spoke into the receiver.

"Dean, it's Gus. How's Katie?"

Dean filled the technology wizard in and then asked what he needed.

"Besides checking on Katie, I just wanted to tell you that the CPU was a bust. It just had too much damage to retrieve anything. One of the bullets bounced off the power supply and sliced through the hard drive. We tried to go through the shredded stuff, but he had a cross cut shredder. It's proving impossible to reconstruct anything."

"I figured that would be the outcome. Are any of our jailbirds singing?"

"Nah. Tightest bunch of lips I've ever seen," Gus replied. "And that Dimitri character...all of a sudden, all he can speak is Russian! He'll be the toughest nut to crack."

"Yeah, you're right on that one." Dean paused then added. "Look, as soon as Katie comes up from the recovery room, I'll be in."

"Dean, there's nothing you can do here right now. Bruce and I are working our butts off to crack this thing, so you just stay there and get some rest yourself, okay? You won't be any good to us dead on your feet. I'll let you know if anything breaks."

"Yeah, I know you're right...but I'll be in as soon as I can," Dean answered, then said, "Thanks," before she hung up the line.

Another hour passed before the women heard the wheels of a gurney squeak as it rolled down the hall. The door opened, and a recovery room nurse dressed in scrubs and Dr. Berg, now in her street clothes, came in, wheeling Katie's gurney. They expertly transferred Katie to the bed and then the nurse wheeled the gurney out.

"She's in and out, so don't expect too much for a few hours. It'll be best if we let her just sleep it off," Beth said as she checked Katie's vital signs one more time.

"Did she remember anything when she woke up?" Tracy asked softly.

"Just her name. She has no idea what happened or where she is, but she did remember me, so that's a mark on the plus side," Beth said with a smile. "I'm sure she'll be fine. It's just going to take some time."

The four women sat in silence, watching the young blonde lying in the bed. Finally, Dr. Berg stood to leave. She explained that she and Dr. Randall were going to be running some tests on the drug samples they were able to secure from the lodge. She promised to stop back later to see how Katie was coming along.

****

"Andre, I'm afraid there's some bad news," Natasha said as she entered the general's office at the embassy. "It looks like Dimitri and the others will not be coming. I've just heard a report on CNN about a tragic resort fire in the Catskills that claimed the lives of five men and one woman. Dimitri must have had a problem with the accelerant."

"That is too bad; he was a dependable man," he said simply, as he continued to read the papers on his desk. "What about the others?" This he asked with more interest.

"In an unrelated story on CNN, they described an incident with two SUV's losing control and going over a bridge. All eleven of the foreign visitors were killed at the site. The state police are recording it as a weather-related accident," Natasha said with concern. "How badly will this affect our plans?"

"We will have to supplement the Japanese contingent. Their job is crucial to the success of the plan. I'll contact the New York members to help replace the others." He finally looked up from his paperwork.

"Not to worry, Natasha, everything will still go as planned. Now what have you learned from that little bitch Lin?"

"She is not talking. She is very tough for that small frame, but I will break her yet. I've administered the mind control drug. It will be a few more hours before I can interrogate her again," Natasha said with a wicked sneer.

"Just do not 'break' her before she talks! You should have administered the drug immediately instead of using your archaic methods," Kasimov warned. "If there is anyone else out there that knows anything, we must find out soon so we can be prepared and...I have plans for her. At least that smug little maid is out of the picture."

"Yes, and don't worry, Andre, I'll take care of everything." Natasha left to go back to the interrogation room and her semi-conscious victim, thinking that she preferred her "archaic" techniques to using modern medicines. It gave her so much more pleasure.

****

At 1900 hours, Katie opened her eyes for the third time, but this time they stayed open. Dean was first to her bedside and glad to see the emerald eyes starting to look a little more brilliant.

"Hey," Dean said softly as she placed her hand tenderly on the young woman's cheek. "How're you doing?"

"Umm. I kinda hurt all over, but my head is killing me," she answered truthfully in a raspy voice. "Are you a doctor?"

"Ahh...no. I'm...a friend." The tall woman was in obvious pain over Katie's lack of recognition, but she swallowed hard and continued. "Do you recognize these two?" she asked, smiling down at the confused emerald eyes as they scanned Tracy and Colleen.

"No...but I'm guessing they must be friends, too, right?" came the apologetic response.

"Right. This is Tracy and this is Colleen," Dean offered with a smile. "Would you like some ice chips to suck on? It sounds like your throat is really sore."

"Yes, that would be nice. Thank you," came the tired, scratchy reply.

Colleen went over to the bedside table and scooped some ice chips into a cup, then went back to the bed to help Katie. Tracy and Dean said they'd be right back and left the room. They walked across the hall to the visitor's lounge and sat on the hard institutional couch by the window.

"Damn it, Tracy, she doesn't remember us!" Dean said in a quiet but forceful tone. "This is all my fault! If I had been one...two minutes sooner, she wouldn't be here like this."

"You don't know that for sure. Dr. Berg said she received three blows to the head last night. Any one of them could have been responsible for this damage," Tracy offered, in hopes of assuaging some of her friend's guilt.

"No. I saw her before that last blow. She was still fighting. She spat on the creep. I should have

moved faster!" Tears started spilling from the ice
blue eyes as though the ice in them was melting. "I
never should have allowed them to investigate."

"Dean, you can't take blame for that. They're
both grown women and trained agents, too. They
knew the risks involved. She was doing her job,
that's all," Tracy said a bit more emphatically. "You,
of all people, should know how things can sometimes
go wrong without it being anyone's fault."

Dean put her elbows on her knees and held her
head in her hands while sobbing uncontrollably.
Tracy lifted Dean's torso and tucked Dean's head onto
her shoulder. She put her arms around her friend,
holding her tightly as the tall woman let her grief roll
out of her body with every tear. When it seemed she
could cry no more, Dean pulled back, wiping her face
with the sleeves of her sweatshirt, and said a simple
"Thank you."

"No problem, that's what friends are for," Tracy
offered with a smile.

"Trace...what if she never regains her memory?"
Words failing, Dean just looked into Tracy's hazel
eyes.

"Dean, she fell in love with you once; she'll fall
all over again. Trust me on this, okay?"

Dean nodded. "I hope you're right." The two
women got up and went back into the room. Katie
was sleeping again, and Col was sitting at her bedside, holding a hand that was grasping hers tightly.
They watched as a series of grimaces appeared on the
blonde's face before she finally relaxed into a deep
REM sleep. At 2100 hours, Beth, Leigh and Dr. Stein
stopped in to check on Katie. Her vitals were good,

and color was returning to her cheeks. All three of
the doctors reinforced the opinion that Katie would be
fine, and that it was just going to take time to see
what, if any, of her recent memory returned. By nine-
thirty, they sent Tracy, Col, and a reluctant Dean,
home for the night.

Sunday, 0800 hours

Dean spent the night with Col and Tracy. The
three cats decided to make their bed on top of Dean,
snuggling with her familiar scent. Dean didn't mind
their company. It was preferable to an empty bed at
the cabin. By eight she was up, showered, and ready
to tackle the assignment once more. Since it was Sunday, Tracy and Colleen proposed staying at the hospital, and Dean was thankful that Katie wouldn't have
to be alone on her first day of recuperation. Dean
hoped to be there by noon, provided things were
going okay at the court building.

It was a beautiful sunny day; the roads were clear
now, so travel was improving around town. It was
hard to believe that a snowstorm had literally shut
down the area only thirty-six hours earlier. Dean
pulled her SUV into the neatly plowed parking area
that Byron had cleared the day before. *I've got to
remember to thank Tracy's staff for all their help.*
Dean mused as she walked into the building. "Morning," she said to the sergeant that was on duty at the
door.

"Morning, Colonel. How's Agent O'Malley?" the
young soldier asked earnestly.

"About the same. Thanks for asking, Sarge." Dean smiled at the young man and then continued to her office. On the way, she called over to Bruce and Gus to join her. When they entered the office, the three of them sat down and began to outline the progress they had made the day before.

"The calendar we found had two dates high-lighted—the twenty-seventh and the thirtieth. We know that the twenty-seventh is the date that all the participants are to be in place, so we are assuming that the thirtieth is the target date." Gus presented their conjecture.

"Makes sense. What else have you theorized?"

"Well, the only thing out of place in his quarters was the video on the United Nations. Why would he have that mixed in with a bunch of porno stuff?" Bruce continued.

"Our guess is that the target area is the United Nations building in New York City."

Gus jumped in with a continuation of their theory. "We know the city water supply has been compro-mised, so we're looking for the action to take place there. Then this video shows up, and the highlighted calendar."

"If that's true, then why drug the entire city?" Dean questioned. "And the thirtieth won't see much action at the UN building, will it?"

"We're checking on that now, but they're not tell-ing us much," Bruce reported. "I've got a call in to General James, but his aide said he's on leave for the holiday and won't be back in the office until tomor-row. When I told him of the urgency, he said that the general was in Montana skiing with his family, and they'd do their best to get him to phone us."

Then it was Gus's turn again. "We're trying to reach the Secretary of State, but she's out for the holiday, too. They'll keep trying to get her on the horn."

"What about the helicopter? Did it get tracked?" Dean was beginning to feel anger and irritation at their inability to contact the higher ups.

"No. The copter must have flown below the radar's detection level. But our sources in Washington saw Natasha there yesterday, so we're assuming that she took Lin there to the Russian Embassy," the ex-SEAL explained.

"Okay. Not much we can do there, for now. Have your sources keep tabs on the movements of Kasimov and Natasha. Make sure they keep an eye on their copter pad, too. I want to know about anyone that moves in or out of that embassy." Dean stood and began to pace the office. "Have either of you gone to the trooper's barracks today?" Both heads shook in the negative. "Fine. Let's go see if we can give their 'guests' a singing lesson."

The three of them left for the barracks at 1000 hours. When they arrived, they were immediately escorted to the waiting lounge, then finally into the Commander's office. Major Vance introduced himself, then asked to see everyone's ID—which he then had the desk sergeant run for authentication. When he was satisfied that they truly were government agents, he asked to be briefed on the assignment. He was none too happy about having a surveillance operation going on in his district without prior notification, so he was not too eager to cooperate now.

Dean did her best song and dance, finally winning him over when she found out that he was ex-Army and had served with General James during Desert Storm. After that, they were treated with all due respect and allowed access to the prisoners. They spent nearly three hours interrogating them using a variety of tactics. "Good agent/bad agent" didn't seem to work on the first batch. The general consensus was that if they exerted a little more effort and switched tactics, good agent/bad agent/psycho agent might yield results with the second batch, but not today. Dimitri was unfazed by any of it and refused to speak, even in Russian. He did give away his surprise at seeing Dean again, but then became even more close-mouthed.

"Well, that didn't accomplish much," Bruce complained, on the way back to their temporary headquarters.

"Yeah. I sure wish we could use that mind control drug on them...then maybe..." Gus's comment must have struck a chord because Dean brightened at his words.

"That may be our only chance," Dean said as she pulled into the parking lot. "You guys call me if you hear anything from the general or the Secretary. I'm going to check in at the hospital and see if the docs are making any progress." Then she backed out and headed out the Quickway to the hospital.

It was nearly 1400 hours by the time Dean parked in the visitors' lot at the hospital. Her first stop was the pathology lab where she found the docs with heads bent over microscopes. So far, the substance that was found at the lodge was identical to the one they had reproduced from the autopsy samples, so

there would be no quick fix to the search for the stimulus. Now that they knew it was identical, they would
continue to expose the substance to as many different
variables as they could imagine might have been
present on the night of the murders.

Before Dean left, she asked Dr. Berg if she had
seen Katie yet that day, and how she was doing. Beth
told Dean that she had indeed seen Katie first thing in
the morning. She was nearly back to normal, as far as
the effects of the anesthesia wearing off, but she was
still having difficulty with her short-term memory.
As far as they could calculate, the last complete memory she has was from early November when she had to
take Sugar in for a seizure episode on a Friday morning. Tracy, Colleen and Beth had already filled Katie
in on the progress of the assignment up to the time of
her arrival at the hospital, but left out any mention of
the personal details between her and Dean, figuring
that topic was best left in Dean's hands.

After the lab stop, Dean detoured to the gift shop
and picked up several bunches of flowers and chocolates, knowing how the young woman loved those.
When she walked into the room, she found Tracy and
Col snoozing on the couch, while a very awake Katie
was staring out the window. Dean knocked softly on
the open door and then smiled as she saw recognition
on the young blonde's face.

"Hi," Katie whispered, gesturing Dean to enter.

"Hi, yourself!" Dean responded. "You sure look
a lot better today. How are you feeling?"

"Still a bit fuzzy, but the headache is starting to
subside. Of course, I have this to put up with too."
Katie pointed to her right shoulder with her uninjured

hand. She looked at Dean's armload and then smiled. "Ooooh. Are those all for me? Or are you visiting half of the surgical wing?" She chuckled at the amount of flowers Dean was carrying. It looked like she had wiped out the florist shop. "Did you leave any for anyone else?"

"Ummm...ah...no, I mean, yes...they're for you, and I did leave a few wilted ones behind." Dean chuckled at her sophomoric display. "I guess I went a little overboard, huh?" Visibly blushing now, she placed the flowers on the small table in the corner then turned and handed Katie the chocolates. "I didn't ask if you could have these or not, but I can't see them being bad for you."

"Oh...oh, yeah. These will be bad for me. Unless you can figure a way to keep me from eating them all in one sitting." She paused as she opened the box and popped one in her mouth. "Mmmm. I wuf twuffles," she said around a mouthful of chocolate. "Wunt wun?"

"No, you go ahead and enjoy," Dean said, chuckling as the emerald eyes sparkled back at her. Their laughter woke Tracy and Colleen. They were surprised to see Dean, and even more surprised to see Katie munching and smiling.

"Now that's what I call a recovery!" Colleen said as she looked at Katie then back at Dean. "How'd you get her to perk up like that?"

Dean just shrugged. "Magic! Just produce a box of truffles and voila!" They all had a good chuckle, then settled down to more serious talk.

Dean asked Katie if she was able to remember any more since she talked to Beth earlier. Katie shook her head. She told Dean that she was trying to concentrate on the case and see if it would start to shake anything loose, but nothing happened. Tracy and Col had helped her try to remember the past few weeks, but still nothing seemed familiar. Nothing, that is, until now. Somehow, when she saw Dean at the door and when she watched her blush, she felt something stir in her—something familiar. She couldn't put her finger on it, but she promised herself to keep trying.

"Well, don't give yourself another headache. Hopefully this will pass and you'll be able to remember what you had for breakfast for the last fifteen days," Dean said cheerily. Inside, she was hoping the young blonde's recovery wouldn't take long. She missed her friend, partner and lover and wanted her back...now!

Talk turned to the case at hand, and Dean filled in the trio on the visit to the trooper's barracks and the interrogation of the prisoners. She proceeded to her recent chat with the docs and the still elusive stimulus.

"You know, Dean, I just have this feeling that there's something there on the tape that we're missing," Colleen commented. "I know we've looked at it from every possible angle...but I just have this feeling. I can't explain it...it's there."

"I hope you're right, Col," Dean answered. "It's going to be the only thing that will turn this mess into a success for us. We've got to find out what that stimulus is, and before Thursday."

"Well, I'm off this whole week, so I'll work on it round the clock if I have to," Colleen offered. "I just know it's got to be something simple."

"Trust me, Dean, once Col gets a bug about something, she doesn't quit until she figures it out," Tracy interjected.

The rest of the afternoon went quickly while the four women talked shop. By 1700 hours, the activity was obviously wearing on Katie, and she was beginning to fade out of the conversations. Tracy and Colleen decided to leave, especially since Col was bound and determined to discover the mystery of the tapes. Dean made herself comfortable on the couch and just watched as Katie slipped off into dreamland. Soon, she joined her, only her dreams were not of a benign nature. She kept reliving the moment that she entered Kasimov's quarters. She saw Katie spit on the guard, then everything went into slow motion: the dive into the room, the shots ripping through the guard, the blow hitting Katie's temple, her falling, the death of the other guard...until she was cradling Katie in her arms. The dream kept repeating itself, with the same ending over and over. She was late again. Just too late!

****

Katie awoke to the cries coming from the figure on the couch. It only took her a moment to realize that the cries she heard were the result of a bad dream. She carefully climbed out of the bed and crossed to the restlessly sleeping figure. *What's tormenting you so?* thought the young woman, as she gently reached down to wake the sleeping woman. It was not the smartest thing she could have done, for as soon as she touched Dean, she found herself in a precarious position—neatly bonding with the wall behind her.

The movement was so quick and fluid that she wasn't hurt by the action; however, she was disturbed by the ice-cold look in the otherwise warm blue eyes she remembered from earlier in the day. "Umm, sorry. I was just trying to wake you from a nightmare you were having." She smiled apologetically at the now embarrassed Dean.

"Oh my God...I'm...I'm sorry...did I hurt you?" Dean gently released the young agent and checked her over carefully.

"No, I'm fine really." Katie took a seat on the couch. "I guess I just wasn't thinking. I really should have known better than to try to wake someone having a bad dream." Dean sat down next to her, beginning to shake visibly. Katie reached over and gently placed a hand on Dean's arm. "Are you okay? Is there anything you want to talk about?"

"I could have really hurt you," came the soft reply from Dean. "I'm sorry, I shouldn't be here." As she got up to leave, she felt a strong left hand hold on to her, keeping her in place.

"Nonsense!" came the simple reply. "I happen to enjoy having you here, so just don't think about going anywhere, okay? Besides, who's gonna help me eat all those truffles?" She bent her head to peer into the pained expression on the tall woman winking as she made eye contact.

A surprised Dean nodded and winked back, smiling at the ease with which Katie was able to control her. Anyone else would have found themselves sitting alone in the room by now as the somber colonel would have quickly left for fear of doing damage or letting her guard down. With Katie, however, it just seemed so natural to let her take over and calm the turmoil within. She silently wondered if Katie felt anything for her other than a budding "renewed" friendship. "Okay. I guess I wouldn't want you to eat them all and get sick enough to have to stay in here."

"Well, I guess that's settled then." Katie reached for the box of chocolates and offered Dean some. "How about we start at the beginning, and you tell me how we came to be working on the same case."

Dean felt a little apprehensive at first, but decided that the telling might jog Katie's memory. So, she began the tale—as the Mad Hatter suggested to Alice—from the beginning. She did edit the personal side of the account, not sure if she should be including their feelings for each other. They both relaxed into the telling and the listening, and Katie found Dean to be a very detail-oriented person. She decided that she liked her—very much—and wondered if they were just partners in the work sense or more. *Certainly something for me to think about in the lonely hours of the night,* thought the blonde as Dean continued the tale.

It took nearly three hours of narrative, interrupted at times by dinner, medication, monitoring of vital signs, and several questions by the blonde. By the end of the evening, Katie felt she had a better understanding of her role in the case and also a better understanding of the colonel in charge. But unfortunately, none of it was familiar to her. At 2100 hours, the charge nurse came in and threatened to physically remove Dean from the room so her patient could get

some rest. Dean tried her most intimidating stare but
found she had met her match. She acquiesced to the
demand, knowing that it was best for Katie in the long
run. She promised to return the next day.

Monday, 0330 hours

The insistent sound of Dean's cell phone finally
raised the Army officer out of a deep sleep. Picking
up the phone, she heard Bruce's voice on the other
end, filling her in on his conversation with General
James. It seemed that the general had just returned
from his holiday ski vacation and was disturbed at the
turn of events. He wanted Dean to fly to Washington
immediately to update him on the situation. "Great!"
muttered Dean. "Any idea when the next flight is
available?"

"As a matter of fact, if you leave in fifteen minutes, you can catch a flight out of Stewart Airport and
arrive in D.C. by six a.m." Bruce offered to pick her
up and take her to the airport, but Dean refused, pre-
ferring to drive herself in her SUV. Bruce had made a
reservation for her and gave her the flight number and
time. After a very quick shower and a change into her
military uniform, Dean left her cabin with three minutes to spare.

The trip to Stewart Airport wasn't bad considering that the area had suffered a major snowstorm only
two days earlier. There was something to be said for
those massive plows in this part of the country. They
could really push the snow out of the way! The flight
left precisely on time and actually arrived five min-

utes early. At this time of the morning, she didn't have trouble catching a cab and was at the Pentagon by six forty-five. Her appointment with the general was at seven-thirty, so she went to the café and waited for it to open at seven. *Just what I need...*thought the colonel as she sipped her tea...*a day with the bureaucrats! Well, they had better make this quick. Time may be running out on us.*

At seven twenty-five, Dean entered General James' office, ready to answer his questions and try to get a few answers herself. The general was already in, and she was immediately directed into his office. After the formal military salute and report, Lieutenant General James ordered Lieutenant Colonel Peterson to be seated, then dropped the formality altogether. "Just what the hell happened, Dean?" he asked in earnest.

"Jack, I can't tell you exactly, because we don't know exactly. The cartel reps were moving out gradually, and the last group was scheduled to leave on Sunday. Our undercover op was going to do a little search and seizure on Saturday night with one of the cartel moles, but somehow the schedule changed and they went on Friday. We weren't prepared for it. Next thing we knew, they were compromised. We activated our insertion team immediately, but there was one hell of a snowstorm blowing and we couldn't get out. By the time we got there, Natasha had flown off with the cartel mole and left orders to kill our op and destroy the records. We believe Lin Yamakura was taken to the Russian Embassy here in Washington. I barely got there in time to stop them from killing Katie, but the records were gone.

"Katie?" the General asked inquisitively.

"Yes, sir." Dean could feel a little heat start to rise and managed to control it. "She's the DEA agent that I told you about."

"Oh...yes, I remember. Go ahead."

"Well unfortunately, our op, Agent O'Malley, was injured during the process. She received three concussive blows to her head, and now she's having trouble remembering anything about the past two months." Dean continued. "We did have some luck, though. We've narrowed down Kasimov's target date to December thirtieth and we're pretty certain it will involve the United Nations building."

"The UN huh? Are you sure? Have you contacted them about any events on the thirtieth?"

"We're about 99% certain, and yes, we've contacted them. But they're not being very forthcoming. The UN security force is extremely efficient, sir, and I'm sure they want to check things out themselves." She stopped and looked out the window. "We tried to contact the Secretary of State to see if she knew of any special event at the UN on the thirtieth, but she's been out of town, too. I'm hoping you'll be able to get us that information, Jack."

The general sat there thinking for a bit before he spoke. "I'll do better than that, Dean. I have a meeting with the Secretary and the Attorney General at eleven. I want you there to fill them in. We should be able to get some answers then."

****

Dean walked down to the small office she used between assignments, figuring that she would use the time to touch base with her team. The office was just as she had left it—plain and simple. The only personal adornment was a certificate of completion from her Command and General Staff School at Fort Leavenworth. Except for her nameplate on the door, anyone entering this office would have thought that it was an unassigned space.

Dean put her coat and hat on the rack by the door and then sat behind her desk gently rocking in her oversized leather chair. An old but well cared for leather chair that she had purchased at an estate sale; it was her only concession to comfort in an otherwise austere room. She would often sit in that chair and gently rock until she came up with the answers that were eluding her.

After half an hour of rocking and thinking, she decided that it just wasn't working today, so she picked up the phone and called her team. Thirty minutes of conversation later, she found that they were still on square three, having progressed from square one by two leaps with the date and assumed site. What they needed now was a good roll of the dice to come up with double sixes. She began listing the known elements on the left side of a sheet of paper, the assumed elements in the center of the paper, and left the right side for the unknown. Right now it came down to: who were the targets; why pick the UN; why drug an entire city the size of New York; and finally, what caused the drug to become active?

At 1045 hours, she straightened the papers on her desk and left to meet with General James and the two bureaucrats. When she arrived at the general's office, she was greeted by his aide and led directly into the meeting room adjoining his office. Already seated in the room were the general, the Secretary of State and the United States Attorney General.

"Ladies, this is Lieutenant Colonel Deanna Peterson, who is in charge of the operation we were discussing. I asked the colonel to come to this meeting so she could inform you of their progress and request the assistance she needs." The general motioned Dean to sit in the empty chair at the round table. "Colonel, the ball's in your court."

Dean thanked the general and reviewed the operation up to the present—giving a very succinct overview without missing any pertinent details. She informed the women of the possibility of the target site being the UN on the thirtieth of December, and of their inability to obtain information from the UN Security Force regarding any unusual event scheduled at the UN on that date. She concluded with a request for their intercession with the UN for information. General James stood after Dean was finished, thanked her for her concise report, and escorted Dean to the door, requesting that she return in one hour.

Then he returned to the table to discuss what options they had.

"I don't know," the Secretary began, "if the President would even consider canceling his speech before the UN General Assembly on a 'guess' that something is going to happen on the thirtieth. There's absolutely no solid evidence to support her beliefs."

"And for security purposes, the fact that he is making this speech has been one of the best kept

secrets in the world. Even the media will not be noti-
fied until the last minute," commented the Attorney
General. "Every head of every nation that belongs to
the UN will be in attendance. The entire General
Assembly Hall, all 1,800 seats, is expected to be
filled. There will be more-than-sufficient security in
attendance, supplied not only by the UN, but also by
the Secret Service, as well as the personal protection
services of all the member nations," she stated.
"Every possible safeguard has been considered to protect these heads of state. If we cry 'foul' now, without solid evidence, our country will look quite
foolish."

"Ladies, I understand your point of view, and
know that you must consider the political ramifications of this request, but I also know Lt. Colonel
Peterson. If she believes that something is going to
happen on the thirtieth at the UN, then...it's going to
happen. And we had better be prepared to act!" the
general said almost too forcefully. "I highly recommend that you take her conjectures seriously and consider giving her information on the Millennium
Presentation."

The two women looked at each other and nodded.
Then the Secretary of State spoke. "General, we will
take your concerns and your recommendation under
advisement, and let you know what actions the President will take. Please be advised that you are not to
discuss any of the events for the thirtieth with Lt.
Colonel Peterson until you hear from us. However, if
any hard evidence should surface, please inform our
offices immediately." With that, the two women rose
and left.

"Gods be damned bureaucrats," mumbled the general as the door closed behind the women. "Damned politicians get this country into trouble, then call on the military to pull their asses out of the fire!" The general stomped into his office and pulled out a cigar, lighting it and deliberately ignoring the no smoking ban in the building.

When Dean returned to the general's office she found him puffing away in his chair, facing the window that looked out on the Washington Monument. "Sit," he said as he turned to face Dean. "Well, they're going to take your warning under advisement and let you know what the higher ups decide," the general said, rather sarcastically.

"You mean they're not going to intercede?" Dean, totally shocked, sat in the nearest chair.

"As I said, they are taking your request under advisement and will let you know," the general repeated.

"Jack, what's going on? Don't they believe what we've told them?" The sincerity and frustration were evident in her voice.

"Until you have hard evidence that something is going to happen at the UN on the thirtieth..." He let the sentence trail off.

"Jack, there is something going on at the UN on the thirtieth isn't there?" Dean persisted.

"I didn't say that!" Jack responded.

"You've got to help me." Dean continued, "Kasimov is a madman. He's got to be stopped!"

"I...I can't. Not right now." Jack rose and crushed out his cigar in the ashtray he kept on his desk. "I'm sorry, Dean, but I can't give you any information. Not until I'm given permission, or you get that hard evidence. I have to follow orders, too."

Dean lowered her eyes and shook her head. "Damn politicians!" She looked up at the general. "Thank you Jack, I know you tried. I'll work on getting that hard evidence for you." She stood, saluted, executed a crisp military turn, and left.

****

Dean took the 3 o'clock flight back to Stewart Airport where she picked up her vehicle and headed back up to the Catskills. She called in to her temporary headquarters to let them know she'd be back that evening, after she made a stop at the hospital to see how Katie was doing. Pulling into the visitors' lot at the hospital, she saw Tracy walking toward the entrance and ran to catch up with her.

"Whoa, you look pretty spiffy, Colonel. Almost had me saluting!" chuckled Tracy as Dean caught up to her. "Where have you been off to in your official duds?"

"General James called me down to the Pentagon this morning. Took the 5:00 a.m. flight out of Stewart and just got back." Catching her reflection in the revolving door she grimaced, then added. "Guess I should have changed before I stopped in, but I didn't want to waste time going up to the cabin and then driving all the way back here. Hope Katie doesn't mind."

"Ummm, if she's anything like me she won't. I've always been a sucker for a woman in uniform!"

Tracy was still chuckling as the elevator door opened on the third floor.

The two friends walked into Katie's room where Colleen had been telling her a story with a very funny outcome—about a call she once went on to fix a computer. They were still laughing and didn't see Tracy and Dean enter. When they did notice, you could have knocked them over with a feather the way their jaws dropped at Dean's appearance in full uniform. Tracy just stood back and enjoyed the look on their faces and the confusion on Dean's. *She has absolutely no idea how damn gorgeous she looks in her uniform. She really cuts a superb figure.* Tracy smiled inwardly. *Now that's a recruitment poster if I ever saw one!*

"What?" Dean asked as she stared back at the slack-jawed women. "You never saw a woman in uniform before?"

Colleen was the first to recover. "Well, let's just say that Tracy never looked that good in her uniform." At that, Tracy took the gloves she was still holding and flung them at Colleen, which led to an outbreak of laughter all around.

"Yeah, well...I'm just not tall enough!" came Tracy's retort, which led to another round of laughter.

"So, why the uniform?" Katie finally asked, still chuckling.

Dean related the early morning phone call and her trip to Washington. She filled them in on her meetings with General James and the one with the Secretary of State and Attorney General.

"You mean they wouldn't tell you anything?" Katie asked in amazement.

"They're taking it under advisement," Dean answered. "In the meantime, if we want to see anything happen, we're going to have to make it happen. If we can get some hard evidence, I know Jack will go to the President himself if he has to."

"Well, short of a signed confession," Tracy said, shrugging her shoulders, "what else will they accept as hard evidence?"

"Looks like that's going to be our only way out," Dean concluded. "The lodge came up empty, Lin's in Kasimov's hands, and we've got empty canisters of a drug we can't get to work. Our only hope is to get one of those jailbirds to talk, preferably Dimitri."

"Time to lean on him a little?" Tracy suggested. "Can I help?"

Dean raised an eyebrow and stared at her friend. "No, you can't help. And I don't think he's the type that will turn from just being leaned on. I need to be able to use that drug on him. We've got to find out how to activate it!"

"I haven't given up yet." Colleen interrupted. "I was up half the night going over and over that tape. Just about the time I'd think I was getting somewhere, Brutus would interrupt me by banging the door open to go out, or whining to come in. As soon as I'd get started again, bang... and he's outside again. I swear, he has been a real pistol for the past few weeks!"

"Well, I appreciate your efforts, Colleen, but I'm going downstairs to lean on the docs a bit." As she turned to leave, her stomach rumbled very loudly. "Umm, anyone care for dinner in the cafeteria? I haven't eaten since yesterday, and I think my stomach is protesting."

She had three volunteers to join her in the cafeteria. As soon as Dean got permission to take Katie down, she snagged a wheelchair and the foursome was on their way. Since it was on the same floor as the pathology lab, they made a brief stop in the lab. Finally they were seated in the cafeteria actually enjoying the food, since this hospital happened to have a decent culinary staff.

When they returned to the room, they spent the rest of the evening working with Katie by trying to stimulate her recall. Unfortunately she still did not remember anything between the beginning of November and Christmas night. The good news was that she was, hopefully, going to be discharged Wednesday. Dean's mood picked up visibly at this piece of news, and she wasted no time in insisting that the young woman stay with her until she was able to fully recover. Katie was surprised by the offer and was actually relieved that she wouldn't have to stay in her trailer alone with just her cats. At nine p.m., visiting hours were over, so they said their good-byes to Katie and headed out. Tracy and Colleen went home, and Dean headed to the court building.

****

When Dean entered the building, she immediately called the task force together to go over her day's meetings. Emphasis was placed on finding the hard evidence that would be needed before they would be able to plan any offensive or defensive strategies since they were still in the dark regarding any special events at the UN. They reviewed several scenarios that could possibly occur in New York City, since they were 100% sure that the city was the general target location. Scenarios encompassing the World Trade Center, Wall Street, the universities, etc. were all discussed.

"What if he's just going to hold the entire city hostage for some reason?" supplied Quentin from Bruce's team. "How do we deal with that? There are not enough of us to handle a block party gone bad, let alone the whole friggin' city. I mean, granted, not everyone drinks the water that comes out of the tap...but in a city the size of New York, even if it's only 50%, we're talking about one hell of a lot of people!"

"Good point, Quent. We certainly don't want to have the National Guard called in to help us...especially if the members come from the city," Bruce said thoughtfully, "But we could call in the military from bases outside the city...those that don't rely on the city's water system."

"I'll call General James in the morning and see if he could coordinate a multi-service force for back-up. Have him set up a 'training exercise' that we could activate quickly." Dean made a note to herself. "There's only two days to get on top of this folks. I want your teams to brainstorm worst-case scenarios and then come up with possible measures to counteract them. We'll meet again at 0800 hours and see what you've got!" The teams immediately broke up and went to their areas to begin work on their tasks. Dean walked over to Gus and asked how the work was proceeding on finding the stimulus. He just shrugged and waggled his hand from side to side. Tired, agitated, and frustrated, Dean directed him to keep on it, and then went into her office.

The answer has got to be out here somewhere. We've been over the same territory over and over, we're just not seeing it. It's got to be something so simple that we just can't see it. Dean kept going over the lists she drew up in her office at the Pentagon as she rocked in her chair. At two a.m., the ringing phone startled her out of a deep sleep. She reached for the offending phone and heard an excited voice on the other end.

"Dean, it's Col...I've found it!"

Groggily Dean asked, "Found what?"

"The stimulus, Dean. I know how he does it! We'll be right there!" Then all Dean heard was a click and a dial tone.

****

It took all of three seconds for Dean to register what Colleen had said and then she stood and walked out to the cot where Gus was getting a short rest. Waking him gently, they returned to her office to wait for Colleen and Tracy. By three o'clock, the four of them were sitting around a table just outside Dean's office.

"Okay...let me start from the beginning," Colleen told the group eagerly waiting for her commentary. "Remember how I was complaining about Brutus pestering me?"

"Yeah, and me too, Dean. Remember how I was telling you he kept wanting out of the house?" Tracy added.

"Well," Colleen picked up the conversation again, "Tracy and I got to talking about it tonight as I was listening to the tape for the umpteenth time...and Brutus was going through his antics...again! Then it finally hit me: what if the stimulus is a sound above the hearing range of humans, but still in the range for animals like dogs?" Colleen smiled. "So, we did a little experiment with Brutus. We took off the tape and played with him. Then I would go to the tape player and put on the tape; and Brutus would get antsy and go out the back door, while Tracy was still trying to entice him to play. We'd take off the tape, bring Brutus in, and start all over again—with the same results. Every time the tape was on, off Brutus would go out the back door! We repeated this several more times and got the same results."

Gus smacked his forehead at the simplicity of the stimulus. "Human hearing peaks out at 20,000Hz, so it's got to be higher than that and still within a dog's range. We need to get an oscilloscope to measure the frequency he's using. I'll get one here by morning, sooner if possible." He stood and crossed to the phone banks by the silent surveillance equipment.

"We should probably have the docs prepare a dose of the drug and test it," Dean said as she picked up the conversation. "We'll also need to know if only one voice can give orders or if several voices can give orders. If this works we could use it on Dimitri to get the hard evidence we need and find out what Kasimov has up his sleeve. We've got our work cut out for us."

"Yeah. We figured the sooner you could get on this the better your chance of beating the deadline. Whatever that may be," Tracy commented.

Tracy and Colleen were about to leave when Dean stopped them. "Hey...I don't know what to say other than thanks. You both really came through for me." She stood and walked over to the two women embracing each one. Knowing that it was strictly against regulations, and that they had earned the right, regardless, she continued, "Would you want to come back in the morning to see how it's going?" Dean asked with a questioning eyebrow.

Tracy and Col looked at each other, then nodded in agreement. "Yeah! Of course we would!" said Tracy. "But, are you sure it's okay for us to be around? I wouldn't want you to get in any trouble for involving civilians."

"You leave that to me. I'll make sure you two have clearance. I'll give General James a call and update him on this breakthrough. Once he hears who made the discovery, you'll be sure to have that clearance," Dean said enthusiastically as she embraced each woman once more and then walked them to the door. "Better get some rest now...and thanks again!"

After Tracy and Colleen left, Dean went over to Gus's area to discuss the testing that would need to be carried out before they could use the drug on Dimitri. Gus had already contacted the two sleepy doctors, who said they would be in with the drug sample by seven a.m. Gus suggested that Dean get some rest in the interim since there wasn't much she could do until morning. She concurred, and they both returned to their former status...napping.

Tuesday, 0700 hours

At precisely seven o'clock, Doctors Berg and Randall arrived at the court building. Gus was already hooking up the oscilloscope so they could determine the frequency of the sound waves that Dimitri used. Dean was up and showered and on her second cup of tea when she met the doctors entering through the door.

"Looks like we've got a break," commented Dr. Randall.

"Of course, we'll have to do some testing first to determine the length of time the subject needs to be exposed to the ultrasonic frequency and how the vocal commands are controlled," added Dr. Berg. "I realize we don't have much time, so the sooner we get started the better. Do you have any test subjects in mind?"

"I've asked for volunteers, people who would not be involved in the mission once we move it to New York City. We have about fifteen people ready to act as guinea pigs for you," Dean replied. "I'd like to have a task force briefing at 0730 in front of my office so we can determine our game plan for the next two days."

The two doctors nodded and took their supplies over to an empty area in the center of the courts where several tables and cots were set up for them. They were using a liquid form of the drug because it was more controllable than the gaseous version. It wouldn't be good to accidentally drug Dean or any of Bruce's team. At seven-thirty, the doctors met with the rest of the task force by Dean's office.

Dean stood and began the briefing. "As you know by now, thanks to a couple of friends, we've discovered that the stimulus that activates the mind control drug is an ultrasonic frequency of 24,000 Hertz." Dean introduced Colleen and Tracy and explained how they made their discovery. "We could have been searching for years and never have found the stimulus without a dog in the lab." Someone in the back of the area shouted that there was something to be said for pets in the workplace, which led to a round of laughter. "All right...all right!" Dean said, smiling as she held up her hand. "Let's get on with it, shall we? Doctors Berg and Randall will explain how they are going to do the testing. Doctors?"

Beth stood and explained that they would be using a small amount of the liquid drug on the individuals who agreed to be used for testing. Then they would be exposed, one at a time, to the ultrasonic sound waves and commanded to do some task which they would otherwise hesitate to do—such as climb a ladder to the ceiling, for someone who was afraid of heights. Questions came from the assembled group on how the sound waves worked and if it would hurt them.

"Not at all," replied Dr. Randall. "A sound wave is just a transmission of energy through a series of vibrations. Normally, a human's hearing is receiving sound waves against the eardrum, causing the drum to vibrate. This vibration of the eardrum, in turn, moves the hammer, anvil and stirrup located within the middle ear, and, eventually, the fluid in the cochlea of the inner ear. From there, an electrical impulse is sent to the auditory nerve, which carries the impulses to the brain for interpretation. It's not necessary to get into the physiology of that process."

They all heard someone mumble, "Thank you," to which she responded, "You're welcome. Ultrasonic waves are waves that are emitted at a frequency higher than the human ear can register. Ultrasound technology has been used for NDT for years...that stands for Non-Destructive Testing. Sonograms are the most recognized use, but they are also used to test for structural integrity of aircraft, railroad rails, and even nuclear reactors. Basically what happens is that ultrasonic waves cause an oscillation of atoms. In this case, the oscillation releases the drug, the drug in turn affects the central nervous system, which in turn causes a response to the voice commands given. Does everybody follow so far?"

As Leigh continued, she explained that transducers are used to generate the ultrasonic waves. It suddenly dawned on Dean that the assignment Trina Carbon's cartel team received was to place and operate transducers *not* transformers. The doctors finished the background on the testing procedure and the stimulus. The information that they needed was threefold. First, did the person only respond to the first voice they heard after the ultrasound treatment? Second, did the ultrasound emission have to continue throughout the command process in order to be effective? And, third, what dosage of the drug was necessary before a reaction would occur. After answering a few questions, the doctors turned the briefing over to Dean.

"Here's what we need to do. Testing group: report to the doctors immediately after we dismiss. Bruce's team: I'll be over to review your worst-case scenarios shortly. The rest of Gus's team: finish assembling the transducers for testing. Any questions? Dismissed!"

****

After several hours of working with Bruce's team, they settled on the most probable scenario. It would involve as many New Yorkers as Kasimov could expose to the sound waves via the transducer emissions. These individuals could then be used to cause a human gridlock in, around, or near the UN building. Police, who could also be affected by the ultrasound waves, would be sent to control the crowds and try to contain the chaos. Every time someone would enter the ultrasound stream, more chaos would result. With that going on outside the UN building, Kasimov would be free to carry out his plan inside the UN. He might even try to penetrate that body with ultrasound waves, thus causing more chaos...or...destruction...and she needed to know what, exactly, was scheduled for the UN on the 30th.

Tracy and Colleen had left to drop in on Katie and inform her of the developments as well as to confirm that she would be released from the hospital the next day. With the situation going down to the wire, they had offered to pick her up and bring her to the court building or to Dean's cabin, whichever she was up to doing. Dean had stayed behind at the court building in case the docs made a breakthrough on the dosage and timing.

Wednesday, 0500 hours

"Damn it, Bruce! We're going too slow. I've got to get to Dimitri and find out what Kasimov is planning!" Dean began to pace back and forth waiting for the results of the doctor's testing. It was nearly 0500 hours, and they were still trying to determine the amount of dosage and time in the system needed for effective results. There was also still the question of the command voice. Dr. Randall was noting changes on the cellular levels of the subjects, but the full effect was not yet being achieved.

"Maybe we got this all wrong," Dean said, beginning to doubt her ability to get the results needed. "Maybe we missed something." She was sitting, thoroughly exhausted, on a bench by the doctor's partitions when she overheard Leigh giving another round of commands to the last set of their charges. Only this time, they did what they were told! She repeated another command, and the subjects followed through. Finally, they were given the ultimate command. They were each told to pick up a pistol and fire point blank at their partner. Though they believed that the guns were loaded, they did it! Then Beth gave the commands, and they did not respond. Dean was so excited that she could have kissed the doctors and everyone in the building; instead she calmly walked over to the physicians for the results.

"Eighteen hours! It has to be in the system for eighteen hours!" bellowed Dean. "That doesn't give us much leeway, Beth. By the time I get it into Dimitri and then get the info to General James, he gets it to the bureaucrats, then we get permission to respond... hell, we'll be lucky if we have time to breathe. If the plan is for Thursday night...well, maybe...but we're screwed if it's for the morning!" She took the proffered dose, and she and Bruce headed out to the trooper's barracks.

"How are we gonna get him to take this?" Bruce asked during the short ride.

"We'll think of something," was all she responded.

When they entered the barracks, they asked for Major Vance and were told he wasn't due in until eight o'clock. They asked to see the prisoners and were refused admittance. "Damn it, man...this is a case of national security! Get me the major on the phone!" Dean insisted.

After five minutes of refusal, Dean had about had it and was ready to bull her way into the prisoner's quarters. Finally, the desk sergeant that was on duty the last time they were in walked into the barracks. They approached him and finally got in to see Dimitri at six a.m.

When Dimitri entered the interrogation room, he sensed that this was not going to be a friendly chat and began speaking English for the first time, demanding his rights as an embassy official. Nonplussed, Dean motioned for the corporal to leave the prisoner with them. As the trooper closed the door, Bruce stepped up behind Dimitri and held him still. Dean carried over the dose of the drug and calmly asked Dimitri to open his mouth. When he refused, she reached up and held his nose until he finally had to gasp for a breath. At that moment, Dean poured the drug into his mouth and then held his mouth closed until the drug had enough time to be swallowed and absorbed into his system. She and Bruce both had on surgical gloves and Teflon coverings over their clothes, just in case. As it turned out, Dimitri was a good boy and didn't spill or spit any of it out.

"Well, Dimitri, I'll bet you know what you just swallowed, don't you? So I guess we'll be back a little later to have a chat," Dean said with a feral smile. She called for the trooper to take him away, cautioning that Dimitri was a potential suicide and should be put on a suicide watch and have anything that could be dangerous moved out of his reach. The officer nodded and took a seething Dimitri away to a private cell. On their way out, they ran into Major Vance and updated him regarding Dimitri and the drug they had just administered. Major Vance was not too happy to hear that they had drugged one of his prisoners, but Dean gave him General James's personal phone number to call if he should get nervous. With their mission accomplished, they left.

On the ride back, Dean let Bruce drive. The case was taking its toll on her, and she decided that she had better make the best of the next few hours and get a little rest. Once back at the court building, she went directly to her office and crashed on her couch until she was awakened at one-thirty by the sounds of voices greeting Katie as she slowly made her way into the building.

****

Tracy and Colleen led a wobbly Katie into Dean's office. "Hey," Dean said, smiling as she greeted them.

"Wow, this is really strange," Katie muttered. "All these people know me, and the only person I know is Beth...and of course you guys, now. I certainly hope my memory comes back!"

Dean carefully led Katie over to the couch where she helped her get comfortable. "So, how are you feeling today?" Dean asked.

"Not too bad, really. A lot better than I look." The bruise on Katie's temple was just turning that ugly yellow-green-purplish color. "The cuts on my back must be healing okay 'cause the stitches are itching like crazy and the fuzziness is finally gone from my head. Only thing I've got to concentrate on now is this shoulder, but I won't be able to start any real therapy until the surgery is healed." The blonde looked up into Dean's sapphire blue eyes and got lost for a long minute before she recovered. "So...umm, what's been going on here? I understand Col found out how to stimulate the drug."

"Yeah." Dean smiled up at Colleen and then went through their progress up to this point. "We've got to go back and interrogate Dimitri, but we have to wait for the drug to take effect first." She looked at her watch, then added, "That will be in about eleven more hours."

"Eleven hours!" came the response from the three women. "That's the soonest?"

"Yeah, it's definitely going to cramp my style," Dean replied, "but there's not much else we can do. It's our best shot at finding out Kasimov's plans."

"What can we do in the meantime?" Katie asked earnestly.

"We," she moved her hand around to indicate herself, Tracy, Colleen, and the rest of the task force outside the office, "are doing all we can to get ready. "You," she pointed at Katie, "are going to do nothing but rest and heal."

"Hey, no fair, I can do something... can't I?" she asked, batting her emerald eyes seductively. Dean had been a sucker for those eyes since she first met her in the diner, so she stopped, smiled, and told the young agent she could answer the phones. "The phones!" Katie protested, but Dean just shook her head and told her that was just as important a job right now as anything else going on.

Wednesday, 2300 hours

By eleven p.m., Dean and Bruce had been over their worst-case scenario several times; the last time was on a conference call to General James. The general had agreed earlier to put a multi-service response team on emergency training drills. One division of Navy SEALs was tasked with the job of seeking out and destroying any transducers or public address systems they could detect. Another division of Army Delta Force soldiers would stand by to enter the UN building and disarm-without-injury anyone with a weapon. The third division of Marine ReCon troops would infiltrate the warehouse in New Jersey to terminate any media broadcasts, and three divisions of Military Police would be assigned to control the chaos outside the UN Headquarters. The Air Force was on standby to airlift Dean's team to the UN Headquarters and the other divisions as close as possible to their designated areas in the city.

The trick would be getting them there quickly. Moving that many troops in a few hours was a monumental task that would normally take months of planning, practice and execution. They had barely forty-eight hours to gather the teams and develop the plan. Timing was going to be everything, and it all came down to whether the politicians would give the green light to the military or would try to talk their way out of it. Dean was not a talker—she preferred action.

At midnight, Dean, Bruce and Katie made the trip to the trooper's barracks to interrogate Dimitri. Katie talked her way into going along, but she was relegated to the observation room. When the trooper brought Dimitri in, he had obviously tried to commit suicide because they had him confined in an old-fashioned straight jacket and he had a motorcycle helmet on his head.

"Well, Dimitri, looks like you've been trying to hurt yourself." Dean watched as he was forced to sit in a chair. She opened a box that Gus had prepared for them and flicked the switch to the transducer. Dimitri's eyes were wild with apprehension, but as soon as Dean spoke and began giving him commands, he became as docile as a newborn lamb. "So, Dimitri, what is Kasimov planning with the cartel?" She turned on the tape player.

"Andre is going to take over the world, with their help."

"And how is he going to do that?"

"With his mind control drugs."

"Be more specific, Dimitri. What is he planning to do on the thirtieth of December?"

"He is going to have everyone in the General Assembly Hall at the UN terminated."

"How?"

"He has contaminated the entire city water supply with the mind control drug. At a set time, he will introduce the ultrasonic sound waves to activate the drugs. There will be a media blackout, and then his voice will be the only one broadcasting, telling the people of New York to go outside their buildings and into the streets to demand an end to the United States interfering with the politics and decisions of other countries. This will make it virtually impossible for any help to reach the UN complex."

"Looks like we called the chaos thing right, Colonel," Bruce whispered to Dean.

She nodded and then continued. "Yeah, then what?"

"He also has transducers planted in the General Assembly Hall and throughout the UN Headquarters. They are set to emit their ultrasonic waves during the Millennium Conference when the President of the United States addresses the assembly. Anyone in the complex who has drunk from the city water supply will be affected."

"When does the conference start, and how will he terminate the assembly?"

"Nine a.m. on the thirtieth. There will be many guards in the room because of all the heads of state present. They will be carrying a variety of weapons. They will be instructed to open fire on the assembly and the dignitaries on the dais. The assembly will be told to kill the people around them any way they can. The UN security force will also be commanded to enter the Assembly Hall and open fire on the crowd."

Mentally, Dean was calculating that they had only eight hours to stop the slaughter. "How can we stop him?"

"You can't. Everything is already in motion."

"That's what you think, buster. I won't be late this time!" Dean said as she turned off the tape and nodded to the wide-eyed trooper to take Dimitri back to his cell.

"You can take the jacket and helmet off. Let him do whatever he wants now," Bruce told the trooper as he led the docile Dimitri out of the room.

As soon as Dean turned off the tape recorder, Katie flew out of the observation room and was waiting in the hall for Dean and Bruce. When they exited the room, Dean's face was a picture of pure determination. "Let's go," Dean said as they hurried out to the SUV to return to their headquarters.

In the vehicle, she placed a call to General James and played the tape for him. "Jack, we gotta go with this ASAP or we're screwed." Dean spoke into the phone after the tape finished. "Yes, I know that!" she muttered into the phone. "They what? Tell me this is some kind of a joke! Jack, don't let me down on this one!" She hung up and immediately let out a string of curses that made Bruce blush. She was remembering Kasimov's speech to the cartel representatives at the lodge when he said he was going to "level the playing field."

"What's the plan, Colonel?" Bruce asked after she had finished.

"The general is under orders to report to the White House before he orders any troops to converge on the UN." Dean was obviously beyond enraged now. "Seems he was reprimanded for coming up with the 'training exercises.' Some member nation let it slip that the US military was performing training exercises on an aircraft carrier just outside of New York harbor. It made some of the UN member nations uncomfortable to know there were military exercises in progress so close to the city, and he was told to put them on hold." She slammed the dashboard with her fist. "None of the teams are ready for anything...let alone deployment!"

"Fuckin' assholes! Just how do they think they'll stop Kasimov now?" Bruce was now registering in the "very angry" range on the emotional rating scale. "Don't they know you can't move troops that numerous without planning?"

"Dean, that Assembly Hall holds 1,800 people!" Katie said as she looked into Dean's eyes.

"Let's get back to the task force. We'll have to come up with our own plan," Dean said with a growl.

Wednesday, 0130 hours

"That's where we stand right now." Dean concluded her briefing on the interrogation and the call to General James. "Any ideas?"

"There's no way we'll be able to locate and destroy all the transducers in time," commented Gus. "Besides I don't think the UN security force will give us access to the building with all those heads of state arriving shortly. I sure as hell wouldn't!"

Bruce pulled out the blue prints for the UN complex. "Gus is right on that one. They'll be on high alert with the dignitaries coming, so they won't be too cooperative. This is the security force headquarters." He pointed out the location on the plans. "They have additional stations here, here and there in the Assembly building alone. Our best bet is to try and get into the Assembly building and then work to keep everyone else out."

"Okay, but how do we keep from getting killed by the 1,800 people in the Hall?" This question came from Katie. "If we can't stop the transducers or the broadcast, that is."

"Good point, Katie." Dr. Randall said before she stood to continue. "Dr. Berg and I have been discussing possibilities to counteract the drug all evening. We believe, and we have tested this on our human subjects, that if we can anesthetize them...put them to sleep... they won't be able to respond to the commands. The problem now is, how do we do that to 1,800 people all at once?"

"Damn, Leigh, that's a great idea!" Dean exclaimed, as she grabbed the building plans and looked for the maintenance schematics. "Bruce, can we get to the HVAC system?"

Bruce looked over the blueprints and nodded in the affirmative. "It's right inside the roof entrance; we can do it."

"Gus, how much gas would we need to knock 'em all out?"

"Depends on what gas we use. If we use the KO237 series, we'd need probably twenty-five of the big tanks. Any other gas and we'd have to double that. And it'll take time to get it all in there. Those containers will take up a lot of space! KO237 is a heavier gas too. It'll float right down to the floor as soon as it comes out of the vents." Gus calculated a bit more then told the group it would take at least thirty minutes before the participants would be on their way to dreamland.

"Colonel, why don't we just keep them out of the Assembly Hall instead?" This came from Quentin.

"Too risky, Quent. If we leave them out on the street, we can't control the situation. There's no telling how many innocent lives may be lost with the chaos going on out there," Dean told the young agent. "It's better to let them in and keep the rest out. We're in control that way and can keep them safe." She looked around the room. "Any other questions?" When none came, she decided. "Okay, that's what we'll do."

Dean grabbed the phone and dialed General James. "Jack...have you heard anything yet?" She shook her head and sighed. "Well, we've got a plan, but I need your help...No, we won't use your troops unless they consent...Yes, it could cost you your stars." Dean outlined the idea they had and requested thirty tanks of KO237 to be airlifted to West Point. She also needed at least three choppers to then transport the tanks and her crew to the city, and enough gas masks for all of them. "We'll be waiting for them at Point. You've got my cell number...and Jack...thanks." When she hung up, everyone in the task force was watching her. "Now, how do we keep everyone else out?" Dean asked with a smile, as they looked over the blueprints one more time.

It took them nearly an hour more before they had the plan worked out and the assignments made. Katie talked Dean into letting her go as far as West Point where she'd wait until she got the all clear signal to come in to the city with Tracy and Colleen.

They needed to get to the Point as soon as possible, and that might prove to be the toughest part. The roads were clear of snow, and there was little traffic at this time of night, but a little help from the State Police would go a long way. Dean called Major Vance and explained the need to get to the Point. He offered two trooper escort vehicles and guaranteed they would get there in two hours, possibly less. By three-thirty a.m., they were dressed in their black camos with their various agency initials on their backs. The trooper cars were waiting for them on the Quickway. As promised, they were at the Point in one hour and fifty minutes. Unfortunately, the choppers weren't there yet.

"Jack, it's Dean. Are the choppers on their way?" Dean was pacing the small tarmac as she talked. "That's going to be cutting it close, Jack." She nodded as the general spoke then hung up the phone.

"What's the delay, Colonel?"

"Took him longer than he thought to round up thirty tanks of KO237. The ETA on the choppers is 0600, fifteen minutes to refuel, then the flight to Manhattan. We'll have maybe thirty minutes to get in, secure the building and start pumping the gas." She frowned and then added. "The heads of state are due to arrive at 0800. General James told me that at 0830, they're all supposed to be in and seated for a pre-conference concert by a consolidated choir of two hundred children from throughout the city."

"Damn, sure hate to expose those kids to that knock out gas." Bruce shook his head. "They'll have one hell of a headache when they wake up."

"Nothing we can do about it now. We can't wait to pump the gas. The President is scheduled to speak as soon as they're done," Dean told the group. "I just hope they don't fall asleep before the rest of the group because if Kasimov is watching, he's liable to get suspicious and move up his starting time." The group fell silent and checked over their equipment as Dean paced until they heard the far off sound of helicopters.

****

At six-thirty, the choppers lifted off for their trek to Manhattan. Dean had looked for Katie on the tarmac as they lifted off but only saw Tracy. *She must be inside with Colleen.* Dean thought as she felt the pain of her absence. *Poor kid, must be totally beat. I shouldn't have let her come down here with us.*

It was almost seven-fifteen when they began sliding down the ropes from the choppers onto the roof of the Assembly Building. The pilots had muted the props and the sky was just starting to lighten. "Thank God for long winter nights," muttered Dean as she descended the rope. *Any later and we'd be spotted for sure.* It took them only three minutes to totally disembark from the choppers, tanks and all. *So far so good; now, let's get in and get on with it.*

The HVAC area was on the floor directly below the roof so at least they didn't have to carry the tanks far. They weighed in at nearly two hundred pounds each so it would take them a while to get them all inside. Bruce had disabled the security system as soon as he touched down on the roof. He blew the lock on the roof door with some of Dean's magic powder. After that, he scouted the HVAC room with another team member. As soon as he gave the all clear, the rest of the team moved the tanks in. They helped set up the discharge relays on each tank before the team assembled for final dispersal to their targets.

Every member of the team was wearing a communication unit so they could all be in touch and report in once their objectives were taken. "Okay," Dean whispered into her com unit, "Remember, we're not here to hurt anyone. Use your stun guns and knock out sprays first, and only disable with your live ammo if you have to use force. Bruce, give the commands." Bruce gave the signals to each two-man unit to proceed towards their targets. A team of three stayed behind and began connecting the relays with the pumping system they brought with them to tap into the HVAC unit. They had thirty minutes to get everything set and start spreading the gas into the building.

****

The two-man teams deployed silently toward their targets, cognizant of the security cameras on their routes. Each person carried a small set of diagrams of the Assembly building, each marked with their primary route and a back-up route. The hard part was getting to the four security offices as the UN guards started to succumb to the gas, and disabling the guards in each one before an alarm could be sounded.

They had to time the security camera sweeps at each
intersection before they could proceed. This alone
slowed the progress of the teams. At 0829, Dean gave
the signal to don their masks.

****

Kasimov, Natasha, and a docile Lin were in the
communications booth with the now dead translators,
biding their time until the President of the United
States began his speech. Natasha had eliminated the
translators with a quick burst of her silenced weapon
when they had entered. Taking over the communications booth was key to this portion of the plot, since it
was from here that he would transmit the orders for
the chaos to begin in the Assembly Hall. He and
Natasha had just finished entering the commands into
the translations system that each of the non-English
speaking heads of state and their entourages, including security personnel, would be listening to. It was
also from here that he had access to the various security cameras that swept the auditorium and the rest of
the building. Kasimov, being the head of security for
his country, had insisted on stationing himself in this
booth during the ceremonies. The Russian leader had
a large contingent of personal security bodyguards
and felt that Kasimov's presence in the communications booth would be most advantageous, so he went
along with his insistence.

Kasimov had contacted the rest of his army of
cartel members the previous evening to insure that
they were all in place and had no further questions
concerning their duties. Now he was mentally going
over the stages of his plan. Stage one, the exterior
chaos to be initiated by his cartel friends, was due to

begin as soon as the last limo delivering dignitaries arrived at the UN. The Japanese and the New York contingents would be intercepting all the media stations' outputs and inserting their taped broadcasts instead. This would begin in conjunction with the rest of the cartel's people initiating the beginning of the transmission of ultrasound waves through the transducers placed throughout New York City and in some main office buildings, especially the World Trade Center and the Stock Exchange. This would lead to major chaos in the streets, which would multiply once the outside transducers kicked in. The public broadcasts floating out of vacant cabs and other vehicles abandoned in the streets would help ensure that no aid would be forthcoming to the UN to interfere with the part of the plan for which he was responsible.

Stage two, was up to him and Natasha, and that was under control. All he had to do was wait until the President of the United States began speaking, then flip the tape recorder switch and watch the carnage unfold from the safety of the communication booth.

Stage three, well, that would be the best part. Total chaos in the world as governments worked to regroup after their beloved leaders were slaughtered. *It will be so easy to take over after this little scenario is over. World domination! I will be the ruler of all!*

* * * * * * * * * *

The first team to report was Bruce's. Dean heard his code over her com unit. "Tango-1" Then she heard, 'Bravo-1,' Charlie-1,' and finally 'Zulu-1,' report in. All the security stations were secure. Now they had to secure the entrances and exits. She looked at her watch. They had fifteen minutes to get this done. Each team had two exits or entrances to secure. It was going to be damned close.

Dean headed toward the hall behind the main dais. She was not worried about the security cameras now that the four security offices were neutralized. She was in a hurry to make sure that the President and Secretary General were safe. The next series of reports came in—Tango-2, Bravo-2, Charlie-2, and Zulu-2.

Okay, half the entrances are covered... just a little bit more to go, Dean thought as she continued down her corridor towards her objective. Then Tango-3, Charlie-3, and Zulu-3, came over her com unit. *C'mon, Bravo...c'mon.* "Bruce, go see what the hold up is with Bravo. The rest of you, get to your posts."

The communications booth, where Kasimov and Natasha had taken up positions, not only contained the equipment whereby the speeches were translated and relayed via headphones to the participants in the hall. It also contained a full set of security cameras, including one backstage behind the dais. Kasimov started from his reverie when he spied Colonel Peterson on one of the video cameras. "Oh ho...Natasha! Look what I see. It looks like little Lin was right. Lt. Colonel Peterson did figure it out! Too bad she won't live long enough to see the tragedy the United States government has brought to all of these unsuspecting heads of state!" He chuckled as Natasha finished dragging the last murdered UN guard into the booth. "Go see where she's going, eh Natasha?" Natasha looked up at her mentor and smiled with glee at the opportunity to meet her nemesis face-to-face.

Dean had just entered the backstage area behind
the dais. It was now two minutes before nine a.m.
The people in the hall should be asleep, or at least
groggy, by now, but she didn't dare look out to check.
Not yet. As she looked down to check her watch, she
caught a glimpse of movement behind her reflected in
the watch face. She turned and saw a gas-masked person coming at her fast. At first she thought that one
of her team was trying to reach her regarding Bravo,
then she suddenly realized it was Natasha.

She moved quickly enough to avoid the blow, but
not quickly enough to avoid the knife blade that followed. It sliced across her right bicep causing her to
wince with the pain. She reached up automatically
and held her left hand over the wound to control the
bleeding. Natasha recovered from the near miss and
turned towards Dean once more, only this time Dean
was ready. Releasing her hold on her injured muscle,
Dean smiled inside her mask and waved Natasha
towards her.

This incensed the Russian, and she leapt towards
Dean, receiving a solid roundhouse kick to the head
for her effort. It sent her sprawling, nearly knocking
off her mask and causing her to drop her blade.
Natasha stood quickly and shook off the blow to her
head, then began a dance with Dean, each looking for
the next opportunity to strike a blow. Natasha's came
first. Natasha feinted right, then swiftly changed
direction and landed a kick to Dean's injured arm.
Pain shot through Dean as the kick landed, causing
her to stumble backwards and trip on a spool of electrical cable. Natasha jumped on top of Dean and
reached for her mask, breaking the seal a bit to where

Dean inhaled a slight amount of the gas still lingering near the floor. Dean grabbed at Natasha's hands in time and reseated the mask and then the two struggled for dominance.

Using her larger size and leverage to advantage, Dean flipped Natasha over her head and got to her feet. The younger Natasha rolled with the flip and immediately came at Dean once more. A flurry of kicks and punches landed on each combatant as they struggled to subdue one another. Natasha focused her attacks on the already injured arm, effectively reducing Dean's ability to counterpunch with each blow that she landed. Beginning to feel the effects of the gas, Dean backed away, but still managed to land a solid kick to Natasha's side, which sent her sprawling once more. As Natasha began to rise, she noticed the knife by her foot. She carefully picked it up and hid it in her waistband behind her back, then raised her hands in defeat.

"Giving up so soon, Natasha? What's the matter, can't take what you dish out?" Dean growled, as she reached for her pistol. But the gas she had inhaled slowed her reactions.

With lightning speed, Natasha reached behind her back and grabbed the knife to throw at Dean. A silenced round cut through the air, piercing her hand as her motion started forward. The knife clattered to the ground as Natasha reached up to hold her injured hand. Dean looked up, startled by the sudden movement and then looked toward the doorway at the rescuer who was slowly approaching the two women, gun still trained on the fallen Russian.

"Thanks," Dean said as her deliverer approached.

"You're welcome," said the rescuer as Dean came closer. Only then did she realize that the eyes that looked through that mask into hers were the most beautiful emerald green ones that could only belong to Katie.

"What...how?" Dean asked a bit hazily.

The sound of running feet caught their attention as Bruce and three team members came in followed by General James and several Delta Force soldiers. "It's safe to take your masks off now," Bruce said to the two women, who immediately removed them.

"Looks like you got a bit of that stuff in your system, or she never would have gotten the best of you," Katie chuckled. "Here, let's take a look at that arm of yours." They sat on some chairs by the back wall where Katie called Bruce over. "Bruce, we're going to need to stop this bleeding. It's pretty bad. Can you help me take care of this? I don't quite have two hands to use yet."

As Bruce took over the job of bandaging Dean's arm, he whistled softly and told her it was a good thing Katie showed up to save her butt or he'd be bandaging more than just her arm.

"What do you mean? I was in full control of the situation!" Dean shot back.

"Oh...you can catch thrown knives?" Katie raised an eyebrow.

"Well, we'll never know now, will we?" The taller woman chuckled. "Say, that was some pretty good shooting. Where'd you learn to do that?"

"Gunnery Sergeant at Quantico...'Focus solely on your target then squeeze between breaths.' I finally got to test his lesson to see if he was right." The young woman smiled. "Guess he is! I'm also glad he made us train equally hard with both hands!"

The Delta Force troops had finished handcuffing Natasha and brought her over to where Dean, Katie, Bruce and now General James were sitting. "Take her out with that other Russian bastard!" the general ordered.

Natasha swore a blue streak when she realized that the blonde sitting next to Dean was the "maid," and renewed her tirade aiming it at Katie and questioning how she managed to escape. After tolerating her expletives for a heartbeat, Katie just stood up, got in her face and then said, "I wasn't finished cleaning up yet...now I am!" She sat back down to a room full of laughter as they led Natasha out.

"Jack, how are the President and the rest of the Assembly?" Dean inquired.

"Sleeping like little lambs. Unfortunately, he may not be too happy about the hangover!" Then he laughed some more. "We were lucky to get here when we did. Thank God I kept my Delta Forces training!" General James commented. "There's a real mess outside. We're still flying in MP Units to control the chaos. It's going to take a while for things to get back to normal out there."

"So they finally approved the plan?" Gus asked.

"Nope...did it on my own," General James replied. "Guess I'll lose a star or two for disobeying orders. We weren't able to stop the cartel members from their appointed duties since we were down to just my elite troops. I felt the priority was to get in and help your people clean up the mess here and make sure the President was all right. I don't think we'll be able to round them up, especially with the chaos out there. We have cut into their media broadcasts to stop those, but there's no way we can stop what Kasimov started out there in any short period of time. We'll have to wait for more reinforcements, and by then the cartel members will be long gone."

"What about Kasimov?" Katie chimed in. "Did you get him?"

"Oh, yeah. Found him six paces from the communications room door. Guess he didn't realize we'd gassed the place! He must have realized it when he saw Natasha attack you with a gas mask on and tried to escape. Unfortunately there were no masks in the communications room," Bruce informed them. "Can't wait to hear his complaints when he wakes up."

"Jack, what if he claims innocence and diplomatic immunity? He is a member of the embassy staff. Will they let him go?" Dean was obviously upset that he might get away with it.

"Once the new Russian President hears Dimitri's tape, and we get Natasha here to roll over on him, he won't stand a chance," Jack replied, as he stood to walk towards the door. "Oh, look who else we found," Jack said turning back to the women. "She was locked in the communications room with the translators. Unfortunately, the translators are all dead. We'll be able to pin that on Natasha and Andre, too."

Lin walked over toward Katie and Dean smiling. Dean realized that Katie had no memory of Lin, so she walked over to meet Lin and advise her that Katie probably wouldn't remember her due to the blows to her head. General James had stopped to talk to Lin as the Delta Force team was taking the President out on a stretcher. Lin stiffened, then stopped talking to the general, grabbed his gun and pointed it at the President. Jack, although surprised by the action, was able to step in front of the pistol as she pulled the trigger. The loud report of the gun brought swift action by the rest of the Delta Force in the room. They quickly subdued Lin and cuffed her. Dean and Katie ran to where the general was lying on the floor.

"Jack, hang on, we'll get you to a hospital... just hang on!" Dean said with tears in her eyes, as she held his head in her lap.

Jack looked up at Dean, the light fading quickly from his eyes. He coughed, looking up with unfocused eyes. "Guess they won't be able to take my stars away now..." Then he closed his eyes and breathed his last.

* * * * * * * * *

It took the general's Delta Force team all day to help revive and calm the 1,800 people in the hall. Dealing with the children was the hardest part for the rugged Delta Force soldiers. Katie had come to their aid and helped calm the children by telling stories until their group leaders were fully recovered, and it was safe for them to leave the building escorted by platoons of MP's.

Once the heads of state were informed of the plot and the reasons they were anesthetized, reason replaced outrage, and eventually they were all delivered to the safety of their embassies, compliments of the newly arrived Marine and Air Force helicopters. By one p.m., Dean and Katie had been flown to Walter

Reed Army Medical Center; Dean, for treatment of her wound, and Katie, for a complete check-up to insure that she had not aggravated her existing injuries. Bruce stayed behind to help the Delta Force, Marine ReCon, and Navy SEAL units clean up the mess. He also contacted Tracy and Colleen regarding the varied success of the operation, and to inform them of General James' death and Dean and Katie's location. Bruce said he'd make sure they were given VIP treatment at Walter Reed.

"They did one hell of a job on this assignment," Bruce told Tracy over the phone.

"The colonel won't get in trouble over going in on her own will she?" Tracy asked, hoping that she was worrying needlessly.

"No way!" Bruce replied. "I understand that the President himself is waiting for them to arrive at Walter Reed. The Delta Force team air evacuated him there earlier in the day. He's fine. A bit hung over from the KO237, but he'll survive."

"I'd love to be a fly on the wall during that encounter!" Tracy laughed, which brought tears of laughter to Bruce's eyes as they both presented theories of what Dean would do, or rather, what she would like to do.

"Yeah, but you gotta remember, he is her Commander-In-Chief, and Dean is by-the-book military. She'll bite her tongue clean off unless he gives her the opportunity to speak freely."

"Oh, he'll get an earful if he does that," Tracy agreed. "Any idea on when they'll be discharged?"

"Dean's slated for some immediate surgical repair to her right bicep as soon as the President is finished with them; so I'd guess, maybe two days."

"Okay, Bruce, thanks for the update. Colleen and I will take a trip down to Washington tomorrow morning."

* * * * * * * * * *

The next day, Colleen and Tracy found a very wide-eyed Katie sitting in the room with a sleeping Dean. Emergency reconstructive surgery of the right bicep and brachial artery had been completed almost upon arrival at the hospital the day before.

"Hi!" Katie greeted Tracy and Colleen. "How was the trip down?"

"Not bad now that the weather is clear. How's the Colonel doing?" Tracy inquired.

"I'm doing okay," Dean responded for herself, opening her eyes slowly. "I feel like I could sleep for a week, but I'm glad everything is over. For now, anyway."

"So, what's the prognosis? Are you going to be okay?" Colleen asked sitting in the visitor's chair next to Katie.

"Yeah. Pretty lucky, I guess. I'll have to go through some intense physical therapy, but I'll survive," came Dean's response. "It'll probably take three months or so to get back to normal."

The women talked about the therapy Dean would have to endure, and the fact that there could be some limitation of the muscle's actions depending on how hard Dean worked to get it back to full strength. They

talked about the death of General James, and about
Lin being held at the Marine Base in Quantico until it
could be determined if she had been acting under
Kasimov's mind control drug.

An hour into the visit, Colonel Samantha Smitha,
the surgeon, came in to examine her handiwork and
pronounced it a success. She signed the discharge
papers to release Dean the next morning with explicit
instructions to keep the arm quiet in order to let the
healing begin. Dean and the surgeon agreed that the
physical therapy could take place up in the Catskills,
provided the therapist contacted her for the course of
exercises required and on condition that if she had
any problems she was to return to Walter Reed for
reevaluation on the course of therapy.

At 2000 hours, Katie, Colleen and Tracy were
"ordered" to leave, so they checked into a local motel
until the next morning. They had decided to stay at
Katie's apartment in Arlington until after the funeral.

* * * * * * * * * *

Three days later, on Monday, January 3, 2000,
Lieutenant General John R. James was laid to rest in
Arlington Cemetery. His wife and three children, the
President of the United States, and representatives
from every member country of the United Nations,
attended his funeral. Dean, in full dress uniform and
with her arm in a sling, sat next to his wife and children. Katie, Tracy, Colleen, and the entire task force
were also present. The President presented the Medal
of Honor to his wife, and Dean presented her with the

American flag from his coffin. His Delta Force team concluded the interment with a twenty-one gun salute.

EPILOGUE

January thru June, 2000

During the first six months of the new millennium, several of the cartel members who took part in the UN plot were captured and were awaiting trial. General Kasimov, Dimitri, and Natasha had been handed over to the Russian government. Under the influence of Kasimov's mind control drug, Natasha gave damaging testimony regarding Kasimov's plan. The new Russian regime swiftly dealt out justice. Kasimov was executed in mid-April, and Natasha and Dimitri were permanent residents in a Siberian prison. It had taken nearly two weeks to restore order in New York City, but it was going to take much longer to repair the economic damage that resulted from the debacle. Wall Street had had to remain closed for two weeks to insure that no adverse reactions from the drug would influence the financial centers. All the transducers were finally located and destroyed. New Yorkers were told that the water supply had been contaminated, and the government recommended that residents drink bottled water. The government supplied bottled water for those citizens who requested it. Doctors Berg and Randall were able to declare the water system free of drugs four weeks after the event.

****

With Tracy acting as chauffeur, Dean and Katie returned to the Catskills on January seventh. Colleen had gone back immediately after the funeral to work. Katie had opted to take her six-month rehabilitation leave in the Catskills and stay with Dean. They figured that, between the two of them, they had at least one healthy body. Besides, Katie wasn't ready to end her new friendship with Dean just yet, feeling a draw to the enigmatic older woman that she just couldn't explain. The two women spent the rest of January together at Dean's cabin with Katie's three cats, enjoying some rest.

Their daily therapy sessions turned out to be a duel between their individual wills to see who could do the most at each session. At the end of January, Dean reported to the local community college to take up the post of Commander for the ROTC program for the spring semester, while she and Katie continued their physical therapy regimen. That semester went on record as being the most successful since the ROTC's inception at the college. Dean's driven attitude seemed to trickle down to her students, motivating them to earn many awards—both individually, and as a unit.

Tuesday, 1500 hours...July 4, 2000

It was Fourth of July weekend, and the country was conducting its first millennium celebration of this holiday. Parties and parades were the name of the game everywhere in the country. Dean and Katie were at the quiet little cabin having a barbecue with a few friends before they closed up the cabin and put it back on the rental market. Dean was reporting back to duty at the Pentagon in two weeks, and Katie was coming off of her rehabilitation leave to return to the DEA. Tracy and Colleen had arrived a few minutes before Beth and Leigh. Kelly and Byron were in charge of BBQ duty, and Linna was sitting with her boss and the rest of the women on the porch as they watched Colleen and Katie play with Brutus.

"Whatever became of Lin?" Linna asked Dean.

"She was held until Leigh, here, tested her and proved that she was under the influence of Kasimov's mind control drug. He used her as a sleeper in case anything went wrong," Dean said. "We all testified to her assistance in breaking the case. Last I heard, she was back in Japan at her old job."

Laughter came from the back yard as Colleen and Katie played "pickle in the middle" with a Frisbee, and Brutus, the dog, was doing his best as the "pickle." A muffed toss by Colleen allowed Brutus to leap into the air and run away with the Frisbee.

"She looks great," commented Beth. "Her physical therapy sessions have done wonders for her shoulder. You'd never know she had surgery if it weren't for that thin scar."

"Yeah," Dean sighed. "We were able to go through therapy together for a while. She really made me work hard to get my bicep back up to strength. I think the therapy was good for both of us." She paused as she took a sip of her beer. "Helped me work through my grief over Jack, too."

"Has she ever regained any parts of her lost memory?" Leigh asked as she watched Brutus pull on a length of rope, now playing tug of war with the two humans on the other end.

"No...nothing!" Dean sighed again.

"I keep telling her that she ought to let Katie know how the two of them felt about each other, but no. This one's so damn stubborn sometimes," Tracy said miserably. "I mean, it's obvious from the way Katie looks at Dean that she's head over heels in love with her. She's probably just afraid to act on her feelings."

"Tracy...how many times do I have to say this? If I tell her, and she stays with me, I'll never know if it's because she really loves me, or because she thinks she's supposed to," Dean replied a bit testily. "Enough already!" Then she stood and reached for another beer out of the cooler, handing a fresh beer to each of the other women in the process.

"Dean, have you ever seen the Little Mermaid?" Linna asked in all seriousness.

"Of course, what about it?"

"Sometimes you have to 'Kiss the Girl'!" Linna said, as the three other women broke out singing the song.

****

"Katie, have you told Dean how you feel about her?" Colleen asked as the large playful German Shepherd pulled the two women around.

"No, I can't. Every time I get up the nerve, something happens and the moment slips away," Katie admitted sadly.

"You do realize she loves you, don't you?" Colleen told the blonde.

"Yes...I think so, but why doesn't she say something to me? She's so hard to understand sometimes." Katie sighed as Brutus pulled the rope away and started to run with it.

"You two are the most stubborn, obstinate women on this planet. Just do it, will ya! You're running out of time!" Colleen almost shouted and then took her friend by the shoulders. "You love her, she loves you... what don't you understand?"

****

"Hey, you two...time to eat!" Byron called as Kelly finished taking the steaks off the grill.

"Be right there!" Colleen called back. "Guess it's time to devour those humongous steaks Tracy brought over. It's a good thing too, I'm starved!"

"Me, too," came the enthusiastic response from the blonde.

As they walked back up toward the cabin, Brutus spotted a bunny coming out from under the brush on the other side of the stream. He turned toward the rabbit, barking, then splashed into the stream, hot on its trail. Katie saw what his target was and took off after the large dog, trying to get him before he could get his prey. Colleen tried to stop her, shouting that all he did was chase them and not harm them, but she must not have heard.

As Katie made it half way across the stream, her foot slipped on a moss-covered stone, and she fell backward, smacking her head on a rock as she fell. At the cabin, the rest of the women watched as Katie fell into the stream. "Damn!" Dean shouted and rushed off the porch, getting to the stream before anyone else.

"Be careful how you lift her!" cautioned Beth, as she caught up to Dean. Byron, Dean, Kelly and Beth carefully carried the unconscious blonde up to the cabin. By the time they laid her down on the couch, Linna had already called for an ambulance. The two doctors examined Katie and found no injuries other than a large bump on the back of the head. Three minutes later, they could hear the siren as it approached the turnoff to Dean's cabin. "She'll be alright," stated Beth, as she put her penlight away.

"That's what you said last time!" Dean spat out quickly, then immediately regretted the words. "I'm sorry...I..."

"It's okay, Dean...I understand," Beth said quietly, as Leigh came up and put her arm around Beth.

As Katie was loaded in the ambulance, Dean looked around the cabin. "Just go...go!" Linna said as she shooed Dean out. "We'll take care of everything and lock up for you. Now, go!"

Dean bulled her way into the ambulance, much to the dismay of the EMT's. Tracy and Colleen drove their vehicle to the hospital while the docs followed the ambulance to the hospital in Dean's SUV. When they got to the hospital, it seemed like forever before Beth and Leigh came out to the waiting room area. "X-rays are normal. No fractures. She's starting to come around and is asking for you."

Dean brightened and quickly went to the examination room where Katie was lying on the gurney, eyes closed. She tiptoed in and stood by the side of the gurney, hesitating a bit before she reached over and held Katie's hand. Katie's eyes opened and looked up into the concerned sapphires looking back at her.

"Hey...you really gave us a scare," Dean said softly. "Glad there's no broken bones."

"Yeah, me too, only there is something..."

Dean's eyes widened, fear showing on her face. "What? Beth didn't say anything was wrong. What is it?"

Katie motioned Dean to lean down so she could whisper in her ear. "Do you remember the first time we made love?"

Dean rose up in astonishment, eyes even wider than before. "Yes," she answered cautiously.

"Do you suppose we could do that again?" Green eyes twinkled back at her.

* * * * * * * * *

Out in the waiting room, Tracy and Colleen waited for the doctors to give them an update. Beth sat down next to Tracy then looked at Colleen. "Do you suppose there's some place in town we can get dinner? I'm starved," Beth said in her most serious tone.

"Umm, sure. She's going to be here a while huh?" Tracy asked.

"Oh, I'm sure she'll be out in a flash." Leigh winked at them. "She's got her memory back!

Coming next from
RENAISSANCE ALLIANCE

Jacob's Fire
By Devin Centis

Jacob, a university professor/scientist, has found a formula for a cure for AIDS, but if the formula is improp-
erly used, it causes mass destruction. The government
and a private pharmaceutical firm want Jacob's formula, and will go to murderous means to get it. However, the pharmaceutical rep who is supposed to cajole
him into selling the formula to her firm is a Christian
who won't exert unethical means. In fact, she and
Jacob become friends during a time when war is breaking out with Russia and China allied against Israel.
The rep tries telling Jacob that what is taking place in
the world follows biblical prophecy and he should
covert from Judiasm to Christianity.

The formula does fall into the wrong hands, and
plague-like devastation is wreaked on the world. In the
meantime, both Jacob and his new found female friend
find they must escape from the government who wants
the formula to use in battle.

Jacob's Fire intertwines mystery with politics and
attempts to form a "New World Order" on the political,
religious, and economical levels. Jacob accidentally
gets caught up in this web of shadow secret organizations through his daughter marrying a young man who
works for the Vatican as well as the new global president.

Out of Darkness
By Mary Draganis

In a most troublesome period of human history, subjugated by the might of Nazi Germany, two women meet under extraordinary circumstances. This is the story of Eva Muller, the daughter of a German major, the commander of the occupying force in Larissa, Greece in 1944. Through the intervention of the village priest she meets Zoe Lambros. Zoe is a young Greek woman with vengence in her heart and a faith in God that's been shattered by the death of her family. They develop a friendship borne out of this dark time, and they help each other to learn to live and love again.

Silent Legacy
By Ciarán Llachlan Leavitt

Amidst the fast paced world of movie-making excitement, Hollywood deals, long hours, and hard work, two very different women—an actress and a director—come together to create a film. In the process they discover an undeniable bond, which draws their souls together despite the surrounding odds. Before their work is complete, they will test each other like nothing and no one before.

And Those Who Trespass Against Us
By H. M. Macpherson

Sister Katherine Flynn is an Irish nun, sent by her order to work in the Australian outback. Katherine is a prideful woman who originally joined her order to escape the shame of being left at the altar. She had found herself getting married only because society dictated it for a young woman her age, and she was not exactly heartbroken when it didn't take place. Yet, her mother could not be consoled and talked of nothing except the disgrace that she had brought to the Flynn name. So, she finds great relief in escaping the cold Victorian Ireland of 1872.

Catriona Pelham is a member of the reasonably affluent farming gentry within the district. Her relationship with the hardworking townspeople and its farmers is one of genuine and mutual respect. The town's wealthy, however, have ostracized her due to her unorthodox ways and refusal to conform to society's expectations of a woman of the 1870's.

As a bond between Katherine and Catriona develops, Catriona finds herself wanting more than friendship from the Irishwoman. However, she fears pursuing her feelings lest they not be reciprocated. And so the journey begins for these two strong-willed women. For Katherine it is a journey of self-discovery and of what life holds outside the cloistered walls of the convent. For Catriona it is bittersweet, as feelings she has kept hidden for years resurface in her growing interest in Katherine.

Other titles to look for in the
coming months from
RENAISSANCE ALLIANCE

You Must Remember This By Mary Draganis
(Spring 2001)

Vendetta By Talaran
(Summer 2001)

Staying In the Game By Nann Dunne
(Fall 2001)

Coming Home By Lois Hart
(Fall 2001)

Trish Kocialski is currently the Director of Parks and Recreation for the Town of Liberty in the Catskills region of upstate New York. Prior to her career in recreation, Trish was an educator for over twenty years. During that time she had published articles in New York state educational journals dealing with comprehensive school health education and wellness, and has edited a compilation of lesson plans for integrating health education into the elementary curriculum for a U. S. Department of Education grant project. Forces of Evil is her first fictional novel.

Printed in the United States
984400003B